BIGGEST ELVIS

BIGGEST
ELVIS

P. F. KLUGE

THE OVERLOOK PRESS
New York

This edition first published in paperback in the United States in 2009 by

The Overlook Press, Peter Mayer Publishers, Inc.
141 Wooster Street
New York, NY 10012

Library of Congress Cataloging-in-Publication Data

KLUGE, Paul Frederick, 1924–
Biggest Elvis/P. F. KLUGE.
p.   cm.
1. Elvis Presley impersonators—Fiction. I. Title
PS3561.L77B5   813'.54—dc20   9552179

ACKNOWLEDGMENTS

Grateful acknowledgment is made to the following for permission to reprint excerpts from the
following copyrighted material:

"Are You Lonesome Tonight," by Lou Handman and Roy Turk. © Copyright 1926 by Bourne
Co. and Cromwell Music, Inc. Copyright renewed. International copyright secured.
All rights reserved. Used by permission of Bienstock Publishing Company on behalf of
Redwood Music Ltd. for the territory of Canada.
"Suspicious Minds," words and music by Mark James. © 1968 Screen Gems-EMI Music.
Inc. All rights reserved. International copyright secured. Used by permission.
Pledging My Love," words and music by Don Robey and Fats Washington.
© Copyright 1954 Duchess Music Corporation. Copyright renewed.
Duchess Music Corporation is an MCA company. All rights reserved. Used by permission.
International copyright secured

Manufactured in the United States of America
ISBN 978-1-59020-258-6
10 9 8 7 6 5 4 3 2 1

To Pamela Hollie
who keeps me traveling
and has sometimes heard me sing

Part One

Ward Wiggins

You should have seen us when we had our act together, top of our game, toast of the town, walking and talking miracles and—you'd better believe it—the real American thing. We were realer than real, if you ask me, more real than the Original because there were nights back then it felt like he couldn't have opened for us, couldn't have come close to us, not on the best night he ever had, not when you compared it to the nights we were having. I know it sounds crazy but I've got to say it. We went way beyond him. We crossed borders he never traveled, lived in a time he never saw, played in places he couldn't picture.

My name is Ward Wiggins and, though I'm not in that line of work anymore, I used to be an Elvis Presley imitator, one third of a trio of Presleys who played overseas for a while, 1990–1991. If you stayed home, you never saw us and you never will. Our time onstage is over now. There were three of us: the young Elvis, the middle Elvis, and the terminal Elvis, three ages of man, three lives in one, and also, I now realize, three versions of America, as it went out into the world. The youthful romantic, the jaded movie star, and the fat, doomed Las Vegas headliner. That last Elvis, that was me.

We showed up in a lot of places: Okinawa, Japan, Korea, Hong Kong and Macau, Guam and Saipan, all through the Philippines, down to Singapore, Malaysia, Brunei, Sri Lanka. That was our territory, the Pacific Rim. We played the military bases. That's where we started. We entertained more troops than Bob Hope and ours were paying customers, drunk and horny, not some captive audience grinning up at television cameras. We played inside the gate, at officers' clubs and baseball fields, and outside, at some of the roughest venues on the planet. We played hotel resorts and convention centers, we opened casinos, gambling ships, soccer fields, and cockpits, we pounded it out to soldiers and sailors, high rollers and refugees, hookers and nuns, oh yes, we did it all and we did it all over the place, but if I have to go back to just one night, there's no escaping Olongapo, the Philippines city that lived off the big naval base at Subic Bay. Used to live, I should say. The base is gone now and the Americans have left, those twenty thousand sailors who came romping into town, when the fleet was in. The party's over, for better and for worse. But, in its time, it was something to see. A kind of high watermark for America, our power, our party, our mighty good times. The Americans went back where they came from and it's just as well, I think. But I wouldn't have missed it for the world.

I can close my eyes this minute and still smell Olongapo, that mix of spilled beer and barbecued meat, of talcum and cologne venting out of barbershop air conditioners, diesel fuel belching out of jeepneys and taxis, and underneath it all, that blend of shit and urine that the hardest rain couldn't wash away, all of this in that hot, heavy Philippines air, fecund, fog-thick stuff that invited you to drink and fornicate and sweat and rot. I can smell it, all of it, and I can miss it too, right now, that and the noises, the sidewalk hustlers, shoeshine boys, sellers of lottery tickets, satay sticks, newspapers, *anything you want Joe,* and the shills outside of nightclubs, *what you want, baby we got it,* country western, hard rock, mud wrestling, foxy boxing, full-body massage, *what you need, baby we got it,* money for honey, honey for money, quick pop, one-night stand, local wife or partner for life, and the sounds that surged out onto the street and into the traffic, horns, mufflers, and all, the music from a dozen different nightclubs, each one a tributary spilling into that great river of noise, sounds from Detroit and Nashville, New York and Chicago, music from every time and everywhere.

Daytime, Olongapo was nothing to look at: tin roofs and rotting wood, metal that rusted and concrete that grew moldy the day after it got poured. Nothing stayed new in Olongapo and nobody stayed young. It was crowded streets and poor, much-pissed-upon trees and if you looked down at the river that separated the town from the base, it was all gray and bubbly and fermented, a black hole of oxygen debt, like someone popped the lid on a septic tank. Beyond, the bay curved off into the distance, toward those brown, dead Zambales mountains, forests long gone, like the hair that falls out of a cancer patient's head once they start the chemo. Daytime in Olongapo was like a movie theater between shows, spilled popcorn, sticky floors, bad lighting. But at night, it made Manila look like a one-pump town, and especially those nights when the fleet was in and the town opened itself to those thousands of American kids, guilty, guilty, guilty of everything you charged them with and yet—you only had to look at them, six years out of Little League—they were innocent too, clueless and young, the best and worst of all of us, let loose in the greatest liberty port on the planet, paid and primped for Saturday night, stepping across that bridge and into Magsaysay Street, striding past the T-shirt shops—AS LONG AS I'VE GOT A FACE, BABY YOU'VE GOT A SEAT—the phosphorescent jackets with flags and logos and ports of call from Pusan to Diego Garcia; barbershops offering shampoo, haircut, manicure, pedicure, shave, facial, ear-cleaning, shoeshine, and in-chair massage; souvenir shops with whole flocks of carved, screaming eagles, herds of carabao, six-foot salad forks, women with bimbo bodies, men with porn-film hard-ons, all made out of the rarest rain forest hardwoods. Out they'd come into a town that wasn't America and it wasn't the Philippines but some gorgeous hybrid, some scabrous, misbegotten mongrel, anyway just one of a kind, dream and nightmare, and though there are moments when I look back in shame, I'd be a liar if I said I didn't miss it. It was our town. Our world. The burned-off mountains. The bay which swallowed fleets and a town which swallowed the men who came off the ships. Babylon and Fort Lauderdale. Sodom and Camelot. And now, show time! Show time at the ramshackle, pink-and-white-painted one-time movie theater that was known as Graceland.

Chester Lane went out first. He had the hardest job of all, or he would have if he weren't such a natural, if it weren't so effortless for him. It's not easy, step-

ping out in front of a house that's half hookers, half sailors. The girls had seen
the show dozens of times, the sailors acted like they had. The girls were hustling drinks—those 300-peso margaritas that were tea and food coloring, you
could drink a bucketful and never feel it—and the guys were noisily checking out women and walloping down San Miguel beers. This wasn't Carnegie
Hall, these people weren't there to read the libretto by pocket flashlight and
suck sour lemon balls, waiting for the fat lady to sing. You didn't get respect
automatically, not in this town. The Original Elvis had been gone awhile now.
He belonged to these kids' parents. Add to that the scattering of soul brothers
in the house and you get an idea of what Chester was up against, stepping out
in front of a bunch of people who figured our act was a joke, a clown show for
used car lots. Or so they thought till Chester Lane knocked the shit right out
of them.

Of the three of us, he least resembled the Original. But, with Chester, the
look-alike question somehow never arose. He didn't imitate, he embodied,
jump-sliding across the stage, jump-starting the evening, baggy pink slacks
with black stitching, jacket to match, hair piled high. He could have been
Ritchie Valens or Buddy Holly or—hell—Otis Redding, it wouldn't matter.
Puck or Till Eulenspiegel. After five seconds, the crowd's show-me attitude
was gone, replaced by openmouthed wonder. Before he finished "Blue
Suede Shoes" they'd gone from I-can't-believe-I'm-here to I-can't-believe-
what-I'm-seeing. Chester walked onstage and Elvis lived, the drop-dead
good-looking punk angel truck driver from Tupelo, the swivel-hipped whip-
persnapper working his way through the up-tempo early stuff, "Tutti
Frutti," "Hound Dog," "All Shook Up," "Ready Teddy." Chester had all the
early moves, the legs-spread backward lean, the one-foot swivel, the pumping hips, the fall-forward faint, the down-on-his-knees croon, even the
sweat drops coming off the end of his chin, as if it were blood and tears, not
perspiration.

Chester Lane did something I never talked to him about. If we'd discussed it, if he'd started thinking, it would have been gone. If I told Chester
Lane to combine macho bravado with an air of youthful vulnerability—well,
he'd be a lost ball in tall grass. But that's what he accomplished. You could

see it when he shifted into a slow tune near the end of his act, "Loving You" or "True Love" or even "Old Shep": out came that hurt boyish side of Elvis, the poet-in-spite-of-himself, the embarrassed romantic. "From hard-on to heartbroken": that's how Albert Lane described Chester's act. That was Albert's way of talking.

Albert—"Dude"—came out next. He did the middle years, the movie years, the blandest patch in the Original's life, when he cranked out thirty mediocre movies while music passed him by. The rot was already there, the self-destructive games, the fawning entourage, the mother-love and self-loathing. Chester's Elvis was familiar and likable. Albert's Elvis made you uncomfortable. There was a sense of danger, of things getting out of hand. Maybe this was where the audience sensed that the life being enacted in front of them wasn't a happy one. Sure, it was Saturday night in the fun-town of Olongapo and, before long, everybody could get drunk and laid. But what unfolded in front of them was close to tragedy. They weren't counting on tragedy, on loss and death, not with all this fine stuff in easy affordable reach, not here of all places. But tragedy was what they got at Graceland. With music, beer, and girls.

Albert began with the movie stuff, even some of the novelty songs, and at first he came off as a bozo, a genial loafer, leering at starlets and laughing all the way to the bank. But then he did this slow, menacing version of "Devil in Disguise." You could just see the anger and cynicism take over, his shit-eating movie star grin turning into a snarl. Then Albert dashed off-stage, shed his aloha shirt, and came back as the Elvis of the famous 1968 comeback special, black leather jeans and jacket, reprising early hits with new energy, so that they sounded like different songs. Chester's "Jailhouse Rock" was detention hall fun-and-games. Albert cut into "Jailhouse Rock" and it was maximum security, three-time losers, throw-away-the-key. And "Love Me Tender"! What Albert did with a microphone during that song would get him arrested in some states: the gasps, the groans, the timely stroking, the slow stride off of chairs in dark corners of the lounge. Albert's "Love Me Tender" was good for business.

Now, me. My Presley, the final incarnation, bloated and sequined, spaced-out and psychic, druggy and delusional. I was the Presley people remembered. Chester's Elvis was a face on a postage stamp. Albert's Elvis came to you in faded Technicolor, film turning magenta with age. But my Elvis was the one they buried and mourned, the guy they still glimpsed from time to time at convenience stores around America. The demands placed on my third of the act were—well—heavier.

In the matter of appearances, I did not disappoint. At six-foot-one-inch and two hundred forty pounds, I had height and bulk. In my college-teaching years, smoking a pipe, wearing an oxford shirt, a corduroy jacket, jeans, and loafers, I was just another out-of-shape academic, sedentary and slack. Ah, but add those glaring sideburns, that hair all oiled and piled. Cast off those elbow patches and force-feed the whole package into a pair of white linen tights. Yes! And circle my belly with a bejeweled belt that might have been borrowed from the World Wrestling Federation. Then give me a shirt that billowed at the sleeves, a collar that peaked in back of my neck, and generous lapels that opened, like French doors, on my sweating, hair-matted chest. Yes! And then sprinkle me with sequins and with stardust and Elvis lived!

In truth, the Original wasn't so hard to imitate. Elvis was a common American type—possibly the most common—the gone-to-seed athlete, the aging hick, yesterday's wild youth, running to fat and trailing memories of some earlier, leaner, dreaming self. Those earlier selves intrigued me. I was the last stop in the transit from punk to hunk to hulk. An aura of imminent death surrounded me when I walked onstage, as if death were waiting in the wings and, on any given night, if it all came together—maybe when I reached down for those low notes in "Suspicious Minds"—I might offer that final gift which the Original failed to deliver: public expiration. But it was more than the sense of death around the corner. In truth, I was the survivor. I was the last to die, because Chester and Albert had already passed on, only nobody noticed, because there was another Elvis coming along, a newer model. What that meant, unless I'd screwed this up entirely, was that their lives converged in me, they lived on in me. I contained them. I tried explaining this to the Lane brothers one time.

"You . . . *contain* us?" Albert asked. Albert was the smart lazy student in back of the classroom, the guy with the baseball cap turned backward on top of his head and his legs stretched out on the chair in front, a show-me smirk on his face. He was the kid who rated your performance but rarely glanced at the books you assigned. Still, he could fire back at you when he felt like it.

"Youth dies first," I said. "So Chester's Elvis died about the time he went in the Army."

"So we're like dominoes. One falls into the other. . . ."

"I'm not wrong, am I? After, say, 1957, no one ever saw Chester's Elvis again. Because then your Elvis emerged. And that ended when—"

"I see where this is headed," Albert said. "And I think it's kind of sickening."

"We all died. But you two went first. I was the last to die. Also the last to live. So if you lived on at all, you lived in me. See?"

"I'm going to say this once," Albert said, shaking his head. "And I'm going to put it into simple language that everybody can understand. Let's say you have a deer, a maybe ten-point buck, close to a hundred fifty pounds. This is a handsome damn beast. It runs like the wind, it jumps creeks, it flies off cliffs, and it's got big brown eyes besides. Okay?" Albert glanced at his younger brother, who was already deeply absorbed, waiting to see how the story came out, wide-eyed and wondering, like a kid around a campfire.

"Have I said anything you don't understand, so far?" Albert pressed. He had a smart-assed edge I often liked, but not now. "If I have, stop me."

I nodded. Go on, get it over with. I wasn't supposed to know, but Albert had been looking at Filipino movies, the action films they made here, rape and revenge films produced in three weeks. He figured that might be a way for him to get started, the way Jack Nicholson began in low-budget Roger Corman thrillers. He would leave the act someday and not look back, I guessed. Elvis was just a role he played. A role and not—as in my case—a fate.

"So you've got this beautiful deer," Albert continued. "A stag who gets shot on the first day of hunting season. End of act one. Shot, gutted, and strapped on the hood of some drunkard's Wagoneer. Skinned and butchered and marinated and turned into venison. Steaks, chops, sausages, and stew. And that's the end of act two. You with me, Chester?"

"So far," Chester said. The kid was all ears. I wondered whether Dude would take Chester with him and whether he'd look after him, the way Chester needed looking after. Albert was cocky and arrogant. And he kept me honest, deconstructing my notion of the three Presleys, of continuous and cumulative time, of transcending and returning. Albert "Dude" Lane didn't buy it.

"So this deer that becomes venison gets digested. It's attacked and broken down by all kinds of enzymes and acids. And this, music lovers, brings us to act three, end of show, last act, curtains, and I guess you could say it contains the deer and the venison, that it reincarnates them, but from where I sit it looks—and it smells—like a pile of shit. From which I—"

"Wipe ass and walk away!" Chester shouted, beaming. It was Albert's favorite line. He used it to end anything that bored him, a meeting, a meal, a movie, an affair. It was his philosophy of life.

"Nothing personal, old-timer," Albert said. He clapped a hand on my shoulder, the kind of sympathetic pat a baseball manager gives a pitcher he's taking out of the game. "We're doing fine right now and I appreciate what you've put together here. But listen—earth to Ward Wiggins!—this is an Elvis show. It's not the College of Cardinals. Chester is not a priest and I'm not a cardinal and you aren't the pope. Okay?"

"I hear you," I said.

"I'm putting this in the nicest possible way but, with all due respect, I don't want to grow up to be you."

When Albert's act was done, the stage darkened, only for a moment but the moment was crucial. It separated me from them, it put them in the past, it said here is what it came to, this is how it ended. We racked the sound system up a few notches, turned the lights up just a little so it looked like dawn and—wham!—we heard the rumbling of "Also Sprach Zarathustra," which most of these guys knew as the "Theme from *2001*," only they'd never heard it this loud before. I waited a few seconds while the music swelled. I looked around the room, which was a movie theater once, so you had a floor full of tables and a bar on either side and a balcony up top, with what they called VIP suites that had BarcaLoungers, couches, and dark-tinted glass.

On any night, even when the fleet was in, more than half the people in front of me were women I knew. Some of them came and went, of course; one married a serviceman and disappeared, another went off to Brunei or Kuwait or Guam, another visited relatives in the provinces and didn't come back. Still, they were a constant audience, the best women—and the biggest bar fines, 500 pesos just to take them out of here—in town. They were heartbreakingly beautiful, in that high-cheekboned, long-haired elegant Latin Catholic way. They were lean and sleek and refined and—surprisingly—romantic. They came out every night in search of magic. They believed in the lyrics of the popular songs. And this was the saddest part, this was what separated them from the women in all the other ports: they were ready to fall in love with their customers.

I waited offstage, listening to the music. I was always pumped up for this: a boxer entering the ring, a bullfighter facing a charge, a batter standing at the plate, two out, two strikes, bottom of the ninth, which, considering the state of Elvis' health at this stage of his career, wasn't such a bad comparison. What I felt, standing there, was that there was something sacrificial about me, something that said, okay, I'm going to perform for you. And die for you. I didn't know whether the Navy guys got this, right away, but I saw recognition in some of the girls who were raised on saints and martyrs and messiahs, raised in a land of relics and icons, a death-loving and theatrical land, where crucifixions were enacted every year, thorns around heads and nails through flesh. They believed in me. I could see it in their eyes, some nights. If they believed in the thousand-to-one chance that some Navy kid they tried to get to buy a margarita might turn out to be a potential husband, then why not believe in me as well, the second coming of Elvis, their personal savior?

When Richard Strauss boomed loudest, I stepped out onstage and let everybody get a look at me. A moment of recognition, you might say: here is my body, bloated for you. The Elvis of this period was into martial arts and he incorporated some of that into his act, kicks and chops and stances. I did some of that when Zarathustra ended. Then I took the mike and addressed the audience. I sounded jaded but country, the voice of a man who was almost finished, almost but not quite, maybe one performance left in him. This performance, here, tonight. I walked to the edge of the stage, singing the hell out of "Are You Lonesome Tonight."

"You remember me?" I asked, when my first song was done. "You remember me when I was king?"

A light probed in back of me and there stood Albert. Albert hated this part, said he felt like a hood ornament on a car, but the moment worked. Half lit, it was as if he were already receding from me, falling into time, into the past.

"I had everything I wanted and more than I needed and I made some mistakes . . ." I took a step toward him, extended a hand, then realized the futility of it, that we could never touch, " . . . that I would make again." And I nodded good-bye to him.

"You remember when you first saw me?" I ask. Better not wait for an answer. These guys weren't born then. I quickly turn to where the spotlight found Chester, way at the back of the stage, posing with his legs spread, his back arched away from the audience, his guitar pointing toward the ceiling.

"That was the me," I said. "The me that used to be." Darkness swallowed Chester. And, like that, I launched into the most disputed part of our act, a quick medley of early Elvis hits, "Jailhouse Rock," "Heartbreak Hotel," "Blue Suede Shoes," snatches of some of the same songs that Chester and Albert had performed moments before. God, did we have arguments about this! Chester said it didn't seem right, repeating ourselves that way. He called it poaching. But I was determined to win this one and what carried the day was the risk or—as Albert saw it—the likelihood of my humiliation.

"You want to wear my leather?" Albert jeered. "See if you can squeeze that gut inside my motorcycle jacket?"

"That's not the point."

"What's the point?"

"They want to see me try. They want to see me lean backward and hold up the guitar like Chester does, with his head damn near touching the floor, only in my case—I admit it—it's my gut climbing toward the rafters. They want to see me try to be young again and mostly fail. They want to measure the change."

"For the worse, man. Look at yourself."

"Okay. For the worse."

"All right," Albert said. "Go crap on yourself."

It was hard, getting him to see that just as Elvis changed, so did the songs. They traveled with him, but what he brought to them, and what he found, was always different. Chester sang "Love Me Tender" and it was like a virgin's plea for gentleness. Albert tried it, it was whips and boots and people handcuffed to bedposts. I sang it, Sinatra-sad, with all the melancholy of time and loss. We interrogated our material—that was what I'd say, if they pressed me. We asked questions of the songs and they asked questions back at us, hard questions of their own, like what were we doing here and what ever happened to us and how did things get to be that way.

I put all of that in my opening medley, age and weight and even a stroke of clumsiness, as if it had been years since I tried these steps. It was sad to see me even try. I saw glimmers of sympathy in some of the girls' eyes, a trace of embarrassment in the Navy guys: *fat sumbitch looks like he might croak right in front of us.* Leonard Warren, Jackie Wilson, Clyde McPhatter, Enrico Caruso, I made a list of performers stricken onstage. The Flying Wallendas. Did they count too? And—come to think of it—Jesus Christ. Didn't he die onstage? Meanwhile, though, they were hearing Elvis. I haven't told you about my voice. Chester and Albert were good singers but their voices were not their main instrument. Chester was a dancer, Albert an actor. Albert didn't have to worry about growing up to be me: he could never take my part. The later Elvis was a stylish, booming singer, elegant and operatic, closer to Mario Lanza than to his earlier rockabilly self. I had his kind of voice. It was born in a shower, developed in high school musicals, perfected in summer stock. Then I abandoned it, but it never deserted me.

After the medley, it was time for the big songs, a mountain range of crescendos and heavy breathing, of boomers like "The Wonder of You," "Burning Love," "It's Now or Never." I turned "Suspicious Minds" into an aria. I shifted down to "Loving You," up to "A Fool Such As I," down—to the pits, in my opinion—with "In the Ghetto," which I skipped if I saw more than three black faces in the crowd. Then there was no escaping the trio of songs that had been Elvis' patented curtain-closer in his Las Vegas years. "American Trilogy," they called it, and a cunning piece it was. "Dixie" and "All My Sorrows" and "Battle Hymn of the Republic." I sang it like I believed it, and by the time I finished, I did. I believed. And so did the people in front of me.

That was when the magic happened. And this was when the story I'm telling you really began, when I sang "All My Sorrows." For just a moment, I would cut out the posing, the kicks and karate chops, and come way down low and quiet, looking out at the audience, where I'd pick a face, some sailor with his arms around a couple of bar girls, a line of San Miguels in front of him. That's the guy I aimed at, him or one of the girls he was with.

My voice came way down, so that the whole place leaned forward to catch the words of the song—a father whispering to a child, a consolation and a warning, that death comes to all of us. A heartbreaker of a song, a kiss of death buried in a lullaby. That was when they knew this was no clown show, that ominous, lovely moment, tucked in between "Dixie" and "Battle Hymn of the Republic." Sometimes I lingered on "All My Sorrows," I held the moment, repeating the words, and sometimes I almost wanted to go from table to table, passing the word, the black spot, the kiss of death. The girls sensed it, some of them, saw it coming and crossed themselves, hoping what they feared would pass. That little moment is when all of this started.

Then I had one mountain left to climb, one roof to raise, that trying, obnoxious "Battle Hymn of the Republic." It made me earn my pay, but I put everything into it so when I finished my heart was pounding, I was sweating in puddles. I'd stay there, head bowed, arms outthrust. (Albert said it was a good way of pointing the customers toward the exit.) Anyway, His truth went marching on, right into the streets of Olongapo.

Biggest Elvis

• • •

It cheapened the act for me to display myself offstage. A car usually waited for me out back. After the second show, I'd pile my shiny boots, loose shirt and tight pants, my capes and scarves and wrestler's belt into a dressing room corner, put on a pair of chinos and a blue denim work shirt and some scuffed-up loafers. On my way out, I'd grab a beer from the bar and nod good night to a handful of girls who stayed behind, the handful who hadn't hooked up with the fleet or maybe they'd finished their customers off already. There was always a group of them, I'd noticed, right near the jukebox. Not all of them were hookers either, at least not all the time. It wasn't that simple. The game wasn't just money, it was also love. So there they sat, some of the girls who worked fast and some who couldn't find work and some others who chose not to work, all sitting around talking, reading movie magazines, comparing clothing, like a pajama party. It amazed me how they could be b-girls one minute—"spare parts," "u-drives," "little brown fucking machines powered by rice"—and, the next minute, chatty, giggling teenagers. In them, guilt and innocence were tangled together. The first month or so, I passed them by, calling out good night like a man who had someplace to go when work was done. They said good night in return. That was that. And that was temporary. One night I decided to take my time, going home.

"You guys," I said, pausing in front of them. "Don't you ever leave?"

"We are waiting for you, Elvis," one of them said. Priscilla, her name tag said. The names changed. Right then we had a Whitney, a Mariah, a Madonna. Priscilla was one of the sharper girls, fluent in English. She could live off the drinks she sold and be a little choosy about the rest of it.

"You're *all* waiting for me to take you home?" I asked. I counted them, one by one, all six of them. "We'll have to rent a jeepney."

"Oh, sir, no sir," Priscilla continued. "You make a selection from among us."

"Half? Three? Two? One."

"As you like it, sir," she said. It was all a joke. They were laughing and some of them had that way of covering their faces when they laughed, hiding their mouths. It was funny, how shyness survived. And here of all places. They were young but they lived in a country that had been dealing with Americans since the century began. We'd been colonizers and administrators, allies and liberators. We were soldiers and schoolteachers, missionaries and investors. At Graceland we were potential customers. Or lovers. They waited to see how we wanted things to be, never quite knowing. So they hedged. Whenever they said something serious, there was a joke in the neighborhood. And every joke could turn serious. Including the joke they were making now, about taking someone home, if I wanted.

"Take two of us, sir," someone suggested. Like a doctor explaining a prescription. "We are small people and you are . . . so big!"

"And then you know what happens," I said, swallowing some of a beer I'd kept for the ride home. "I come out tomorrow after the show and you're all sitting here but you stop talking all of a sudden. You look, you trade glances, and I know that the word is out on me. What size is Elvis' gun? How fast did he draw it? How often did he shoot it? Did he hit or miss the target? How many targets were there?"

"But sir!" another girl pressed. I leaned forward to check out her name tag. They all had name tags. It was a step up, I guess, from wearing numbers, like the women in Bangkok, sitting behind one-way glass windows, displaying themselves to customers. "Elvira!" I said. "That's you?"

"Yes sir." A top-of-the-line model, in black billowing slacks and a matching blouse and a halter that covered a more substantial bosom than you usually saw in these latitudes. She was more Italian-looking than Filipino: Claudia Cardinale, Sophia Loren. Plus she had that pouting, downward-turning mouth that says, come on, I dare you. Elvira was one of the bolder girls. Others blushed and giggled as soon as you looked at them. Some—Elvira looked like one of them—had been around, to Singapore and Hong Kong. Others were fresh from the provinces, right out of barefoot villages and barrios. Those were the ones with tribal looks, short, flat-nosed, with high cheekbones, and squat, serviceable bodies. Their conversation didn't get past "How you like Philippines?" and "How many children you have already?" Endearingly, they always wanted to see family pictures out of the wallets of the men they slept with.

Now Elvira leaned forward, aware of the edge she had on the other girls, who were watching her make her play. She paused, she purred, reached out and placed an elegant, manicured finger on the top of my hand. And then she did this trick. Later, I saw other girls at Graceland do the same thing when they were getting intimate, late at night, close to closing time, which meant closing a deal as much as closing a bar. But this was the first time for me, and Elvira was a piece of work, when she wanted to be. She took my middle finger—yeah, that one—and gently bent it across the palm of my hand so that the tip touched down about an inch away from my wrist. Then—with all the girls watching, ooohing and aahing—she released the finger and stroked it and gave me this come-on look. The span from where the finger touched when it was bent back to where it reached when extended was supposed to be the length of my love machine. A rule of hand which Elvira seemed anxious to verify.

"You like me?" she asked, running her finger up and down my middle digit, tickling and stroking.

"Elvis and Elvira? Gee, I don't know. I don't think so."

It turned out they laughed a lot, this late-night crew. They laughed about business, about Japanese and Americans and Filipinos. Compare and contrast: how much they paid, how much they wanted, how quickly they finished. They cursed the customers who masturbated beforehand, so the girl would have to work harder for her money. They all deserved a better break, I thought, and I admired the way they came back, night after night, dressed like princesses.

"Baby Elvis goes out all the time," a girl named Whitney said. "And Dude Elvis . . . all night. Every night. But Biggest Elvis . . ."

"Biggest Elvis!" They whooped, they laughed, they high-fived each other, and now I had a name that would stick and Whitney looked around, astonished, no clue what she'd done. Out of the mouths of babes. In the Philippines, nicknames kept on coming, a nation of Babys, Juns, Dings, Dongs, Bings, Bengs, Dodongs and these weren't schoolkids. They could be senators, ambassadors, judges.

"Biggest Elvis," I repeated, acknowledging the inevitable. The nickname would stick. "Enough for one night. I want to thank you all for a lovely evening."

A chorus of complaints arose. Biggest Elvis was getting away, one big tuna slipping out of the net. As I walked away, though, I saw something that stopped me. Three women sat near the jukebox, which cast just enough light for them to see the squares and tiles on a Scrabble board. I hadn't noticed them till now. They didn't banter like the others. They kept a distance which wasn't hostile, they just needed to concentrate. I couldn't resist looking at the board. Later, I asked myself what I expected to see. Was I looking for a game played by Olongapo rules, with BARFINE leading into BLOWJOB and COCK branching into a triple word score QUICKIE? There was a kind of false wisdom you could fall into when you lived in a place like Olongapo, a kind of wised-upedness, a beery, bullshitty I-saw-it-coming, I-told-you-so. That's what happened to me now. Because the words on the Scrabble board were things like EXODUS and QUINCE.

"Wow," I said, pointing to the word DIASPORA. "I didn't think you knew those words."

I should have known better. This was a country that valued education. If you wanted hungry students, this was where you came. The trouble was, they stayed hungry after graduation. You had political scientists driving taxis, biologists diapering rich peoples' babies, history majors sitting in bars, waiting for strangers to walk in. That's what I wished I'd remembered, while the silence lengthened. No one at the table gave me a look. All I heard was someone shaking the paper bag in which they kept the unplayed letters, that and "You Don't Send Me Flowers Anymore" starting out in the jukebox.

"Well," I said, when no one responded to me. "I'll be saying good night."

I prolonged it a little, aware that something had gone wrong and it was my fault. It was nothing that would cost me, nothing compared to the blunders and insults that happened with customers every night. But this was my mistake and I regretted it.

"I'll see you tomorrow night," I added. The table stayed quiet. I walked away. Then I heard a quick sentence in Tagalog and a round of laughter that excluded me.

"What was that about?" I asked, turning back. "Was that about me?"

No one answered. They seemed, not frightened exactly, but intimidated. Americans were nice enough people, but you could never tell when they'd pull rank. One minute they were winning, generous, easy. The next minute: a master race. They were like kids walking down a sidewalk, straddling a crack in the basement, crossing a line by chance. Not watching where they walked.

"Elvira, tell me," I said. She wasn't the one who'd spoken. I knew that. It was one of the Scrabble players. But Elvira had laughed.

"Oh, nothing sir."

"That was it? Nothing?"

"Yes sir."

"That was a long sentence, just to say nothing. And a big laugh, that followed nothing. Why don't you just translate *nothing* for me?"

It didn't take much to bring the colonial out, even in the most easygoing visitor. Heat brought it out, travel and discomfort. *Come here. Now. Take this back. Not that way. I told you not to.* Sometimes the people brought it out in us. They made us be that way. If things got too friendly, they reminded you that they were from here and you were not. When the dancing was over, the bottles empty, the bills paid, they reminded you. They reminded themselves. And maybe they were doing you a favor.

"She say—"

"Who?"

"Sir, I don't know," Elvira protested. It was getting ugly, all on its own. "Sir, I do not see. Please sir. I hear you say, I'm surprise you are knowing this kind word. In English. And then someone say in our language, say to you, I'm surprise *you* know this word. And we laugh, sir. I'm sorry."

"Okay," I said. "It's okay, everybody." On my way out, I signaled to a bartender stacking cases of empty San Miguels. I ordered ten bar-drinks, margaritas, 300 pesos each, which went a long way in Olongapo. At those prices, I hoped he'd consider using some tequila.

●   ●   ●

Olongapo at two o'clock in the morning. It deserved better than it got; it deserved a painter who could capture the crazy play of neon on rain-washed streets, the street kids, down for the night but not out, the last satay peddlers, the flash of jeepneys, the all-night bars and barbershops and restaurants and massage parlors. The smell of butchered forests and polluted oceans, gasoline and perfume, and any kind of sinful possibility.

I got dropped off at Barrio Barretto, in a zone of mom and pop nightclubs except for one place, The Main Event, that featured foxy boxers—female pugilists—when the fleet was in. The Main Event was one of Dude's favorite hangouts, when he escorted movie people from Manila. Dude was an explorer and what he discovered at the Main Event impressed him, watching one girl slam another around the ring. It sounded more like a pillow fight, what with twelve-ounce gloves, but some of those women had moves. Dude insisted, some of them could parry, feint, hook off the jab, throw uppercuts in close, go hard to the body. Those were the ones he liked to buy, fresh out of the ring.

"I couldn't believe it," he told me. "I still can't. They're so pumped up after they fight—if they win, that is. It's like the bed's a boxing ring."

"Sounds fun," I said.

"No, no, don't do that deprecating thing, Ward. It's like fighting and fucking are . . . you know . . . the same thing."

"The Marines have known this for years," I said. "The only question is, which comes first."

"You get one sweaty, passionate armful, that's all I know," he said. "So ready—"

"Willing and able," I completed. I wished I could give more to Dude sometimes, when he tried to talk to me. We canceled out each other's thoughtful moments.

"I've got just one question for you, old-timer." Dude stuck a finger into my stomach, right below the navel. Then he pushed and it sank, readily, down past his knuckle.

"I can't feel a thing," I said.

"I'll bet you can't," Dude said. "Tell me, Ward. I'm just wondering. How many years since you could stare down and see your cock? What'd the Original call it? Little Elvis?"

"Oh, it's been years. But some other people look in from time to time."

"Yeah, sure," Dude said. "I don't believe you, Ward."

An alley led off the highway, right past the Show Me Bar and Nightclub, which showed me one barmaid, head down on the bar and, farther in, the glow of a television set, like a fire in back of a cave. Past the Show Me, a hard-packed path went through some garden plots, corn, beans, eggplant, down toward the beach. The feeling changed as soon as you left the main road. Along the highway, you had air-conditioning, cold beer, hot music. They danced the latest dance, they wore the latest threads, they talked that MTV talk. Out back, you were in another country, where people lived in square wooden houses with tin roofs, or in open-sided thatch-roofed huts. Wood smoke curled my way, and I could smell caged pigs and tethered goats. Some mornings, I'd come across schoolkids dressed in uniforms, whole columns of boys and girls, and women carrying plastic tubs of laundry to where a stream emptied into Subic Bay. That was during the day. But the real magic happened at night. I'm talking about a certain moonlit night, the same night I talked to the jukebox girls for the first time, the ones I'd noticed crossing themselves when I sang "All My Sorrows." I walked home and an old-timer came toward me, came out of the fields, gesturing for me to wait awhile. Up close, I saw he had one good eye. The other was just a socket. He was a skinny, shrunken fellow wearing baggy khaki shorts and an old T-shirt that said DAIRY QUEEN. Out in the fields, he might be mistaken for a scarecrow. He moved toward me and I saw that he had a rooster in his arms, a fighting cock, cradling it like a mother holds a child in a nativity scene. He held the rooster toward me and there was plenty of moonlight to show me those shining feathers, some red, some brown, and the glint of killer eyes. The old man held the animal out for me to touch it, saying nothing, just humming what sounded like a lullaby. I reached out, hesitated. He nodded again. I just brushed the animal behind the neck. The feathers felt smooth and oiled. The scarecrow nodded his head, thanking me. "That's all," I said. "That's it?" He backed away and crossed the flooded field. Communion complete.

You could laugh about it all you want. But this Elvis business wasn't just an act. If I were doing a low-rent lounge act in Henderson, Nevada, it might be different but in this part of the world, spirits hovered and sometimes I could feel them in me. I saw it in the audiences at Graceland and in moonlit fields at Barrio Barretto and I sensed forces, fates, larger somethings that I couldn't see. For the record, I'm agnostic. I put Christ a couple rungs higher than Elvis and I put Elvis somewhere above Santa Claus, all of them on a ladder that leads right into space. But still, something started happening when Elvis came to Olongapo. Every night I felt it, that sense of something impending, something that was headed my way and I didn't have to do anything but wait for it. Sit and wait, the way bar girls waited for lovers, the way the port looked for ships. Something coming.

Built by some Manila bigshot as a weekend retreat, the place where I lived sat right on the beach. I liked it the first time I saw it, a one-room building, concrete and wood, with a porch along the front, looking out at the bay. In back there stood a water catchment, an old concrete cistern that caught rain off the roof and released it onto a concrete slab below. I liked my shower, when I came home. The beach wasn't much, rough brown sand that the tide covered with Pampers and Clorox bottles and broken rubber shower sandals, as though returning unwanted gifts. A little farther inland, clumps of grass and vines and morning glory ran above the water line.

On the porch, three in the morning, Biggest Elvis hunkered down into a chair that protested at the two-hundred-forty-pound hunka-hunka-love dumped into it. The steps complained also, the very floor I walked across. I inconvenienced the world I lived in and some nights, when it rained, or mornings, when the sun heated the tin roof, snapping and creaking as it changed temperature, it sounded like the roof was complaining about me too. Oh, I was something, really something. I needed Dude Lane with me, to keep me honest.

Chester was popular. Not like a sailor. Chester was a friend, not a customer. The girls ironed his shirts and combed his hair. They brought him local food, from *lechon* to locusts. They gave him their pictures, invited him to family parties, baptisms, weddings, funerals and if he screwed them— which I doubted—it was almost certainly for free, as if they were teaching him a new dance step, *show me how, show me now.* He was learning the language too. Chester approached this country the way a kid rushed down a beach, splashing into the water. I worried about Chester. I worried that time was not on his side. He had turned me into his guardian. Just recently, he'd asked me what it meant to be Catholic.

His brother, Albert "Dude" Lane, could be a pain. He was selfish, sarcastic, ambitious. The girls saw Chester and everything was for free. They saw Albert and they flipped the meter. But Albert was smart. Every conversation with him was a combat, with winners and losers. Everything he did was part of an overall campaign. He wanted to make it more than anyone I'd ever seen, a score, a killing, a name for himself. He spent half his time in Manila. Three hours away. He weekended in Cebu or Palawan. He didn't report to me but I could read the names of resorts on the towels he stole, on bath gel, shampoo, and little bars of soap he kept in our dressing room, laundry bags and coat hangers, stationery and shoeshine cloths. That was Albert. Driven by dreams. Or nightmares. The nightmare was what he'd told me: he didn't want to be Elvis forever, to grow up and be like me.

It was still dark when the roosters started crowing. Maybe the one I blessed was one of them, the leader of the pack. I sat out on the porch a while yet. Some dogs came trotting down the beach, shadowy figures in gray light. Someplace down the beach, a radio went on loud. They weren't getting their money's worth unless it was going full blast. The Eagles sang "One of These Nights" on Armed Forces Radio, followed by Wilson Pickett's "Land of a Thousand Dances." It was odd how songs found us, moving through the air, bouncing around time zones, orbiting the earth and landing in a place like this, Subic Bay at dawn.

Bedtime. I left the porch and stepped inside, undressing in the dark. I'd turned on the air conditioner and the overhead fan. It was redundant, like wearing a belt *and* suspenders, but I liked the whooshing of the cold air overhead. Another treat to myself came next. Over my bed hung a mosquito net, finely woven, my teddy, my tent, my kind of shroud. I rolled beneath, enjoyed the cooling of the room, the stirring of the net. It would be late afternoon before I emerged. Meanwhile, my younger selves made up for me, all through the night. The Lane brothers got their share all right, they evened the score. But Biggest Elvis slept alone, another American waiting for his fate to find him.

Colonel Peter Parker

I was one of those World War II veterans who got a taste of the Pacific and never quite made it home. It wasn't just the Japanese who left stragglers behind, hiding out in caves and taro patches thirty years after the war was over. After the war, I hooked up with the Trust Territory government as a business adviser, based on Guam. Guam made sense. It was midway between the Philippines, where the war had started for me, and Japan, where it ended. Guam was an American place, way out in the Pacific. It was also a good place to turn a buck. Not at first, though. Those early years you needed a government job; back then, the private sector didn't amount to spit. Scrap metal and copra, that's all. Everything was small-time, secondhand, and down-home. A store was a place that sold canned corned beef and mackerel and warm beer. A hotel was a Quonset hut with a broken toilet. The airports were World War II fighter strips, the roads were all potholes. It was a tropical version of West Virginia. And the Palauans and the Trukese, the Chamorros and the Carolinians were like the Hatfields and the McCoys.

I liked it fine out here, back then. But you can't stop progress. Or you can't stop the people who say you can't stop progress. They wanted those concrete air-conditioned houses. Forget the thatch. Forget outrigger canoes and sailing by the stars, when you can blast around in a fiberglass shell with three hundred Evinrude horses behind you. Well, it wasn't up to me. They decided what they wanted and I helped them get it. I got in on the ground floor. You wanted to do business in paradise, I was your man. I knew about long-term land leases that were really sales, I knew about local proxies. You wanted a garment factory in the boondocks, a hotel on the beach, I was your man. Interested in cable TV systems, time shares, tuna fishing, talk to me. Casino gambling, garment factories, golf courses.

There's something about islands that draws people with money. Carpet-baggers, we call them. When they came, they came to me. I helped unpack their bags. Some things worked out, others didn't. But it was all business. I took the money I made from them, plus money I'd married and money I'd saved, and I put it in beachfront property in the Northern Marianas, mostly on Saipan. Not the high-priced parcels on the sandy side of the island, right on the lagoon. I bought the rocky places, cliffs and blowholes. I wasn't the first but I was one of the first to figure that tourists don't care about beaches, they only think they do. They like to look at them, they like knowing they're there, standing by. But when it comes to swimming and sunbathing, God never made a beach that could compete with a clear, clean, filtered swimming pool. So after ten years I made money, and for ten years after that the money I made made more money.

All I can say about the Elvis show is it sounded like a good idea at the time. The Elvis thing wasn't work, wasn't even a sideline or a hobby. It was a joke like—I don't know—the Tin Man, the Scarecrow, the Cowardly Lion. It was something I did for my boys. It began in a nightclub down on Marine Drive, the Tiger's Cage, the only night I've ever been there. Or ever will. It burned down last month, suspicion of arson, surprise, surprise.

"Uncle Pete, just take a look," Albert said to me. He was twenty-one at the time, a junior at the University of Guam. "Just come out with us one night. There's something we want to show you."

"Is it your girlfriend?" I asked, fearing the worst. Chester and Albert were my sister Patsy's kids and they'd been with me for ten years, ever since their mother got herself killed in a highway accident at Welch, West Virginia.

"No, Uncle Pete," said Chester. "We have an idea. A family business

venture." I started worrying right then. Ideas weren't Chester's strong suit.
He brought home C's from the University of Guam, where he was a fresh-
man. It broke my heart to see how kids from Truk got higher grades in math
and Vietnamese ran rings around him in English. And the comments on his
papers! Sometimes just a line drawn across the middle of the first page: "I
stopped reading here."

"We could make money," Albert said. "And have some fun." He was the
older smarter brother but that didn't make me feel any better. He wasn't *that*
much smarter. Dude's last business venture that I know about involved a
$500 overseas telephone bill to a phone sex operation in Skokie, Illinois. Af-
ter I straightened him out, Chester did the same thing. But he—Chester, the
criminal mastermind—tried calling collect. "I only wanted to talk," he said.

I loved these boys like they were my own. I loved them from the minute
they stepped off that plane from Honolulu at three in the morning, all lost
and groggy, milling around in a mob of tourists, looking for me. They were
easy to handle when they were boys. But lately the sap was rising and the
grades were falling. Albert was squeaking through, in "dramatic arts."
Chester said he was thinking about majoring in oceanography, mainly because he liked boats. He might as well have said tap-dancing. What they
needed was work and the only thing that interested them both was music. I
was a Mantovani fan. Ferrante and Teicher. I couldn't even listen to my boys
practice on their guitars. Practice makes perfect they say but as far as I
could tell, they were getting worse. But I helped them out. I rented them a
warehouse in Tamuning they could practice in, an old Quonset hut next to a
Toyota dealership, and a cockpit. Overnight, it became headquarters for the
restless youth of Guam. Now the boys wanted me to endorse their next move.

The Tiger's Cage was the nastiest place I'd ever been. A cracked linoleum
dance floor, a moldy carpet, plywood booths, rusted card tables, plastic
tablecloths, nothing, absolutely nothing, you couldn't buy at a yard sale. No
napkins, no glasses, no toilet paper in the john. A local place, for sure.
Japanese tourists come to Guam by the hundreds of thousands. It's Florida

for office girls and low-middle management, traveling on tight little pack-
ages that involve Japanese airlines, Japanese-owned hotels, tour buses, and
duty-free shops. But the Tiger's Cage was for local layabouts and losers, for
slumming military, for Filipinos and Trukese who worked docks and ware-
houses and construction, on and off the books. This was the underside of
Guam, and my boys were welcome there, met with friendly waves and high
fives. And then I realized what they wanted out of me, the whole idea. They
wanted me to buy the place.

"So when do they start the fights?" I asked.

"Just hold your horses, Uncle Pete," Chester said. "Relax and enjoy the
show."

"I hate drinking beer straight out of a bottle," I said. The boys made a
fuss and eventually the waitress brought me over a peanut butter jar she'd
mostly rinsed out.

The show Chester wanted me to enjoy started with an all-girl band out
of Korea that was hard on my eyes and rougher on my ears. "Lolling,
lolling, lolling on the liver" was the name of their first song and they
worked their way down from there. "Climson and Clover." At the end they
sang happy birthday to one of the customers, a Guamanian guy in a soft-
ball uniform. "Happy Birthday to each and evlee one of you," the lead
singer said.

After that there was sort of an amateur night, with men from Anderson
Air Force Base doing Willie Nelson songs and a big Palauan offering up a
Don Ho medley, "Tiny Bubbles," "Beyond the Reef," "Hawaiian Love
Song." The best by far was a little Filipina who put all she had into "The
Way We Were." She amazed me: she took over that song and she owned it.
What Streisand sang was a donut. What this girl offered was a cake, with
layers, icing, and candles. Every note had meaning, every note was held a
little longer than possible, and oh . . . the looks, the profiles, the tears. That
little no-name girl could sing! When she finished I wanted to get up for a
standing ovation. Then I noticed that, though I was clapping loud and hard,
I was clapping alone. And the boys were looking at me, snickering.

"Trouble is, Uncle Pete . . ." Chester started, and stopped. Long sen-

tences slowed him down. But he had a good heart. I wouldn't change him.
Even here, when the waitress dropped a can of beer, picked it up, opened it
without thinking twice, and everybody got sprayed with foam, he smiled and
told her it was okay, just bring us another.

"The trouble," said Albert, finishing the sentence, "is there's a million
like her. You've seen one, you've seen them all."

"She was good," I repeated.

"But it's ho-hum," Albert said. "Question of supply and demand. Maybe
she'd light up a room in West Virginia. Those redneck mouths would drop,
they'd sell their trailer for one slow dance. But here . . . they're like
cockroaches."

"You shouldn't talk that way son."

"Oh, okay, Uncle Pete. I take it back. But you saw what happened here.
Ho-hum. She's somebody's housekeeper. She cooks, she irons, washes,
watches the kids for a hundred and fifty dollars a month. And she sings on
the side. So what else is new?"

"I thought she was good," I repeated. It still didn't seem fair.

"Hey!" Chester nudged Albert. "He's here."

"Who's here?" I asked, looking around to see who'd just come in, maybe
the owner, who'd tell me what a great business opportunity I could have
here, with a little fixing up and the right promotion. But all I saw was the
same gang as before, slugging beer, slipping out to the parking lot for drugs.

"Heading to the stage," Albert said.

Squinting up into a pink spotlight, running fingers through his hair, fussing with a screeching microphone, was the man I came to know as Ward
Wiggins. He was a rangy kind of fellow, running to fat and not caring about
it. He leaned back to pour a Budweiser down his throat, the way a mechanic
might feed a quart of Quaker State into a clunker before taking it out on the
highway. You could see the shirt he was wearing pull apart above his belt
and his belly button peek out, like a kid poking his head out of a pup tent,
wondering is it okay, can I come out and play. He belched then, and I
turned to Chester, like it was time to go now, I'd heard enough, when all of a
sudden the man began to sing some song—was it called "Love Me"?—that

I hadn't thought about for years, any more than I'd thought about Elvis since he died, since before he died, but that didn't matter because this was the kind of thing you see in the supermarket newspapers: ELVIS ON GUAM! He did three or four songs, not saying anything in between, not even noticing applause, and when he was finished he walked offstage, right past our table, where he hesitated for just a second, nodding at Chester. "Hello, sir," Chester responded. Then he was gone, out into the parking lot, and half the customers followed, as though reporters might be asking what he was driving and which way he went. It was over fast.

"That guy scared me," I admitted. "And I never even cared about Presley."

Chester and Albert got this look on their faces, the way boys do when they think they're one step ahead of you, trying to convince you that a swimming pool makes sense, just from a real estate point of view, improving property values, like it's an investment.

"Uncle Pete," said Chester. "You know those papers I bring home from school? My introduction to literature course? The one I call farewell to literature? Those nasty comments in red ink? Those zingers?"

"Sure."

"That's the guy who writes them."

"Who?"

"Just got done onstage. Singing Elvis. That's Professor Wiggins."

"Well, son, your professor has got himself an interesting sideline."

"That's what we've been wanting to talk to you about," said Chester triumphantly. And what he said that night made sense. That night. The next few days I called some people I know. And then I went to call on Professor Ward Wiggins at the University of Guam. I took Chester along to show me the way.

We waited out in the hall an hour to see Professor Wiggins, who was much in demand that day. One or two at a time, people went into his office, emerging ten minutes later, some of the students red-eyed, with crumpled papers in their hands, and sometimes with parents who were flushed and angry, asking directions to the office of the department chair, the dean, the president. It felt like a doctor's office, on a day that all the tests came back positive. I know all about doctors' offices, on days like that, walking out with a death sentence and a bill to pay.

"Sir, can we come in?" Everybody was "sir" to Chester. His brother called everybody "dude." They called him Dude back and it became his name. But nobody called Chester "sir."

"If you're next in line," Wiggins said from the other side of the door. When we came in, we saw him at this desk, facing out the window, looking at a rectangle of brown grass, concrete sidewalk lined with some scraggly plumeria.

"Hi, Chester," he said. "You too, huh?" He was wearing exactly what he'd worn at the Tiger's Cage: short-sleeved shirt, tan slacks, running shoes. He glanced at me, then back to Chester. "You bring some help?"

"This is my Uncle Pete," Chester said. We shook hands. "He's my guardian, sir. My father, as far as I'm concerned."

"Glad to hear you say that," Wiggins said. "I've been thinking a lot about my own father lately."

"He coming to visit you on Guam, sir?"

"He's been dead for twenty years, Chester."

"Oh. Sorry . . ." Chester looked at me and shrugged like maybe it was wrong to offer condolences, if someone's been dead for so long.

"It's okay. You never get so old you don't look around for someone to intervene in your life. Someone who'll say, now Ward, that was a little out of line. Or way out of line. . . ."

His voice trailed off. He turned away and looked out the window again, to wherever our folks have gone. But when he came back at us he was smiling.

"Okay, Chester. You're a good kid. I'm inclined to make this painless. But you've got to help me out a little. I can't do it all on my own."

"Sir?" Chester didn't know what he was talking about.

"A little pick-me-up, am I right? A make-up quiz, extra credit, nudge the needle out of the red zone? That's what I've been doing all day. In your case, Chester, I don't mind. I liked you."

"Thank you," Chester said, still confused.

"Okay!" Wiggins spun around in his chair. "*The Adventures of Huckle-berry Finn?* Remember that one? The first book we read?"

"Yes sir," Chester said. He sounded shaky, that boy of mine. "The first book we read."

"Excellent. Now just tell me this. What kind of vessel—what kind of craft—do Huck and Jim travel down the Mississippi on?"

Poor Chester looked lost. Later, he confessed he hadn't read the book. Still, he'd kept showing up for Wiggins' class because he liked hearing him talk, liked the way he walked back and forth, getting excited. The book was kind of incidental. The book was an orange, Chester said. Wiggins was the fellow who squeezed the juice.

"Think about it, Chester," Wiggins said. "There's no rush, son."

He got up and started taking armfuls of books and putting them in empty cardboard boxes. The books weren't on shelves and they didn't look like they ever had been. They were in stacks and Guam's climate hadn't agreed with them.

"How are we doing, Chester?"

". . . kind of craft?"

"That's right!" Wiggins shouted. "A raft. You got it. The C is silent. And—speaking of C's—is that okay? I can't go much higher than that."

"Sir . . ." Chester finally had it. "This wasn't about my grade. That's not why we came. That wasn't it at all."

"I asked Chester to bring me here," I said. "But this isn't about him."

"Then . . . who?"

"You. I wanted to talk about you." I let him chew on that while I turned to Chester. "Have you got a way of getting home from here on your own?"

"No problem, sir." He nodded to Wiggins. "Don't worry about that grade, sir. Anything you give, it's all right with me. I'm not so much of a student. But I want you to know I didn't sell the books back. I'm keeping them with me."

"Well, then," Wiggins said. "I guess this is good-bye. I liked having you in class. Keep up with the music."

"Not really college material, is he?" I said after Chester was gone.

"Never mind that," Wiggins said. "He never missed class, not once. And he's the only one who dropped by just to talk, not to get an extension. Or massage a grade."

"He's a good boy," I agreed.

"Well then, mister . . ."

"Colonel, actually. Colonel Parker." For a moment his face lit up, as if he'd just thought of something funny.

"Your first name wouldn't be Tom?"

"Peter," I said. "I caught your act at the Tiger's Cage the other night."

He was surprised by that. He hadn't noticed me sitting at the table. Now he stared at me awhile, looked me over.

"You disapprove? A professor out in a bar like that, singing Elvis?"

"No."

"If not, you must be curious. What's a man like me doing in a place like that?"

"I'm curious, all right. Why you're throwing books in boxes. Why you said good-bye to Chester like you'd never see him again."

"Because I probably never will," Wiggins answered. "I'm out of here. My appointment ends next week."

"Did you jump or were you pushed?" I asked. I'd gone too far and he recoiled. First I sensed resentment: it was none of my business. Then he smiled and came back with a question of his own.

"Why do I get the feeling you already know the answer to that question, Colonel Parker? You've been checking me out, haven't you? Who are you anyway?"

"Your next employer," I said. Before I could get any further there was a knock on his door. Wiggins got up, cracked the door open, faced another angry student, a girl, and this one had brought her brother, a weight lifter in military fatigues and sunglasses. So Wiggins gave another pop quiz, something about what color was a whale. When they were gone, he turned back to me.

"If you want to talk, we'd better get out of here," Wiggins said.

We walked across campus slowly, out to the parking lot, where Henny, my driver, was waiting. When he asked where to, I motioned a circle, a signal he was used to. We headed inland, into the boondocks.

"Henny went ten rounds with Flash Elorde," I said. "In Flash's hometown. You follow boxing?" Wiggins shook his head. "They gave Elorde the decision. A hometown decision. In the Philippines, that's what most decisions are. He's been working with me ten years. Everything he hears in here, he forgets. I want you to understand that. I do a lot of business in this car."

"I haven't heard anything yet," said Wiggins, "that sounded like business."

"All right. Try this. Ward no middle name Wiggins, born Lakehurst, New Jersey, June 2, 1949. Isn't that where that big German blimp crashed, right when it was landing?"

"The *Hindenburg*. Not a blimp. A dirigible."

"Public elementary and high schools. Rutgers University. Football scholarship. Fraternity man. B.A., M.A., Ph.D. The apple sure didn't fall far from the tree. Ph.D. was in 1977. *Decline and Fall: The Later Novels of James T. Farrell*. What was that about?"

"A ticket to Guam," he answered. "You can read it."

"Teaching career starts at Drew University, three years, University of Arizona three years, Long Beach State two years, then there's a gap in there. . . ."

"I got married."

"And quit work?"

"To write. It was complicated. It didn't work out. Say, Colonel, I'm not enjoying this. I'm not having a nice time."

"What happened next?"

"I came here. My wife died a couple years ago."

"Wasn't she your ex-wife then?"

"Where the hell did you . . ." He squirmed in his seat, concentrated on looking out the window, where there wasn't much to see. These islands, once you get away from the beaches, could be Oklahoma. The heat waves come off the road, the wind kicks up spirals of dust out of red clay, dogs slouch around gas stations and mom and pop stores, little clusters of houses cut into tangan-tangan brush. "Yeah," he said. "If you're a stickler for chronology. She divorced me and then she died. Not the other way around."

"Then . . ."

"It's not the oldest mistake in the book, but it's up there. Moving to a new place to save a marriage. Especially a place like this. It's like taking a sick fish out of a goldfish tank. And putting it in a puddle on the sidewalk."

He was talking more than he meant to. The car worked that way for me. These rides were like confessionals. Also, it looked like he hadn't had any-body to talk to for a while. That bit about missing his father rang true. As if those old-timers would've been able to straighten us out, if only they'd stuck around.

"So now you're going to be a nightclub singer?"

"I don't think so," he said, waving the thought of it away. "The Elvis thing just happened. After my wife was gone. It's nice being someone else for a while. But you can't make a living at it."

"Yes, you can," I told him. And, in the time it took to drive back to Agana, thirty minutes or so, he was mine. Our conversation went the way I'd wanted it to. The secret was in the homework, the phone calls, the informa-tion I had going in. That's what primed the pump. Forget about invasion of privacy. People are flattered when they find you've been asking around about them, taken the time to snoop, cared enough to listen to the gossip. Spy on them? They love it. Take notes on them, compile a file? They're tick-led to death, thinking they're important enough to be followed around. They like feeling that way and so, to keep the feeling alive, they talk about them-selves. It's the father thing again, the lost authority. We want to know that someone's keeping track, keeping score, a pat on the head, a kick in the ass, it's that simple. And Wiggins would have talked to anyone. He was about the loneliest man I ever met.

Albert "Dude" Lane

Wipe ass and walk away! What could you say about a country where they chilled the air and boiled the water, fished with cyanide and watched chickens kill each other for sport? Where they did bad things to bad parts of pigs and called it cooking and, if they ate vegetables, they washed them off with Clorox first? I kid you not. After three months I still hadn't taken a solid shit. Later things got better, a lot better, but right after I arrived, this whole country was a bad case of wipe ass and walk away.

At the Ninoy Aquino Memorial Airport, when we arrived, I saw chunks of concrete coming out of the ceiling, holes in the wall with wires trailing out, and the carpet was like something they'd use in a carpet-cleaning commercial, before they break out the magic cleanser. "There will be some delay in offloading the baggage," the PA announced while we walked to customs and immigration, "on account of some problem." Yeah, sure. Took time to open all those suitcases.

Flying down from Guam, I'd thought about how we were on the road again, the Lane Brothers, Dude and the Chestnut, how we flew across the world years ago and now we were headed to another strange place. It touched me, seeing the Chestnut staring out the scuffed-up window, trying to decide what was a cloud and what might be an island. My kid brother and me. I felt good about that until I looked across at this pile of suet which made us a party of three, digging into his third package of free peanuts while he read some book by Elvis Presley's hairdresser. Then I started feeling not so good, having Uncle Buck along for the ride. And I wasn't clicking my heels about this Philippines adventure either. I was doing it for Chester. It was his idea. I was doing it for Uncle Pete, who made it sound like it was the last thing he was asking of us. The way he looked, some days, he might be right. He had this kidney thing we didn't talk about because it might upset Chester. Anyway, I was in this for the sake of other people. There wasn't much in it for me. That was odd, too, because I'm the one who's supposed to be a me-first guy.

The sidewalk outside the terminal was a feeding frenzy and we were the food, so many meatballs in a tank full of piranhas, of guys surrounding us, yanking at our bags, hotel sir, air-con taxi sir, first time in Philippines sir? The sidewalk was jammed and the road was worse, cars and vans and these stretched-out jeepney things, covered with paintings and tassels and names like LOVE MACHINE, two dozen Filipinos squeezed into them. The music and the shouting and the heat could give you instant migraine and it wasn't just that, it was the air which wasn't only hot and wet—we had plenty of that on Guam, God knows—but filthy air, like in a tunnel or a parking garage. Wipe ass and walk away, I mean it. I was wondering what to do when I noticed this wasted-looking American with sunglasses and an aloha shirt and khaki pants.

"Stay here," he said. "I'll get the car." Off he went, seriously gimping, and when he came back it turned out his name was Jimmy Fiddler and he worked for Baby Ronquillo, who owned the nightclub we were headed for.

In a minute, he was fighting through the worst traffic I've ever seen. Calling it gridlock would be a compliment. You had four lanes, two one way, two the other, but bit by bit people got pissed off, moved out into the oncoming lane and didn't duck back in on account nobody would let them, so then there were three lanes going one way and then four until the team on the other side organized and mounted a counterattack, pushing through, only now it wasn't four lanes anymore, it's like six, because space between cars, back to front or side to side, was wasted space. This wasn't a traffic jam, that would be like calling a lump of coal a dead plant. This was hell and we were all going to die here in the poisoned air because everything on the

road was burning coffee grounds and the visibility went as far as the side of
the road, where I saw a line of stores, more like stalls, places with pots of
food on tables, stacks of retread tires, wicker furniture, signs advertising
BED SPACER TO RENT and GO-GO DANCER WANTED and GOATS FOR SALE. And
there were people along the road, kids and dogs just watching us not moving, like they were fishermen on a riverbank, casting a line out into traffic,
pulling in an aerial or a rusted muffler. Would you believe there were kids
out on the highway, thin kids in shorts and T-shirts, selling cigarettes one at
a time, selling chewing gum, newspapers, handkerchiefs, flowers? Some of
them wore headbands like Arabs and had cloth over their mouths. There
were beggars too, a kid leading a blind man, a woman hefting a baby up into
car windows, like merchandise she was trying to unload, something that fell
off the back of a delivery truck. She pointed to her mouth and stomach, the
kid's mouth and stomach too. They saw we were Americans and soon they
were all over us. "Hey, Joe, very hungry. Hey, Joe, give me peso." We'd
moved maybe five yards in the last five minutes. Then we edged out into an
intersection, turning left, turning right, and following the coast. Ahead of
us, half smothered in haze, was a city or what used to be one. I saw high-
rise buildings with cranes on top only you couldn't tell if the buildings were
going up or coming down. On the beach side, on low swampy land that
stuck out into the bay, there was a bunch of shacks that were worse than
anything I'd ever seen, acres of shacks, laundry, mud, and babies. Those
folks were squatters, Jimmy said. Then, all of a sudden, there were these
lawns and palms and big buildings, hotels and convention halls and the-
aters that Imelda Marcos built, Jimmy said, but the place felt down and
mean, like nobody's plans had come true and everybody was pissed off. The
walk along the ocean might have been nice, once upon a time, but there
were people in rags, camped under the trees and running after tourists and
stepping out into the traffic at stoplights to beg. The palm trees looked like
they'd been planted there for punishment and the grass was raggedy and
you just knew that if you walked through it you'd have shit on your shoes
and not dog shit either.

"Look, Dude!" the Chestnut exclaimed. Count on him to see the sunny side of things. "Look at all those ships!" Damn if he wasn't right. Manila Bay was still something, all full of ships, dozens of them anchored in the harbor, and out behind the ships you could see some mountains come tumbling down to meet the sea.

"Makes you wonder where they're going and what they're carrying," the Chestnut said. "Makes you want to take one. Any one."

I have to tell you I loved my little brother, when he talked that way. "When we leave here, Dude," he said, "can we leave by ship?"

The way I was feeling, I'd have paddled out to one of those ships right then. The country was a dump, let's face it, the country was for losers like our driver. What ever happened here since World War II that mattered? I'd been wondering about that, ever since Uncle Pete set this up. When was the last time anybody said, hey, let's all go to a Filipino restaurant? What's your favorite Filipino movie? You went to most countries and there was one certain something you had to see, the Eiffel Tower, the Pyramids, the Taj Mahal, the Great Wall, the Grand Canyon. So what's your destination here? You want to go shopping? What for? I asked Ward Wiggins, the professor, if he could name a single Filipino writer and he came up empty. Embarrassed but empty. Quick, anybody, name a Filipino who isn't a Filipino politician. See what I mean?

"I guessed you'd want a peek at Manila before heading to Olongapo," Jimmy said. "How long you staying?"

"As long as they like us," the Chestnut said. "That's if they like us."

"You guys do Elvis, right?"

"Yes sir."

"You don't do nothing else? Beatles? Rolling Stones? Hank Williams? Only Elvis?"

"Yes sir."

"Sounds like a couple weeks to me. We got lots of imitators. We got the Philippines Patsy Cline and the Philippines Willie Nelson at the O.K. Corral. We got the Philippines Prince and Jackie Wilson at the House of Soul. Plus there's always a James Brown and Chuck Berry and Jerry Lee Lewis around. They do okay. For a while."

"And . . . what then?" I asked.

"What do you think? Something else comes along. People got short attention spans around here. They get tired of the same old act. It's like one of them cheap watches, look just like a Rolex, keep time for a while. Then it stops. Don't nobody repair them. Throw them out and buy a new one. I give you boys a couple weeks. A month, tops."

"We'll be staying longer than that," Ward Wiggins said. It gave me a queer feeling because a couple of weeks sounded fine to me, it sounded generous. But Ward sounded real sure of himself. I was afraid he might be right. It was all that crazy, the whole Elvis act. "You'll see," he said.

I promised Uncle Pete I'd give Professor Ward Wiggins the benefit of the doubt, which I had surely done, on Guam, while we were putting our act together, arranging material, buying wardrobe, hiring some backup men— Filipinos—who could harmonize and play instruments behind us, keyboards, drums, flute, guitar. Anybody would have had to wonder what a college professor was doing at two in the morning, singing Elvis in the lowest bar on Guam. That was a warning in itself. There were others.

I'll be the first to grant that Ward had the voice, the body, the flair. He was a hard act to follow so it's a good thing he came last. Fair enough. He had his third of the act, my brother had his third, I had mine. Only then he started in with this business about how we ought to mix up the material, so maybe he'd end up singing an early song like "That's How Your Heartaches Begin" and Chester might try a later song like "The Wonder of You." And, he said, since I was the middle Elvis, I had the unique advantage of traveling through time in either direction, past or future, all the way from "Love Me Tender" to "Suspicious Minds."

"Don't you get it?" he said. I had asked why he was confusing all this stuff. "I'm the senior Elvis. I can't go forward. I've got no future."

You can say that again, I thought. What happens to an Elvis impersonator who grows old, anyway? Do you pretend that you look like what Elvis would have looked like if he'd lived? Or do you go into something else? Orson Welles?

"And Chester, he's got no past. He's the young Elvis, with the whole world still in front of him."

"So? So what? Why mix it all up? You mix up the songs, you mix up the audience."

"This is about tradition and the individual talent!" he said. It was like he was lecturing back at the University of Guam but they dumped his butt and now he was our problem. "This is about time and change. When we take a song out of the time it appeared, when we take the text out of context, we interrogate it! Damn straight, Dude! That's what we're doing, we're interrogating these . . . confluences . . . of wax and sound . . . words and music . . . time and place . . ."

"Well, shit," I said. Then, all of a sudden, he laughed and I couldn't tell whether he was laughing at himself or me.

"Listen, Dude, it's no big thing. A couple songs now and then. Wild cards, okay? New wine in old bottles, old wine in new, that's all."

The benefit of the doubt meant lots of doubt and not much benefit. If he'd just do his act and leave us alone we'd be okay, I thought, but he kept mixing things up. Synergy. Juxtaposition. Horseshit.

"I think you've got the surface Elvis," he said to me another time. We were back on Guam and we had our backup musicians with us for the first time and I was wearing my black leather pants and jackets, I just knew I'd kicked ass. And here he came, out of shape and out of work, telling me I got the surface down.

"Thanks a lot," I said. Hell, I'd leave it like that, if he would. The surface was a fine place to be. The surface was where you lived, that's what I thought. You went deep, maybe you drowned.

"Don't go getting touchy on me, Dude," he said. He pulled me aside and motioned I should sit down on a couple of beer crates. He was in costume too, one of his rhinestone Liberace suits and it made me uncomfortable sitting across from him decked out like this, like it was . . . I don't know . . . Miller Time for clowns. "What did you do before this?"

"In music?"

"No. Drama. You were a drama major, weren't you?"

"I did *Bye, Bye, Birdie*. I was Billy Bigelow in *Carousel* and El Gallo in *The Fantasticks* and Sky Masterson in *Guys and Dolls*."

"All the singing heroes, huh? My wife and I went to see that *Carousel*. You were good. Almost too good. I just about had to throw a bucket of water on her after you came onstage.

Yeah, I thought, and from what I hear about your marriage, the bucket of water missed. Then he asked if I'd ever done any nonmusical drama and I told him *Orpheus Descending* and *Picnic* and *Look Back in Anger*. And then I figured it was my turn. I was entitled to a question of my own.

"What did you ever do, Ward, if you don't mind my asking?"

"Besides impersonating a professor? Is that what you're getting at?"

I shrugged. Some students loved him. Others hated him. It's usually that way, I guessed. Everybody was somebody's asshole.

"Don't discount the professor role, Dude. That was drama, fifty minutes Monday–Wednesday–Friday, eighty minutes Tuesday–Thursday, three hours on seminar nights. That, by the way, is when I started doing Elvis. After seminar."

"You change personalities in a phone booth someplace?"

"I never acted in my life, Dude, and I've never sung for money, if that's what you want to hear. As a matter of fact, I'm not singing for money now."

Then what the hell for? I wondered. I held off on saying it. I sat back and got another portion of bullshit.

"I want you to think of this as more than an act. More than an impersonation. It's an incarnation." He stopped and checked my eyes, to see if I got it, like it was a deep point. What I got was a feeling that he'd be serving up poisoned Kool-Aid before much longer. We were talking weirdness. I just listened.

"You've got the music down, Dude. But think . . . dramatically. The music they can get on cassettes. You can be as good as those cassettes, but you can't be better. What you can do is take this Elvis . . . deeper. Give them more than they ever got from the Original. More than they'll ever get."

"Him being dead, you mean?" Nothing like a brown-nosing question to move a lecture along.

"Yes! They want . . . they come to see . . . to get close. And, the way art refines life, selects and arranges and lies . . . we do that too. All I'm asking, Dude, is this. When you're up there I want you to feel what's gone before you. Chester . . . the young Elvis . . . what it was like for him . . . to be him . . . to be . . . and to have been . . ."

The tenses were kicking up on Professor Wiggins, no doubt about it. It was hard to keep track of time out in the Twilight Zone, I guessed.

"And then, Dude, if you can do it without gagging, I want you to look ahead. At what's coming. I want you to look at me."

My nod of agreement wasn't enough for him. I was studying my boots and I felt him reach out a hand, touching my chin, raising up my head, to be sure I was looking at him.

"There. Take a good look. That's what's coming. I'm the third act and there is no fourth. Time plus you equals me. Put that in your act."

After two months on Guam, we were ready to perform for real. We were tense, edgy, wanting whatever was going to happen, good or bad, to happen soon. That's when Uncle Pete announced he was going to try us out on the road, which is an expression that doesn't mean much on Guam. I was hoping for Hawaii. Maybe not Waikiki, up against Don Ho, not right away, but maybe someplace nice on Maui or the Big Island. But Uncle Pete decided to send us to Saipan. A disappointment but not, all things considered, a bad choice.

Saipan was half an hour's flight from Guam, part of the same chain of islands, the Marianas, only Saipan is a U.S. commonwealth and Guam is a U.S. territory that calls itself a commonwealth. Anyway, it was far enough away so that all of my brother's adoring pals and my druggy unsavory friends wouldn't come trailing after us, to boo and cheer. But if it wasn't home territory it wasn't foreign ground either. Uncle Pete did a lot of business in the commonwealth and took us up there for vacations, when we were little. I'd always liked Saipan. It was quieter than Guam, greener and less crowded. On one side of the island there was this long, sandy beach, shaded by soft-needled ironwood trees. That's where we passed the hot part of the day, moving from picnic to picnic, folks offering us plates of chicken and fish and ribs wherever we went, local folks relaxing, good people, I thought. This was along the invasion beach and, in the shallow lukewarm lagoon and out on the reef, there were tanks and landing craft that were rusting away right where they'd gotten hit. We'd go out there, looking for bodies and stuff, and sometimes, right at the edge of the reef, where the ocean turned serious, we'd scare ourselves, chucking pebbles that would sink to the bottom of the world. I didn't mind trying out our act on Saipan. But as soon as we landed, I started feeling sick. Not the Chestnut. He was Mr. Don't Worry, Be Happy. Not the Professor, not that I could see: he'd sniffed failure a time or two before. The man in the middle, the middle Elvis, was the one who worried.

Saipan was changing, getting to be Guam all over again, a murderer's row of high-rise hotels along the beach. The laid-back place that I remembered, maybe it was still there, but you'd have to look a lot harder to find it. What I saw was Japanese tourists and Filipino worker slaves, just like Guam. When we turned into this Las Vegas–style hotel, when I saw a showroom big enough for the Republican convention, I started to sweat. Elvis pictures were all over the place—someone had gone out and papered the town—and that made me feel worse, like they were wanted posters. I got sick as soon as we arrived. Then I went outside. They had one of these irregular pools, shaped like a kidney or a liver, jungle-looking, with dozens of Japanese tourists around the edge, smoking cigarettes and burning the skin off their backs. I hated the idea of trying to entertain them, of my songs going into those ears, like water down a drain. Clueless sunstroke victims, duty-free dipshits, slide-rule club on vacation: our first audience. Karaoke kids. I found a chair in the shade and told the Filipino to bring me a club soda. The whole setup felt no-win. The club soda felt like it was going down the up staircase. I turned the chair around so it faced the beach. Trying to get a grip. Funny, they make a big deal about putting hotels on the beach and then they forget it, it's just where the sun sets.

"Some hotel!" Chester came up from behind me, just bubbling over.

"There's a refrigerator in our room all filled with stuff. And did you see that fruit basket! They got grapes!"

"Great, Chestnut. My big thrill was snapping the paper band around the toilet seat before I vomited."

"You going to be all right, Dude?"

"Yeah, sure. Never better. I'm jet-lagged is all."

"Dude, it's a twenty-five-minute flight."

"Shut up, Chestnut."

"You know what I thought of when I saw you sitting out here across the swimming pool? It was just like one of those Elvis movies, *Blue Hawaii* maybe, or *Paradise Hawaiian Style*."

He was smiling down at me, certain he was cheering me up. I'd never watched a whole Elvis film but I pictured lots of women in out-of-date bathing suits and stupid fight scenes and songs coming in out of left field. Old, stale movies. Was that my world now?

That afternoon, after sound checks and rehearsals, we sat together at a table in the empty showroom. Professor Wiggins had polished off a plate of egg rolls and now he contemplated ice cream that my brother said wasn't bad at all. I couldn't eat. Chester had picked up a postcard that was on a table near the front door. You know the kind: it shows the place with all the tables set, flowers on every table, ready for Japanese money to come walking in.

"How come," Chester wondered, "these postcards always show the place when it's empty?"

"What?" Now I was in negotiations with my stomach: I'd settle for a cease-fire. But my stomach said, vomit now or vomit later, it's up to you. How long can a stomach hold on to food anyway, before it has to go down? Or come up?

"They always show what the place looks like with no customers. It looks empty."

"You're deep, Chester," I said.

"I mean it. You go to a restaurant, it's not to look at restaurant furniture. I want stains on the tablecloth, people facing desserts they can't resist."

"You leave Ward out of this," I said. The eldest Elvis was reconnoitering something called an Island Sundae: pineapples, maraschino cherries, sliced bananas, and kiwis. God, if I ate and vomited that against the wall I could be an art major.

"Huh?" said Chester. "Oh . . ." He laughed a little to please me, then worried he shouldn't have laughed because Ward's feelings might be hurt, though he didn't look to be in any particular pain right now. At least the Filipino took away the dish before Elvis licked it clean.

"Another Island Sundae, sir?"

"I'll wait awhile, thanks.'

"Check on him twenty minutes from now," I suggested, and went upstairs to vomit again and put on my leather. The things we do for love, right? My brother Chester didn't have many ideas but when he did, it was a lulu.

That first time onstage is like the first time you get laid. Mainly, you want to get through it okay, complete the performance. And later, when you think about it, it's hard to sort it out, what worked and what didn't, when you should have slowed it down some, or speeded up, the was-it-good-for-you and do-you-want-to-do-it-again. You just want to get through it and the truth is I don't remember much.

The showroom was full, I noticed, and they were all Japanese tourists, not counting the Filipino waiters. I saw some of the same people I'd seen around the swimming pool. Maybe a sunburn is a kind of status symbol in Japan, it shows you've been away, you walk around Tokyo with the skin peeling off your nose. Anyway, they were out there, drinking in groups, smoking in groups, and—I could picture it—getting ready to walk out in groups. They were a young crowd, low-budget, just like Guam. No time for a slow tan, I guessed: just go out and microwave yourself. Some could hardly move in their chairs. A few of the girls looked sharp, though. Small but sharp. You heard these stories about Japanese tourist women, how they kicked up their heels away from home.

So it began. Our careers as Elvis. The backup guys were playing "Don't

Be Cruel" and offstage, Ward was reading about how it was 1956 and Eisenhower is president and Marciano is champ and Ed Sullivan is on TV. . . . all for this audience of Japanese! Then, he said, a poor man's son was born in Tupelo, Mississippi—in a manger, probably—and a few years later, having moved to Memphis, he picks up a guitar and so forth. It sounded like a Christmas pageant and I'm worried they'll walk out on us. Then, oh my God, my kid brother was onstage singing "Blue Suede Shoes" and the whole room lifted off the ground and it was going to be okay. We were going for a ride tonight. We were driving. The Professor had it right, I guess. When Chester Lane came onstage they moved in their chairs. When I was onstage, they were moving in bed. I could feel their eyes, peeling that black leather right off me. Nice Chester, giggle and cuddle, jitterbug and neck, Mama won't mind, and then, when I was up there—"I want you, I need you, I love you"—I could feel them sliding off their chairs, reaching for their room keys, those nasty girls from Nippon. Before I know it, I was standing next to Chester, waiting to join the Professor for the closing tableau and I put my arm around the kid. In front of us, Ward boomed "Suspicious Minds," he poached "Loving You" and made it sound like a loser's last chance, then karate chopped his way through "Burning Love."

"Is it just me," I asked Chester, "or is he singing 'Burning Love' for the sunburn victims?"

"He's singing to everybody," Chester whispered. He had this serious side, solemn almost. He was the kind of kid who gets one of those you-already-have-won letters from the magazine subscription company and looks for Ed McMahon to come up the driveway. On Guam.

"We could cut a deal with Coppertone," I said. Chester shushed me and we walked onstage for "American Trilogy" and I swear the audience gasped, seeing us standing there together, it was like one plus one plus one adds up to eternity. Ward was crooning "Dixie" and now I saw what he was aiming for with this act of ours. Chester took them to Memphis, to truck stops, radio stations, roadhouses. I brought them to Hollywood and Hawaii, movie sets and beach resorts. Ward took them to Las Vegas and died and went to heaven. No encores after that.

"Okay!" I said to him as soon as we were offstage. "You were right!"

He just nodded. He was flushed and out of breath and sweating harder than anybody I ever saw. "Could I borrow your towel?"

"It's just like you told us," Chester said. "We're larger than life."

"Larger," Wiggins said. Then he caught my eyes. What he said next was for me, no mistaking it, and later he said the same thing to Jimmy Fiddler when he drove us in from the Manila airport. "Longer too. You'll see."

"Many Americans love it here. They come here and they never want to leave. Sometimes, if they go stateside, they come back." That was what they said in Olongapo. I can't remember where I heard it first. Maybe it was from Jimmy, or from one of the Filipinos we hired for backup after we arrived. No, wait, maybe it was the woman who ran Graceland, the day we checked out the place, Malou, the brainy-looking one who didn't put out. Anyway, you heard it all the time. And it was true. Americans loved it, all right. And the dumber they were, the more they loved it. The place was paradise, if you're a certain kind of American, if the most important things in your life were steak and pussy. You got the steak, lots of it, top-grade, choice, served the way you like it, at 1950s prices, inside the base. And you got the other stuff, young or old as you want it, served the way you like it, on the other side of the fence. At 1950s prices.

Some people could be happy forever with a setup like that. I admit I was in hog heaven for a while. The Professor took us aside when we arrived and gave us this talk about the birds and the bees. No matter what else we did, he said, we shouldn't mix business with pleasure, shouldn't do business with the girls who worked at Graceland, even though they'd be wanting to do business with us. He was appealing to our professionalism and our pride, he said. And that night, as a matter of professionalism and pride, I started working my way through the girls.

It was easy. There's a rule I heard about out at Subic City one night, the rule of the haircut. Some old chief petty officer announced it to me like he was serving up the law of gravity. The wisdom of the East. The rule of the haircut: everywhere you go, far and wide, high and low, the price of a woman is about the price of a haircut. "The high end might be a wash and blow-dry at a hairstylist, a couple hundred bucks maybe," this old redneck said. "That could last all afternoon. The low end is a five-buck trim near the bus terminal, in and out in twenty minutes."

I went wild, the way anybody would, with all these fine cheap women around, two or three a night, one or two at a time, kiss me good night and wake me up in the morning, the pitter-patter of little feet. Elvis needs you, darling. Newcomers fresh from the provinces, foxy boxers right out of the ring, ex-convent girls and Arabs' mistresses, the snooty-looking Spanish senorita types and the dark and funky Malays. It tickled me, sometimes, to look around Graceland and count the ones I'd had. First, a minority, a loyal opposition, then a quorum, a majority. And if it weren't for Malou—I'm still not sure what she does for fun—or her highness Elvira and a couple of others, I'd have had them all. Matter of professionalism, Professor. Matter of pride.

It's hard to say what happened next. Kind of embarrassing. The bottom line is that, after a month of take-a-number-please, fall-in-line fornication, I'd had enough. The girls of Graceland were still fine-looking, don't get me wrong, and I was still waking up wanting it, every morning. But a couple things got to me. At Graceland, I'd see them working the tables, hustling drinks and fines, slipping into the VIP lounges, out into cribs or cars, coming back and going out again, turning two or three tricks a night, and I'd look at the guys they were going with and it bothered me, it even hurt some, picturing what they were up to. Or I'd see some cheerful Dolly or Priscilla out back washing some guy's come out of her hair. And humming a tune. I'd thought they were lining up for me. Then I saw I was wrong. I was lining up for them. And it wasn't just about sloppy seconds. It wasn't that I didn't want to be last in line. I also didn't want to be first. I didn't want to be in line at all, in any line including all those bodies I'd seen in gym class, red-blooded American boys, waiting to unload on them. Fucking unfair, I thought. And sad, besides. I'd be onstage singing "I Want You, I Need You, I Love You" and across the room I'd spot someone I'd been to bed with, sitting next to some bench-press crewcut kid, his hand on her butt, hard-assing her about springing for a margarita and she'd flash me this look which said—which begged—*rescue me*. I saw that look so often. Pretty soon, it seemed, I saw it everywhere I looked. Or, if I passed them out back, they'd sing a little bit of a song, not exactly aiming at me, just putting it in the air, "Are You Lonesome Tonight" or "True Love." They'd say they didn't mean anything by it, if I asked, they were only singing a song, what's the difference, but I knew better and it bothered me, having songs I sang come back at me that way, like lies. It bothered me, too, admitting that the Professor was right, to have him teach me a lesson about professionalism and pride, him living on the beach, all by himself, loving nobody, no kind of role model at all. Anyway, I cut down—and out—on the fine women of Graceland. I'm embarrassed to say it, like all of a sudden I wasn't a man. Failure in the sack, that's what it sounds like. But it wasn't like that. The problem was someplace else, in my head or maybe my heart. I don't know. I just didn't want to be part of the party that was going on there. Me of all people, the sexiest Elvis, bailing out.

Once I turned off Graceland women, Olongapo got old for me, small, dirty. And I couldn't see a way out. Chester was loving it. And the show, the Elvis act, kept packing them in. The fleet sailed away but the act sailed on, guys from the base taking up the slack, repeat customers and—this surprised me—people driving over from Manila. We had valet parking all of a sudden and a gift shop that sold Elvis souvenirs, books and records and pictures, not just pictures of Elvis either, but pictures of *us*. That was weird, I thought, and I told Ward I thought it was weird, imitation Elvis getting tangled up with the Original, and we had another Twilight Zone dialogue.

"I don't like it either," he said, nodding his head, then shaking it with regret. "It's the commercialization I don't like. I hear it was the owner's idea. Baby Ronquillo. Do you happen to know . . . is Baby a man or a woman?"

"A woman," I said. "Though we could always get a second opinion." I was already acquainted with the legend of Baby Ronquillo. She'd climbed the ladder right out of here. Then she bought the ladder, just for old times' sake, and, now and then, climbed back down to look at where it all began for her.

"Well, it's her place. But I don't like it. I think it's . . . tacky. Just to make a buck."

"Hey, Ward?" I asked. "Earth to Ward?"

"Yes."

"I've got news for you. This place is a business. It is commercial. We sell beer and whiskey for money. The girls sell their bodies, for money, and we get the bar fines. Coming and going, we make money."

Ward let me finish but he had this way of shaking his head, no, no, no, right when you were talking, as though he were saying you started out wrong and the more you spoke, the wronger you got. Annoying habit.

"You're not telling me anything I don't already know," he said when I finished. "It's a business, sure. But there's more than that going on here, Dude."

"What might that be?"

"If you have to ask . . ."

"Thanks a lot, then. I guess I dodged a bullet. Remind me not to ask."

I didn't have to ask, though. I knew. It was happening all around us. Graceland was changing, taking on airs. They dressed up the outside of the building to look like a southern mansion, with columns and a porch, and then they ran neon all around the edges of the building, so that at night the outlines of it were traced in pink. Vanilla ice cream with a raspberry swirl. They took down the sign that said GRACELAND. They'd put it up, just for us, right after we arrived. Before that, Graceland was Genghis Khan's Tent, Da Place, Burning Inferno, the Chicken Factory, a jinx location, too plush for the local market. At first, Graceland was just another name and the smart money said that in a month or so they'd be taking the sign down. The smart money was right, but for the wrong reasons. We didn't need the label, any more than the Taj Mahal needed a sign out front. People found their way to us. They weren't customers, they were pilgrims.

"No end in sight," I said to the Professor one night. We usually talked at the start of the show, while Chester was onstage. I could hear him singing "My Wish Came True." "I thought the novelty would wear off."

"We're not a novelty act," he answered. "Tiny Tim was a novelty act. Sha Na Na. The Village People. There's lots of novelty acts. Fifteen minutes of fame, like the man said. Not us, Dude. We're stayers."

Calm and confident as can be, he delivered all this, and I had this sickening feeling I was trapped in Olongapo, stuck in a black leather suit, singing Elvis tunes and when I died they'd drive me to the graveyard in a damn jeepney. I'd been thinking weeks, okay, months. He was talking till death us do part. When it came to the PI—the Philippine Islands, that is—I had a bad case of been there, seen it, done it. But Ward was only settling in.

"Business is only getting better," he continued. "You see that for yourself. It's not just the fleet and it's not only the naval base. We've got Filipinos driving over from Manila, we've got vans and buses in the parking lot, you notice? We're getting press too. Manila papers, airline magazines, *Stars and Stripes*. Have you seen this?"

He handed me a book in Japanese or Chinese, I couldn't tell which. I should start from the back, he said. I should turn it over.

It was a tourist guide, I guess, that had pictures of Manila Bay and Corregidor, of beaches and rice terraces and . . . of us. There we are, two glossy pages to ourselves and a photo of three of us onstage at the end of the act, Chester with his legs spread and back tilted, guitar up at the roof, and me with this fight-me-or-fuck-me look, and Jumbo the Elephant wiping his jowls with one hand, pointing his finger heavenward with the other, as if thanking God for our material. I thought I'd signed up for a music act, not a cult.

"I'll tell you something," the Professor said, and warning lights flashed on in my head. He sounded as though he were saying something that had just occurred to him, struggling to get it out, so I should be patient, listen carefully, not interrupt. But I was feeling like a character in a script he wrote, a script I was trapped in, the same script night after night. Hell, movie actors got to change roles, travel to different locations. Even in a sitcom or soap, at least the story moved along, things changed, people left town or died.

"He'd have come here."

"Excuse me?"

"He never played overseas. They say Colonel Parker—his, not ours—had immigration problems. I don't know. The whole world was there for him. But he played Hollywood and Vegas and a hundred pissant towns. You know where he was headed, when he died? The first concert they canceled? Two nights in Portland, Maine. The night after that, Utica, New York."

"So?" Portland and Utica were sounding pretty good to me.

"This is his kind of town. The navy base, the clubs, the beach, the neon strip, the audiences we get . . . the air we breathe . . . the air . . . the funk, the sex, the rot, the bloom . . ."

If you asked me to pinpoint, down to the second, the moment I thought Wiggins wobbled out of orbit, this was it. You could get into Elvis, I guessed. I didn't understand it. I didn't understand the people who did. But okay. You could be serious about the work you do. It was good to care about your work. But Ward was turning into Elvis' ambassador to planet earth, appointed for life. So, *caught in a trap.* I knew if we put this to a vote, right now, I'd lose, two to one. Chester would vote against me and Ward knew it. Out onstage, Chester was singing "Any Way You Want Me." After that, "Teddy Bear." Then it would be time for me to turn my trick in the House of Elvis.

"I know him better than you do," Ward said. He couldn't let go. "It's his kind of town."

"He's *my* brother," I reminded him.

"I'm not talking about your brother, Dude. I'm talking Elvis."

The Chestnut was coming offstage. I heard them wanting more but we didn't do encores. Elvis returned to earth on his terms, not ours. That's why he picked Olongapo. *His* kind of town. Our kind of town. All according to Ward. Sometimes he made it sound like the Original's life was just the start, an opening act, a rough draft. That the Elvis masterpiece was yet to come. Sometimes it scared me, hearing him talk. Other times, it pissed me off.

"I've got news for you, Professor," I said. "This was never supposed to be forever. You can stay all you want. But at the right time, we're gone."

"Who's we?" he asked.

"That's me and my brother," I snapped back. I was inside my leather, already sweating, feeling surly.

"I don't think so," the Professor said. "Your brother's stay here could outlast either of ours."

"Is that so?" That knowing manner irritated me. But the truth was, I hadn't seen so much of Chester since we arrived in Olongapo, especially after I started poking the Graceland cuties. He'd been hard to find, rushing in and out of the apartment, like there was always someone waiting for him. "Out with it," I said.

"You should hear it from him," the Professor said. "Brother to brother."

"Just . . ." It was time for my show. "Don't play with me, Ward."

"All right. I guess you didn't notice. While you were jumping the help here, your brother was falling in love. He's proposed, I hear."

The lights went dark just then and I stepped onstage. "Return to Sender."

The night Ward dropped that bomb on me, I left Olongapo for Manila. We worked Wednesday through Saturday night. Sunday through Tuesday was a slow time for me. Chester was always taking off someplace, out to provinces with some of the girls. He invited me along but I knew better. Piling into a jeepney with some off-duty hookers wasn't my idea of fun, or riding in an interisland boat with no schedule and no lifeboats. Besides, I'd seen that look of disappointment when they knocked on the door and I answered, two or three girls with some food for Chester. It didn't matter if I'd had every one of them, every which way, it wasn't me they cared to see. But Chester was fair game. I thought about him that night, on the bus, passing through villages and rice fields on the way to Manila.

Put it this way: suppose every day, somebody threw a party for you, so that you couldn't step through a door without a bunch of people yelling "Surprise!" That, roughly, was how my brother Chester got through life, ambushed by everybody's love for him. Was I jealous? Damn straight! Who wouldn't be? But I was more worried than jealous. You had to fear the worst for a guy like the Chestnut. It got to the point I'd walk around thinking, okay God, if somebody has to lose a girlfriend or have an accident, grow a tumor in his brain, and it's between me and my kid brother, if it's between Conrad Birdie and Billy Budd, let it be me Lord because I can hack it and Chester can't.

And the Philippines! Bringing Chester to the Philippines, all these women, it was like asking a puppy to play in traffic. He was bound to get hit. I deserved some of the blame. I got distracted after I arrived, I got carried away on the sexual side of things. I was like a baseball player who doesn't want to get out of the batting cage. I had that stroke, man, getting good wood on the ball, knocking them out of the park. Home runs, baby. I figured Chester, in his own small way, was up to the same thing. Who wouldn't be, except ex-Professor Ward Wiggins? But I never dreamed my kid brother would fall in love here in Olongapo. That's plain crazy. That's like going to the stockyards, the damned meat packing plant, and saying, could I please adopt this here little lamb as a pet?

"What's up, Dude?" he had asked when I finally caught up with him after the show. It was hard for Chester to act innocent. He either was or he wasn't and in this case he wasn't.

"You know what, Chestnut," I said. "And don't pretend you haven't been ducking me."

"I just don't want to argue with you, Dude," he said, and I could see he was getting ready to feel all choked up and torn.

"Who's arguing?" I said. "I just want to be in the loop."

"Then you'll argue," he said.

"Try me," I said. And then, when he sat there, tongue-tied, I decided to help him. "So," I said, "I guess you think you're in love."

"I know I am," he said right back.

"I see," I said. And I waited a couple beats, almost as if that settled things for good. "How do you know you're in love, Chestnut?"

"You know," he said, looking straight at me but—it seemed—he was talking down, as if he were reporting on a trip to some country I'd never visited.

"*How* do you know?" I asked. "Enlighten me, little brother. Is it like in the movies, you walk around and you hear music all the time?"

"Honest, Dude, I don't think you'd understand. You're lots smarter than me and more experienced too. Maybe that's why you wouldn't get it."

"I see," I snapped back. "If I'd had less experience and less brains . . . if only I were a little dumber and younger, maybe I could figure it out."

"Come on, Dude," he pleaded. "Don't do this."

"Well, do I get to meet my future sister-in-law?"

"In a while . . . " he said. "Sure . . ."

"In a while." Suddenly the Chestnut was an expert on timing. "How the hell well do you know this woman? You even met her family?"

"Yes . . ."

"Visited her home?"

"Yes."

"You got any kind of idea where you want to spend your life? Where your home is? Your work? Because this Elvis thing won't last forever."

"We have plans, Dude," he said. "We talk all the time."

"This girl from the boondocks—"

"Her name's Christina."

"Well, what do you talk about with her? Her favorite color? *Your* favorite color?"

"Come off it, Dude."

"What could you possibly . . . " I didn't even bother finishing: *have in common.* I sensed that, across all the gaps, passport and sex and race and everything, they were two of a kind, two clueless people, two of the kind who never quite figure it out. Love makes you stupid, I guess, but you come out of it. Unless you weren't so bright to start with. Then it's like a nap turning into a coma.

"You do anything besides talk?" I asked. And as soon as it was out, I saw my kid brother's face turn into a kind of a fist. So I asked again, whether they did anything but talk, and he still didn't answer and so I kept going because I was falling fast, I knew, but I hadn't hit bottom yet.

"You given her a tryout, Chester?"

Now his eyes filled with tears but he was crying for me and how cruel I was, or pathetic. So I got a little crueler and more pathetic.

"You'd take a car for a spin . . ."

"She's no car," he protested. "And she hasn't been used."

"If you say so," I answered back. Out of nowhere, I pictured somebody crawling under the dashboard, ass in the air, setting this woman's mileage back to zero. "Still . . . all the more reason. . . . Just try it. . . . Everybody does it. They expect you to. If you don't they'll laugh at you. And you don't want that, do you, Chester? *More* people laughing at you?"

In Manila, I stayed in a hotel a few blocks in from Roxas Boulevard, slept through lunch, slept after lunch, and, at sunset, I walked along the seawall, checking out the ships that my brother had gotten so excited about. I passed the U.S. Embassy, through the park they call Luneta, the children's playground at the edge of the park, kids running from sandbox to slide to seesaw, this endless supply of Filipino kids, nannies and parents looking after them. Then I sat in the lobby of the Manila Hotel, sat there for hours, enjoying marble that was so smooth and cool it made you want to roll across the floor and walls and ceiling that were dignified dark wood, with a luster like leather. I watched people come and go, people with schedules and serious business out in the world, plane tickets and reservations out across the dateline, expensive-looking people with places to go. Not all of them, of course. A couple dozen Taiwanese tourists could turn the place into Disneyland and there were always a couple of lounging Filipinos, carrying cordless phones the way cowboys pack six-shooters. Still, it wasn't Olongapo. It felt good, being out of there, being in a place where no one knew me, where I could be anyone. I liked checking out women—some of those perfect haughty beauties who worked the reception desk and probably didn't live off bar fines. I wondered what it would be like, sitting down and talking to a woman who didn't reach for my zipper after she'd used up her ten words of conversational English. I wondered if I still had it in me to fall for a woman or make a woman fall for me, someone with a little class and refinement, someone like one of those reception-desk girls, manicured and multilingual and computer literate. Olongapo had contaminated me. It leaked out of my pores, dripped off my tongue. It threw a scent that nothing could cover, no change of wardrobe could disguise. Elvis used to be my act. Now Elvis was me and everything else was a performance.

Later I ate alone at a German restaurant on Del Pilar Street, watching a months-old soccer tape. I walked past money changers and barbecue stalls, barbershops and VD doctors and hostess bars. I passed labor recruiters' offices. Wanted: a go-go dancer, a construction worker, carpenter, pipefitter, attractive hostess, driver, able seaman, nurse, for Kuwait, Taiwan, Saudi Arabia, Singapore, Saipan, Malaysia. Everywhere but here. And everyone but me. No call for Presley imitators so far as I could see. And no way out for one. Here I was, an Olongapo star, an Elvis clone, aching to escape but no idea of how to do it. Every idea I had sounded ridiculous, like a porn star wanting to make a serious film. *You can't get there from here.* I looked around whatever bar I was in, another room jammed with Filipinas climbing poles and studying themselves in mirrors.

Way past midnight and already drunk, I turned into a nightclub on Mabini Street. I sat at a bar and watched midgets. The doorman was a midget. A midget was playing guitar onstage, "Take Me Home, Country Roads," all that hick whining stuff, so far from home. The first ten minutes was between me and my beer. After that, I looked around. This was the Hobbit House: all midget staff, the emcee, the waitresses, barmen, the comfort room attendants. And I'd arrived on the best of nights. It was as though they'd been waiting for me to come through the door. Because the emcee was announcing a contest. For dwarfs. Who sang. Elvis Presley.

Now I ordered shots with my beers and watched them do their thing, which was our thing, only more so. Smaller—obviously—but more exaggerated. Shrinking magnified them, the way a bacteria stuck between a glass slide looks bigger under a microscope. It was like watching my life, all stretched out in front of me, smaller and smaller all the time. Chester's Elvis was more childlike, my Elvis was more macho, like the anger had gotten compressed. Ward's Elvis launched into "In the Ghetto," the voice of an opera singer out of the body of a fire hydrant. They'd copied what we copied. That about clinched it, I thought. They were kids playing a kid's game and so were we. We weren't actors, we were imposters, dressing up in someone else's clothes, and songs, and life. Ward Wiggins could say whatever the hell he wanted. He could call himself Elvis the way a hooker would call herself Whitney or Dolly or Madonna. But at the end of the day we were all cheap tricks.

"Out scouting the competition?" someone asked. I turned slowly on my bar stool and looked into sunglasses, scarred skin, and the mouth of a muskrat. "I like these guys more than your act," Jimmy Fiddler said. "These guys have a sense of humor about themselves. They *know* they're ridiculous."

I signaled for my check and wished I were out of there already but checks take forever to arrive in the Philippines. They don't trust the help to add, I guess, so there's always a Chinese-looking woman behind a teller's booth, keeping tabs.

"Your drinks are taken care of," Jimmy said. "There's someone wants to meet you."

"No thanks," I said. My guess was that Jimmy wanted to bring me over to meet all the baby Presleys. They'd pull me onstage for a song, maybe hang on my arms, sit on my shoulders, scoot between my legs, like Santa and his little helpers. That would tickle him no end.

"Baby Ronquillo wants to meet you," Jimmy said. "Does that register with you?"

"The person who owns Graceland?"

"Shit, you don't know the half of it. Graceland's nothing. A toy. She owns a five-star hotel in Palawan and a logging concession in Mindanao and a golf course on Cebu. Then there's the movie studio. . . ."

That got my attention, though Jimmy wasn't done yet. "A French restaurant in Makati. Condos in Alabang. A placement service for overseas workers. She ships them out by the planeload. Shipshape, the company's called."

While Jimmy talked I looked over at a woman dressed in a black suit, tailored-looking, that had threads of silver and gold woven into the sleeves. Good legs, I noticed, hair in a bun, still black. While I was looking at her she was looking at me, so there were two of us who were making an inventory. The famous Baby Ronquillo. From bar girl to boardroom. At Graceland, they said her big break came back in the Marcos days, when there'd been some international meeting in Manila—was it the World Bank?—and the local talent had been trotted out to welcome visitors, $3,000 a pop. Baby stayed attached to her banker and when she left him, months later, she was off her knees forever. Or so they said at Graceland, where they told it as if it were a Cinderella story. Now the living legend was staring at me from across the room, wanting for us to meet. I wondered why. I asked myself, why not? And then I got scared. I realized I was in deep. I was up against quality. And I was drunk. This was one deal I couldn't screw up. I turned back to Jimmy.

"Tell me about the movie studio."

Malou Ordonez

Biggest Elvis walked away and we laughed at him. Then the drinks came, the bar drinks that he ordered for us, blue margaritas which tasted like melted candy and we earned half the cost of the drink, which matched the daily minimum wage in a country where the minimum was negotiable because we could always go a little lower. The Americans knew it, even the first-time sailors, the R & R boys, when they bargained for bodies, how much for a short time, how much for all night, for one hole, two holes, three holes. So it was cheers, Biggest Elvis, though we poured your drinks into the toilet, here's looking at you, Biggest Elvis.

"Malou, you spoke fresh to him," Elvira said. "And he makes me put what you say into English."

"You could have told him I said anything. 'What a handsome man!' 'I love the way you walk.' 'The bigger, the better, the biggest, the best!' "

"I could not think so fast," she said. This was so. Elvira, we said, had a limousine body. A beautiful woman, built the way that Americans liked, and Arabs, and Japanese. She had the body, the fall of hair, that Spanish nose, those breasts—her "moneymakers," the other girls called them. Men took her on trips to Singapore and Hong Kong and she returned with whole wardrobes of clothing. "If they undress me, they can dress me too." Not only nightclub clothes, Olongapo things, but hats and shoes, sweaters and leather jackets and furs that she would never wear here. Souvenirs, she called them. But she always came back to Olongapo. Elvira the beautiful, the bountiful, the forgiving and forgetting. She didn't come to the club every night. She never went with men for short times. She sat, she flirted, and when the moment came, she quoted an absurd price, four or five times higher than the other girls. Still, when the fleet was in, Elvira met them. In Olongapo, we all waited for the fleet.

"Biggest Elvis," Elvira said. "Is it true he never takes a girl?"

"He leaves here alone. Every night is like tonight."

"He has someone in his house, maybe."

"No," I answered. "The bartender—Remy—his family lives near there. He says Biggest Elvis stays by himself. He sleeps all day."

"I think . . ." I knew what she was thinking. I knew how the sight of Biggest Elvis going home alone could grow into a love affair, a marriage, a life together away from here. "I think Biggest Elvis is lonely," Elvira announced.

"Here," I said. "Eat something." I passed over some green mangoes and a plate of salt. To fill her mouth and to stop her dreaming.

"Baby Elvis is very popular," I suggested. "Everybody loves him."

"He's a nice boy," Elvira said. But she wasn't interested. Even now, dipping mango in salt, Elvira had elegance, holding the mango between thumb and forefinger, pointing her little finger outward as she put the slice between her lips. Elvira was royalty. Our Marie Antoinette. She loved hotels, air-conditioning, airports, duty-free shopping. She loved meals prepared at her table in five-star places, pepper steak and Caesar salad, cherries jubilee, bananas flambé, Irish coffee. She brought back menus to Graceland, menus from room service at the Oberoi, the Grill at Raffles. She brought baskets of perfume, bubble bath, shoeshine kits and shower caps, stationery. She brought back ballpoint pens with no caps and clothes hangers without hooks. She brought Bibles and city maps and copies of *What's Doing in Perth* and *This Week in Hong Kong*.

"There is the middle Elvis," I said. "Dude Elvis. Very available."

"I don't want him," Elvira said, cocking her head toward the VIP rooms along the balcony. That was where Dude Elvis took his friends, Manilenos and foreigners, for special parties behind dark glass. One night, we saw

Baby Ronquillo there and Dude Elvis joined her, after his act was done. Elvira did not compete with Baby Ronquillo.

"I don't want that Dude," Elvira repeated, shaking her head. "But Biggest Elvis . . ."

No, I thought, this was another Elvira mistake. They had all been mistakes, all her men. At least she had her souvenirs and no babies. Many others had babies and no souvenirs, red-haired freckle-faced babies, babies with wide African noses.

"No, Malou," she was saying. "I do not think of Biggest Elvis for myself. "I think of him for you."

It took time for me to answer. My friend Elvira was not a smart woman. But she had instincts. She looked at a man and right away it was yes, no, or maybe. "If I can picture something happening, it can happen," she always said. "If I can see it in my mind, never a problem." Now she pictured me with Biggest Elvis. "You could have him, Malou," she said. Not a doubt in her mind. Finished already. Elvis and Malou.

"For what? What do I want that man for? I had one American already. As you know."

"It's up to you," she said. Behind her, just then, was her driver. Where Elvira stayed was only a minute away, an air-con apartment a man from Brunei provided for her. But Elvira did not walk the streets. She stood up, brushed some grains of salt off her lips. She couldn't help it. Everything she did was sexy. Sometimes I thought I would like to make love with Elvira. That was something *I* could picture. There was something about Olongapo, the Navy talk, the world they brought and the world we brought to them, those thousands of cocks, that made us look at each other sometimes and think of other ways, the chance of something fond and gentle, soft not hard. So we found ourselves, sometimes, staring and wondering about what love might be.

"Think about him, Malou," Elvira said. She left, taking three other girls with her, newcomers from Visayas. She had some clothes for them, she said. And a place to stay, if they needed it. The other girls, the ones who slept upstairs in the empty VIP rooms, disappeared up the steps. Then I closed the club for the night, though it was never really shut, never empty. In the PI, no place ever closed. A bartender slept in the back, plus some girls upstairs and a guard who was also a doorman, blue-uniformed and carbine-carrying, sitting in the doorway all night long, dozing between oversized cut-out figures of the three Elvis Presleys. And if the boys from the fleet came back at four in the morning, Graceland would open once again, open anytime, open as wide as necessary, one size fits all.

I gave the boy who watched the car ten pesos and drove down Magsaysay Street. The windows were up, the doors locked, the air-conditioning on. Where the road went into the base, American sailors piled out of jeepneys, buses, taxis, three-wheelers, a mob of drunken boys leaving a trail of spilled beer and semen from here to Subic City. On my left and right, they walked across the Santa Rita Bridge. A line of cars preceded me to the gates. I dimmed the headlights and rolled down the windows. Some of the Americans noticed me. "That baby takes unleaded premium." Meaning no harm. The Filipino sentries knew my face. The American guards knew the plates, the sticker, the papers in my hand. They waved me through.

Subic Bay was an American place. It was not ours, not yet, though the newspapers said that someday the Americans would leave. Not ours, not yet, but I was a child of this place and when I drove over the bridge, across the river they called Shit's Creek, when I drove through the gate, the traitor in me relaxed. If you hear of a military base you picture gates, fences, guards, patrols, dogs. Subic had all of those things. But, consider the barracks, like college dormitories, the clubs, snack bars, shops and restaurants, the ice-blue swimming pool, the beaches and baseball fields, the lawns, cut and watered and smelling sweet. No jeepneys, no noise, no garbage, no crowding, no horn-blowing. Why not say it? No Filipinos. And why not admit it? I felt at home there.

I first entered the base with my mother, who worked as cook and *lavandera*—washerwoman—in the house I stayed in now, until recently the quarters of Commander Andrew Yauger. Mrs. Doris Yauger was a thin, golf-playing woman with a smoker's cough and a whiskey voice, who later left for a hospital in San Diego. The Yaugers had no children. Commander

Andy encouraged my mother to bring me to work. To play. I had television, swimming pool, hamburgers, ice cream, stereo. Commander Andy was a kind man and a good American. At the base he was in charge of civic action projects in the barrios around the base, dispensaries, roads, schoolhouses. He sponsored handicraft cooperatives, handicapped Olympics, Little League Teams, scholarship raffles, dozens of good works. He sponsored me. I was one of his good works.

In my high school years, I helped my mother with parties that Commander Andy and Doris would give. That was me, a tray of *lumpia* in my hands, circulating among officers and wives, not a servant so much as a friend of the family, a bright young Filipina who devoured good books, won spelling bees, memorized the U.S. and Philippines presidents. And I spoke such wonderful English. "Very" not "berry." I recited Edna St. Vincent Millay's "Renascence," *lumpia* tray in one hand, napkins in the other, "above the earth is stretched the sky, no higher than the soul is high . . ." Thanks to Commander Andy, I had pen pals in Korea, Spain, Germany, and Chicago. I wonder if they wonder what became of me. I was headed for the University of the Philippines under Commander Andy's sponsorship. Yes, I was planning to major in English and business administration, a poet with a pocket calculator, very impressive. *Would I like to visit America? Someday, of course, perhaps, but only just to visit, for my home is the Philippines, my country which I love, to be made a better place.* I had all the answers. And Commander Andy Yauger beamed.

Sometimes, Commander Andy would take me with him when he went into the barrios. I would sit with him through sweltering meetings with barrio leaders, school groups, women's clubs, watching him greet and joke, watching him stand and join in singing the Philippines national anthem. Often, he was the only one in the room who knew all the words, though those were the only Tagalog words he knew. After the national anthem, he needed an interpreter. That was me. Commander Andy was at his happiest out in the barrios. No speech was too long, no request too small, no building too hot. He arrived on time, when meeting halls were empty, and he was always the last to leave, never declining a meal of local food he could never guess at, local food he praised. Then, on the ride home, I would watch him wince and sweat, it never failed, yet still he asked for seconds and cleaned his plate, even though he knew he'd be sick, pulling off to the side of the road, to vomit. Sometimes he had diarrhea. In this way, in our own way, we became intimate.

The Urban Farmers Cooperative was one of Andy's favorite projects. Commander Andy had noticed that in even the worst parts of Olongapo, in the squatter settlements along the river or the shack colonies up in the hills, Filipinos did what they could to make things better. They put flower pots in the meanest alleys, tin cans filled with soil, bougainvillea trained to cover tarpaper walls, papaya trees fighting out of tiny squares of baked, dead clay. Commander Andy arranged for a hillside plot high above Olongapo to be divided into gardens and offered to local poor. He arranged for a water pipe that would run from the base to the gardens. He established a schedule for a jeepney that would take people up to the gardens and back down and—just to be safe—he arranged for some old men to keep watch on the gardens, day or night. For those who did not eat all of what they grew, he promised that base restaurants would purchase anything they offered. What I have said sounds simple but, oh, the meetings, the requests, the excuses; the poor so hapless, the landowners so predatory. The driver wanted extra money for carrying vegetables. The barrio people wanted to be paid for permitting a water pipe to run in front of their houses. The farmers wanted an advance on crops they hadn't harvested. Others tried to rent out, sublet, even sell plots they hadn't even planted. Still, in the end it worked: eggplant, tomatoes, onions, pepper, garlic appeared. Miracles. There were flowers too and benches with a view of the city and the base, where people could sit while children ran from plot to plot, watering vegetables, splashing themselves, squealing with delight.

We would often stop at the gardens on our way back from other projects, many of them unsuccessful. The Olongapo way was to take as much as you could as quickly as you could. And the place to get things was the base. How could it be different, when all that separated a first-world superpower and a third-world city was a polluted river? With the Americans, the only question was how—and how quickly—you could turn their presence to your advantage. And there was this: no matter how much you got, you'd never get even.

Once, shortly after he had returned from home leave, we drove past Subic City, to a village in Zambales where Commander Andy had donated materials for a basketball court: concrete, hoops, nets, lights—so the people could play at night—and benches, so that old people and children could watch the games. It was the idea of the garden all over again, a project for the whole community, Americans just getting it started, contributing the missing pieces and then backing away. "The sooner it becomes a Filipino thing, the better," Commander Andy said.

In this case, it had become a Filipino thing a little too quickly. In fact, before it was built. Muddy puddles marked the place where the basketball court should have been. Cement, lumber, fencing, and wiring, all had been delivered, all were gone. Nothing had changed. Nothing had moved, except the materials themselves. Commander Andy sat behind the wheel of his car, a white Chevrolet which everyone in the barrio had learned to welcome. But this time no one came out to greet us.

"Tell me I wasn't kidding myself, Malou," Commander Andy said after a while. "This wasn't something that was just my idea, was it?"

"No sir," I said.

"They all wanted this basketball court, didn't they? They were all on board. At least they said they were. You were there, most of the meetings. Was there something I was missing?"

I shook my head. I was ashamed of myself for being from the Philippines. And angry at Commander Andy for making me feel ashamed. And also a little grateful that I was better, already, than the people who lived here. It had started raining again, harder than before, and the puddles came together on the would-be basketball court and soon it was underwater, all of it.

"We could go out into the rain, Malou, and go knocking on doors," Commander Andy said.

"If you want sir, I can . . ." I was already reaching for the door handle.

"Sit still, Malou," he said. "It's raining too hard. And besides, you already know what happened. Don't you?"

"Yes sir."

"So tell me."

"Tell you?"

"Sure. Tell me what happened here. Tell me a story."

"Sir?" I didn't like the way he was pressing me. At one moment, he confided in me, he shared. We were partners. Now he used me: Local testimony. Specimen. Exhibit.

"I need an explanation, why this particular photo opportunity for the admiral isn't coming off on time. Unless they want to come out and make mudpies."

"All right, Commander Andy," I said. "Someone stole your equipment. Someone came and took what he wanted or he sent some boys to take it for him. Not in disguise. Not in the middle of the night. They came and took what they wanted while everyone was watching and nobody was doing anything to stop them."

I gestured toward the houses around us. Poor, small places, hammered together with wood and tin that had been part of other houses, before typhoons came along, and after the next storm they'd be part of other houses. In the meantime, they were homes to families of ten and twelve. Homes where there was always someone awake and always someone sleeping.

"Maybe someone came out and spoke to them. Someone who was at your meetings, someone who asked—" I stopped to catch my breath. "Someone who asked who sent them. And the boys mentioned a name and that was the end of it. The name of someone who can take what he wants. And that was the end of it. Because the person who asked wasn't supposed to die defending the money of U.S. taxpayers. Was he?"

"Okay, Malou," he said. He'd softened now. He was smiling.

"I'm not finish," I said. I corrected myself. "Finished. Because after they took what they wanted there was something left behind. A bag of this or that. Some loose nails, maybe. A few boards. Scraps and garbages . . . garbage. Little things. And the people who live around here and saw what happened and did nothing to stop it because there was nothing they could do . . . then they came and took what was left and they became part of what happened, until there was nothing left but what you see."

He sat quiet for a while after I had finished, looking out at the rain. The whole place ached with failure and guilt, it seemed to me. Then, even as the rain kept pouring down, some children ran onto the court, four or five of them, splashing, diving, sliding, rolling around and covering themselves with mud, then standing up and letting the rain shower them clean. Commander Andy watched them and I knew he'd already forgiven them, and their parents, that tomorrow he would try again, here or somewhere else. "Look at them go!" he said. "Kids and puddles. Put a puddle next to a swimming pool, a puddle always wins."

By the time we drove through Barrio Barretto, the rains had passed, and also his bad mood. Everything was clean and dripping, the road steaming and the air so fresh, we rolled down the windows. "Let's go watch the sunset from up high," Andy suggested. "And smell some flowers."

With this my heart sank again, because something had been happening at the Urban Gardens. Andy hadn't noticed it but the farmers had spoken of it, not to me but around me, and I knew it was only a matter of time. And that there was nothing to be done. Meanwhile I listened to Andy, fully himself, renewing our argument about whether we would see a so-called "green flash" at sunset, an explosion of gases he claimed to have witnessed many times at sea but which I had never seen in Olongapo. He teased me about it, even as we pulled into the Urban Gardens, or what was left of them. And then the teasing stopped.

The plants were all gone, except for a few dead cabbage leaves, brown as tobacco. The benches and fences had vanished also, all of it as if it had never been. Andy was dumbfounded. The basketball court had never been born. But the gardens had flourished, for a while. Crops had been harvested here, money earned, meals eaten. "What happened?"

"The water pipes," I said. "Illegal connections. One by one. So first the farmers have plenty water and then a little less and then a trickle that becomes a drop. And now . . . the result is what you see."

"*The result is what you see*," he repeated. "That's profound. Really, Malou. The result is what you see. So excuse me. I'm going to see the result."

He got out of the car and, from the way he slammed the door, I knew better than to follow. I leaned against the car, watching him move from plot to plot, although the borders were eroded and only little sticks with seed envelopes on top showed what had once been planted there. They looked like cemetery markers now.

"You knew about this one too," he said when he came out of the garden. "I sensed you weren't too happy about coming up here. You knew."

"I heard the farmers talk about it. Then . . . whenever I came here . . . I tried the water. Always it was less."

"Sure, I see." He turned away from me, sighting across the ruined garden. The sun had set behind the Zambales mountains and we had not even seen it go, it just slipped away. "I have a question or two for you, Malou. A bunch of questions. Like how long have I known you? And why didn't you tell me what was going on, why the hell didn't you tell me, or did it kind of tickle you, seeing me walking around stupid?"

That, I think, was the moment things changed for me. Because, when it had started, I was every Filipina confronted by an American. I was the maid who spills a drink, the *lavandera* who burns a shirt, the cook who puts a prime steak into the oven for two hours and turns it into pot roast. "Yes, mum." "Sorry, sir." The bowed head, the downcast eyes, the explanations that evaporated, English sentences falling apart under pressure. The customer was always right and the American was always the customer.

"The water," I said. "If I told you about the connections, you would turn off the water. You or the people you told. I did not like that. All over this country you see people carrying buckets of water from wells and faucets to their houses. Or they carry dishes and laundry to the water. Their clothes, their pots, their dirty bodies. And the water is never clean because this is the Philippines. There is always someone upstream, sending their dirt down to you. And there is always someone downstream, cleaning themselves in your dirty water."

I took a breath and gathered myself. I had Andy's full attention. He wasn't used to outbursts. He was a good man but—as I was learning—not as smart as I was, in some ways. Looking back, I see that I learned everything I needed to learn about Americans from Commander Andy. That night, a few lessons from him awaited me, but I could see them coming.

"I'm sorry about the basketball court. People took what they could. It's a shame. So the cement goes into someone's house and the lumber into some-one's roof. I'm sorry about your garden too. But the water that was meant for vegetables and flowers goes into tubs and mouths and pots. That's not what you planned. I'm sorry about your plans."

I could have gone on. There was no end to this kind of speech. The story of our lives, the history of our country. But I'd said enough. The power was already draining out of Commander Andy and toward me. Enough. More words would have been a waste. The Americans were curious about us, in the way that travelers are curious. They wondered aloud, they asked ques-tions, they immersed themselves in things. But, at a certain point, they stopped learning. They learned as much as they needed and they stopped. We kept on learning because we never stopped needing.

"All right, Malou," he said with a sigh. "My job is giveaways, goodwill, public relations. That's what they told me when I came. And I said, no, that's not my style. This is about community development. This is about nation-building, even. That's what I did. Thought I did. Tried to do. Now you're telling me I'm a Santa Claus after all. Reparations."

"Reparations?" I did not know the word and by now I'd learned never to fake it, when I did not know. And sometimes the people I'd been speaking to were fakers themselves.

"Repairing something that is broken . . . only you're the one who broke it," he said. "And maybe you can never fix it, even if you try. So you try and you pay. Understand?"

I nodded. And, before long, the issue of reparations arose again.

I'd felt it coming. There were those increasing confidences, first about work, then about his wife. She was ill, he told me, she was unhappy, she was with-out joy in him or for him and that, he said, went for every room of the house. So it happened, in a car, parked near the Binictitan Golf Course, a sudden lunge, a coupling so pent-up and so quickly over, it was almost as if the same song was playing on the radio when we were finished as when we began. Then the tears came. His, not mine. He leaned forward, head in his hands like an athlete who'd let down his team. What team, I wondered as I watched him, and what game? This was the game they all played in Olongapo. He hadn't let down the team. He'd joined it. Maybe that is why he was crying. Anyway, I knew he was mine then. My American. My first American.

I waited for his tears to pass, guessing that when his sadness was over he would want sex again. What should I tell him? Should I tell him—would it make any difference?—that he was not my first man, not quite, or should I let him blame himself for ruining me? What should I say? "That's all right." "These things happen." "We were friends before and we will be friends again." "I still respect you." Those were things that men said to women, not the other way around. Suddenly the whole thing was comical. I was glad his face was away from me, so that he could not see my smile. I decided not to tell him he was not the first. Something would have been lost, his pride in me, his shame in himself, the purity of the occasion, something that I could use, in the long run, to my advantage. I ran my fingers through his hair, patted his head. "Never again, Malou," he said when he pulled himself behind the steering wheel. It was a promise I was sure he would not keep.

I saw Commander Andy through the years at the University of the Philippines. He would come to Manila, sometimes on business, but eventually I knew he was coming to see me only. The one-sided relationship slowly faded; for him, as his departure for America grew closer, the guilt outweighed the pleasure. I say that now, as if I'd known what I was doing, yet part of me always believed that, when he left, he'd be taking me with him. And that, when he asked me, I would smile, I would think that I had seen this coming, I would compliment myself on having made it happen, and I'd have gone to America. There were two kinds of Filipinos. There were the ones who were destined for local consumption and others who were meant for export. I never doubted which category I was in. Commander Andy was my ticket out, I supposed. And I wasn't wrong. But, in the end, I miscalculated. My big mistake.

When I had finished at UP, I returned to Olongapo. Now, Commander Andy was short, headed home. His wife was already stateside. In a hospital. I knew all this. I was Andy's houseguest. And, once again, I was his project, answering questions about courses, grades, transcripts, prospects, boyfriends, all of it touching and tiresome, and, lurking beneath it all, was the knowledge that he still wanted me. It was in the air, in his every word and look. His life was at a crossroads. Down one road, an alcoholic, neurotic, sickly wife. Down the other, his Malou: his pride and friend and partner.

I worked and slept late and he was gone during the day. Those were the hours I loved, when I had the run of the house. I stretched out in a tub of cold water, I read a book in an air-conditioned bedroom, looking out the window at the wall of bamboo, and sometimes, when the wind blew, I'd hear the bamboo clicking, like so many chopsticks, tapping out a message. And the message was soon . . . soon . . . any minute now.

All the time I was there, I waited for him to come into my room some night. I wished he would. I tempted him. I tortured him. I felt sorry about the guilt he felt for me. I also wanted to use that guilt. And I realized what a weak foundation it was. At Graceland I charted dozens, hundreds of penetrations, all without love and without guilt, yet Commander Andy was filled with both. So I wanted to go to him and I waited for him to come to me, even as the days before his departure dwindled. I waited too long. I waited until the night before his departure. Then I decided the future wasn't for Commander Andy to decide. It was up to me. I left Graceland early and was in my room when he came home at midnight from a farewell dinner at the Officers' Club. I heard him open the sliding doors, step out onto the terrace, sit heavily in a chair. I walked softly across the living room and stood in the doorway in that delicious, wasteful place where cold air meets the humid night, where you could feel a cool breeze at your back and yet hear the sounds of birds and bamboo.

Commander Andy was sitting there, looking into his last Philippines night. I tiptoed behind him, put my hands on his shoulder. I leaned forward and my hair, left loose, came down upon him. I kissed him on the forehead, the way a daughter would kiss a father, saying good night. Yet he could feel my hair, when I leaned down to kiss him. And my breasts, just behind his head.

"May I join you?"

"Malou," he said. He touched my hands, which were still resting on his shoulders. "Yes. My God. I was just thinking . . ."

"Think aloud," I said.

". . . that I'm supposed to be happy, getting out of here. That was the theme of the evening. Nobody seemed to know how happy I've been. Except for you, Malou. You were my big screwup. There was nothing you couldn't have done. Now you're back here keeping tabs on . . . let's face it—a whorehouse."

"That's not your fault."

"I was there at the beginning," he said. "I got you started. I really believe it."

"You blame yourself too much."

"I've wanted you every night you've been here, Malou. I thought it was over. I was set to go back . . . you know . . . do my duty. Now . . ."

"Commander Andy," I said. "It's not the things we do that we regret. It's the things we don't do." And this time I left no doubts. I kissed him on the lips, I gave him my tongue, I pressed against him. "It's up to you, Commander Andy." I went back to my room and waited for him to come. How hard could it be for a man to choose happiness? How long could it take? I waited. I showered. I prepared myself . . . not that preparation was required. He was mine.

Then, after half an hour, I heard a door close. I heard him starting his car, backing out, driving away fast, as though he were rushing to separate himself from me. In the kitchen, I found house keys and a duplicate set of keys for the car, which he had left at the gate, before hiring a driver to take him to Manila. The house was mine for two more months. He had also left an envelope with ten $100 bills and a letter.

Dear Malou—

This is not the ending I hoped for. Believe me when I tell you that if it were in my power, I would be staying here, even if it meant staying forever, and you would be the one boarding the plane, even if it meant you'd never come back. There was another ending I pictured. You did too. The two of us going on that plane together. Impossible but I wanted you to know that I spent every night—including this last one—picturing that. That was the dream I had. You tell me we regret the things we didn't do, not the things we did. All right then, this money is for the things I didn't do. Goodnight, Malou. Goodbye.

Yours,
Andy

I showed the letter to Elvira. She read it and laughed. "No sale." Then I told her about the money Commander Andy had left behind.

Now, at night, driving inside the base, Graceland felt far away. The museum of Elvis. I was at home inside the base. I was at home inside Commander Andy's white Chevrolet, his parting gift to me. His house was mine for one more week. Past the small boat harbor, I lived dangerously, speeding through the darkness, turning off the headlights for just a moment, wondering what it would be like to drive all night like that, fast and straight and alone. I slowed down when the road divided. Right went to Cubi Point airstrip and the beaches. Straight led to the naval magazine where they stored bombs and poison in the rain forest. I turned left, into some low hills. My headlights flashed against trees that rose in straight lines, one hundred feet tall. Groves of bamboo waved me home to Commander Andy's house but not to Commander Andy. Monkeys sat on the retainer fence, seeing no evil.

Just after making the turn, I saw some headlights a hundred yards behind and knew that someone was following me. The base police, I guessed, but it was too late to regret my sprint through the dark, with headlights off. Thank God it was harmless. *But officer, I'm a silly girl and no one was hurt. I am sober, as you see, and I am almost home and do you notice my English, how carefully I speak?* I drove slowly, entering the housing area, and suddenly I was in America, among dozens of houses at the top of a green hill, a street like the America we see on television, every house the same, lawns with bougainvillea, hibiscus, croton, yards with slides and swings and toys, with well-fed, much-loved dogs, golden retrievers. I put on the right-hand turn signal—*see how thoughtful I am, most of the time?*—and turned into Commander Andy's carport. I turned off the headlights and pretended to fuss with my purse and waited for the people following me to pass. But the car stopped, right outside. Headlights went dark, but I could hear music from inside, Willie Nelson and Julio Iglesias, "For All the Girls I've Loved Before," and now I was frightened. An American car with no markings and two men inside. I saw them in the streetlights, in this well-lit, well-kept neighborhood where no harm could come to me. At last I took the house keys out of the purse and got out. I closed the car door at the same time two other car doors were closing. It was all one sound. They walked toward me and I was frightened in this American neighborhood. In the house behind me, lights shone in the laundry room downstairs, in the living room and kitchen above, but they were lights that I'd left on. Commander Andy Yauger was gone forever. No one was home. To the left and right, no sound of voices, no glow of television. Help, if I needed it, slept behind the hum of air conditioners. I stood next to the car, watching them walk toward me, come into the light. In the front was a Filipino I recognized, Doy Valencia, the son of a former senator. We were classmates once but that would not help me now. Doy was a rich man's spoiled son, running a resort outside of Subic City. In school, we called him "senorito." Now people went to him for passports, loans, favors, drugs.

The other man was an American in a Hawaiian shirt, with white pants and sunglasses and the walk of someone wounded. Him, I knew and feared. He played small parts in movies produced by Baby Ronquillo. He was her escort and bodyguard. Worse yet, he claimed to be in love with me. I had met him in the time before Elvis, when the bar that became Graceland was called Genghis Khan's Tent. "The house of pagan pleasures." There were carpets and pillows in the VIP lounges—that was the Genghis Khan touch. "Love on horseback." The main floor was the same, tables, stage, bars. My place was by the jukebox in the corner. It was a good place to hide. Perhaps the bar was rougher then or I was younger but many nights I curled up and made myself as small as possible. That was when I started dressing blandly—loose T-shirts, baggy slacks that would not show my shape, a turned-around baseball hat to cover my hair. Elvira said I looked like a lady's room attendant, in my disguise. Still, it failed. Jimmy Fiddler saw through it.

The fleet was in. Normally, Genghis Khan was slow: no Graceland. The tents were empty, the pagan hordes went elsewhere. The place was sad. A ninety-percent-empty Olongapo bar was the saddest place on earth. It was two bad things combined, a party that no one was coming to and a business that was facing failure. The girls would sit by the jukebox and if a customer or two appeared they were rushed, swarmed, ambushed. The girls were like salesmen, pressing too hard to change their fortune, to make that first sale, to get the party started. When the customers retreated, the mood was worse than before. It is bad, I think, to sell yourself to men. It is worse if you make that decision and cannot find a buyer. But when the Seventh Fleet came in, Genghis Khan filled early and stayed busy until late at night. As the evening passed, the place grew wilder. I wore earplugs to muffle the noise of the band. I wore sneakers to step through spilled beer and old clothes so no one would notice me. But someone did.

Toward closing time, I felt that someone was staring at me. I glanced up and saw a table of Americans. They were not military, they were business-men or tourists. They had some girls with them already, girls straining to sell themselves before closing time, so the bargaining had gotten harder, the whispers more suggestive, hands were placed on knees, straying north to make a certain point, lips were pursed in a way that left nothing to doubt. There was a girl for every man at the table, rough girls, none of them among my particular friends, part-timers who came in from the provinces when they heard that the fleet was in. A girl for every man but one. He was staring at me and—worse—I sensed he was talking about me, entertaining the table with his appraisal. *I like them shy, I like them lean, I like the ones who put up a little fight.* The girls nodded and smiled, encouraging him, wanting him to approach me, waiting to see what happened when the comic Ameri-can made a move on cold, stuck-up Malou. I made myself small, I returned to my column of figures. I could not leave until closing time. I sensed the American working himself up, the others urging him on. *That nothing*

T-shirt, I'd pay ten bucks just for a peek underneath. More laughter. I heard one of the girls say my name. Now he knew Malou. She added something else, that I am not available, maybe. *Abailable,* we say. He pounced on the *maybe,* he lurched to his feet, he parodied our accent. "Maybe," he said, "we can turn not *abailable* into *available.*" He stood facing me and suddenly he half-sang, half-shouted, "Malou, Malou, the most beautiful sound I ever heard." No ignoring him now. I met his eyes. I shook my head. No, no, no. I raised my books, I showed him my pen. *See, I'm a bookkeeper.* But he moved toward me, limping.

"Malou?" His voice was polite up close, but his face was narrow and mean. In movies they called him "Daga." The Rat. I looked in his eyes. I saw pain, anger, humor. A terrible energy. The life of a party I didn't want to attend.

"What's the bar fines for those four girls over at the table?"

"Three hundred pesos each, sir." He handed me two 1,000-peso notes. I wrote the girls' names, Eva, Flor, Donata, Maricel. Second time tonight for Donata and Eva. That's the trick. Go out once, return to the club, go out again. Doubleheaders. I then said what I always said. "The bar fine, sir, repays Genghis Khan's Tent for the loss of an employee's services. It does not compensate the employee for any additional service you may wish her to provide once you have left these premises. Those charges are negotiable and additional. Do you understand?"

"Sounds like the Miranda warning."

"Sir . . ."

"I love the way you say your speech."

"Thank you, sir. We must be careful." I turned back to my accounts.

He put a 1,000-peso note right on top of the open page.

"That's your bar fine, Malou. I like the look of you. That maybe-I-will, maybe-I-won't, I-could-live-with-it, I-could-live-without-it expression. That's hard to find, especially around here."

"No."

"No?"

"No." I handed him back the money. He turned to his table, where his friends—and the girls—were watching us. Now he decided to make a skit of it. He took his wallet and turned it upside down. Peso notes rained down, thousands, hundreds, lesser denominations. Behind him, his table applauded and others too.

"I said no," I repeated.

He reached into his pocket for change, a half dozen 1- and 2-peso coins that clinked down on top of the pile of paper money. He turned his pockets inside out. This, in its way, was funny stuff. *What does it take to win your love, Malou?* Now he dropped to his knees before me. The Rat was begging. He sang an old movie song, "True Love." He had a fair voice too, so when he finished, all of Genghis Khan's bar cheered him. But I got up to leave.

"Don't . . ." He grasped an ankle, held it very tight. He wasn't drunk at all. He spoke like a lawyer, his voice measured, his eyes calm. "Don't embarrass me in front of my friends, Malou. Don't. Those are some important people. And even the ones who are unimportant . . . I don't want them laughing at me either."

I shook my head. "I'm leaving now."

"All right, I made a mistake," he said. He sounded like Commander Andy now. Desperate. The room turned silent. If I picked up his money and went with him—if only I were a good sport—what a rousing cheer there'd have been. *Hey, that Malou, that woman is . . . I mean we're talking . . . tough.* He might have settled for that, my agreeing to save his face. But I had a face of my own to save.

"Good evening, Malou," said Doy Valencia and, at the same time, and less politely, the American said, "Good morning."

"Yes?" I said.

"You going to invite us upstairs, Malou?" asked the American, and the way he said *upstairs* was nasty. Upstairs for a quick one, stopping off on the way home from work.

"I do not know your name, sir," I said, though in fact I did. I was acting stronger than I felt. The American scared me and I realized that was why he came.

"Name's Jimmy," he said. "Jimmy Fiddler." He kept scratching and tugging at himself, at his crotch. "Okay? Now can we go upstairs? I'm a big fan of yours, Malou. You remember? I went down on my knees to you, darling. Around here, it's always the other way around."

"We will do our business here," I said. "And quickly please. It's late."

"Christ," said Jimmy.

"And . . . Doy." My voice had the artificial tone that Filipinas take on when we speak English for the benefit of Americans. A classroom recitation. "Would you please tell your friend Jimmy to keep his hands off his thing? He won't be using it here."

"Son of a bitch!" Jimmy exclaimed. "I guess I won't. Not unless I want to. If I want to, I will. I ride bareback, darling. And I ride for free."

"Malou," Doy pleaded. "A question only and then we go."

"Ask your question, then," I said. "And go."

"You work at Graceland. You manage the place, no?"

"You keep track of the bar fines," Jimmy interrupted. "That's for the girls who screw outside the bar. And you keep track of the action up in the VIP lounges, right? You use cameras? Or get down on your knees, Malou, and peep through the keyhole? And, let's see, you keep count of that hair tonic the girls are hustling, the so-called margaritas, and the champagne-for-chumps. And every week you take a convoy of jeepneys that you fill up with whores and you truck them down to public health so that they can get their licenses renewed. Once a week—more often if the fleet is in—you take the money and you deposit it in the account of a Filipino Chinese accountant who cooks the books for Baby Ronquillo. I know all about you, darling. I could write the story of your life. So let's cut to the chase."

"Some people are asking about this Elvis group," Doy said. "About the boss."

"Biggest Elvis?" Now it seemed a long time since I'd seen him. *Diaspora. I didn't know you knew that word.* "He looks after the Lane brothers. He handles the money for them. For the musicians." I was not telling them what they wanted to hear. I was filling the air with words. "The songs, he selects, every night. Never the same program—"

"This is getting very boring, Doy," the American complained.

"Malou," Doy said, working to keep things calm. The American scared me but I could not help feeling sorry for Doy. Fat, pampered senorito, class clown. The anxious host, the sweaty eager-to-please local. If a drink spilled at a sloppy table, if glasses broke, he was the first to wave for another round, no harm done, even though the American made the mess. "Malou," Doy said, "what do you know about Colonel Parker?"

"Is he from the base?"

"Colonel Parker!" the American shouted, the way they do, as if saying something louder will make us understand.

"You mean . . . the manager of the real Elvis Presley?"

"No, darling. That was Colonel Tom Parker. This is Colonel Peter Parker. He lives on Guam and he's got a lot of money that he keeps quiet about."

· "Now he's here, Malou," Doy said. "You see?"

"Is he? I haven't seen him."

"No," Jimmy said. "He's not here this minute, not as far as we know, but he's got this Elvis act. The punk, the hunk, the lunk, whatever the hell . . . and no one believes that's the end of it. More like a beginning. People are wondering about his plans."

"This doesn't make sense," I said. "This . . . colonel? He is not here, am I right? And he doesn't know me. And I do not know him. Correct? And you are asking me about his plans?"

"The Lane brothers are his adopted sons, Malou," Doy said.

"And he confides in them? Then ask them . . . if you think they know anything."

"No," Jimmy Fiddler said. "It's the older Elvis. The fat fuck. He's in charge. In charge of the act and the sons. That's what I call a position of trust. Sending flesh and blood to Olongapo. Skinny-dipping in a sewer. The man must have something in mind. You find out."

"There may be nothing," I said, and before I finished, Jimmy Fiddler

stepped toward me, grabbed my hair, which I had pinned up. The brooch
fell on the sidewalk. My hair fell loose behind my shoulders, the way I had
not worn it in years.

"I've been wondering how far down it went," Jimmy Fiddler said. What
he saw pleased him. I could tell. "Wear hair like that, it's all the clothes
you need."

Now he took my glasses also, slipped them off me carefully. My Gloria
Steinem glasses, Elvira called them. They made me look scholarly. Now
they clattered on the sidewalk. Jimmy Fiddler stepped, left, then right, a
one- and a two-dance step, and crushed them.

"Well then, Malou," he said. "I think you'll find something out. I really
do. All we're asking is what kind of a fish is Colonel Parker. Is he a shark?
Is he a whale? Is he a friendly little dolphin? Understand, love?" You
wouldn't let me down, would you? Break this poor heart of mine twice?"

I did not say anything but I had not stopped thinking. Jimmy Fiddler was
a movie character, a cowboy in the tropics. An actor, a bad actor, nothing
original about him. And he was weak, the way Americans were, American
men. I could master him, in time. I saw this, through my fear.

"You understand?"

"Yes sir," I said.

Now he stepped back and glanced at Doy Valencia. "Give me a minute,
buddy." He walked out of the carport and into the garden. What now? Then
I heard him pissing in the sandbox, a hard, sudden stream, as though a pipe
had broken. Doy came over and handed me a handkerchief so I could wipe
my eyes.

"I'm sorry about this business," Doy said. Though he was worthless, I believed him. All things being equal, Doy would be good. But if Jimmy Fiddler made a joke on the way home—a joke about me—Doy would laugh on
time. It was not easy, being a man around Americans.

"Why didn't he talk nicely to me? Why this way?"

"Malou, believe me, he has ideas about you." That was all he said but
Doy wanted to say more. "It's not a nice place, here. It brings out the worst
in all of us."

"Nice or not nice," I said, "it doesn't make sense. Why ask me? I only work at Graceland. Why not ask Baby Ronquillo? She owns the place. She made all the arrangements. Ask her what she knows about Colonel Parker."

Doy flinched when I mentioned Baby Ronquillo. Knowledge is power, they say. That is why people lie so much. Doy was tempted to lie. Or he could tell the truth for old times' sake and that would make me a little stronger and him a little weaker. He looked over his shoulder, to make sure the American was still pissing.

"We cannot ask Baby Ronquillo," he said.

"Why?"

"She is the one who is asking."

I watched them drive away and then I walked upstairs into Andy's place. The movers had come and gone already. Gone, the baskets and carvings from the mountain tribes, the seashells and miniature brass cannons from Sulu, the hardwood tables and chairs that gave him such pleasure and remorse, "parking my butt on what used to be the rain forest." What stayed behind were things that Andy thought that I could use or sell, odds and ends, dishes and sheets, books and CDs, a popcorn maker, a rice cooker, a portable radio. His car.

Now, Andy seemed far away and the house confirmed it. My vanished American. No help for me now. Cassettes and dishes, hair dryer and toaster, crumbs for mice. Base housing once again. In a few weeks someone else would move in. The houses accepted us, our photos and furniture, books and souvenirs. They went along with the program. They waited for the next customer. New occupants. Children, to play in the sandbox Jimmy Fiddler pissed on.

I threw what I wanted into some shopping bags and carried them out to the car. I could not sleep here anymore. One last time, I walked through Commander Andy's house, closing windows, turning off lights, saying goodbye. The house was empty, the house won again. I drove slowly out the main gate and across the river. I felt that a part of my life was ending. Commander Andy time. My first American. Good-bye, Commander. Now I was a citizen of Olongapo again.

An hour before dawn, I drove down Magsaysay Street. I saw drivers asleep in jeepneys, guards in doorways. Dogs crossing from side to side, foraging pizza crusts, scabs of Navy vomit. People going out early or coming home late. The edge of a new day in Olongapo. Foxy boxing. Mud wrestling. Country and western. College-girl fashion show. Graceland. On the sidewalk, cardboard cutouts of our three Elvises, young, middle, and biggest.

Part Two

I, I, I'd like you folks to know that I was
the hero of the comic book. I saw movies
and I was the hero of the movie. So every
dream I ever dreamed has come true a
hundred times.

Elvis Presley,
quoted in *Elvis*
by Albert Goldman

Father Domingo Alcala

At the curve of Subic Bay, at the foot of the Zambales mountains, at the end of the road from Olongapo, my parish reposed, a few dozen buildings, only two of them more than one story, shops that were sheds, stores that were stalls, people who lived off what they took from a tired land and pulled from a polluted bay. The days were blindingly hot, nights humid and still, and what I waited for, every day, was late afternoon, when the sun relented, the heat subsided, winds stirred, and all my disappointments receded. It was possible, in this time of rich golden sunlight and playful breeze, to forgive, to bless, and to hope. I could try to tell myself that this was a place among many similar places. But it was all a lie. This was a place like no other. This was the most evil place on earth. Or the saddest. Or—if it was possible— both. No escaping it, even as I walked among my people, as I greeted parishioners, patted heads, chatted amiably outside garages, lifted lids off pots in *carinderias,* sat in doorways with old women. This was Babylon. This was Sodom and Gomorrah.

After a few years in Subic City, I could feel the Americans coming. I could sense the Seventh Fleet's movement toward my village, could count the long days at sea that separated the carriers and cruisers, destroyers and submarines from their last sight of land, Perth or Pusan or Diego Garcia, the dwindling distances, the miles and hours that kept them from my village, from the night that I would go to sleep, feeling the wind blowing off an empty bay, and awaken to find that the fleet was in. I could feel it in my legs, in the palms of my hands, I could feel them coming. I had my ritual, when the fleet was in, my private ceremony. I mounted the steps of one of the town's two-story buildings. The sound of the jukebox grew louder as I climbed the steps. "Macho, macho man!" The main floor was empty, just one girl in a chair at the bar, a pile of hair curlers in front of her. She jumped up, mistaking me for an early customer. Then, seeing her mistake, she backed away, ashamed or disappointed. Down below, in the darkness slowly falling, my parish transformed itself from ramshackle barrio to sin city. Farmers lived off the land, fishermen off the sea, yes, yes, but their daughters lived off the fleet and—see how the evil compounded!—fathers, mothers, brothers lived off the daughters who lived off the fleet, off the fleet and what followed it, tourists with special tastes, a United Nations of furtive catamites and sodomites, pederasts and pedophiles. My people prepared themselves. Smiling acolytes lit charcoal fires for satay sticks, older brothers emptied truckloads of San Miguel beer into refrigerators. While the sky turned orange and purple, swirls of neon pink and lime celebrated Marilyn's, Blow Hole, Ace of Hearts. And, like candles in roadside shrines, jukeboxes came to life, the Eagles promising "One of These Nights," the Three Degrees wondering "When Will I See You Again?" The joy of arrival, the melancholy of departure, everything was ready. If you were a priest in Subic City, you knew all the tunes. You knew venereal diseases. You knew chlamydia. You knew T-shirt slogans. EXCUSE ME: YOU OBVIOUSLY MISTAKE ME FOR SOMEONE WHO GIVES A SHIT.

I could feel the approaching Americans and the town could feel them too. Lassitude and randomness yielded to calm, confident purpose, inaction to strenuous effort, ordinary humanity to something that was more and less. Even now the Americans passed through the gates, they crossed the river, onto Magsaysay Street, into the liberty port. They decided to save Magsaysay Street for later. Graceland's first show was ten P.M. Meanwhile, they commandeered jeepneys and, beer by beer, advanced toward my parish.

Let me make clear that I did not hate the Americans. I enjoyed my missions inside the American base. I envied their youth and good cheer. I loved the jukebox music that accompanied my life, music for every occasion, first meetings, flirtation, consummation—Donna Summer, that would be—and departure. Sometimes it seemed that the songs didn't underscore emotions but that they replaced them, so that what it came to was a loss of feeling, atrophy and numbness rolling in, men and women reduced to jukeboxes, and it was all a matter of feeding coins into slots and pushing the right buttons, again and again, night after night. "You've got to give it to the Filipinos," I heard a sailor say one night. "They just keep coming." A double entendre, a dirty joke, all right, a table full of snickers. A profound truth, nonetheless. Jan and Dean were right. "Two girls for every boy."

Now the women came out. They were always here, wives, mothers, and daughters, but now they clustered around jukeboxes, they loitered in doorways. At one moment, a single girl stood outside Blow Hole, brushing her hair. Then another, then three. The moment arrived. Contact. The sound of horns beeping, horns that sounded like wolf whistles, tapes playing. The first arrivals disappeared into nightclubs. The second wave, the third milled around on the street. How like an invasion! No wonder we used the same words for love and war, foreplay and softening up, first contact, hit the beach, slow dance, fast dance, touching and embracing, penetration, planting the flag on foreign soil. Jeepney after jeepney of hard muscular bodies, institutional haircuts, high school faces. Love and war, mongrel and hybrid, a beast with two backs.

Now I retreated. Render unto Caesar. Render along the beach, in cubicles and cribs at the rear of nightclubs, under tables in the game of smiles. On your knees, on your back, render. The game began. I left my people behind, where I could not help them, where the very sight of me would contribute to their pain or—conceivably—spoil their pleasure. I retired to my quarters, a modest bungalow, half-residence, half-office, behind my church. Sitting in darkness on this night of a thousand couplings, snatches of music drifted my way, that pounding disco, those forlorn love songs, vulgar and hypocritical and yet each of them, in its own moment, persuasive.

The Americans had to go, the sooner the better, no matter how much they paid to stay, no matter how much their leaving cost. Sail away, sail away. Loving them, hating them: never mind. Maybe there would be a nation here someday. Maybe not. My people would have to sort it out among themselves. I knew the arguments on both sides. Safeguarding democracy, projecting the free world's presence, Russians in Cam Ranh Bay, only ninety minutes away. Forty thousand Filipinos on the payroll at Clark and Subic. Ripple effect. Indirect employment. Hospitals and schools, golf balls and shell casings, all the things that Americans gave, that my people took. And, against this, the talk of sovereignty and pride, exploitation and debasement, my arguments, but just as much a litany—a list of songs on a jukebox—as the others. I had heard them all, all through the Marcos years. Now the yellow-dressed housewife played the jukebox. Cory Aquino. The bases must go. One song. Or we could raise the rent and shorten the lease. Another tune. Stay a while longer, a little while, and pay a little more. One song melting into another, the jukebox gone haywire. Subic and the fleet and the shattered nights. "Perpetual peace is a dream and not a very happy dream at that." Von Clausewitz, K-4 on the jukebox. The hour before dawn is darkest. Notes from the journal of a country priest. "Liquor in the Front, Poker in the Rear." Music adrift in night air. "I've Been Loving You Too Long." Too long, indeed. Meanwhile, I had the case of Teresa de Guzman to contend with and, though I did not know it, the meeting with Elvis Presley.

"Padre Paternity?" I asked.

"Oh, come on, Father," the lieutenant said. "You know how people are about nicknames. Does it surprise you that Americans pick up the habit? Knock, knock."

"Who's there?" I asked.

"Domingo."

"Domingo who?" I asked again.

"Domingo to court to sue your ass." Lieutenant Porter leaned back in his chair and laughed. A Navy lawyer in an air-conditioned office on the second floor of headquarters, inside the base, he was a short, pugnacious humorist. He passed out business cards for a Subic City establishment that offered "the finest cocksuckers in the Philippines." Around his office he exhibited the most obnoxious local handicraft available, carvings of eagles and carabao, velvet paintings of the Kennedys, the gaudiest of sunsets.

My report: a certain Teresa de Guzman, employed as a cultural dancer in a Barrio Barretto club, attempted to escape the unwanted attention of an American Marine attached to the USS *Peleliu*. She tripped and broke an ankle, which injury had caused her pain, cost her substantial sums for continuing medical care, the final outcome and sum of which could only be estimated and, moreover, her injury deprived her of the opportunity to earn her livelihood and pursue her career, thus impoverishing not only Ms. de Guzman but her entire, and entirely dependent, family. So I said.

Lieutenant Porter savored my presentation. We had done this a dozen times before, he and I. Now it was ending. Where he was going, he would trade in subdivisions and wills, he would incorporate businesses, avoid taxes, plan estates, and miss "da PI."

"I love it," he said when I concluded. "What will I do without you? What will you do without me?"

"The best we can," I said. "A greatly overcrowded occupation."

"I don't suppose you'll ever get to the Allentown-Reading area?" he said. "Farms turning into subdivisions, factories into outlet malls. Pennsylvania Dutch selling pies and pretzels. Taverns where men sit and watch TV all night long and the only woman in the place wears overalls and a flannel shirt."

"Not like here."

"Well," he said, picking up a file. "Before my eyes tear over altogether." He read the file while I waited. "Tsk, tsk," he went. Or "Oh, my!" Or "Naughty, naughty." Then he threw the file on the desk. "Cultural dancer? That's beautiful. Go-go girl, takeout girl, escort service, maybe. Hooker, u-drive, spare part, I thought I'd heard them all. But cultural dancer? That's stylish. This woman—"

"Teresa de Guzman."

"—works out—or out *of*—a place called Fountain of Youth. A water sports place, pools, saunas, showers, and all the local . . . cultural . . . extras. It says here that at the end of her . . . performance? . . . she sits in a tub in a T-shirt which I surmise is a wet T-shirt and she invites some members of the audience to help her soap up . . . some of those hard-to-reach locations. Lance Corporal Reese responds to the invitation and, the floor being wet . . . he stumbles forward. Teresa de Guzman interprets this as an attack. She gets out of the tub, she arises—with a modest shriek, no doubt—and . . . that wet floor again . . . down she goes."

"I have a signed statement, I have witnesses."

"By the jeepney load. Sure you do. So do I."

"In light of this disagreement, Lieutenant, I suggest we go to court. The 1965 amendment to the bases agreement provides for adjudication in local courts of offenses charged against American servicemen. I therefore request, on Teresa de Guzman's behalf, that Corporal Reese be placed on international legal hold—"

"—until the Philippines courts have settled. Tell me, Father, how long does it take to reach a decision, these days?"

"Maybe . . . a long time," I responded. "Lawyers, witnesses, translators. A crowded docket, a sadly overloaded system. . . . I'm afraid the *Peleliu* will have sailed long before Corporal Reese has a decision."

"Sailed! Did you say his ship will have sailed? By the time your courts get to a decision, the ship will be decommissioned, melted down, recycled into hubcaps."

"Then again . . ."

"We could settle. All right, Father, the moment approaches. How much will it take to make cultural dancer Teresa de Guzman whole again? What's the market value of an ankle?"

"To a lawyer or a priest, sir, very little. But to a cultural dancer . . ."

In a moment more, our work was done. It would be a long while before the other parts of Teresa de Guzman's body matched what her ankle had earned for her. Lieutenant Porter escorted me out of his office and was surprised to see a woman sitting outside in a chair.

"Is this . . . ?"

"Lieutenant Douglas Porter, this is Ms. Teresa de Guzman." Shifting to Tagalog, I told the woman that she should keep her eyes on the floor, downcast, and her face sad. Then I told her she was 5,000 pesos richer but she must stay serious and not thank the American or it would be harder for all the women who followed her here.

"God, she's young, she's a kid," Porter said. And he was right. Teresa de Guzman was a nymph, an angel. A woman, surely, but newly so, small and young and irresistible. In Olongapo, she tempted—she invited—defilement. Someone should have spanked her and sent her home.

I was surprised by Porter's surprise. Teresa de Guzmans greeted the fleet by the dozens, by the hundreds. They were women only intermittently, as the market demanded. Mostly, they were girls. Expect no courtesans here, no erotic magicians. These were Girl Scout troops turned feral. Confronted with this, Porter seemed chagrined. He invited me to lunch, detailed an escort to accompany Teresa to the front gate.

"I notice the ankle isn't bandaged," he remarked. "Which one was it, anyway?"

"I'm not sure."

"She's pretty." We stood together outside headquarters, watching Teresa and her escort walk away. I prayed that she wasn't inviting him out just then. At the very last minute, rounding a corner, she looked back at us and waved and—how couldn't you love her?—she skipped away, hair flying behind her. Porter leaned back and laughed. I almost joined him, then stopped myself. Life in Olongapo had its comical side. But there was pain too. Abandoned mothers and children, a generation of half-American half-orphans. Broken promises, unanswered letters. It was better not to be amused. Once you started laughing, you might never stop. Humor was corrosive here. So were tears.

People noticed when we stepped into the Officers' Club. Porter might have been making a point about me—the red priest was a regular guy, liberation theologians put on their pants one leg at a time, and everybody likes french fries. I was his trophy radical and he steered me from table to table, making much of our friendship. "I know who you are," some officers muttered, not looking up from their food. "Heard all about you!" others good-naturedly exclaimed. That was Americans. Inconsistent, unprincipled, clumsy, strong.

"Sorry," Porter said when we reached a corner table. "It felt like we were bride and groom, moving from table to table."

The Officers' Club was on the beach, directly across from the headquarters building. From the bar—an air-conditioned alcove with clean carpets and endless peanuts—I could scan the bay. Though a few ships remained, the Seventh Fleet was back at sea. Like a pan of water left on a stove at low heat, the famous bay stretched out, idle and empty.

"Where have all deflowerers gone, huh, Padre?" Porter asked. He'd read my thoughts. On Saturday night, when the fleet was in, Olongapo was grotesque, appalling, but alive. When they were gone—I had to admit—it felt vacant. That was something you could blame on the Americans. Add that to the long list of charges. A few small fishing boats out toward Grande Island, smoke coming off the Bataan mountains where it surprised me, that they found something left to burn—what was the point of it all?

"I've liked doing business with you, Father," Porter said. "I don't care what they say. I can't tell you the dinner parties that have been ruined for me because I spoke up for you. Believe it or not, there are people here who think that this base is a good thing. Good for world peace, good for the balance of power, good for the balance sheets. Good for the Philippines . . . as every poll taken in the area emphatically confirms. Your mayor agrees. Your senator, your chamber of commerce. The opposition comes from outside, from university mouth-offs and newspaper columnists who never get out of their chairs, and politicians who scream about nuclear war and national sovereignty when we know it's all about renegotiating the lease. You don't hear that kind of talk on the street. The jeepney drivers, the lottery salesgirls, the waitresses. No problem. None, anyway, that can't be solved. They love us. Or they say they do. And I'll do them the compliment of believing what they say. Of taking their word for it."

"I'll say this once, my friend," I interrupted. "This place dishonors you and it dishonors us."

"Maybe so. Just don't put it to a vote. Anyway, we've worked some things out. I tell people I like you and that I've got a sneaking suspicion—which I won't ask you to confirm—that you like me. Sometimes I ask myself what it's going to be like here, years from now."

"Business as usual?" I suggested. I felt that way sometimes, that it would never end. I felt that way when my cheeseburger arrived, a wonderful thing, impossible to duplicate outside the base. Is it the beef, American not Australian, or the texture of the cheese, the grease on the grill, or the Stars and Stripes flying overhead? Business as usual. Activist priest, portfolio of problems, a broken ankle, a trashed apartment, cases settled out of court. Cheeseburgers, later.

"No, Padre. No more business as usual." This was important enough for him to put down his cheeseburger and wipe the catsup off his lips. "That's what I wanted to tell you. You didn't hear it from me and never mind where I heard it. But your good thing—your bad thing—is coming to an end."

I waited for him to resume. This could be everything or nothing. We specialized in crying wolf, in claiming victory, in paper triumphs and false alarms. Marcos had used the bases against the Americans: as long as he remained in power, Clark and Subic were safe. Aquino had equivocated. The bases had to go eventually, she said. Meanwhile, however, the lease might be renegotiated. Three years at $481 million per year—one third of what we'd originally asked—was enough for us to permit our sovereignty to be violated until 1991. Meanwhile, negotiations continued. We were still selling ourselves.

"It's just not worth it," Porter said, "that's what they're saying. Putting up with your bullshit and paying more to listen to it. It's not official yet. Your politicians might change their mind. It wouldn't be the first time. But we think they'll vote the next treaty down and we're not too upset about it. We're walking away. It'll be a year, eighteen months, before the great moment arrives. But it's starting now."

He might be wrong. That was my first thought. No American knew what violations of language and logic Filipino politicians perpetrated every day, how they posed and postured, how they changed positions, switched sides, betrayed their allies, their constituents, themselves. He might be wrong, I thought. Then I realized that I wasn't thinking he might be wrong. I was hoping; anyway, half-hoping.

"I wanted you to know," Porter said. "I wanted to be the one to tell you. That way I could ask you something and get you to answer before you have much time to think about it. . . ."

He gestured around the dining room. I saw tables full of Americans, most of them at coffee and dessert. Ice cream or pie. Ice cream and pie. Beyond them, the beach, the baseball fields, the ship repair facility, machine shops, offices and barracks, airstrips, golf course. Would the aborigines move into the housing? Would the rain forest prevail? Would the meek inherit the base?

"Tell me . . . tell me what you think. . . ."

I couldn't say.

"You're going to miss us," he said.

"I admit it," I said, recovering a little. "I'll miss you. That doesn't make me want to keep you. And it shouldn't make you stay."

Teresa de Guzman, cultural dancer, waited for me at the front gate and sat happily in my car, riffling through my collection of cassettes as we drove back to Subic City. I thought I might ask what she would do with 5,000 pesos. But when I thought of the things that 5,000 pesos could buy I realized it wouldn't make any difference, it wouldn't change her life in any important way: three or four bags of rice, a Sony Walkman, a crib for someone's baby. Her family would nibble away at it. Or she'd spend it all at once and I would notice the Technicolor flicker of another television set along the road.

"*Sus, Maria,*" Teresa shouted when she saw Tina Turner among my tapes.

"Research," I responded.

"Research," she repeated.

That's what we'd been doing in Olongapo, I thought. The whole community was a laboratory. We incubated diseases and we indulged dreams. We made love, we made money, we made babies, we made—as they say—beautiful music together. It was hard for me to believe that the Americans were going. End of research, of study abroad. Study a broad.

"*Sus, Maria,*" Teresa repeated, when I pulled the car into the courtyard outside my quarters. She rushed off, crossing herself. On the step of my front porch, as though waiting to make a confession, Elvis Presley sat. Not one of him, but two. One was younger than the other but they were linked. They came from different decades, the fifties and the seventies, so they were both out of the past. Part of history. Like America itself, I hoped. News of the Elvis Presley show had not escaped me. Another in a line of grotesques. The hits just kept on coming. I drove past the so-called Graceland whenever I had business at the base as often as two or three times a week, when the fleet was in. I could recite the name of all the clubs, on a street where the names changed all the time. When I saw the cardboard Presley figures outside of what had been Genghis Khan's Tent, I guessed that the entertainers were ex-servicemen, staying on. I never dreamed that the three Elvises had come halfway around the world, a trinity of pilgrims on what the eldest had the eventual effrontery to call a mission from God. All that came later. It started with two Americans on my front porch.

"I am Father Domingo Alcala," I said, walking toward them. Nothing in my priestly vows compelled me to be more civil to Americans. Or to pretend that their visit to my parish made my day.

"I'm Ward Wiggins," the older of them said. "And this is Chester Lane."

"You're the men who sing at the place called Graceland?"

"Yes sir," the younger replied. "My brother, Albert, he's part of the act too, sir. Sir, your name was given to us by . . ." The younger Elvis blushed and hesitated.

"By the girl he's planning to marry," the older Elvis completed.

"Ah, I see," I said. When a military man decided to marry a Filipina, he and she were obliged to go for counseling at the base. The Americans knew that most of these marriages were doomed: that a courtship in a Philippines liberty port was poor preparation for a life in Bakersfield or Fayetteville. So there were lectures and interviews and papers that took time to process. They could slow things down but they could never stop them. And they could never more than dent the Olongapo credo that divorce in San Diego was more valuable than a marriage in the Philippines.

Sometimes—more rarely—the Filipino family put things to the test, sending the betrothed to the hardest possible taskmaster. That would be me. Some of our people had integrity. Others had been through marriage counseling enough times to give the course themselves. Those were the girls I secretly cheered for. The cynics, the opportunists. Cases of true love were more disturbing. Disasters in the making. As I talked to them I wondered which was the greater catastrophe: when the Navy man met the woman's family, a busload of Pinoys looking for a ticket to California, or when she encountered his in-laws, stepping into a living room of polite Americans, watching football on television, waiting to carve a turkey.

"Does the lady work with you at Graceland?" I asked.

"No sir," the younger Elvis replied.

"At what bar does she work?"

"What makes you think . . ." The younger Elvis looked to the older for help.

"The lady doesn't work in any bar at all, Father Alcala," the older Elvis declared. "She's not a dancer. Not a hostess. Not a prostitute."

"I haven't touched her," the younger Elvis asserted.

"I see," I said. His protest surprised me. It sounded quaint. "What is the lady's name?"

"Christina Alcala," the lad replied. "She said you've known her awhile."

"Did she tell you that?"

"Yes sir."

"Did she tell you she was my sister?" I couldn't wait for his reply. I turned away, covering my face with my hands, moving them up and down, feeling my hair and the skin of my forehead, the lips across my teeth, always the skeleton waiting, just below the surface, biding its time. At lunch I'd learned that the Americans were leaving forever. On the same day, by the middle of the afternoon, I was informed that my sister wished to marry one. And, doubtless, leave herself.

"I get the feeling we've surprised him," the older Elvis said to the younger, "in not such a nice way."

"Shh . . . " said the younger. "Priests have families too, you know. How would you feel?"

"Maybe we should leave and come back another time."

"No," I said. "You can stay."

"She's not pregnant," the younger emphasized. "She hasn't been touched. Like I said."

"That's good to know," I said. Temporary consolation. Oh God, in another year they'd have all been gone! "Do you mind my asking . . . how you met?"

"It wasn't supposed to happen is what the man is saying," the older Presley told the younger. My predicament interested him. "It's not what he had in mind."

"Well sir," the younger said. "It's not much of a story. I was at a picnic out at White Rock with some friends of mine from work—"

"Graceland girls?"

"Yes sir, and there was lots of other picnics too—and this other group, they all teach at a school here, it turns out, a school out this way—"

"I know. You passed it on the way in. Sacred Heart. My sister teaches kindergarten through third grade. I'm the principal, it happens. I also teach . . . whatever needs teaching."

"Well sir, whatever you teach, it isn't volleyball. They couldn't play volleyball at all. They were giggling and silly and getting all tangled up in the net and losing track of the score and forgetting to rotate out and I'm telling you, Father, you can't just sit and watch that kind of half-assed . . . oh . . . ."

"Finish your story." Part of me was getting to like this awkward, ingenuous youth. Part of me liked all of them, until I saw the outcome of their presence here, all the things they did and everything they left behind, meaning no harm. You realized that the harm they did had nothing to do with anything they intended, good or bad. I liked them. They weren't stormtroopers or foreign legionnaires. They were boys, meaning no harm. But so was Lieutenant Calley.

"I got up and organized things. Someone had to. Then we had a game, Graceland against your school. Good girls against nasty girls, they called it."

"So who won?" the older Elvis asked. I'd been wondering the same thing, Graceland versus Sacred Heart.

"Graceland, sir. And that's about all there is to it, sir. That's the story of how we met."

"I see. You were at different parties at the same beach . . ."

"Yes sir."

"And after a while, the two parties became one party." I noticed the older Elvis smiling, sympathizing with my predicament, the snail's pace of my interrogation. I felt he'd dealt with the younger Elvis himself and enjoyed seeing someone else attempt to reach him.

"Well sir, we shared food and we sang. Some of the people sort of know each other. Dolly—she's some kind of cousin—"

"So . . . you played volleyball together and now you want to marry my sister."

"No sir."

"No?"

"I wasn't in the game. It was all-girls, both sides. I coached and later I refereed. And someone had to keep score for them."

"Chester?" The elder Elvis intervened. "What Father Alcala is getting at . . . is that you must be missing a few steps. First you play volleyball and next you want to marry her. If that's all it took, then everybody who played volleyball that day would be getting married. . . . See?"

"No sir," the young man insisted. "See, I was the only guy."

"Then why," I said, "of all the women who were there, did you select . . ." The word *select* destroyed me. After I said it, I could not go on. The language of pimps, salesmen, waiters, floorwalkers, and streetwalkers. Select. And now my sister had been selected. Finally, I finished the sentence. Select was the verb. My sister the object. "My sister?"

"Are these conventional questions?" the elder Elvis asked. "I'm just wondering."

"No," I admitted. "They are not." I promised to consult with Christina and to set a date for another meeting. Recovering a little, I conveyed the seriousness of the marriage bond at all times, and special considerations in this case, issues of family and culture. And faith. I wondered if young Elvis—Chester—was Catholic. He was not, of course. That, I realized, was to my advantage.

"But I'm willing to learn," he said. As if the Church of St. Peter were a new instrument for him to play. Then he arose, with the utmost good cheer. "Whatever it takes, Father." He offered his hand. "You're not looking so good, sir."

"It will pass."

"That's okay. It's not every day you run into a brother-in-law. See you soon!"

"Wait outside a minute," the older Elvis told the younger. Chester Lane nodded, waved, stepped outside. I was left facing an older version of my brother-in-law-to-be. It was as though a dreadful film had been fast-forwarded to the closing sequences, so I could picture Christina attending to the wishes of someone like this lout, heavy-faced, fat, sideburned.

"I don't want to prolong what's been a difficult afternoon, Father," he said. "I can tell you're not pleased. But this isn't what you think."

"And what do you think I think?" I replied. I wanted the Americans gone. All of them. Now. Forever. But there was an intriguing familiarity about him, a presumption of equality that I couldn't leave unchallenged. One of the hazards of my calling—of ministering to the poor, the victims, the humble—was that, day in day out, I was smarter than the people I worked with. Not better, certainly, not even wiser. But surely smarter. And when I caught a glimmer of smartness—a knowing smile, a furrowed eyebrow, an ironic tilt of the head—from someone, I responded. I noticed how he studied my bookshelves. I wondered if I had not found another member of that most secret society, scarcer than aborigines, more furtive than pedophiles: a reader.

"I think you're tired of American kids showing up to marry bar girls. I think you're skeptical about love affairs that happen between tricks. I think it angers you when the American leaves with a local girl and it sickens you when they leave the girl behind, and the baby, so what we have here is a no-win situation. Stop me if I'm wrong. . . ."

He waited for me to object. If I did, it would only be to ask who this man was, really, and why he had come to me. I nodded for him to proceed.

"So you're jaded, Father. I understand that. But that young Elvis out there is something special. He's the best of all of us. He's talented and he works hard. He makes friends everywhere he goes. He's a sweet kid. Give him half a chance, you'll see that. That's what I want you to know."

I had a dozen ways to delay or disrupt these marriage plans. I could bring our parents in from the province or send Christina out to them. I could suggest a waiting period, a year or more. Or I could put young Elvis through a daunting course of religious instruction, see how our young troubadour fancied St. Thomas Aquinas, Teilhard de Chardin, Cardinal Newman. That, suddenly, appealed. A dialogue—a double dialogue—with Elvis.

"All right," I said. "Half a chance." And then, because I could not resist, "Who are you really?" And I will never forget the way he answered me, the nonchalance, the effrontery, the . . . humor.

"I'm your dream, Father. Or your nightmare."

"What would that be?"

"Another priest in the same neighborhood."

The next week, Wednesday night, via the back door, I entered Graceland for the first time as Biggest Elvis' guest. The comparison Ward Wiggins had made between us was blasphemous. Also intriguing. If Christ were to return to any town in the Philippines, surely it would be Olongapo. I'd always said so, that our Savior would be drawn to the worst place, just as I had been. And now . . . Biggest Elvis . . . told me that Elvis Presley would choose the same town. For the same reason.

I sat in one of the VIP lounges, where a shy beautiful girl I once knew as Juana—now called Whitney—brought me beer, courtesy of Biggest Elvis. After that, on other Wednesdays, she often sat with me, even when her presence would surely be welcomed by any customers down below. Whitney was diffident, disinterested. Also, completely unembarrassed by the presence of a priest. That first time, we watched the whole performance, the acrobatic gyrations of my would-be brother-in-law and convert, the mean glowering of his brother, the middle Elvis, and finally—what shall I call it, that opening drum roll, that clap of creation at the dawn of time, that crack of doom?—the advent of Biggest Elvis. How shall I describe the melancholy underlying his songs of youth, "Loving You," "True Love," "I Want You, I Need You, I Love You"? Or how the experience of life in a fallen world informed "That's How Your Heartaches Begin"? How he knit his songs together with comments and asides, at one moment cautionary— "there but for the grace of God go I"—at others, mocking. Or how he cast literary quotations out at waitresses and sailors—"Fly not yet, 'tis just the hour" and, near closing, "Had I but world enough and time" and—before singing "Are You Lonesome Tonight"—"they flee from me that sometime did me seek" and—at closing—"ask not for whom the bell tolls." Sometimes he glanced, though he couldn't see me through the dark glass. " 'Tis better to rule in hell than serve in heaven." In this particular hell, his quotations were unrecognized. He was their source, their author, the wisdom of Biggest Elvis, lord of Graceland, the ultimate G-spot, where the evening ended with "American Trilogy," a wrestling match of drops and falls, kicks and chops, sweat and pain, a parable of birth, death, resurrection.

"See what I mean, Father?" he asked, that first night. "We're in the same business!" Still in costume, wiping himself with a towel, he had rushed up to the VIP lounge while the girls of Graceland sounded last call down below.

"It's quite a show," I granted.

"Show?"

"What else?"

"All right. All I'm saying is that we both work for men who died that people don't want to get rid of. They inspire shrines and relics and miracles and visions and talk of second comings. And holy music. And rituals, Father, rituals that are routine to us, our bread and butter, but they mean a lot to people's lives, while they're waiting."

"Preposterous. . . ."

"Then talk me out of it. Tell me I'm just a singer in a rough bar in a bad-assed town. That's what He was!"

"It's an impressive show," I said. "Can't we just leave it at that?"

"It's more than that and you know it. You saw what was happening down there. You felt it. There's something else. Something more. I don't know what."

"Neither," I said, "do I."

I asked the lovebirds to wait a year and, to my surprise, they acceded. Chester's religious instruction proceeded, all too easily. "Whatever it takes, Father." Chester already believed in Santa Claus and the Easter Bunny, his sharp-tongued brother remarked, so he wouldn't have any difficulty with the doctrines of the Church of Rome. My hope was that time or accident would end this engagement. Granted, the young American's respect for Christina was remarkable, his behavior impeccable. Still, it could not be. Meanwhile, though, I had a new friend.

Biggest Elvis! In a perfect world, we'd have traveled together, walked dogs, met for breakfast every morning, retired to the same small town. We were that well matched, not the odd couple, but the even. And, as we grew old together, needing less sleep, staying awake longer as though that might reduce the risk of death, as though being awake when death came might permit some last-minute negotiations, we might talk of Subic and the fleet, raise our voices, what was left of them, and sing old, profane songs. We'd been walking through wastelands before we met, deserts of nods and non-sense, rote learning and ritual, excuses and extenuation and, sighting each other, we saw salvation. We shared newspapers and magazines and detective novels. I relaxed around Biggest Elvis. More than that, I confessed my doubts, certain confessions that took me aback, after I had made them, confessions that, in the end, were warnings. He brought out the despair in me, the mockery I kept to myself, the obscene voice I had only heard in dreams, often enough to recognize it as my own.

"Slow down," he said to me one night when we were out driving. Between Barrio Barretto and Olongapo, the road climbs and curves and, around a single turn, there is a cemetery on the left, a true city of the dead, a subdivision of mausoleums. Headlights wash over tombstones, plastic flowers, snapshots of the dead. On the right, sprawling for miles, the town, the base, the bay, the mountains of Bataan. "Look at that!" Biggest Elvis exclaimed. "Pull over."

There they were, America and the Philippines, rubbing up each other like slow dancers, with a polluted river in between. The base was as trim as a university campus, the town a boiling pot of neon lights, clotted pink and red, like an infected wound.

"Sometimes I wonder," I said, "if we will ever have a nation here." I kept talking, once I'd started, about that little time when the Philippines mattered. Yellow ribbons, People Power, marching nuns, martyred exile, avenging widow. "The Filipino is worth dying for." "Only a Filipino can stop a tank." (Provided, I could not resist adding, the tank was driven by another Filipino.) Those had been great days—dislodging an American-backed dictator while the world watched. Then, another great day: that morning that the skies over Olongapo had darkened with gray ash from Mount Pinatubo, ash that had clogged sewers, soiled laundry, scratched windshields, and—as if God had heard my pleadings—buried the American base at Clark Field. Great days. But Subic remained and things had not changed. We were still a poor country run by rich people, a nation of servants, at home and abroad.

"You're down, tonight, Father," Biggest Elvis said.

"You noticed." I knew I'd gone too far.

It's hard for me to say exactly when I realized that Biggest Elvis had to go. The very pleasure I took in him persuaded me. He brought out the doubts in me, the weakness, the despair. And the subversive affection for an America which he epitomized. But those were problems I might have lived with. I might even have endured his colleague's marriage to my sister, although my nights were filled with grotesque imaginings of what our Filipino journalists would make of this. I pictured myself presiding at a ceremony with men dressed in pink and black suits, the bridal couple in a Cadillac, the church wired for sound, my sister decked out like the Original's Priscilla, a nymph buried under a beehive of hair, gazing upward toward a sideburned, thick-lipped sensualist, winking at me as he kissed her deep and long, right in front of me, as though part of the priestly office was to confirm that a large wad of chewing gum had successfully transited from mouth to mouth.

That was bad. But there was more and it was worse. On Wednesday nights, watching the three Elvises—the trinity—I saw that Biggest Elvis might be right. He *was* competition. He was another priest in the neighborhood. It was ritual and passion—*payson*—it was parable and moral. I saw the pattern of it, the response Biggest Elvis elicited from an audience of whores and sailors. When I compared what happened at Graceland, these waves of emotion, with my strained pieties on Subic City Sundays, the apathy and routine of it all, I despaired. We were mismatched. And we were becoming more so as the show improved, as postulants and mendicants arrived from far and wide, devotees and pilgrims, always more of them and more loving, all the time. "We're in the same business," he kept telling me. A joke, I thought. And yet we were. In these islands, we welcomed prophets and messiahs, Baltazar, Papa Isio, the League of Honor, the Colorum, sects, movements, faith healers, now this.

Biggest Elvis had to go. If fate cast me as his Judas, so be it. The shrine, the relics, the half-holy music, the incarnation and reincarnation, death and return, absolutely fraudulent and utterly convincing, it was happening here and fast, so that its triumph seemed shockingly easy and years from now I might look back and say, of course, I should have known, it was all so perfect, where else but here, who else but him. Him. The god of Graceland.

II

Ward Wiggins

When Colonel Parker found me on Guam, he had asked what Elvis meant to me. It was a harmless question in itself but what he really wanted to know was whether I was nuts. Was I one of those pathetic nobodies who attach themselves to larger personalities, whether as lost love, best friend, missing child, separated twin, or—not to dance around the key question—reincarnated self. Was he entrusting the Lane brothers to a head case?

"I've listened to the records," I answered. "Not all of them. I've read some of the books. Not all. I could say that about a lot of people I've studied, from D. H. Lawrence to James T. Farrell. I've done some homework, that's all."

"Sure," Colonel Parker countered. "But you don't go into a bar at night and do a . . . was it Lawrence? . . . routine. Whatever that would be."

"Fair enough." I wanted to give the man an honest response. I hoped that one would occur to me. "Look, I admit it. Things haven't worked out too well for me. I haven't done the things I thought I would. And the things I have done . . . haven't pleased me. Or anybody else."

"Meaning?"

"My book. My marriage. My teaching. You name it."

"I won't ask about the marriage," he said. "That happens all the time. All over the place. But I'm wondering about the teaching."

"I wasn't happy. That's the short answer."

"So you just . . . chucked it . . . ?"

"Time to move on, Colonel. Before time runs out. Look, I've been a dis-appointment to myself. And, lately, whenever I was way down, I all of a sud-den found myself singing."

"Singing . . ."

"That's right. In the shower, singing Elvis songs. Then, out of the shower, in front of my mirror, my hair, still wet and soap in my eyes, grinning, scowl-ing, posing. Coaxing those sideburns south, a quarter inch at a time. He'd come to me. Elvis. At home. Or driving, especially at night, around the back of the island. Listen . . . you don't have to worry."

He looked worried, though, downright alarmed. I'd gotten carried away and that business in the shower didn't sound healthy. Sideburns on my face? Why not hair on my wrists? What would it take to kill a resurrected Elvis?

"This isn't Jekyll and Hyde," I assured the Colonel. "I know who I am and I know what I'm doing. I'm Ward Wiggins and I'm sorting out a way of living that makes sense and that . . ."

"Yes?" I'd gone too far but there was no avoiding it. The Colonel had a way of opening people up.

". . . that has some magic. Because what I found, Colonel, was that the happiest part of the day was when I was walking around as Elvis. That part was magic. The rest was so-so. I decided to follow that magic and figure it out. That's it. That's all. I know what I'm doing."

"You're sure about that, son?"

"This is something that I step in and out of. I know when to stop and where it ends. Trust me."

I gave the Colonel a straight answer, I thought, based on the best infor-mation available at the time, as they say in court, when they're on trial for perjury. But as the weeks in Olongapo slid into months, as I got into a pat-tern of afternoons on the beach, nights and early mornings at Graceland, the coming and going of the fleet, I realized that, if the Colonel asked the ques-tion again, my answer would be different. I was getting further and further into the role I played. Notice, please, that I did not say I was *sinking* into it: this isn't about immersion, drowning, disappearance. Better to say I was advancing into it, day by day, and better still to say that it wasn't a role, with lines all written, exits and entrances. No: this was a fate. This wasn't something I was reading. This was something I was living, that I didn't know the ending of.

Magic. Maybe it came to me on Guam when the sound of my own voice, singing, lifted me out of the dumps. Or on Saipan, when I saw those Japanese secretaries turning sentimental about the death that they knew awaited me, offstage. But that was nothing, compared to what happened in the PI. When an old man waited for me in the moonlight, so I could bless his fighting cock, that was magic. Or, late afternoons, when I stepped out of the bungalow and walked along the beach, sailing a few notes toward the sunset and the kids surrounded me, dozens of them, "Hey, Elvis, hey Elvis," and when they followed me along, singing scraps of songs, spinning around in the water, using driftwood for guitars, yes, that was magic too. Or seeing the girls of Graceland cross themselves during "All My Sorrows." Moments like that, everything flowed through me, all kinds of connections were made and I became—wisecracks aside—part of something big. And more, I sensed that something was about to happen, that I wouldn't be waiting long. I could see it the way people looked at me, when I was onstage.

People were staring at me wherever I went, staring at me as though they'd have to testify about what I looked like the last time they saw me. Filipinos stare a lot, unself-consciously. *Gawk* should be a Tagalog word. They were credulous and I think some of them believed I might be the original Elvis after all, the one who never died, who faked his death and hid out and showed up here, in the best of all possible disguises, as his own imitator. Or—this wouldn't play in cold climates but it was plausible here—Elvis did die, and was buried and was raised from the grave and where else to return on earth but Olongapo, the worst booking his heavenly agent could make?

Graceland relaxed when the fleet was gone. The house was full, don't get me wrong, but it was a different kind of crowd. On weekends we got outsiders from Manila, tourists and expats and rich locals, older and more refined. They got the standard show. But on weeknights we drew guys from around the base. They weren't like the fleet; in fact, they disappeared when the fleet came in and for a week after that, giving the girls time to get checked and cleaned up at public health. The station guys were repeat customers, savvy consumers, our most discriminating audience. I changed the act for them. I talked more, segueing in and out of songs, raps on Elvis returning to Olongapo, Elvis philosophizing about women, about death and time, about other performers, about meeting the Beatles, about singing with Sinatra, about shaking Richard Nixon's hand. I had Elvis wondering about people who died before him, like Hank Williams, Eddie Cochran, Buddy Holly, Chuck Willis, Johnny Ace, and about people who came after he died, Prince and Michael Jackson. I talked around the songs and sometimes around Chester's and Albert's also and then one weekday night I was watching Chester working on "Don't Be Cruel" and I had an idea.

"Don't Be Cruel" was a tired song. It combined sad, predictable lyrics with a daffy, mildly upbeat tune. And everybody knew it, top to bottom, front to back. Chester sang it because someone had to and his vitality could pump it up. Still, it was the flattest part of his act, maybe of the whole show. One night he turned to us while we were watching and rolled his eyes.

"You know something, Ward?" Albert said. "That old dog won't hunt anymore." He enjoyed his brother's discomfort. It's not that Chester was dying out there—he always had the audience on his side—but he was working awfully hard. "It's a good thing the girls like him," Albert continued. "Go figure. I screwed most of them and paid the going rate. Chester calls them ma'am and gives them a big grin. He's the one they bring the food to. 'Is Chester home?' I open the door, it's ho-hum, Monday morning at the office. Shit, he's in pain out there tonight, though. And before long, Professor, all our songs are gonna feel like that one."

"So you think."

"I know. These songs are like clothes or cars or women. They get used up. I know that you're a professor—or you were—and you like thinking things last forever. But not this stuff. I guarantee it. These babies are way past ripe."

"Is that so?" I asked. "Watch this." Right then, Chester was a third of the way into the song and out onstage I stepped. A look of true alarm crossed Baby Elvis' face, as though I were pulling him offstage. The guys in back stopped playing. Not a clue. Then I began to sing "Don't Be Cruel" the way my Elvis might have done it, if he'd had the strength to try new things and the heart to look more deeply into old ones. I sang it slow and bluesy; Chester's song was about making up and breaking up, heartbreak and hard-ons. I came to the song across a gap of time, drugs, divorce, obesity, and boredom, and I sang like it was my last chance of love and not much of a chance at that.

I nodded to Chester and he came back in, up-tempo. You didn't have to explain to him. He got it, sometimes too quickly. And when he finished, up-tempo, and I was ready to come back with a second helping of sadness, Chester waved me off: he sang the way I'd sung, as if he'd just learned what life was about. Then, with this mischievous grin, he passed off to me so I had to sing it upbeat. Now the audience understood what we were doing— the girls were the first to notice any departure from the norm—and I was just about finished when out walked Albert with his own reading of "Don't Be Cruel," the crueler the better. When I think back on our time together, that's the kind of thing I remember, Ward Wiggins, Chester Lane, Albert Lane reinventing "Don't Be Cruel." We crossed oceans. We skipped date-lines. We jumped backward and forward, hopscotching time. We rescued what was lost and revived what was dead.

After that, the rule was anybody could step into anybody else's tune. But only on a Wednesday or Thursday night and only with fair warning and never in connection with our closing song, "American Trilogy." That was off-limits. So Chester would walk up to his brother, smiling, ask whether he planned on doing "Return to Sender." Dude nodded, knowing what was coming. "Company's coming," Chester would say. Or—once misdirection was permitted—I'd come sauntering out and Dude's "Return to Sender," which was about a love letter not going through, became something differ-ent, because I sang it as though I'd had all the mail I ever wanted. They were fun nights and they served a purpose, too, because it made old songs new. And from that it was just one short step to my worst-ever idea.

"You know about the Sun Sessions?" I asked the brothers one night.

They both shrugged. They left the homework to me. I told them fast: that before he'd signed with RCA, Elvis had recorded with Sun Records in Memphis. Some of those early recordings had been released, rough stuff but loaded with talent and pleasure that had drained out of his later recording. "Good Rockin' Tonight." "That's All Right." "Mystery Train."

"I do those songs already," Chester reminded me. "Good Rockin' Tonight" was the Graceland theme song and "Mystery Train," all eerie and sinister, raised regular goose bumps.

"What I think . . ." I hesitated. "There's always been talk of other people who dropped by. You know. Carl Perkins, Johnny Cash, Jerry Lee Lewis. Jam sessions. The future of music, getting born."

"You know what he means," Albert said. "Like in one of those movies that shows a bunch of kids in a playground and—guess what?—the one with four eyes says let's build a rocket ship and go to the moon and before you know it—"

"You don't like it?" I asked. I was almost relieved. This was an idea that made me nervous. Sometimes I liked having Dude around. I could count on him to express my own doubts. He never let me down, that way.

"Jesus, Professor! A birth-of-rock-and-roll pageant. A passion play. A nativity in Olongapo. Come off it!"

That, I supposed, was the end of it. But if you could never count on Chester Lane, you could never discount him either. "Oh hell," he said, clapping his brother on the shoulder. "Let's give it a go."

A few nights later, on a Wednesday, when the club had emptied, we tried it out. I'd asked the girls who weren't out with guys to stick around, Malou, Elvira, and some others, a dozen in all. A sample audience. I ordered drinks from the bar and I sent out for food, chicken and satay.

"You pay their bar fines, I guarantee you they'll love it," Dude said.

"That might not do it," I replied.

"Maybe not; those girls have *some* principles," Dude agreed. "There are some things even money won't buy."

The women sat around at the front tables, acting like customers, while we took the stage. Before we started, I tried to explain what this was about, the start of rock and roll, not what happened but what might have happened, legends in embryo, poets in their youth. And so forth. Yawn.

It was a disaster. Chester carried off the young Elvis effortlessly. Albert was enough of an actor to make a believable Johnny Cash. But my Jerry Lee Lewis—my attempt at "Great Balls of Fire"—was grotesque. I jumped up on the bench, I karate-chopped the piano, I danced and pranced and, through all the noise I was making, I heard the girls of Graceland laughing. Then I saw Chester rolling on the floor, howling, and Dude advancing toward me with a towel in his hand, shouting, "Stop the fight! Stop the fight!" And when I thought about it later, I guessed I'd learned a lesson. I wasn't an actor. I wasn't an impersonator, skipping from Cagney to Cary Grant to Edward G. Robinson. I was Elvis. Biggest Elvis. So long as I stayed within his life's generous borders, I'd be all right. When I walked in his shoes, inhabited his skin, I was better than okay. I could move back and forth and feel his power. If I shared my wonder about the years he hadn't lived to see, his power sustained me. When I left him, though, I was finished.

Malou sat where she always sat, at the table near the jukebox, which cast enough light—pink and yellow though it was—for her to do her accounting or read a paperback or lay out her Scrabble board. I walked over to her that night, after the Sun Sessions fiasco. The other women had left, still giggling. That was one of the nice things about Americans. When they made fools of themselves you could laugh at them aloud.

"Just how bad was it?" I asked.

"Terrible," she answered. "I could not stop laughing. When you climbed on that poor piano bench . . ."

"That thing was already cracked! You know it."

"Now it's firewood."

"Thanks. With friends like you . . ."

She gave me that look of hers that I'd come to know, nonplussed, amused, a lift of the eyebrow, a pout of the mouth, but mostly a shrug of the shoulders. Half here's looking at you kid, and half tough shit.

"I know it's late," I said. "Do you want to . . ."

She reached for the box, the board, the tiles. Some of the girls were sleeping up in the VIP lounges, the guard in front, the bartenders in back. Graceland was tucked in for night, when our Scrabble game began.

"I'm too much for you," she said. She dressed in T-shirts and slacks every night, wore glasses, kept her hair in a tight bun, as if her world might fall apart if she released it. Maybe it would. "Still, if you insist."

Malou Ordonez

While Baby Elvis fell in love, Dude Elvis slept with all the women he could purchase. He was big, they said, and very fast. He wanted his women three ways and when he finished he felt sorry for them, and for himself, and sent them home. He never had the same girl twice and they never stayed for breakfast. Now, they said, he was the good friend of Baby Ronquillo. Meanwhile, Biggest Elvis was there for me. Elvira thought I should take an interest. Jimmy Fiddler ordered me to. Still, I resisted.

He always paused to spend a while with those of us who gathered around the jukebox after the last show. First he talked a little, still standing. Then he'd sit and eat with us. Next he paid for the food. He stayed longer and longer, until sometimes only two or three of us were left. When he pulled himself up out of his chair, he seemed sorry to go. Biggest Elvis was lonely. And it would have been so easy for him to make a selection from among the women of Graceland.

"He stays for you," Elvira said.

"He speaks to everyone *but* me," I corrected. This was true, at first. He interrogated Elvira about her boyfriend from Brunei, the apartment he kept for her, her shopping trips to Singapore and Hong Kong. Priscilla had worked on Guam. They talked about that place. And Whitney! The beautiful Whitney, the deep eyes, the swanlike neck, the endless legs, the pianist's tapering fingers, the utterly vacant mind, no one talked to Whitney. After Elvira, Whitney was the loveliest woman at Graceland. Maybe before Elvira. She was also, by unanimous testimony, the worst, sexually. "A total corpse," said one American. Some of our girls loved sex. Others tolerated it. Whitney was puzzled by it. And by almost everything else. Yet Biggest Elvis spent time talking to her. And Whitney responded.

"Tell me, Whitney, the man of your dreams."

Whitney looked around for guidance, for someone to give her the correct answer.

"Elvis Presley?"

"No, I mean someone you would like to spend your life with. Someone you want to have children with."

A number of girls were listening, expecting to laugh. Often they made jokes about her. "What does Whitney say to the man of her dreams?" Dolly asked. And answered: "Are you finished yet?" "What does Whitney say when she makes love?" Answer: "I can't feel anything."

"Just talk to me," Biggest Elvis told her. "What kind of man do you want?"

"I want . . ." She was tired of the teasing, determined to answer. "Short or tall, I don't care so much. Tall is better. Not so old." Then she smiled. "Not so young." She caught herself laughing.

"Where is he from, this man of yours?"

"I don't know," she said, as if the question had never occurred to her. "Let me think . . ."

"From Olongapo?"

"No."

"Where, then—from the Philippines?"

"I don't think so." It was not an answer. It was a reflex.

"A rich man?"

"Is better, yes."

"We haven't narrowed it down much," Biggest Elvis said. They sat together in silence and a miracle happened. Like a child in a classroom, Whitney raised her hand.

"I'm wanting . . . ," she said, "a serious man."

I sat quietly, night after night, adding figures by the light of the jukebox, drinks and bar fines, half-listening to the never-ending story Biggest Elvis was hearing from the girls of Graceland: old boyfriends, broken promises, a ship to Manila, a job in a beauty parlor, a problem with a boss or a father, then the move here to try the Americans. Words to go with the music of my numbers, drink for customer, 75 pesos; ordinary drink for bar girl, 150; margarita, 300; visit for short time to VIP lounge, 300; bar fine, 500. This was the money for Graceland, money for Baby Ronquillo. What happened to the girls upstairs or outside was up to them. Some of the girls bragged about how much they earned, others never said. The ones who wanted to fall in love, they sometimes worked for free. And kept quiet about it. About making love for nothing.

Night after night, Biggest Elvis talked to everyone but me. Elvira said that just as Dude had worked through all the local bodies, Biggest Elvis was working his way through all the Graceland minds. And hearts. Advancing toward me. Saving me for last. Meanwhile, I did nothing to encourage him. That was my response to Jimmy Fiddler. On the other hand, I didn't run away. Then there came a night when I was working late, my weekly summary. I looked up and Biggest Elvis stood in front of me and all the girls were gone. My turn.

"May I sit?" he asked.

"As you wish," I answered. He noted my coolness. What I felt for Jimmy Fiddler I directed at him. Another American. *"I ride bareback, darling, and I ride for free."* Perhaps I should have approached Biggest Elvis, learning things about Colonel Parker, but I could not bring myself to do it. I could tell myself that I'd been playing distant, hard to get, all part of a strategy. In fact, I'd done—and planned to do—nothing. That was my whole plan. Do nothing. That was our way, when dealing with Americans. It was as close as we came to fighting them. Go slow, go slower, stop. Misunderstand. Do nothing. Sooner or later, they forgot. Eventually, they went away. So I told myself, knowing all the time that Jimmy Fiddler would not forget and leave. He would remember and return.

"Everybody's gone but you," Biggest Elvis said.

"And you," I answered.

"Place is different when it's empty."

"Upstairs. In back. Someone is always nearby. You're never by yourself in this country."

"I am," he said. Just that. How should I respond to that? I wondered. How does anyone? There were perfect answers somewhere. That being alone was not a bad way to be, most of the time. Or that his loneliness was his business. That we get what we deserve.

"I've been wanting to talk to you," he said.

"Oh." I gave him a businesslike look. Was it water on the dressing room floor? Seating of customers during "American Trilogy"? "How can I help you?"

"By accepting my apology."

"What for?"

"Apology for *diaspora*. It's been bothering me. I waltz over to the Scrabble board and say, I didn't know you knew those words. That was out of line."

"It's all right," I said. "I'd forgotten already. And also, you bought a round of drinks for everyone. The first of many."

"You fired back at me," he said. I wondered if the point of his apology was to confirm that I had been the one who retorted in Tagalog. *It surprises me you know those words.*

"You were the one, weren't you?"

"Yes," I said. "And I would do it again."

"That won't be necessary."

The next night, Biggest Elvis stayed until the others had gone.

"How does the jukebox work?" he asked. "I mean, is there a distributor who brings around the records and you pay him and if a song isn't getting played enough he takes it out?"

"Not here," I answered. "It's just songs that the girls like. They bring the records. When they leave, they take their records with them."

"Do you have any songs in there, Malou?"

"No, not me. That's for the other girls."

"Then . . . ," he reached into a paper bag and pulled out three records, three forty-fives, "could you just tuck these into a corner of the machine?"

There were no labels on the records. I pointed to the jukebox. Some labels were printed, half handwritten, but every song was identified. "What are these songs? And who are the singers?"

"There's no need for that. Just leave them blank. Nobody'll notice them. And . . . would you mind not playing them?"

"No . . . not at all." At first I guessed that, like any hopeful singer, Biggest Elvis had recorded himself. Singing Elvis songs, no doubt. Hoping that no one could tell the difference. Sad, even for Olongapo.

"Unlisted records?" Elvira asked.

"He said not to play them."

"He's not so fat, you know. You see him onstage in those Elvis clothes, he looks very big. But in normal clothes . . ." She gave up looking for coins. "You know I never carry small money. Give me some pesos."

"I promised him," I said. And handed over some coins.

"See?" Elvira said. "I put the money in the machine. And my finger wanders. Is like an accident, no? What's this . . . no labels? . . . I'm curious. . . . Let's see . . . so I push buttons . . ."

She sat down beside me. I'd told her what I expected to hear. Biggest Elvis copying the original. Anonymously placing unlabeled records in the jukebox. Secrets within secrets. We all had them. Elvira was mine. We sat and watched the machine find its way to Biggest Elvis' hiding place. The first song I knew, Phil Collins' "One More Night." The second song was a black man singing "I've Been Loving You Too Long." The third was a woman, I didn't know even the title, but it must have been "Every Little Bit Hurts."

"Those," said Elvira, "are the three saddest songs in the world. Biggest Elvis is lonely. And he wants you to know."

"You have to work hard to be lonely here."

"He's telling you," Elvira said. She gave me that matchmaker's smile. In Elvira's perfect world, no one slept alone. It was like wasting food.

"Why me?"

"Don't you see? He thinks you're lonely too."

"Where's Whitney?" Biggest Elvis asked.

"Sick," I said.

"How sick?"

"Every month sick."

"And Dolly? I haven't seen her for a while."

"With a man in Boracay. A man who works for United Nations. Water Development Project. She goes with him, when he comes."

"True love?"

"Not Dolly," I said. "Dolly comes back. I'm sure."

He asked me how I could be so sure, how I knew. I shrugged at that: women's intuition. But he wasn't content. He asked me about the place we now call Graceland, that used to have many other names, and about the women—the hundreds of women—who have passed through here. I told him more than I wanted. There was history in the place and some fairy tales as well. We had a winners' circle of marriage and money and escape. I knew some of these women. Elvira might yet be one and—though I doubted it—Whitney also. I saw some of these women when I was little, or when they came back to visit from the States, Australia, Italy, trailing husbands and families. Others had passed from history into legend. Lucy Number One, Baby, Donna, Bing, Lucy Number Two, Connie, Aurora, Maggie. Graduates with honor, stars, exports. Hall of fame. Sometimes they wrote for a while, Christmas cards with family photos, for a while. Our Cinderellas.

Marriage was not the only happy ending. A few of our women had moved from affair to affair, cashing in, trading up, money and power accumulating. Our Evita Perons. They began on their knees, servicing sailors, and they ended in limousines, discarding lovers at will. That was the story of Baby Ronquillo.

"These marriages, do they last?" he asked.

"Not important."

"If that's not important," he said, "what is?"

"You're not in a classroom anymore," I answered.

"What does that mean?"

"You shouldn't ask a question when you already know the answer."

"But I don't."

"Then you should."

A hilarious night. Tables full of grilled fish and chicken, courtesy of Biggest Elvis. Elvira modeled some clothes the sheik bought for her, strutting up and down the stage, lip-synching "What's Love Got to Do With It?" Back from Boracay, Dolly did an imitation of Chester attempting to teach Whitney a dance called "the monkey." I do not understand this kind move . . ." Dolly's Whitney protested. "I hate this monkey business." When they left, the tables were covered with chicken bones and paper plates of yellow rice, empty boxes from the Donut Hole, dripping cartons of Selecta ice cream. Biggest Elvis stayed behind.

"There's a saying," Biggest Elvis said to me. "Or maybe it's a line from a song. I really don't know. A saying in the form of a question."

"So . . ." His elaborate prefaces irritated me. I didn't like to talk to Biggest Elvis about our business here. I did not like being called on as a friendly expert witness. It reminded me of Commander Andy. All these foreigners who claimed to know us.

"*What can they buy as good as they sell?*" He recited it as if he were onstage, a fine, wise line. He seemed so pleased with himself, with the poetry of it. I slammed down my book and got up. This was one question too many.

"What can they buy as good as they sell? You should know the answer, my friend. Food!" I started moving from table to table, collecting trash, sweeping the mess into a pile at the center. His mess. His leftovers. Suddenly I hated him for feeding us, for caring, for asking clumsy questions.

Then he was standing next to me, holding a garbage can he'd gotten from behind the bar.

"I'm sorry." He held out the can. "Push the stuff in here."

We moved from table to table, as if this were something we did every night, cleaning Graceland, working as a team. He followed me behind the bar, waited while I washed my hands, then washed his own. He would not leave. He was what I needed. But not what I wanted.

"What do you want with me, Biggest Elvis?" I shouted. "Night after night, you sit, you watch. You ask questions. What do you want?"

He did not answer. He just stood there. Was he at a loss for words? Cathouse got your tongue? Or was he afraid of saying the wrong thing?

"You want a girlfriend?" I asked. "You have so many from which to choose. Elvira! Who would not want Elvira? You'd have to be sick, not to want Elvira. Shall I speak to her for you? Some night when the sheik is not in town? Or Whitney? What about Whitney? Sleepy but beautiful. You might be the one who awakens Whitney. Her Prince Charming!"

"Stop this," he said, holding up his hand. "This is whore talk."

"This is whore town. Why not Lucy Number Three? No complaints about her from anyone. She loves her work. Or Erlinda. Or Priscilla. What do you want, Biggest Elvis?"

"I'll tell you," he started to say, but I wasn't finished. I wanted to burn my bridges. Jimmy Fiddler wasn't going to be my matchmaker, one American pushing me toward another. No matter what.

"In the biggest bar in the best liberty port in the Pacific, you're an American, you have money, anything you want is yours. So many choices, short-time, long-time, young or old, mother or daughter, mother *and* daughter, two or three at a time. Are you a leg man? Tits, is it? Ass? Or . . . yes! . . . mouth. Or maybe you're a Billy-boy."

Now he'd heard enough. He stepped toward me. Now it comes, I thought, a slap across the face, just like in the movies. Suddenly I saw it, everything that was supposed to happen. After he slapped me, I would look at him in shock. How dare you! Then I'd tremble and cry and find myself in Biggest Elvis' arms. He'd wipe my tears away, hold me. We would embrace and kiss, a paperback romance, us standing there on the floor of the empty nightclub, the tall American folding the island girl into his arms. The girls in the VIP lounges would awaken and look down upon us from above, beaming. Stupid stuff.

No. He put his hands on my shoulders and turned me around, as though I'd been a child walking in the wrong direction. He steered me back to the jukebox, pulled out my chair, made me sit, and then he took a chair himself, sat facing me, his arms folded across the back of the chair.

"You're the only person I've met in years who's interested me one bit," he said. I started to answer but he held up his hand. "Just bear with me, Malou. This isn't rehearsed."

He looked down at the floor, ran his hand through his hair. "Why do I want to know you? Because you're smart. Because you read. And while I'm punching gut and sweating bullets, you're here, doing your books or reading something. The kind of woman who always brings something along to read because she might get bored, the book is like a warning to the world she's in, that if the people she's with aren't up to expectations, in a minute she's out of here. . . ."

He picked up tonight's book, turned it over. *Love Medicine.* Elvira had laughed when she saw it, as if the hero would be French Tickler or Spanish Fly.

"There you are, with those glasses and black slacks and the same white T-shirt with nothing on it, every night, extra large, with room for you to hide in."

I made a T for time-out with my fingers. "Actually, not the same shirt, all the time. I have many like it."

"I say to myself, she's smart. You make a mistake, she'll nail you. And she's moody, she'd got all kinds of moods. You run into one of those moods—not if, but when—and you've got a problem. And she's alone. Funny wiring for a place like this. Or anywhere. Now here's where I start sounding like a kid. I say to myself, I think Malou is neat. I'd like to get to know her. I wonder if that's even possible. I wonder . . ." He laughed, shaking his head. "You're right, I guess. Who wouldn't want Elvira?"

"I do, sometimes." I could hardly hear myself but I said it. And he heard, he nodded. He wasn't shocked.

"Who wouldn't want Elvira? Or—dream the impossible dream—Whitney. Fine and willowy Whitney. She smiles at me, ever since we talked. We're friends now. That's something."

"She said she wanted a serious man," I recalled.

"I guess I don't always say the wrong thing. Or ask the wrong question. Only now and then. And only to you." He almost reached out for my hand. He started, caught himself, withdrew. I saw it all. "Could we be friends? All right. You're a woman, I'm a man. Which generally leads to fucking, not friendship. You're from here and I'm from there. So it's money and passports. And a lot of questions I can't answer. Still . . ."

"I don't know what you want," I say. Olongapo is bottom-line. How much, how long, top or bottom, here or there. A certain act, a certain price. That's the deal. A price for what you want.

"Talk. Spend time. Do things together. Get to know each other. . . ."

Talk to each other. In Olongapo you talk while you wait to get hard again. *Spend time.* Time is money here. Spend time in VIP lounge, hotel, apartment, beach. *Do things together.* What kind of things do you want me to do? Once you think Olongapo, everything becomes clear and specific. What he says is vague. *Get to know each other.* We do that all the time here. Some do it several times a night.

"I'm sorry," I said, "I do not think it is possible. What you say . . ."

He nodded, almost too readily, as if he'd heard what he expected to hear. "Well then . . ."

He walked away. Biggest Elvis sleeps alone again, I thought. Malou, also. An offer of friendship, rejected. A thousand other Americans reached into their pockets for money and then they opened their pants. Biggest Elvis was different. But he was still American and I'd had one American too many.

"Biggest Elvis!" I called out after him. In the movie I would run to him. We would walk out together, onto Magsaysay Street, neon reflections gleaming on the shower-wet street. And then the movie ended, the picture blurred, the part of it that I could imagine. I could not imagine us together, not here or anywhere. Still, he turned when I called out to him.

"What's the harm in it," I say, "if we talk sometimes?"

The next night, Biggest Elvis tried for a seven-letter word every time. He accomplished this twice in the first game, once in the second. He lost both. He shook his head and left, thanking me. I told him "You're welcome" and watched him walk away. Just a friendly game, which I won. Twice. Elvira would have told me to let him win, at least once, and afterward, to stretch my body in front of him, to stretch back and yawn luxuriously. She begged me to discard my T-shirts. I sat alone, wondering about Biggest Elvis. What was his story? His personal history? No one came to anyone clean, beyond a certain age. We had records. Was it better to share the past or ignore it? I closed my eyes and rested my head in my hand and I heard him walking toward me, coming back for me. What now?

"Pardon me, sweetness, I was just out looking for a blow job. I know it's a little late . . ." Jimmy Fiddler stood there, his crotch at the level of my face. He smelled of aftershave, a heavy scent. The same Old Spice that Commander Andy used. These Americans.

"I see you're getting to know Fat Stuff. You fucked him yet?"

The look I gave him took him by surprise. He pretended to be shocked.

"Whoa . . . sorry, darling. I forgot. You don't do that kind of thing." He pulled out a chair and sat down, uninvited. "Thing I can't figure out, is dykes made or born? Did you come onto the planet saying, gee I was put here to chew the carpet. I was born a rug muncher? Or is it something that you discover after a real bad date?"

I stayed silent, waiting for him to leave, knowing that—like the other American—he would leave when he decided.

"Enough chitchat," he announced. "Time's short. What do you know?"

"Nothing."

"Oh," he cheerfully replied. "Nothing. Okay. Well, I guess I'll be on my way then." Suddenly he spun around and wiped everything off the table, glass, Scrabble board, tiles, all over the floor. "I don't think you're even trying. When this person I know asked for me to check out Colonel Parker, I could've played it any number of ways. I could've made friends with one of the three stooges. But I didn't. I thought of you, darling. Do you know why?"

"No," I said. But I knew.

"I like mixing business with pleasure."

I knew that. He'd thought of me. He wanted me.

"But I'm not having so much fun," he continued. "Not yet. I don't even think you're trying to make this work. I think you just forgot about me. I remembered you. You bet. But you forgot about me. I guess I'm just not . . . memorable."

"No," I said. "I didn't forget." I disappointed myself. I lacked the courage to defy him. Like so many other Filipinos who talked to Americans, I said one thing and meant another. I told the American what the American wanted to hear.

"You have a plan. . . ."

"Yes. I have a plan."

"Where's the board?" Biggest Elvis asked the next night.

"I gave it to Dolly," I lied. "She wanted to play at home." In fact, I'd picked the board and tiles off the floor, tucked it all in back of the jukebox. An *A* and an *H* were missing. Underneath the jukebox, I supposed.

"Oh. What are we going to do, then?"

"We could talk," I say.

"The two of us?"

"It's what you wanted, no?"

He nodded, sat down, and looked at me. "I don't know what to say. I don't know where to begin."

"Take your time," I said. I tried sounding relaxed and playful. Teasing. Elvira did this so well, Dolly also. Not me.

"I say the wrong thing, you'll get mad."

"Trust me," I said. Jimmy Fiddler, my matchmaker, my coach. How artificial I sounded, as though reciting lines someone else had written. Someone who didn't know me. I'd noticed how a silence sometimes fell over Olongapo tables, when music stopped and drinks were ordered and it was still too early for bar fines. How little—once we stopped talking business—how little there was to say. "You were a professor, they tell me. Who discovered you? Was it . . . this . . . Colonel Parker?"

"You really want to hear this?" he asked. "I was a professor. And a husband. And somebody's kid once too. You want the whole thing? What's your pleasure, Malou?"

"As you wish."

"You'll return the favor sometime? I don't mind going first, if you promise you're next. But if it were just me—out there alone—I don't need it. It's not my style. So this is for you, Malou."

"Thank you," I said.

He said he'd never liked those books that began with somebody's birth and ended with somebody's death, books that went marching from the obvious to the inevitable. He liked stories that moved back and forth, recovering and reconsidering the past, visiting the future, returning to a present that was enriched from both sides and if he hadn't gotten that to work in a book he'd once written or the career he used to have, he had it now, everything coming together like magic, time and place, the way the Elvis act had come together here in Olongapo. He'd had bad times, false starts, dead-end jobs, and a marriage that ended just before his wife's death. Just four months ago he had thought of himself as a failure, till he'd opened his mouth in front of a mirror and an Elvis song came out. And was that—I asked again—how he met Colonel Parker? Or had he met the Lane brothers first? He didn't heed my question. He was telling me more important things, he thought. Now, he felt, he'd found himself. Even as he put himself into another man's life, his own life was enlarged. He was amending and continuing Presley's time on earth and it might seem crazy to someone who'd never been there but there was power on the Graceland stage. He stepped right into that power and it trailed him offstage, it followed him home, magic. Colonel Parker must be pleased, I ventured, detesting my own clumsiness, wondering if I weren't going out of my way to fail, even hurrying my failure along. He stopped a moment, puzzled, as if he'd heard a wrong note. Then he continued. The best thing when you're happy is not to examine it, he said. He'd have been happy to just have a new life in a new place, where every note and each breeze and every blink of neon elated him. But then he'd seen me sitting at the jukebox, solitary and unmoved—"outside of the magic"—and, though it was pushing his luck, he wanted something more. Happiness was something you shared, he believed, though sadness was better faced alone. He looked at me, distant and skeptical me, and wondered if his happiness could touch me. Or not? That was the chance he was willing to take with me. We could talk about his life some other time. Everybody had a history. You show me yours, I'll show you mine. But that wasn't what he wanted me to know. That wasn't the most important thing. No need for me to respond now. If I walked away, he'd understand. Maybe I hated Elvis—both the dead and living—and maybe I found him repulsive. He could understand that.

"So what do you think?" he asked.

"I don't know," I said. I was overwhelmed. I was touched. I still hadn't found out what I needed to know. "I don't know."

"That'll teach you to give Dolly the Scrabble board."

That, perhaps, was when I should have spoken, when I should have been as honest with the American as he had been with me. I should have said I'd lied about the Scrabble board, that I needed to talk to him. I needed information. I was in trouble and I should have told him. But I was Malou and I did not. My mistake. He seemed at ease. He'd trusted me and he didn't regret it, yet. He stepped behind the bar, reached into the cooler, a San Miguel beer for him, a Coke for me. He beamed as he neared the table, he seemed buoyant, relieved.

"Your manager," I said. "This Colonel Parker. Does he manage many acts like yours?"

He stopped and stood still. He took a swallow of beer, right out of the bottle, not bothering with the glass. He almost always used a glass. He looked down at me and I could not meet his eyes.

"Know something, Malou? I counted five times you asked me about Colonel Parker. At the beginning and at the end and three times in the middle. Makes five."

"I was only wondering. . . ."

"No, not five times, you weren't only wondering. You were pumping me. You want to tell me what's going on, Malou?"

I stayed quiet.

"You're in a jam, you should tell me. I'm done talking. I'm ready to listen." Still, inept as I'd been, deceitful, I could not bring myself to confess to the American. Knowledge is power. So we lie. Or keep our mouths shut.

"Of course you'd be taking a chance, talking to me. You'd be way out there, wouldn't you, walking the wire with no net. Hell, Malou, I'll make it easy for you." Out of his pocket, a wad of 100-peso notes. Americans repeating themselves on me. They brought out the worst in us. And we returned the favor. Commander Andy to Jimmy Fiddler to Biggest Elvis. Money men, material girls. "I'll pay you to tell me what's the matter. How much does it cost for you to trust me? More than a quick pop but less than for all night? Somewhere in there, I guess. . . ."

Now he reached behind the jukebox, found the Scrabble board I'd hidden, and handed it to me.

"Was this your idea of subtle? Get me to tell my life story and oh, by the way, about the man you work for, you wouldn't happen to know . . . know what, Malou? His bank accounts? Investments? Deals? It must be that. It couldn't be anything personal. No one would go to you for something personal because we all know how far your personal interest extends." He thrust his hands far apart, like a man crucified, and then he narrowed them slowly. Look at the size of this fish I caught. And kept narrowing. "We know how far." Now his hands were closer together, narrowing the distance between the finger and thumb of one hand. "About an inch."

The next few nights, the food came as usual. More than usual, even. Whole barbecued chickens, grilled fish, plates of rice, cartons of ice cream, all courtesy of Biggest Elvis, who did not appear. That didn't stop any of the girls from eating. But some of them wondered. Christmas was coming to Olongapo and Christmas was a puzzling time, especially for Americans. The Americans thought they knew us. They saw Filipinos running up and down basketball courts, playing their hearts out at a game in which, because of their lack of height, they could never prosper. They always came up short.

Biggest Elvis was to be our Santa Claus, I heard. He hadn't spoken to me. I'd heard him singing "Blue Christmas" and "I'll Be Home for Christmas." Christ and Elvis in one show: it surely appealed to him. If he imitated the one, how long before he followed the other? Biggest Elvis was a strange man and part of me regretted that I would never get to know him. Jimmy Fiddler pushed us together and—because at the last moment I rebelled, if failure can be rebellion—Jimmy Fiddler had kept us apart. I saw that now.

"You had a fight with Biggest Elvis," Elvira said.

"What makes you—"

"That was a statement," Dolly said. "Not a question."

"This is the question," Elvira said. "Did the fight come *before* or *after?*"

"Is better if it happens after," Dolly said. "Then you take the money and you leave."

"No, no," Whitney disagreed. "Before. Then you don't have to do anything with them. No bother."

"Bother?" Dolly asked.

"I like to keep the man waiting as long as possible," Whitney announced. Smiled like an angel.

"In your case, Whitney," Elvira said, "that sounds like good policy."

Whitney smiled at the compliment and then Elvira turned to lecture me. "First you get the American. Then you decide for how long, for how much. *You* decide. You stay in control. But first you have to get him. Now, Malou, you tell me. Did you get him?"

"No," I said. "I don't think so."

"Are you going to get him?"

"Yes," I said. "Soon."

• • •

I got out of the jeepney when it stopped near a bar called Show Me and found a path that led through vegetable gardens down toward the beach. Three children came running toward me, just to take a look.

"Where does Mr. Wiggins live?" I asked in Tagalog. Shrugs and puzzlement came back to me. They'd never heard the name. One of them pointed me back to where I came from. I should ask at the bar.

"Show Me . . . Elvis!" I commanded. They broke into laughter and pulled me along. One of them pointed across a rice paddy to where an Elvis figure scared off birds. There were Elvis scarecrows all around, like a field of crucifixes. On a chicken coop, hand-painted: ELVIS LIVES! HERE!

At Biggest Elvis' house, people were sitting on picnic mats, splashing out in the bay, standing over fires and cooking. Elvis costumes were flapping on a clothesline in back, beady, gaudy things, like paintings hung out in a gallery of rice paddies, offerings to birds and dogs and naked children. I could hear Elvis singing "Burning Love" and I couldn't tell whether it was the living Elvis or a recording, until I came around the corner of the house and saw that it was both. Biggest Elvis stood on his porch, dressed in shorts and T-shirt, barefoot, singing along with a tape player, so that the dead and living voices could not be separated. Then it ended and he saw me. And I saw who was with Biggest Elvis and it was not someone I would have expected to be there, out of uniform as well.

"Hello," Biggest Elvis said. "Come on up." As I climbed the steps I saw the people on the beach watching me closely. Who is this woman who comes to visit Elvis? They were suspicious. They did not necessarily approve. Was I good for him? Good enough?

"Want a beer? Soft drink? There's food." He was cordial but I sensed some wariness. He turned down the tape recorder. "You know Father Alcala?"

"We've met."

"Yes, hello, Malou. Nice to see you." I sensed it again, the terrible artificiality of Filipinos abandoning their own language around Americans. We become like characters in foreign films, our voices dubbed, our words out of place. "I didn't know you knew Biggest Elvis."

"She works at Graceland," Biggest Elvis answered. Was there anyone left in the world who called him Ward Wiggins? He could be ironic about Elvis, he could be scathing about other imitators. But when I saw him here, among signs and scarecrows, surrounded by local people, I wondered. His doubts were for the record, something he used to gain the confidence of skeptics, but in the end, at home, he believed. In Elvis. And Biggest Elvis.

"I work as a bookkeeper," I added.

"Well, someone has to, I suppose," Father Alcala said. He'd taught at the high school I attended. Once, we traveled together to Manila, where I won a spelling contest. The winning word was *sacrilegious.*

"Is she the one . . ." Father Alcala turned to Biggest Elvis.

"I was telling you about? Yeah."

"*Diaspora.* I should have known it was Malou! We don't get many students like Malou. I'm surprised to see you're still in Olongapo."

It sounded like reproach, as if I'd disappointed him. Here, leaving was a measure of success. The longer you stayed away, the greater your triumph. If you came back to visit, you were welcome. If you stayed, you were suspect.

"Come see me, Malou," he said as he got up to leave. He nodded at Biggest Elvis and stepped out onto the beach. In these islands, you didn't just walk away. You went from person to person and that is what Father Alcala did, shaking hands, listening, laughing, gesturing toward the porch I now shared with Biggest Elvis. I watched this good man move among his people. We were all proud of Father Alcala. Not because he was a priest. There were many priests. And not because he was a good man. It was because he stood up to the Americans. He spoke out. He talked back.

"Is it true what they say?" I asked. "That he comes sometimes to Graceland?"

"Why not?" Biggest Elvis asked. "He's my friend."

"That surprises me."

"And my enemy. It's complicated. We're something, the two of us together."

"And today? What is this?" I gestured out toward the beach, where the picnic was over but the table remained piled with food. As people left, they took home piles of fish, cuts of pork, mounds of rice. "Was it loaves and fishes? Your miracle? Or his?"

"San Miguel, chicken, ribs, and fish. Every Sunday. On me. It didn't seem right to live here and not do anything."

"And you sing?"

"Just a little number now and then. On the house." The sun was setting now and, as the sky turned color and the wind pushed little waves to shore, the party on the beach was slowly ending. People came up to the porch to say good-bye. "Well, all right," Biggest Elvis said, and "Any time at all" and "You know where to find me" and, to teenagers, "Take care of business, now." The old men shook his hand, bowing slightly, and women held up their children so he could touch their foreheads, the same foreheads they'd offered to Father Alcala a short time before. Two or three groups remained, building fires out of driftwood.

"Nice out here right now," he said, as if we'd shared many Sundays out here and our argument had never happened. "You should see it when the fleet's in, all covered with ships."

"I have," I say.

"From here, I mean. It's like they all came just for me. Wow, what did I do? They sent the Navy after me!"

Sooner or later, I would have to say what I'd come to say. Out with it. I couldn't do that sitting down, relaxing. I got up, walked the length of the porch, braced myself.

"It's not true, is it?" He interrupted me before I began. "You live here all your life and you take sunsets for granted. Is it?"

"There was an American officer I knew. He said you have to give it an hour, before you make up your mind. The best comes after sunset. He rated them, ten to one."

"So we'll watch and see how this one turns out."

"I notice the sunset. But to you it says, look at this, look at me, look at where I've gotten to. I look at the sunset and it tells me where I haven't been." I couldn't wait any longer. "I came here for a reason."

"Let's have it."

Like most Filipinos, I fit my words to my audience. We tell the audience what it wants to hear. That afternoon, I tailored nothing. Baby Ronquillo, our club owner, had gotten curious about the interests and intentions of a certain Colonel Parker, manager of the three Elvises, guardian of two. Worried and tempted by a wealthy American's unexpected interest in Olongapo—why here of all places, why now of all times?—she might have gone to Guam and asked a direct question. But that wasn't Baby Ronquillo's style. A direct question amounted to a confession of weakness—of ignorance—and an expression of interest carried the risk of rejection. Why exert herself when she could permit her driver—a B-movie villain—to insult and demean a Filipina employee, to coerce her to extract information by any means, preferably sexual, from an American who might, or might not, be in Colonel Parker's confidence?

"So intricate," I said when I was done. "So dumb." Biggest Elvis stayed in his chair, looking at me, and past me to the beach, where sunset turned the mountains purple and campfires were flickering on the water's edge and it was possible to notice the first stars overhead. "The result," I said, "is what you see. I repeat the same mistake. I do the complicated stupid thing and I do it badly. I hide the Scrabble. I induce you to talk to me the way that you've been wanting to talk and I abuse your confidence with questions about Colonel Parker and I do so badly that even you can tell—"

"*Even* me?" he said. "That hurts. I thought I was perceptive."

"I thought *I* was obvious. In any case . . . the whole thing collapses because I did not do what I should have. I should have come to you and told you that I was scared and needed your help."

He didn't answer. He sat in darkness and I stayed against the porch railing, the evening sky behind me. He could see me but I could not see him. "That's what you're doing now? Asking my help?"

"As you see," I said. I leaned back against the railing, relieved. Whatever happened next might be bad, but now that I had shared this story, it would not happen only to me.

"I don't know about Colonel Parker," Biggest Elvis said. "They're wrong."

"You've met him?"

"Sure. When he hired me and a couple times after that. He's shrewd. I can tell you that and you can tell them. When we talked it was always about the Lane brothers, or the act, or travel or business. And me. He wanted to know all about me. He picks you clean with questions and you don't even mind. The next day, you realize you gave a lot and you got nothing. He was here when he was young, he told me. I remember that. I asked him when, what year. He said 1941, 1942, part of 1943."

"That was . . ."

"Not a good year for Americans in the Philippines, I know. He was a prisoner."

"You said 'part of 1943.' Did he escape?"

"No. That's the part that really sticks with me. And that's the only time he wasn't just on automatic pilot when we talked. They put him on a freighter with a couple hundred other prisoners, packed into a hold, hotter than hell and no light from above. Pails of water and slop passed down that people killed for. They drank their own piss. They drank blood. All the while they were heading for Japan, through an ocean full of American submarines, he was more than half hoping that their torpedoes would hit the mark and put everybody out of their misery. All he asked, he said, was to be out of that hold, out of that ship, before he died. It wasn't drowning that bothered him, but going down inside that freighter—the *Nagasaki Maru*, it was called. All he asked was to be in the water, looking up at the sky. He didn't want to go down inside that ship. 'A sardine can for a coffin.' That's what I remember. It won't impress Baby Ronquillo."

"No," I said. "It's only a story."

"Only a story?" He seemed surprised, maybe a little disappointed in me.

"I don't see what—"

"It's a story, Malou. Not 'only' a story. And, for what it's worth, that's the one time I felt I was seeing Colonel Parker." He got up out of his chair and stretched. "I'll see what I can find. Meanwhile, if Jimmy comes at you again, tell him that you tried your best with me and that I sensed your curiosity, which I did because I'm so perceptive."

"Because I was so clumsy!"

"Tell him that I told you I know plenty but I want to talk to him directly, without some woman in the middle. If he wants to know about Colonel Parker he talks to me. That should work."

"For a while, only."

"It'll buy time and get you out of it. You're off the hook. So there." He looked pleased to have been of some service to me. Now the next move was mine. "It's not your problem anymore."

"There's more," I said. "I'm sorry for all this. I feel like I missed a chance with you. I'll never know what might have happened." And, because I am Malou, I had to add a line. "Maybe nothing."

"Maybe nothing. There's always that possibility." Then he touched me and it came as a surprise, that he touched me at all, and at this time, and the way he did. He put his hand at the side of my face, on my cheek. He kept it there, as if giving me a chance to know the feeling of it, to recoil if I wanted. I feared I might, too, instantly, instinctively, before I could do anything about it, before I could fake affection. I would flinch because he was Biggest Elvis. Or an American. Or a man. But nothing like that happened. I did not recoil. "Maybe nothing," he repeated, drawing me closer. Gently. Biggest Elvis had a gentle touch. No grabbing, no force. He only guided me into his arms.

"Maybe nothing," I repeated. We could have been dancing, but there was no music now. I felt my head against his chest, my body against him, his hands moving down the sides of my body, confirming things. Now his hands rested, ever so lightly, on my ass. I moved in closer, accepted the inward invitation, the decision to proceed. "I can go now," I said, but the words meant nothing.

"Stay," he said. I liked being with him. I felt that I had passed a test, already, but more tests awaited me. I wondered what it might be like, awakening in the morning—if I could sleep at all—walking out to the main road, at the same time the children went to school. I wondered about the old people in the fields, watching me pass in the early morning, and Elvira, waiting for me back in Olongapo, asking, "How big is Biggest Elvis?"

"It's not tonight," I said. "But tomorrow and the day after that. I have no trouble thinking about tonight."

"Just how far ahead do you need to see, Malou?"

"Can you tell me I'm not making a mistake?"

"No. Not for sure."

"All right then," I said.

"I can walk you out to the road," he answered, and I realized he had mis-understood what I said—"all right, then"—or how I said it.

"What I meant was, all right, I'll stay."

"You'll stay?" He couldn't believe his ears. He pulled away from me a little, held me at a distance to see what he had, and I knew then that he was mine. "You're fine."

"You're lucky. Shall we go inside and see what happens?" Then, the same thought occurred to both of us and we said it together, Biggest Elvis and Malou. "Maybe nothing."

I liked having Biggest Elvis. It pleased me and it surprised me how much I was pleased. I'd wondered whether it was possible, in a place like Olongapo, to have sex in a way that did not make me feel like I was renting my body. The good thing about Biggest Elvis was how grateful I made him, how much he wanted to do for me, how unworthy he felt. The body that I'd hid delighted him; the body he showed the world caused shame. In bed, he con-tained himself almost forever, waiting for me to tell him that I wanted him, that it was time, high time, and he wanted to hear it again, just to make sure it wasn't a mistake, that it was all right and, until the very last, he'd have stopped—I swear it—if I told him to. I did not. Then, at a certain touch from me, a certain whispered word, he exploded.

I dreaded what might happen afterward. I feared that our intimacy would entitle Biggest Elvis to questions I wasn't ready to answer, my last time with a man, my first time, what it meant then, now, where it would lead and when would we meet again. After a moment of silence, I got off his bed and tip-toed around the room, retrieving my clothes. I pulled at a door in the back of the room.

"That's my closet," he said.

"I was looking . . ." I paused. I couldn't say I'd been looking for the door, the exit, the way out. ". . . for the shower." He didn't ask me whether I al-ways took my clothes along into the shower.

"Come on," he said. He'd looked normal enough, on his back. Rolling out of bed, he was massive. His height saved him from being comical, but it wouldn't save him forever. "It's in back. I'll show you."

I stood on a concrete slab, naked, while Biggest Elvis climbed up a lad-der. He turned something, a valve or faucet, and looked down at me. I was enjoying the stars and the night breeze off the bay.

"You ready?" Biggest Elvis asked.

"Anytime," I said, reaching for some soap I'd seen on a crossbeam. "Ai-iii!" Water slammed down from above, so cold it took my breath away, as though someone had emptied out an iceberg on me.

"Sunday special," Biggest Elvis said, coming down the ladder. "It's left-over ice from the beer cooler. It goes into the tank. They put it there while we were inside. You didn't hear them because the air conditioner was on. Anyway, we were busy. You like it?"

"It . . . surprised me. Yes, I love it. Look." I was laughing like a little girl. He hadn't heard me laugh that way before. "Goose bumps."

"Move over," he said. "We have only five minutes of cold water. And I'm not used to sharing." He stepped into the waterfall and made funny gasping sounds—uh-huh . . . huh . . . uh-huh—as he hopped up and down, jogging in place. "I can hack it, I can hack it, I can hack it."

I laughed at him and Biggest Elvis grabbed me, lifted me up, right into the stream, right where it came out of the catchment, turning around with me until I was dizzy and he was badly out of breath. Then he stopped and let me slide down, so that his lips were on me as I descended, between my legs, on my thighs and stomach, my breasts and lips, and the water washed over us.

"Talk about clean," he said. Now we swayed together, side to side, and I knew that I wouldn't be leaving soon, that I wanted him again, that I'd be here in the morning.

"Now it begins," I said, in his arms. I detested myself for not simply going back inside, not thinking. I always had to show I knew enough to worry. I had to be the first to ruin something so that no one else could ruin it for me.

"What's that?"

"The what next. I hate that part. Can't we just say . . . no obligation. . . . Each of us . . . is free."

"Sure we can say that," Biggest Elvis said. "It's been said before. Thing is, it's usually the sailor says it to the woman. Not the other way around."

"We'll just take it—"

"A little at a time." He was against me now and I was going to want him soon, right here perhaps. "A little at a time." Standing. Lifted up a little. Wondering what the wet cement would feel like. "A little at a time. You're stepping on my lines, Malou."

Morning.

"No public displays of affection," I said.

"Yes, ma'am."

"You're making fun. You're condescending. But this is important. When we meet, it's as if nothing has happened. Do you understand?"

Another nod and I was down the steps, no parting hug, no farewell kiss, no future date. I was already in practice for tomorrow. Only I paused a little, not for his sake but only because of our custom: you don't just walk away.

"None of this talk about living together," I said. "You have your place, I have mine." I had meant to say something kind but this was what I said. The fires were out, the beach seemed empty. "Well, thank you," I said, walking away, knowing that from here on everything was going to be awkward.

"Malou." The sound of my name came from behind me.

"Yes?"

"Nothing. I just wanted to say your name. Malou."

* * *

Biggest Elvis was never more carefully watched than when he next came to
Graceland. I had moved into Elvira's place, after leaving the home of Commander Andy Yauger. She had the most luxurious apartment in Olongapo,
certainly the most cluttered, and a headquarters for the Graceland women.
When the sheik took up residence—once a month, usually, for a long
weekend—we cleared out and moved into the VIP rooms at the club. If only
the Japanese businessmen who entertained themselves on black Naugahyde couches, with Johnnie Walker scotch and karaoke tapes for between
shows could see how, within moments of their departure, these pleasure cubicles turned into girls' dorms, littered with food cartons, makeup, laundry,
as if the part the women played with visitors—seductress, innocent, slut,
blushing bride, as you like it, sir—were only an act, readily cast off. I had
expected Biggest Elvis to try to reach me, Monday or Tuesday. I was ready
to scold him for tracking me down. In the end, I was sorry he didn't call.
And I could not avoid smiling when I remembered how he gasped and
jumped under that icy shower we'd taken together. "I can hack it, I can
hack it, I can hack it." Or that sigh of, what?—release, pain, ecstasy?—
when I'd permitted—invited—him to come. And the way he'd stood behind
me on the porch, calling out my name, just my name.

"How's everybody doing tonight?" he asked when he walked in around
eight P.M., an hour before the showroom opened. Our front bar—the day
shift—was open from noon, staffed by waitresses who didn't go with men,
some married, some cherry girls. The women who worked the showroom
appeared around eight, half-dressed, fussing with makeup, combing out
their hair.

"Good evening, Biggest Elvis," some of them said.

"The Lane boys here yet?"

"Chester yes, Dude no," Dolly answered.

"I guess he's coming in from Manila."

"Is it true he makes a movie for Baby Ronquillo?" Dolly asked. "Someone told me."

"It wouldn't surprise me," he said.

"If Dude Elvis becomes movie star," Whitney asked, "what is becoming of Graceland?"

"Well, I don't know. It has to be the three of us. The Elvis trio. You know how it works."

"Father, Son, and Holy Ghost," Whitney said. It surprised me, that sort of talk from Whitney, that she had come to believe in him that way.

"It won't work with just two of us. Or one. It wouldn't even work if the Original came back on his own."

"The Original?" asked Whitney. "You mean the other Elvis?"

"Yeah. That guy. Him." He fell silent for a minute, studying the jukebox crew, looking at Elvira, bounteous and overdressed, at Whitney, beautiful and blank, at the perky, teasing Dolly, and at Lucy, a flat, high-boned Visayan who was already famous—Lucy Number Three—because the sight of her body stepping across a room had caused a Marine to faint. Long ago, Lucy Number One had married a Navy guy. Later came Lucy Number Two. She went away with an Australian. So, Lucy Number Three.

"Sometimes I wonder," he said. "Sometimes I think that, every day we live, we should live like it's our last, we're going to die the next morning. So we should . . . get closer to everything we do. Every meal, kiss, piss, song—"

"Piss?" Dolly asked.

"You know what I'm saying. Because it could all end tomorrow. But then I say, no, that's crazy. Too much pressure. What would it be like, if you knew your next meal were your last? Could you taste the food? Or, if someone says to you in bed, make it good, it's the last time ever."

"Whitney says, 'Oh no, not again,' " Dolly joked. "And Elvira says, 'This will cost you extra.' "

Elvira laughed but Whitney was hurt. Lately, she'd started looking to Biggest Elvis for guidance. He shook his head, waved his hand, as if to tell her it was nothing to worry about, they'd talk about it another time.

"So do you go about your business as usual, like you're going to be around forever? That's what happens, I hear, when people learn they've got, say, six weeks to live. First they vacation, they pig out, they gamble. Then they come back to work. They take it a day at a time. Hey, am I right, Malou?"

"This is nonsense," I answered. He'd been talking to me all along and everybody knew it. "You probably won't die tomorrow. And you certainly won't live forever. Nonsense."

The girls of Graceland weren't accustomed to hearing someone speak so sharply to an American, especially to Biggest Elvis. They fell silent, waiting for him to respond. The silence grew deeper, longer. Even I wanted Biggest Elvis to break it.

"I'll do what I can for you, no matter about Dude," he said. "I'll do what I can." He got up, stretched. His pants slipped down a little when he raised his arms. "Damn if I'm not losing weight," he said to Dolly. "Did you see that?"

"Biggest Elvis, you're melting away," she responded. "Soon you'll be *pretty* big Elvis."

He reached into his wallet and placed two 500-peso notes in front of me. "Let's get something special after the last show. Call it a Christmas party. Some of that fried pork for me. With the skin."

"You shouldn't," I said.

"I'm worried my cholesterol's too low," he said. "And, like you say, no-body lives forever." He walked back to the dressing room he shared with the Lane brothers. "Or dies tomorrow."

"He's not losing weight at all," I said. "He hasn't lost a pound. He's fat."

Soon afterward, the first customers arrived, the ones who wanted the best tables and girls. It felt like a department store just opening, floorwalkers heading to their counters, salesgirls near the front door, offering a taste of this, a scent of that. When the other girls had drifted off, Whitney came over to me. Usually I intimidated Whitney. It was nothing I set out to do. Nor had I done anything to correct it.

"Pardon me, mum," she said. The language of a schoolgirl or maid.

"Yes, Whitney?"

"Excuse me, but I do not think you should be speaking so hard to Biggest

Elvis. He is trying hard to take care of us. He is buying us food and he give us money for medicines and he never bother us for monkey business. I'm sorry, mum, but I am not liking the way you talk to him."

"Thank you, Whitney," I replied. I almost laughed out loud, watching her walk away, like a student going from blackboard back to desk. Here was Whitney rising to the defense of Biggest Elvis, who never pressed the girls for monkey business. Poor Whitney. Whitney with a crush. If only she knew what satisfactory monkey business her idol and I had transacted. It was better not to tell her. Besides—and now my bad mood returned—it might never happen again. I didn't know how I felt about that. I tried relief, I tried disappointment. Neither one felt right.

That night we dined on *lechon*, just as Biggest Elvis ordered, and chicken and prawns. The girls of Graceland laughed a lot. Dolly imitated all three Elvises but she did Biggest Elvis best, the singing and the moves, the spoken parts between the songs.

"I'm thanking you very much," Dolly said, pushing out her stomach, toweling herself just like Biggest Elvis. "This song 'Burning Love' I'm dedicate to all the sailors and hostesses who drop by clinic on Monday. . . . No . . . no . . . never happen at Graceland . . . finest bar in Babylon. . . . All women are beautiful all men are handsome here. . . . We don't rush show, we don't water drink, and everything you are see is real."

And with that Dolly took the towel and shoved it into the crotch of her slacks, breaking into a few lines of "Suspicious Minds." When Biggest Elvis laughed, he gave himself over to it completely, holding nothing back, flushing and convulsing. I resented that and I resented her and I resented myself for letting it bother me. I watched in vain for the least sign of possessiveness toward me and when I saw none, when he included me in the same cheerful farewell that included everybody else, waving good-bye, that bothered me too.

• • •

"Biggest Elvis sleeps alone," Elvira said, later that night.

"I suppose so," I replied. "So?"

"If you plan to treat the American like this," Elvira asked, "why did you sleep with him?"

Elvira knew. It escaped the others but Elvira knew. She could look at anyone and tell. She had taken me home, turned on the air conditioner, slipped into a terry-cloth robe that said RAFFLES HOTEL, and started in on me.

"Two theory," she said, holding up her fingers.

"Theories," I corrected. She ignored me.

"Number one theory. Pay me now. U-drive theory. Taxi theory. You go with the American and he pays from beginning. Cash and carry."

She paused and drank some tea she'd made. One of the pleasures of air-conditioning, she said, was that it let her enjoy things the sheik had introduced her to in other climates. So she would walk over to the aircon and say that she felt like October. Or Christmas. And out would come wool scarves and cashmere sweaters. Or there'd be soup on the table, or hot rum, or mint tea.

"Number two theory," she said. "Very hard and very rare. My theory. You make the American—"

"The American from Brunei?"

"American is meaning everybody rich," she said. "You make the American fall in love with you. No money down. Maybe you don't do monkey business with him, first time. No money. No money talk. But later you have apartment, you have car, you have commissary food, you have trips. Maybe when the American goes, you go too, as wife or something."

Elvira's voice trailed off. This was all theory now, even to her. When it came to marrying the American and going away, she was in the realm of legends, Navy Lucy, Australia Lucy, and the other Graceland legends.

"You . . ." she said. "I don't know what to call what you do. You sleep with Biggest Elvis one time, for nothing. And then you make insult. No money for you now, no money for you later. You give your thing away and you get nothing back. Malou, what is this?"

●   ●   ●

The next night he did not appear until after the food he'd paid for was eaten and the girls were gone. I sat by the jukebox, finishing my accounting—bar drinks, bar fines, VIP lounge. I wished my life could be summarized as neatly. Columns for love, friendship, work. Now and then. Here and there. Yes and no. Theory number one. Theory number two. No theory at all. Living as though I would live forever, living as though I'd die tomorrow, living like this. In Graceland, Olongapo, Philippines, a recording angel. And then he came, not from backstage, but from the front.

"It's late," he said. I nodded yes. We were like nocturnal animals—bats, maybe—who awaited sunset and hated dawn.

"Okay if I sit with you awhile?"

"As you wish."

"I was out talking to Father Alcala. About military bases and Philippines history and the Catholic church. About all kinds of things."

"You like these talks?"

"I do." He nodded. "But now I'm tired of talking."

"Oh?"

"To him. I wanted to talk to you."

I waited for him to say something more. But he sat there, looking at me, waiting for me to respond, which was the cleverness of an old man or the awkwardness of a boy, I couldn't tell, when it came to Biggest Elvis. So we looked at each other and the silence continued, serious silence, embarrassing silence, and—suddenly—silence that was funny. We both laughed at the same time.

"What is it?" he asked.

"Sitting here, not saying anything . . ."

"Are you thinking what I'm thinking?"

"It's just as if . . ."

"I know," he said. "As if we'd been together forever."

By accident, we'd broken through. I told him he'd ignored me, just the way I'd told him to, but I hadn't liked it when he did it. He said he'd been walking on eggshells around me, that he worried about doing the wrong thing, about violating any of the many conditions I'd called out to him as I left his house. He didn't want to take me for granted. He didn't want to ruin his chances, which might be no chance at all, so he did nothing.

"Malou, we're all still kids," he said. "We never grow up. Not in these things. Unless you're different."

"I just can't picture us together here," I said. "And I cannot picture us anywhere but here."

"Look," he said. "The time we spent together. It wasn't so bad, was it? Or was it?"

"It was good."

"Because I was worried. I thought maybe you'd decided once was enough. Maybe once was too much."

"No." I shook my head. "And I really like that shower. Is that only on Sunday?"

"For you, every day of the week. For you, I'll buy an icemaker." Now he turned toward the jukebox.

"There's a switch in back," I said. "Only I know about it. Which one do you want?"

"One of mine. Any one."

I reached for the switch, pushed the button for one of his songs, and it was "Every Little Bit Hurts."

"Did you and your wife have songs?" Sometimes I wondered about my ability to say the wrong thing, to ruin the moment. A defense mechanism, a mood killer.

"Yes," he said. "But not these. Not this. Now don't sit down. Come here."

Biggest Elvis stood there. And it was just like the movie scene I'd pictured and laughed at a few weeks before. The empty tables, the bottles and beer nuts and napkins, waiting for the morning cleanup. A cave in one of the VIP lounges, the one that Whitney called home and I guessed that, when they heard the music, Whitney and her suite mate, Lucy Number Three, had come to the window and even now were watching me slip into Biggest Elvis' arms, slowly dancing to a song that wasn't quite as sad as it had been before. Biggest Elvis could move. We saw that every night. But this was an embrace, not a dance. The song was our background music. It must have seemed to Whitney that we were characters in a romantic movie. I felt that way myself, something in me answering to this fat American. If it hadn't been there, I couldn't have faked it. But it was there.

"Shall we . . ." I said.

"It's late."

"Shall we go?"

"As you wish," he said. My line. I pinched him in the side, where his love handles crept over his belt. "Malou!"

"I don't know what to call you."

"You know my real name, don't you?"

"Ward Wiggins. Yes. I don't like it."

"Me neither. It sounds like the name of someone in a western movie. Not the hero."

"Then there's no choice."

"No, Malou." He had a habit of smiling whenever he said my name, as if the sound of it pleased him, almost as if he could taste it.

"Biggest Elvis."

IV

Albert "Dude" Lane

Whenever there's poor folks around you know there's a rich neighborhood hidden away someplace. The only thing you've got to do is find it. It's not like the States where you can drive all day around a place where people live pretty much the same, same size houses on the same size lots, same kind of car in front and, out back, the same size pool above the ground, ripped at the sides, so they don't even bother to take it in when winter comes. I've seen plenty places like that. Everybody goes shopping together.

In the Philippines, it was as though you needed something rich to balance out what's poor and God knows, there was plenty of poor in need of balancing. Actually, Olongapo was better than most places, ratty and chewed up as it was, because it could live off the base. Between Olongapo and Manila it was worse: all these sad little towns where fixing tires—patches on patches—was the main trade. Was it going to be hot and dry or raining and steamy, that was the only question. Would there be water in the potholes? Mud or dust, on the way to Manila? And then, when the traffic thickened and the air turned brown, you knew you were coming into Manila. That's where you got *Guinness Book of Records* poverty, because it wasn't dumpy cinder-block towns anymore, not villages of wood shacks with tin roofs, but people living under highway overpasses or wall-to-wall along the railroad, or along the seawall on Roxas Boulevard, or on landfill near the harbor, picking through garbage. My condolences went out to anybody born there, my heartfelt "Sorry about that."

The morning after I got drunk on Mabini Street, I got a call that someone was there waiting for me, Jimmy Fiddler down in the lobby. He opened the car door for me, put on a tape of Johnny Cash serenading criminals, and when the concert ended, we'd covered a mile, tops. No side roads in Manila shortcuts, backstreets. It was like playing musical chairs in a parking lot. We spent twenty minutes at one intersection, locked in, so I decided I'd take in the whole screwed-up scene, the cinder-block buildings, the soot-covered wood, the rusty roofs, the balconies hung with laundry, the oil-covered, cracked-up sidewalk, yet you had to give it to these people, they stayed busy. They sold stuff, they blew horns, they laughed and pissed and littered and, in spite of everything, they smiled like so many kids— orphans, really—born into a bad world, praying and singing and smiling on through, even though the hour was late and the odds were long. That's what the Chestnut had fallen in love with, I guessed, one of those convent schoolkids you saw squeezing in and out of jeepneys, covering their mouths with handkerchiefs. You couldn't help believing that they deserved better. He was making a mistake, no doubt about it. Marrying someone isn't like collecting Halloween treats for the UN, one for me and one for them, this was Chester's life we're talking about. Yet I could understand what he was doing. I've got a little sympathy too. And brains. But, if it was up to me, when our helicopter lifted off the roof of the embassy, Miss Olongapo wouldn't be sitting next to us.

There were billboards all around the intersection, advertising Filipino films, eight or nine of them. In the States they'd have posters, posters blown up for still photographs. Here they had these crude paintings that turn movies into comic strips—which is exactly what they were—heavy-handed, gaudy-colored, glaringly lit. I sat through some of these things in Olongapo. They sold tickets to everyone who came, forget the number of seats, and they kept coming all through the movie, they talked when they wanted and laughed at all the wrong spots and when you saw what was up there, you couldn't blame them. There were two kinds of movies. One kind was a love story. You had one man and two women on the poster. The man looked like an over-the-hill dance instructor, mustached and overweight. One of the women was hot and sexy, the other saintly and weeping and the plot of the movie was, everybody fucked. The other movie, there was a Rambo-looking guy—sometimes called "Kumander"—and a military bad guy and a guerrilla beauty and the plot was, everybody died. Sometimes they combined the two kinds and they screwed and then they died: massacre movies, these were called. So I sat in traffic, studying billboards and, right there, above traffic, three times the size of life, sneering down from the corner of a billboard, was the same guy who was sitting behind the driver's wheel, Jimmy Fiddler, a.k.a. "Daga." The Rat. His name was on the list of actors, four or five down from the top, below some stars nobody outside the Philippines ever heard of or ever would.

"Hey, that's you up there," I said.

"You noticed, huh?"

"Was it hard?" How hard could it possibly be, I thought, if this guy did it? And how good could it possibly be, if he was sitting here in traffic, driving me around?

"Wasn't nothing to it," Jimmy said. "I'm a natural."

"You die in this one?" I asked, nodding toward the billboard.

"Shit . . . are you kidding? You think I kill the good-looking guy and kiss the girl at the end of the movie?" He turned and faced me, letting me see just how ugly he was. At first I thought they called him the Rat because he looked like one: chinless face, nasty teeth. Now—when I saw that pitted skin, noticed those red eyes, I thought he looked like something that a rat had eaten. "Me getting up close and personal with Gretchen Barreto, do you think that's something anyone would pay to see?"

"I guess not," I allowed.

"Of course I die. It's the order you die in that's important. First to kill, last to die, that's me."

"But you never get the girl," I said.

"Hey, stud-muffin," he answered. "It's only a movie." Now he turned off the main highway. We passed through a gate where some blue-uniformed pistoleros saluted Ratso or maybe what they saluted was the sticker on his windshield. And suddenly—I mean, like presto—we weren't in the Philippines anymore. It was that rich neighborhood I was looking for. Now I'd found it. And I was through the gate.

"What's this placed called?" I asked.

"Forbes Park," Jimmy said, turning one syllable into two: *For-bis.* In Forbes Park the street curbed smoothly under arching shade trees, branches meeting overhead, making a green tunnel for us to pass through. The house sat behind walls and gates but I could still sneak a peak at Beverly Hills mansions with fussy lawns and gardens that looked like pictures out of children's books. Lifestyles of the rich and famous.

Then, right then, I started to worry. A flash of alarm, flop sweats, like me onstage and not knowing my lines. I was on my way to visit Baby Ronquillo and all I knew was that she owned the club I worked at and lots of other businesses besides. A movie studio. I was hoping there might be something for me in them, that she might put me in cheap flicks that would get me started. And—what else?—she had an employment agency that sent locals overseas. That was all I knew. Shit, I was flying blind. How did she get where she was? Who did she belong to, if she belonged to anybody? And who belonged to her? And what did she want with me? It wasn't fair. Her court, her rules, her crowd, her game.

We turned into a white crushed coral driveway lined by tall, straight palm trees with little mops up top, barbered and polite. The house was yellow stucco with a red-tile roof, Riviera-looking, if you could say that something reminded you of a place you'd never been. Right then I was beginning to feel I'd never been anywhere. Born in West Virginia, raised in Guam, working in Olongapo. Shit!

I got out of the car, stopped and stretched, trying to relax myself or at least appear relaxed, in case anyone was watching. I liked the way the flowers grew around the second-floor veranda, purple bougainvillea against the sand-colored stucco. Out on the lawn, a Filipino was edging the grass with what looked like nail clippers. Another one was watering the grass, slapping at it with the water that came out of a hose. In this country, it was cheaper to hire a man than buy a sprinkler.

A maid opened the front door and gestured me inside. I could hear people laughing in back of the house. On my left I spotted a dining room with a long, shining table. On my right a staircase went up to the second floor, the kind of staircase you make a grand entrance on, all polished marble, watching your step so you don't go down on your ass. The marble was orange and white, like a Creamsickle.

I stepped outside the house into a field of sunlight and the first thing I saw was a color I'd almost forgotten, that light, clear swimming pool blue, like a whole pool of aftershave lotion, Mennen skin bracer maybe, a color that didn't exist in Olongapo, that kind of blue, not in the water and not in the sky. A big lawn surrounded the swimming pool, several terraces on different levels, each terrace bordered with flowers and ferns and hedges, all of them leading up to a wall that ran around the property, with shards of glass, clear glass and beer-bottle brown, politely embedded in the top. There were some trees that you don't plant and you don't grow, you just move in under them and stay.

I looked around plenty. I had time. There were two dozen people. None of them was Baby Ronquillo and none of them paid any attention to me. They'd seen me all right, I sensed, and they'd decided not to bother with me. Fair enough. I walked over to the bar, got a club soda, and just stood there, taking it all in.

Three fashion-model types were perched at the edge of the pool, lean and haughty, with expensive don't-even-think-about-it looks on their faces. Precious and delicate, not like our Graceland girls. A couple others sat at the table teasing with some guys in white linen slacks and silk shirts, no threat to anybody. Billy-boys.

I wondered if Baby Ronquillo was going to show up at all. Two more groups of people arrived after I did, more of the same, fitting right into giggles and gossip that didn't include me. I was standing there alone, me, myself, and I. They talked about me—I picked the words "Elvis" and "Olongapo" out of the chatter—but no one came over to say hello. That was strange. Somebody arrived at a party, he didn't stand alone for long, not in this country. Filipinos were friendly people, I'd found, maybe too friendly, but they didn't just leave you hanging, feeling as out-of-it as I was. Someone always came over. This bunch was different.

I tried walking over to one of the tables, four or five people sitting around, picking at cheese and grapes and things, drinking white wine and paying no particular attention. Land this bunch on a desert island, you wouldn't worry about any monkey business, that's for sure. Monkey business: Olongapo talk for screwing. Right on the money too, I thought, the way we climb and ride and roll and poke, it was hardly even human. I'd been working in a zoo, no doubt about it, a zoo where every bedroom was a cage and every meeting was a trick and there was nothing monkeys did that money couldn't buy. And I'd climbed right through the bars of the cage, at first. Now, it shamed me.

"Elvis?" One of the girls sitting at the table looked up at me, over her shoulder.

"Yes?" I responded.

She started to laugh at me, as if the point had been to see if I responded to that name. Her buddies joined her. "The Elvis of Olongapo," one of the guys said. That kicked up more laughter. They shifted back and forth from English to Tagalog and left me standing. All right, big deal, they knew two languages and I knew one and it might be asking too much for them to accommodate me. But if I only spoke Tagalog, if I were some humble Filipino, holding a free beer, I doubted they'd be any nicer. It would all be English then.

"Hong Kong . . . Seoul . . . San Francisco . . . New York," said one of them, the hostess of a show I'd watched on television.

"No, no," said a guy everybody called Bong. "Singapore . . . Honolulu . . . Los Angeles . . . New York!"

"Nonsense," said this beauty who looked to be one sigh away from anorexia. "Hong Kong . . . Bangkok . . . Rome . . . London . . . New York!"

I was in a nest of frequent fliers, arguing about the best route to New York and later, the best hotels in town, the Mark, the Plaza, Helmsley. They called out names the way the girls at Graceland called out numbers—K-3,

G-7, W-9—as soon as a customer walked toward the jukebox. And then I realized that if the revolution that never comes ever came, if a bunch of hostess girls and jeepney drivers, lottery salesmen and cigarette vendors grabbed some guns and came over the walls of Baby Ronquillo's property, if they got their shit together and left patches of T-shirt and skin on the cut glass, if they put us all against the wall, sure, it would suck to be me, but I couldn't argue with it, just a matter of having been in the wrong place at the wrong time.

After twenty minutes, I'd had enough. I stepped to the edge of the pool. The water looked good to me and nobody was in it. So all right. If they weren't paying attention to me, I wasn't paying attention to them. I took off my shoes and socks and no one cared. My shirt came next, neatly folded, far enough back so it wouldn't get splashed. I pulled off my jeans, nonchalantly. This wasn't a striptease. This was Elvis in Hollywood. The film he should have made. He could have been something, it was written all over him, a combination of Marlon Brando and James Dean, the sneer, the loneliness, that cornered, restless feeling, hunter and hunted. He could have been great and Ward told me he knew what he'd missed, making those twenty-nine moneymaking piles of shit. Not one of which you'd pay to see today. Sure, he combined Brando and Dean, in a way. He got fat and he died young.

My boxer-style underwear went last and I heard some comments behind me. Was it that I'd stripped naked or was it that I wore boxers? This was a bikini-brief crowd, male and female, phosphorescent candy-stripers that left little to the imagination. Minus my boxers, I left nothing. I walked around the edge of the pool right past the three models—" 'Scuse me, ma'am,"—and stood at the deep end of the pool. They'd be laughing if they could see this at Graceland, I thought. Olongapo seemed far away from Forbes Park. They'd told me Olongapo wasn't the Philippines. But what was? Was it this pampered gang of switch-hitting, frequent fliers? Well, check it out. Elvis goes a-skinny-dipping.

I swam back and forth, several lengths, just showing off—I knew they were watching me—but then I got into it, my breathing and my stroke, my underwater turn, and I kept at it, even if they weren't watching anymore. Back and forth, back and forth, it was just me, nobody else, and when I finally stopped at the end of the pool it was as though time had passed, the quality of light had changed, shadows had moved across the lawn, and people had left the pool and gone to tables beneath the trees where I sensed a line of snow, a whiff of pot, out there in the shade. Then Jimmy Fiddler came to the edge of the pool, handing me a towel.

"She'll see you now," he said.

"She's seen me already," I answered.

"Come on, smart-ass," he said. I followed him across the yard toward the house. We were almost inside when he stopped and turned, standing in my way.

"I figure you don't take advice from anybody," he said.

I shrugged. "I listen. It depends."

"Well, listen to this. Watch yourself upstairs. Whatever you think . . . it's probably wrong."

"Anything else?"

"The thing about this country . . . you've got to know when to leave, that's all."

"You haven't left."

"See what I mean? Watch yourself."

He led me into the house, carrying my clothes for me, and after I got dressed he pointed me up those marble steps, to where Baby Ronquillo was waiting, in a chair that looked out a bay window, onto the lawn and the pool. She was dressed in a terry-cloth bathrobe, enjoying coffee and a cigarette while someone did her nails. She was that kind of woman. Her house was guarded, her yard was gardened, her pool vacuumed, clothes tailored, body massaged and manicured, and when she moved around town it was in an air-conditioned bubble. The air she breathed was different from what I sucked in and out. She scared me.

"Well done," she said. She looked me up and down, the way the Navy checked out Graceland girls. In a minute, I bet, the manicure would be over. I was ready. At least I think I was. Ready or not, here I come. The legend lives. This particular series was going the full seven games, I bet. "You remind me of the Colonel."

"How's that?" I asked. I never saw Uncle Pete go naked. Come to think of it, I never saw him in swimming trunks. But Baby Ronquillo had known him before I did. And maybe she'd know him better.

"My Gary Cooper," she said.

"Your *who?*"

"My American. My cowboy. My . . . how do you say it? . . . my *something else*. Are you surprised?"

"No," I said. "Actually . . . it's nice to hear."

"He had none of that American guilt. Do you follow? I don't think you do."

"Uh . . ."

"In bed. Between the first time and the second. With others it was 'What does this mean? Where does it go? You know I love my wife, Baby, I really do!' But Colonel Parker smoked a cigarette between times. And held me. Just like in the movies."

I couldn't think of a single thing to say. Anyway, there was no need. Baby Ronquillo was looking way past me, smiling, and it was a moment before her attention returned. And then it was to dismiss me.

"You'll be hearing from me," Baby Ronquillo said. "Jimmy will drive you home."

And that was how my career in movies began. My bits as a mercenary, a drug peddler, a kidnapped missionary, a multinational businessman. The scripts came to Olongapo on a Thursday. I read them over the weekend, hopped into a hired car after the second show early Sunday morning, and headed to wherever they were filming, Manila, Batangas, Laguna, Zambales, Baguio. Baby made films fast—second takes were rare—and she made them all in a bunch. I gave up keeping track. I took what she gave me, no questions asked. Later, though, she invited me to read scripts, to jot down ideas, wondered whether she could come up with something that might attract a Stateside audience.

I'm not stupid, I told myself. At first I figured she wanted me to go to bed with her, especially after what came to be called my "audition" in the swimming pool. But that didn't happen. I wasn't a boy toy, not yet. She seemed more interested in what Uncle Pete was up to. His plans, his prospects, his business strategy. I couldn't help much but she took it good-naturedly enough. She liked having me under contract, it seemed. And she praised some of the ideas I came up with. Elvis Presley showing up in the Philippines: that's the one she liked the most.

V

Chester "Baby Elvis" Lane

"This Philippines business," Uncle Pete had said, way back on Guam. "It scares you, doesn't it?"

"Yes sir," I said.

We were sitting out back, late at night, in two lawn chairs at the edge of the property, the edge of a cliff really, because it was a couple hundred feet down to Marine Drive. We couldn't see the traffic, because the road ran right against the bottom of the cliff, but we could hear it all right, beeps and honks during the rush hour, drunks and drag racing and sirens late at night. We couldn't see the buildings, either, all the malls and clubs and shopping centers, but we could catch the glow, which made it hard to see the stars. You've got to go way offshore to see the stars, way out on a boat, and then you've got to turn off the cabin lights and the running lights and that's when the whole sky comes out.

"Fear of failure?" he asked.

"Not exactly, sir. I mean if we stink, I guess, it doesn't matter *where* we stink. And if we're good . . . It's just that . . . ."

"What? It was your idea, this whole Presley act."

"Yes sir," I said. "Only I guessed we'd end up playing in lot of local clubs. Or a room at one of the hotels on Tumon Bay. Up to Saipan once in a while, sure. I saw us playing in places we know. Playing for friends. But this . . . you've got us going to a whole different country."

"That's it, huh?"

"Yes sir."

"But that's not all of it, is it?"

"Sir?"

"If I were sending you to, say . . . France . . . or England . . . or Japan . . . that would be a whole different country too. . . . It's about the Philippines, isn't it?"

"Yes sir." I took my time about answering. Uncle Pete didn't mind. My answers were slow in coming, he said, but they were worth waiting for. At the University of Guam, they were still waiting for some of my answers. Multiple-choice tests were murder. I always pictured situations in which two out of three answers might be true, sometimes three out of three. That took some thinking, some looking into things. But they only wanted one answer.

"Sir?" I said when I was ready. "We've got plenty Filipinos on this island, don't we? More coming all the time, they say. They do all the shit jobs, the ones the locals won't take. They work cheap. They get treated bad sometimes. Still they keep arriving and they're always hustling and a lot of folks don't like them because . . . they'll do anything, you know. It's like they don't have a home at all, like their home was a ship that sank someplace and Guam is their life raft . . . I don't know . . . I haven't had any problems . . . but they're so . . . so . . . all over the place."

"Like cockroaches?" asked Uncle Pete. I knew he remembered what we said, down at the Tiger's Cage, that night the Filipina was singing Streisand and no one cared. It was harsh all right, but that's the way it was, no point denying it.

"Yes sir. Me and Albert, we'll go where you send us. But we can't work up too much enthusiasm about going to the place those people come from. Sorry, sir."

I was sorry, really, because Uncle Pete had always been there for us, especially when Dude got busted with marijuana and some pills, but that didn't stop Dude from going ballistic when Uncle Pete said where he was sending us. The Philippines was a dump, Dude said, and everybody knew it. If we went, he said, we better sew our wallets into our pockets and dip our cocks in creosote.

"The thing of it is . . ." Uncle Pete began lots of sentences like that. He'd say "The thing of it is" and you knew something important was coming. "The thing of it is, an island like this, you get too comfortable. You settle in. You know every mile of road. You know the boondocks. Every beach, every curve of coast. No matter how much you screw up, there's always friends around to get you home and home isn't far. If you're a local boy, you've got protection. And, oh hell, Chester, you could play music for your friends, you could marry and make babies and watch me grow old—grow older, that is— and that's not so bad. . . ."

He stopped and it felt like he was picturing it and it wasn't so bad, him sitting out like this, with us around him, all the family he had. Then whatever he was picturing, and liking, he erased.

"But you come to a certain point . . . and you realize you've never been anywhere . . . you've been so happy staying put that you don't know where you could have gone . . . or what you could have been. That's the disease of islands."

"But you've done okay, Uncle Pete."

"I didn't come here straight from West Virginia, son. There were lots of places in between. Lots of places."

We always wondered about Uncle Pete's life. We were vague about what he did now, his business out in the garage. Uncle Pete said that being powerful meant that nobody knew your name and that being rich wasn't about the car you drove but the calls you made, and the people who called you. He kept his name out of the newspapers. When people asked at school, we told them Uncle Pete was a retired U.S. Navy officer and a private investor. Dude laughed at that. "Dim bulb," he said, "how many retired military you know got money to invest? Retired military private investors. That's a thin book joke. Retired military wait at the mailbox for their monthly checks. They buy their pot roast at the commissary and they line up to die at the VA hospital." Now that we were talking, I asked Pete about the places he'd been, after West Virginia and before Guam, because whatever he told me would be big news, something that I could bring to Dude. Dude figured Uncle Pete was Mafia or CIA and that maybe the Witness Protection Program had sent him to Guam.

"Don't start quizzing me, son," Uncle Pete said. "You have to leave, that's all."

"Because you don't want us to be big fish in a small pond? Is that it?"

"Small, shallow pond," Uncle Pete replied. "No room to swim. No room to drown."

If you're nice to people, people will be nice to you. That's the last thing Uncle Pete whispered to me at the airport, the day we flew off to Manila. He whispered something else to Dude and, as soon as we passed into the boarding area, we traded.

"That's lovely," Dude said. " 'Be nice to people and they'll be nice to you.' "

"What'd he tell you?"

"To watch out for you," he said. "In case being nice to people doesn't work, I guess."

Being nice worked fine, though, from that first day until now. I knew it would work out from the minute we came down the hill that led into Olongapo, every street jammed with life, chock-full of it, people sitting, hammering, drinking, crawling, smoking, hawking, shitting, flirting, napping. It was all you could do to take it in, all that life. I didn't know the world could get so full. The whole place got me excited. And then, right away, we walked into the club, which wasn't called Graceland yet, it was still Genghis Khan's Tent, and once we were inside there were maybe two dozen girls sitting around, late afternoon, no customers, nothing happening. The place wasn't open yet, really. Mrs. Ronquillo had the girls who were going to be hostesses cleaning up the place, vacuuming and dusting and all, and that's what they'd just stopped doing when the three of us came walking in. So the first time I saw the girls of Graceland they weren't dolled up and dressed fancy, they were wearing cut-off jeans and T-shirts that said DAIRY QUEEN and BAN ANIMAL TESTING. They wore hair curlers and kerchiefs. It was a good thing I saw them that way, with mops and buckets and Ajax and Windex. It showed me that they weren't just . . . I hate the word . . . whores. They were this bunch of girls, scrubbing and wiping, making a party of it like they tried to make a party out of almost everything, no matter how bad it was.

I'll never forget that minute, them looking at us, sizing and measuring the way women do, and us, the three Elvises, looking back at them, like we'd returned to earth and they were what we saw. For Dude it was simple, looking over that crew. Wow, I got my work cut out for me. Who's first? Later he changed—he became a monk almost, and after that he changed again. But he came to Olongapo angry and the minute we walked through the door, I knew Dude was going for a fuckathon. The girls knew it too, the girls could tell.

Ward was different, of course. He walked around the edges of the room, he stepped up onstage and stared out at a house that hadn't been filled for a long time. The windows in the VIP lounges were smudged and dirty, one was missing so you could see underwear and stockings hanging inside. The whole place was cruddy but—swear to God—Ward acted like he'd just bought his dream house. He was like a minister and this was a church he'd been sent to preach at, his own church. He motioned me toward him. He put his hands on my shoulders, looking me hard in the eyes. "This will work," he said. You ask me, that's when Biggest Elvis was born.

While Ward was sniffing around onstage, Dude went backstage to check out our dressing room, which, it turns out, had empty cases of San Miguel bottles wall to wall. So I was alone, standing near the girls, feeling a couple dozen pairs of super-experienced eyes on me and it made me nervous as prom night, no kidding, so I walked over to the jukebox, reaching into my pocket for change but I didn't have any Filipino money yet. One of the girls—Malou, it turned out—got up and reached into the back of the machine, saying something in Tagalog, all of which I missed except two words of English. "Cherry boy."

The jukebox was a museum. We're talking rock and roll heaven, musical grooveyard, memory lane. Half the song titles weren't even printed, they were handwritten. I leaned down to read the songs: Del Shannon, Loretta Lynn, Screamin' Jay Hawkins, Roy Hamilton, and Fats Domino. And then this girl, Dolly, came up behind and leaned hard against me and linked her hands around in front of me, except one finger was making these little circles around my belly button. I knew it was a joke and she knew it was a joke and everybody knew it was a joke but my body wasn't in on the joke, it didn't have any sense of humor at all, it was getting seriously excited and those circles around my belly button kept getting wider, like someone dropped a stone in a pond, those circles were rippling out, taking in more territory. She was turning me on and she knew it. So, like it was pulling the eject button on a shot-up airplane, I reached for the jukebox, pushed the first song my fingers could find, and it was an early Miracles song, "Mickey's Monkey," and as soon as the first notes rang out, cherry boy was in charge.

Dolly was good. She copied every move I made, the way I hunkered down, the way I rocked back and forth on the balls of my feet, the way I stretched out my arms and threw my shoulders, she caught on but she didn't catch up because when it comes to dancing, I've got a million moves. So, by the time we finished, all the girls were breaking up, seeing Dolly get more than she bargained for from the cherry boy. She stood there, smiling and surprised and out of breath. I said what I'd been raised to say. "Thank you, ma'am," I said. And she gave me this look—I wouldn't know what to call it. Surprised? Flattered? "You're welcome," she said.

That moment got us started off right at the place that was later known as Graceland. Because we weren't johns and they weren't hostesses, no one was the boss and we were in it together. I wanted the whole Elvis thing to work, for their sake as much as ours. They were depending on us and I didn't want to stink out the place, that's all. Dolly and me were pals. She adopted me, she protected me. Some of the others maybe wanted to take a shot, for money or just to say they'd done me, but Dolly headed them off.

Graceland was like no nightclub I'd ever seen. It was one huge room, with a main floor that came down in three levels, from back to front, down towards the stage. Not a window in the place—it had been a movie theater once—except where what used to be the balcony had been divided into private lounges, like the places you see around the top of basketball arenas, where the big shots sit and drink and watch the replays on TV. There were three bars, one on the right as you came in, one in back under the balcony, and another out front where the lobby used to be. On the left, there was a jukebox and a table. That was Malou's place, where the girls checked out with customers on their way upstairs or to hotels. Our dressing room was a joke—on us, Dude said—out in back of the stage, next to the storeroom and the toilets. Through the years, folks had tried to decorate, with flags and pennants, calendars and snapshots, Christmas lights that never came down. But—Dude said—these were like drawings on the walls of a cave. Empty, even half-full, the place was death. It needed a packed house.

Our second day in Olongapo, they were cleaning while we were rehearsing. It was funny, it was as though we were performing for an audience of maids, and there was Dolly again, up on a ladder, scrubbing the smoked glass outside one of the VIP lounges that ran around the second floor. Now, Dude and me tended to take it easy during rehearsals, just going through the motions, because Dude's mostly an actor and I'm mostly a dancer and we need a full house to fire us up. But Ward never held back. He was more like a priest and you don't half-pray. He sang "Suspicious Minds" all out, so that the opening

We're caught in a trap
We can't get out
Because I love you too much, baby

caught everybody's attention. I doubt they'd ever heard that big a voice before. And then, halfway through, Ward went into the slow part, real husky and low, down on his knees . . .

just don't let a good thing die
when, honey, you know
I'll never lie to you . . .

and then, taking the backup part

    oh, oh, yeah, yeah . . .

and that little slow moment in the middle was when he captured them. There was silence when he finished, like a ghost had gone walking by. Maybe the girls had been wondering if we could hack it and maybe Ward was the one they wondered about the most. Me and my brother had the looks. What you saw was what you got and no complaints. But looking at Ward out of costume, you saw a dumpy guy nobody was going to want to undress with their eyes. But then he'd sung. There are thousands of guys who think they can do Elvis. They look like him—that's the easy part—but they die as soon as they open their mouths. Ward was the real thing. Goose bumps. Silence. Awe. And then, from the back of the club, the voice of someone who couldn't sing at all, Dolly, up on a stepladder, wiping smoke and spider webs off the glass,

    I'm caught in a trap
    I can't get out . . .

and then all of the girls took up the song, just that one verse about being caught in a trap, which maybe they were. But—caught in a trap—they were singing about it.

    That night, Dolly asked did I want to go out and see the town. A bunch of girls were going, she said, like that would make me feel comfortable and I guess it did. Dolly had more mileage in the tip of her tongue than I had in my whole body and that scared me because if I wasn't exactly a cherry boy, I hadn't fallen far from the tree. It was like, one on one, Dolly outnumbered me, but with a bunch of the other girls along, I was okay. It got to be a joke that night. They called themselves my bodyguards. They didn't ask Dude or Ward, only me.

    Soul City was across the street, a black and bluesy kind of place where the brothers seemed surprised to see me. The burden of proof was on the white boy, to prove he wasn't an asshole. This was where they went to get away from Navy bullshit and white bullshit. The jukebox was all rhythm and blues. Hall and Oates wouldn't have lasted a minute. So I got some sorry stares from the customers and—this surprised me—from their girl-friends too. The girls were Filipinas, just like Dolly and the others I came with, but there was something about them that was different, as though, af-ter all that music, dancing, and the rest of it, some soul had rubbed off on them. You could see it in the way they danced and the way they laughed, the way they flipped their hair, Tina Turner–style, and the way they looked at me, like I was last year's movies. Dolly put on some music and I guess they wanted me to dance, show what the white boy from across the street could do. It didn't feel right, putting on an act, here's the blue-eyed soul brother. I sat down at the empty end of the bar, nursing a San Miguel and minding my own business.

Even the room made me nervous, no windows at all, no view, just yellow and black striped walls. Ward said white places, bars and taverns, had win-dows all around, exits and entrances from all sides, so you could wave peo-ple in off the street or see who was pulling into the parking lot. But black places were like caves with one entrance and when the door opened every-body got to check out the visitor while the visitor was helpless, adjusting to the dark. Ward had a lot of theories like that.

"Hey, kid . . ." This guy was two stools down from me, a light-skinned black man and no kid. If he was military, he was career military, maybe re-tired. I relaxed a little, knowing he'd been dealing with whites a while. "Could I just ask you a question?"

"Yes sir."

"What are you doing here?"

"I'm with them, sir," I said, nodding over to where Dolly and the rest were gabbing with the other hostesses.

"I know that," he said. "I saw you come in. What I mean is what are you doing in the PI?"

"I'm working across the street, sir," I said, "with them."

He laughed and took a swallow of beer and gave me this look I used to get in high school which I call the back-to-drawing-board look.

"I know what *they* do," he said. "I don't know what you do. Unless what you do is what they do."

"No sir, I don't do that."

"I didn't think so."

"I'm an entertainer, sir. I sing and dance." I looked at him closely. He seemed like a nice man. Be nice to people and they'll be nice to you. "I sing and I dance a lot better than I talk."

He took that kindly, signaled the bartender she should bring me another beer. She studied me closely when she delivered it and I guess she thought she was staring at the Original or someone close enough to the Original to be worth staring at. That's part of being Elvis, Ward said. Giving people a good look at you, close up.

"I'm part of an Elvis act," I said.

"Moving in right across the street? You're shitting me!"

"No sir."

"I thought I'd left that shitkicker behind. Elvis Presley! You do him?"

"Yes sir. I'm the young Elvis. From when he was starting out. There's two more. The Elvis who was a movie star. That's my older brother."

"Unbelievable. And . . . let me guess. You got some fat crooner for the third and final act?"

"I wouldn't put it that way, sir. That's Ward Wiggins. He's the brains of the operation."

"Just how much brains does it take?" he wondered. He was nice but he acted as though someone had pulled a practical joke on him. "Right in my neighborhood. How long you staying?"

"It's kind of open-ended. There's a difference of opinion. My brother thinks it'll go a couple months. But Ward thinks longer. Much longer. Maybe permanent."

He shook his head again, studied me the way his bartender studied me, the way Dolly and the others had looked me over earlier in the day. Part of it was simple: they were checking to see how much I looked liked Elvis. That was the first thing, always. But not the last. Sometimes people looked at me and Dude and Ward, back and forth, and it was like they were thinking, well, that's how he began and that's how he grew up and that's how he wound up, there they are, cheek to jowl, the beginning, the middle, and the end. That got to people. It got to me whenever the three of us were near each other, onstage or in back or in a car together. I don't know how to say it. But it was like seeing a whole lifetime of clothes in one pile, everything you wore or were ever going to wear, from the diapers at the beginning to whatever you wear when you die. Diapers again, I guess.

Dolly came over to me and said we were going now, lots of other places to see. The man I'd been talking to shook my hand again, said his name was Billy Bowers and he was the unofficial owner of the place. The bartender was his Filipina wife and the place was in her name and I could walk across the street anytime. I told him to drop in on us sometime. He nodded politely and told me not to hold my breath.

We moved fast after that, Dolly and Whitney and Priscilla and Luz and Esther and a girl they called Lucy Number Three, on account of there'd been two girls named Lucy before her that did real well, married guys and left town, so Lucy was a lucky name. We went to a country-western place called the Corral and a hard-rock place called Hot Wax and a heavy metal place called California Jams and a bunch of others I forget the names of. They got me dancing after a while. I danced with all the girls but Whitney, who said she didn't know how. There were places that specialized in female boxing and massage and mud wrestling and body painting. The farther we got from town, the places got more basic. The last stop was just a cement floor and a tin roof over a pool table, with wooden bleachers on the side and a bar in back and some little rooms behind the bar, where girls and guys could go for "short time." There were always girls around and some of them came to life when they saw me—customer coming!—but Dolly cut that right off. "You can look," she said, "but you can't touch." I danced some more and the girls talked and a pile of food showed up, barbecued fish and piles of rice and a soup called *sinigang*. It amazed me how these women could put it away. They were always up for food, I learned. Later on, when we went for picnics in jeepneys, hell, we wouldn't be out of the damn parking lot and the sandwiches would be gone.

Going home, that first night, around two in the morning, I heard them whispering, consulting, maybe even arguing a little. My name was in it. "Baby Elvis," "cherry boy." My guess was that one of the others—it could've been Lucy Number Three—was saying, well, we've had a nice time on our night out, we showed the kid around but that doesn't mean one—or two—of us couldn't do business between now and sunrise. That's what it sounded like to me, anyway. It got lively in back of the jeepney, lots of back and forth whispering and giggling. The mood changed. Until then I'd been one of the boys, or one of the girls, or something, but now it felt like this-little-piggy-went-to-market. Then Dolly spoke a couple of sentences and everybody got quiet. Something had been decided. Maybe Dolly was saying, back off, he's mine. Maybe she was pulling rank because she was a little older than the rest, and a good talker. Maybe she was the one who would break me in. I hoped not because I liked Dolly for a friend. I'd do what she wanted me to do, I guessed—be nice to people, and all—but I'd have preferred not to. But it wasn't up to me.

Dolly gave directions to the guy who was driving. These jeepneys were funny things, stretched-out jeeps, silvery, splashed with paintings and symbols, with names and sayings, with horses and saints. The driver was up front, in control, hands on the wheel, the horn, the tape player, like captain of the Starship *Enterprise*. We were all squeezed in back. I was wondering where I was going and who with and it was like back in high school, who gets dropped off at the end of the evening, where and in what order, together or alone.

Well, the first was me. The jeepney pulled in front of this apartment they'd rented for Dude and me. It had a bedroom—which Dude took—a living room where I would sleep on a couch, and a kitchen for the beer.

"Good night, Baby Elvis," Dolly said. It was the first thing anybody had said to me for a couple miles. "We see you tomorrow."

It was awkward, getting out of a jeepney, especially if you were packed way in front, right in back of the driver. I started working my way toward the back.

"Thanks, everybody," I said. And I mentioned every one of them by name, Dolly, Whitney, Priscilla, Luz, and Esther, and Lucy Number Three. "I'm grateful for the welcome to town and I'll do my best not to let you down." Meanwhile, I was inching my way out. "Thanks again. I had a real nice time and . . . hey!"

Maybe Dolly vetoed anybody taking me home that night but somebody said something and they all got in a poke, a tickle, a pinch as I crawled by, defenseless. Whitney just tickled my ear with her finger. The others weren't so shy. Somebody hefted me right between the legs. It was Lucy Number Three, I think. She touched me good, like she was putting it on a butcher scale to weigh. I rolled and stumbled out the back, shirt hanging out, everything all tangled up, and if I hadn't gotten laid, I sure looked as though I had. I stood there waiting to see if one—any one—of those girls would follow me out of the jeepney. It wasn't up to me. It was their move. Then the driver gunned the jeepney and they barreled off down Magsaysay Street, loud music behind them and the muffler roaring, and I could hear them laughing like a bunch of teenagers, shouting "Good night, Baby Elvis" and "We love you so much, Baby Elvis."

Dude stuck his head out the bedroom door as soon as I came in. "Where you been, Chestnut?" he asked, walking over to the refrigerator, opening it up, showing me a San Miguel.

"No thanks," I said. "I had plenty."

"So I see. Who with?"

"A bunch from work. They took me around, one club after another. It's some town, Dude. It really cooks."

"It's a shit-pile, Chestnut. One big clip joint. But there's nothing we can do about it right now. It cost you much, tonight? They got a million tricks here. They water drinks or they dope them. They drink tea and charge for champagne. And you go to sleep with one of them in your room, they'll have a yard sale while you're sleeping. And slap you with a paternity suit in the morning."

"We had a welcome party," I said. Something was going wrong here and I didn't know how to set it right.

"It cost you much?" he asked again. "Three hundred pesos for a quickie. That's scale. Don't let them bullshit you. You especially. They look at you, they know you're a rookie."

"I didn't pay nothing tonight, Dude. It was a welcome party. It was for me."

He drained his beer in a swallow, chugged and belched. "Well, that's all right, then. You get it for nothing from a hooker, that's true love."

I just sat there on the couch, taking my shoes off. He didn't get it, not tonight and maybe not tomorrow. But now that I was Elvis one and he was Elvis two, there was some distance between us. We were playing different parts, even when we weren't onstage.

"I got a little welcome party of my own going on in there," he said, tipping his head toward the bedroom. "Not quite over yet. Two thirds over."

So I was in bed and I could hear the sound of my brother and someone working it out. To me, it sounded like they were both onstage, waiting for applause when they finished up. Then, not ten minutes later, the door opened and some woman came tipping into the room, which was dark. I was still awake but I tried to be thoughtful, trying to pretend I was sleeping, and she was thoughtful too, tiptoeing across the room so as not to wake me. Then she stopped by the couch and looked down at me and saw my eyes wide open.

"Baby Elvis," she said. "Cherry boy." So I knew it was one of the girls from work.

"Who's that?" I asked.

"Never mind," she said. And left. I could've asked Dude the next morning who he'd been with but I didn't want to know. Or maybe I did. I wondered. But in the end, I liked it better, not knowing.

Dude always kidded Ward about sleeping alone. He joked about it, about how burning love burned out, how blue suede shoes should be blue suede slippers. The fact is, Dude slept alone too. The women he paid were "tuck me ins" who left as soon as they got finished and "wake me ups" who came over in the morning. I opened the door for them and I hated to see which of my friends he was tagging. Dude went a little crazy when he got to Olongapo.

I got into the habit of stopping in to talk to Billy Bowers, even between shows, still in costume. I'd just grab this plastic raincoat and pop across the street. It tickled him to see me, Elvis at halftime, dressed in black and pink, sitting at a bar with a bunch of brothers who'd as soon go square dancing as watch what was happening at the place we were calling Graceland. Billy had thought a lot about Olongapo. He said it was like this valley in the old Tarzan comic books, a secret valley where elephants went to die, so they left their tusks all over the valley, a treasure of ivory.

"Olongapo is like that valley," he said. "Look around, Baby Elvis. You got a harbor full of ships and a street full of bars like you ain't had in America in a hundred years. Even the air smells old. And you've got all these sidewalk characters, hookers, hoods, newsboys, cripples, out of an old movie, black and white. You've got a bar like this and an old bullshitter like me. . . . You don't find that anywhere but here, no more. It's a junkyard, man, it's a museum, it's the magic valley. Everything that used to be in America—everything that America used to be—it's here. It washed up here. My bar included. And your act."

Maybe Billy was right. There was no place we could have hit the way we hit in Olongapo. From the start I knew that we were part of something special. And it wasn't just, hey, you catch this act, here's a fun place to go. Ward was weird, Dude said, but Ward was right. Elvis was back, the second time around, in triplicate. I wasn't the only one who knew this. It spread through the girls. It was out on the street. And I could feel it, whenever I sat down with Father Alcala. He was tired and worried, quiet when he should have been talking, and laughing when there was nothing funny around, at least nothing I could see. He said that this outbreak of Elvis was the latest local social disease. He was a man standing in the way of something that he couldn't stop. Elvis in Olongapo.

"He is dead, isn't he?" I asked Ward one night. Dude had been going on about how Ward was losing his grip on reality, that before much longer we'd be needing an exorcist. It was one thing, he said, for some street kid to gawk when we walked by, thinking Elvis was back, but it was something else when we started acting that way ourselves, turning a whore bar into a revival meeting.

"Elvis Aaron Presley?" said Ward. "Deader than hell." I'd joined him up in the VIP lounge, watching the house fill. The showroom opened an hour before our first show and the band did fifties music, the sort of stuff that was around when Elvis came on the scene, Ink Spots, Mills Brothers, Bill Haley, Frankie Laine. But no Elvis stuff. "Have you been talking to your brother?"

"Him. Sure . . . and Father Domingo too."

"I'm telling you, he's dead. August 16, 1977. In the bathroom at Graceland, on the floor in front of the toilet. At the age of forty-two. While reading a book. Some say the book was *Sex and Psychic Energy*. Or the Bible. Or something about the Shroud of Turin. His face was purple, his eyes were red, and his body was cold. They autopsied his body, they embalmed him, they put him in a coffin, and they put the coffin in the ground."

"Then what?"

"Father Domingo wants to know whether I think Elvis is back? Tell him he's still in the ground. He didn't pop out after three days. That's his tiger, not mine. Okay?"

Ward had guessed right. Father Domingo was out for us. I was just trying to learn the ropes about being Catholic. I wished there was a book I could read, like a driver's manual. I mean, how hard could it possibly be, if sixty million Filipinos were Catholic already? I felt that I could be a good Catholic. But Father Domingo kept me reading, kept throwing me puzzles. And sometimes he teased me about my act. He'd ask me if I felt Elvis inside me, when I performed. Or what was the difference between saying Elvis lives—which was appearing on signs around town—and Jesus lives. And what was the difference, did I think, between music that was holy and music that wasn't. It seemed we weren't making any progress at all.

"I'll tell you the secret, Chestnut," Ward said. "Keep this between us. Most people die and that's it. They leave some memories behind and people crying. It's pretty much over, though. But sometimes it's different. If a life's been big enough—not good or bad, especially, just big—it leaves something behind that other people can be part of, that they don't want to let go of."

"Second coming?" That was another phrase I'd heard from Father Domingo.

"Second chance."

"For the person who died, you mean?"

"For him." Ward nodded. "And for us. All of us. To try it out again. Sing those songs. Get it right this time. Okay?"

"We're not doing anything bad, then?" I asked. Ward shook his head. "Sometimes it feels that Father Domingo thinks we are."

"I know," he said. "But he gets Sunday. And all of eternity. All I'm asking for is Saturday night."

It was Wednesday, Thursday, Friday, Saturday night, to be exact, plus special appearances that our boss in Manila, Mrs. Baby Ronquillo, arranged at hotels and graduations and once—never again, Dude said—at a cockfighting pit. But that was part of the deal that Uncle Pete had made, she could ship us out on off-nights. So we went by small plane—the Buddy Holly special, Dude said—by ferry, by jeepney, sometimes all three, to places so far out of it they hadn't heard that Elvis had died and others they hadn't heard he'd lived. We were traveling backward through time, it seemed, to places that were from before the beginning. We were like light from a far-off star, carrying images of what happened years before. And—funny thing—it was all my idea. My *one* idea, Dude said. He said it back on Guam, he said it on Saipan, he said it in the Philippines all the time, like when we were at the domestic airport, waiting for a Philippines Airline flight that was five hours late or on a ship where the deck was covered with sleeping passengers and cockroaches owned our first-class cabin and four out of four toilets were clogged. Dude would bitch and I'd nod, not wanting to argue, but God, I was happy, knocking around islands I couldn't pronounce the names of, and waiting to go onstage while they cleaned the blood and feathers out of the cockpit. And I was always happy coming back to Olongapo, because there's no place like home and Olongapo was ours. We owned the place. Also, Christina was there.

Dolly was the one who brought us together. Dolly was my bodyguard, my matchmaker, my chaperone, which is funny parts for a bar hostess to play but what I've learned here is that people aren't just one thing. A hooker isn't just a hooker. And a singer—an Elvis, say—can be more or less than what he seems. That goes for priests, too.

Take Dolly. She was a hustler, all right. I'd seen her work on a table of hard-core petty officers, wised-up dudes who'd done it all, from Pusan to Bangkok. They came into Graceland tough and shrewd and tighter than a crab's ass. "Just beers." They ain't buying nothing extra, you'd better believe it. They'd pour their own beers, thanks—"hands off, darling"—and drink at their own slow speed and that's that. "We need anything, we'll let you know, darling." Nobody could put anything over on them. Girls came over, introduced themselves, asked if they'd like some company. "You can sit with us, darling, but don't talk to me about no bar drinks." That was the part I didn't like, watching these friends of mine, beautifully dressed, hanging around a table full of rednecks in T-shirts who just ignored them—like the guys were the ones who should play hard to get, not these great women. They'd keep talking among themselves. That wasn't polite. I could see this frozen look come over the girls' faces and the life drain out of them, all the spark and smile while these . . . assholes . . . were talking about the base bowling league or something. Something died in me, when I saw that.

That's when Dolly did her thing. She'd drop by the table and start kidding around, tell a joke, get the party going. Before long, the guys were whispering, what they wanted, what they needed, the girls were whispering back, the drinks were coming, beers and whole trays of margaritas. Everybody was pals and the evening was still young. There was nothing official about it, but Dolly was the team manager. Elvira had the looks but she was kind of snooty. Malou had brains but she wasn't so good dealing with customers. "You have three strikes on you when you're dealing with Malou,"

Dude said. "You're an American—that's one—and you have a dick—that's two. And you're here." So Dolly kept an eye on things. On me.

The first time I saw Christina was at the White Rock beach in Barrio Barretto, when we all wound up playing volleyball. I didn't notice her before the game but, once it got started, she stood out. The other girls tended to goof off and clown around. Whenever they did something wrong, they made a joke out of it. Before long, the object wasn't to score a point but to do something cute and funny. Christina got pissed off, I noticed. The others were falling over each other, rolling in the sand, tangling up in the net, playing like they were at a pajama party, like giggles were points. Christina played harder. She was tall for a Filipina, rangy and lanky and athletic-looking. She dug the ball out of the sand and set it up, only to see somebody slap it into the net and worry about a fingernail. Everybody else forgot the score. When the game ended, she walked off toward the beach, waded out into the water like she never wanted to see any of us again. I hadn't seen anybody like her before.

"Who's that?" I asked Dolly.

"That's just Christina," Dolly said, like she was apologizing for the girl's bad manners.

"Dolly," I said, swallowing hard. "I'd like to meet her." Something happened that next minute that's hard for me to describe. Dolly had kept the other girls away from me. I was cherry boy, Baby Elvis, a kind of mascot, everybody's buddy. But maybe, all along, she'd been saving herself for me, or me for her. When I asked about Christina, that chance was gone. We weren't going to be a couple. She adjusted fast, in a damn twinkling, but it was there for just a second, a little worry and a little pity, about what was and wasn't in the cards.

I didn't expect her to go rushing down the beach to bring Christina the good news. But somehow the word must have gotten passed and I'd be surprised if Dolly and Christina were the only ones who knew. Women have a way of finding this stuff out: there weren't any clueless women around here, except Whitney. Anyway, the party broke up and I was carrying a whole load of pots and pans out toward the side of the road, where we were going to snag a jeepney. Stuff was shifting and sliding on me and I was struggling not to drop anything, so I didn't see her coming. She just stepped in front of me, like she'd come to collect a bill I was walking out on.

"Dolly says you want to meet me," she said in a let's-get-this-over-with tone of voice. I fumbled around and finally put my dirty trays and dishes on the ground.

"Hi," I said. "I'm Chester Lane."

"I know who you are." No sign of a smile on her face, in a country where everybody smiles, whether they mean it or not.

"They call me Baby Elvis."

She nodded. "I know that too." Now I felt that everybody on the beach was listening, hell, that the traffic out on the road was slowing for a look, the way you do when you pass an accident. "You wanted to meet me."

"I sure did."

"Why?"

"Because . . ." I forgot why, I almost said. "I liked the way you played volleyball."

"We lost. Fifteen to six."

"You scored the six." That earned a shrug. "I could tell you didn't like it. You took it seriously and the others didn't."

"That happens."

"Well, I thought you were fine." I was feeling a little better now. Not great, but off the critical list. Her eyes never left me, though. She used them like weapons, I swear. First they found you, radar-locked onto target, then they started burning in. "I play at this club here in town—Graceland, it's called—and I was wondering if you'd like to maybe come by and be my guest there and watch the show is all. No obligations . . . 'No salesman will call.' . . ."

"Impossible," she answered. She didn't say why but I figured it out real quick. I could've kicked myself. Graceland was where I worked and I had lots of friends there that I wasn't ashamed of. But asking her there was like taking a prom date to a massage parlor.

"Look, I'm sorry," I said. "I only thought . . . I'd like to get to know you. Sorry." I reached down to the plates and trays, swiping away the flies that were circling around in holding patterns, waiting for a place to land.

"You don't even know my last name," she said. That's true, I thought. And I didn't suppose I'd be needing it. I'd as soon stick my tongue in an electronic socket as give her a call. "Christina Alcala," she said. "Good afternoon." And she walked back down the beach.

Not fewer than a dozen Graceland girls had been watching me from maybe thirty feet away. Of those, half had passed right by us while we were talking, moving real slow. So the atmosphere on the ride back to Olongapo was real sad, everybody knowing I'd just gotten slaughtered. I just sat there, staring out the back of the jeepney, watching the Philippines slide by, all the bars and food stalls and funky beach resorts. Then Whitney of all people tapped me on my knee and broke the silence.

"Baby Elvis," she said. "You are not so good talking to the girl. . . . Next time—"

"There ain't gonna be a next time, Whitney."

"Next time, maybe you sing."

There was a next time, though, thanks to Dolly. Not that I saw it coming. It was just as well. Sometimes it's good not knowing. Sometimes it's the only way to go. If Dolly had told me I was due for a rematch with Christina Alcala, I'd've been sweat-soaked, fumble-fingered, and tongue-tied. This way, I was only hungry.

Our show had kept getting bigger and bigger, folks coming from far and wide, especially after this American TV show did a segment on us called "Elvis on the Beach." Beached Elvis, Dude called it, looking over at Ward. "Beached whale." There was an edge in Dude's voice and if you looked at things through his eyes, there was something to resent. The fame that came to us came mostly to Ward. More and more, me and Dude felt like opening acts, preliminaries for Biggest Elvis. We knocked audiences on their asses, no mistaking it, but, hard as we worked—and you should've seen the pure, nasty competitiveness Dude started pumping into "Jailhouse Rock"—the emotions in the room raised up a notch when Biggest Elvis walked onstage. I asked Ward what that extra something was. It wasn't musical, he said, it was spiritual. I asked him what did that mean. "You're the ones who lived," he said. "I'm the one who died."

Some nights, the show was so draining, I didn't want to hang around the jukebox and eat the food that Biggest Elvis was always ordering. So when Dolly asked would I like to go home, she had something special cooking— some goat meat, she said—I said fine. Let's just get out of here. In a minute I could slip into some slacks and a T-shirt and step out onto the street. People spotted me and Dude but they didn't come at us the way they swarmed Biggest Elvis. Dude said he liked it better that way. He was an actor, he said, and part of being professional was the ability to move in and out of a role, not like some people, some head cases we knew. So it was a good thing, he said, that we could walk down a street and not get mobbed. It meant we were professional. I wasn't sure he liked being a professional so much.

Dolly lived way up the winding road that leads in and out of Olongapo, right behind a row of stores that sold surplus equipment that jumped the fence from the base, uniforms and mess kits, office equipment, first-aid kits, tools, boots, you name it. We walked up a steep flight of steps to where a couple houses held on to the edge of the hill, just barely. Dolly's house was solid, square cement blocks, the roof was shiny new, and, coming nearer, I heard the hum of an air conditioner, spotted the glow of a color television: from a distance it looked like a lit-up aquarium, fish swimming inside. Dolly's two kids were watching the TV and Christina was watching them. She was Dolly's baby-sitter, also her cousin.

"Hello again," she said when we walked in, like oh, what a pleasant surprise. Before I could answer, one of the kids was tugging at my hand, a boy who asked was I Elvis and I said sometimes, it depended. It felt like I was answering Christina. Dolly and Christina exchanged some words in Tagalog. It never bothered me, not being able to understand what they said. I think people need a way of pulling back, sometimes, of drawing a circle around themselves, even if I wasn't inside the circle. Good news, bad news, they get to you sooner or later, anyway. Then Dolly dragged her kids to the back of the house and I was left alone with the Texas Chainsaw Volleyball Player.

"I was rude to you," she said. "Dolly says I was. And I agree."

"It's all right," I said. "I think I deserved it. I just saw you and I said, that's someone I'd like to meet. It's not like I knew what I was doing or anything."

"True, true, true," Dolly said as she passed through and headed into the kitchen. "Oh so true."

"Well," I said. "Everybody seems to be agreed on that one thing. Chester Lane doesn't know what he's doing." Now I faced Christina. "You know what you're doing, all of the time?"

"Yes," she said. "A little." A little was a lot. We wound up talking for hours. Mostly, she talked and I listened. Christina had this very exact way of speaking, as though she composed a whole sentence, looked it over for mistakes, before saying it out loud. Other times, she'd just stop and wait for the right word to come. "Going to the dictionary," we called it later. People like me and Dude just ran our mouths, saying whatever was in us, funny and foul as it might be. Christina wanted everything to come out perfect. So she took me back to that picnic on the beach.

She'd noticed me, she admitted, so slow and soft you'd have thought it was a sin, just putting her eyes on me. She'd seen how the women liked me, not the way a seller treats a buyer but they honestly liked having me around. She'd never seen an American treated quite that way, the way I was teased and watched over. She also liked the way I ran errands, organized games, made a point of talking to everybody. But she didn't want to talk to me.

"He wants to meet you," Dolly had told her.

"What *for?*"

"So he can know you."

"What for, know me?" She was angry at first, she said, angrier than anyone could realize. "These Americans think that every woman here is like the women on Magsaysay Street, waiting to be found by them."

Dolly shouted something from the kitchen then and it wasn't about dinner. She was speaking up for the women on Magsaysay Street, I guessed.

She was letting go of the hopes she'd had for us but she wasn't riding off into the sunset, that was for sure. And Christina better watch what she said about the girls of Graceland.

"You Americans assume that every woman is waiting for you to enter their life," Christina said. Now, when she spoke, it sounded rehearsed, like something from a classroom that she needed to get out all in one piece. "It comes from the base. It disgraces Americans and Filipinos both. It brings us to the edge of war, all in the name of peace. It protected a dictatorship, in the name of democracy. It poisoned the air and the water. It turns us into a race of servants, procurers, prostitutes. It leaves behind a race of orphans, mixed-race, neglected—"

"Bullshit!" Dolly cried out from the kitchen, following with a spray of Tagalog. If Dolly's voice was a gun, those Tagalog words were bullets. And the English words were tracers. They told me where she was firing. Words like payroll and jobs and dollars and nice guys. Christina smiled, kind of asking for my sympathy, but before she could resume, Dolly marched in two of the mixed-race kids her cousin had been complaining about. "This is Marines," Dolly said, pointing to the boy who'd asked me about Elvis. "And this . . . ," she hefted a girl, a year or two younger, with eyes that broke your heart, "is Navy." She made a face at Christina. "My poor, confuse half-caste baby."

"Not everyone is as good as you are, Dolly," Christina answered, kissing the young Marine, the young Navy.

"Not everyone is as bad as you say," Dolly responded. She moved the kids across the living room, then closed the bedroom door behind her.

"Olongapo is a bad place," Christina continued, but her speech had lost energy. The reciting was over. She returned to the story of the beach and how she'd run over to intercept me, once the party started breaking up. *Dolly says you want to meet me. . . .*

She wanted the Graceland girls who were walking by us to know she was turning me down. It peeved her, being put in such a situation, another girl who'd caught an American's attention. At least the Graceland girls could hear what she was saying. But beyond them was a beach full of Filipinos who could only guess: another Navy boy facing off with an angry girlfriend, another love affair winding down when the American's time grew short. That's what she thought she looked like to the people who were tearing open Pringles cans and dangling babies out at arm's length so they could pee into the Navy's rented bay.

There I'd stood, carrying pots and pans, complimenting her on her volleyball play, ticking her off even more because—she already knew, she could tell from the look on my cherry boy face—I didn't really deserve the ration of shit she was handing me. I was another well-intentioned American kid. The world was full of them.

I had asked her to drop by Graceland sometime, catch the act that the town was talking about. On me. Bigger than full-body massage, foxy boxing, mud wrestling, here was the Elvis show. Another Olongapo abomination, the worst of a bad scene. Sure, she granted, there were good Americans here. I might even be one of them. So much the worse. Hadn't I ever thought about what those girls went through night after night, hitting on customers, hustling drinks, what that felt like? Or what it meant to go off with somebody—anybody—who had the price of admission?

Now she was on a roll again. If I studied the history of these islands, she said, the real history and not what got served up in schools, I would know that the story was of abuse and betrayal, one foreign power, Spain, replaced by another, the U.S., with Japan in between. Deaths by the thousands. World War II, a colonists' war, the Philippines caught in the middle, wrecked and ignored. MacArthur rushed off to rebuild Japan, Marshall pumped millions into Europe, Germany included, and the Philippines got no real money, only a phony, strings-attached independence. Business as usual, corruption everywhere. America running military bases to protect democracy, then ignoring democracy to protect the bases. Marcos dancing with Nancy Reagan. Bush toasting Marcos. And Olongapo was at the heart of it all and we were the heart of Olongapo because what happened at Graceland symbolized the whole sick thing: Americans with beers in one hand, money in the other, standing unsteadily while a beautiful nation went down on its knees. And that—she wanted me to know—was why she'd been angry at me. Nothing personal.

Nothing I could say when she finished. I liked the way she spoke to me, the way she put it all together, even though the message wasn't so good. She met my eyes, now and then, while she was speaking. She wasn't just delivering lines, the way people do. She was paying attention to the way I took them in. It's not often someone speaks to you like that. In a country where buildings, jeeps, and probably airplanes were held together with tape, wire, and chewing gum, I'd found a perfectionist. Nothing half-assed about her. I'm gonna get close to you, I said to myself. Any way you want me, that's how I will be. I noticed she didn't smile much. I could do something about that. And I still hadn't heard her laugh out loud, not once. I'd be taking care of that, count on it. And I would sing to her, even if it wasn't at Graceland.

It seemed to me she was placing a mighty heavy load on Graceland. I knew what went on there. I'd see the girls making deals and disappearing for a while, upstairs and outside. Sometimes I didn't like the looks on their faces when they came back in. But I'd seen them laugh and joke too. I'd heard them singing or, in Dolly's case, trying to sing, even dancing together by the jukebox, after closing, when they shot the shit and ate Ward's food. I'd seen how they hung around the place, practically lived there, washing clothes and changing diapers up in the VIP lounges, trading dresses. It wasn't like they had some better place to go. And I'd seen the way they looked after each other and had taken care of me, from the day I walked in until this very minute, and another thing I'd noticed was that if they talked about leaving, or even if they left, they talked about Guam or Hawaii or California. They never spoke about back home. And Graceland gave them a shot at that, not a great shot but the best they had, and until something better came along I was rooting for them. That was how it looked to me. I might be wrong, though, and I decided to keep my mouth shut. I didn't want to make her mad at me all over again. So I was happy when Dolly came out and said it was time to eat.

It was one in the morning but in this country, when there's food you eat.

The presence of food was special, not the appetite. Mostly, Christina and Dolly talked about the two kids, who kept inventing these excuses to come into the kitchen and stare at me, until I volunteered to escort them to bed myself, if they promised to stay put after that. It was a deal, they said. Handshakes and high fives.

Surprise. Double-decker bunk beds for the kids, covered with toys and teddies. And a third bed that was Dolly's, not that different. She slept with them, when she had a choice where she slept. Souvenirs and tourist stuff took the place of Terminators and Robocops. A Statue of Liberty, a map of Singapore, a lacquered coconut crab shell that said GUAM: WHERE AMERICA'S DAY BEGINS. There were framed photos: Dolly at the railing of a boat, Dolly at an outdoor grill, turning chicken, Dolly in cut-off shorts, holding a baseball bat. Some photographs were taken in nightclubs, by photographers who went from table to table: Dolly and different men. Always the same Dolly, always a different man. Bummed me out. It's sad, the way we leave each other.

"You are Elvis?" asked the Marine. Same question as before.

"Sometimes," I said. Same answer.

"When?"

"Whenever I want to be."

"Sing," he commanded.

"You sing," his sister chimed in. She was darker than Dolly, all right. Afro-Amer-Asian. Anybody ever going to sort this out?

"In bed, first," I said. They popped right in. "One song is all you get."

" 'Every Time You Go Away'!"

" 'Don't Worry, Be Happy'!"

They settled for "Love Me Tender." I sang it so slow it put them to sleep. Hell, it usually puts me to sleep. There's no way around it, I had to live with it, though it wasn't my favorite song. But it worked as a lullaby. One minute the Marine and the Navy were watching me with big eyes and I wondered how many other men—nice-enough guys—had come home with Dolly before. What kind of parade had it been? All of a sudden—thank God their eyes were closed—I was wiping away tears. Carried away by my own performance. Surest sign of an amateur, Dude would say. Dolly and Christina both noticed it too, when I came out.

Dolly walked us out to the front of the house, then followed us to where steps led down to the main road. Two in the morning, all's well, dogs sleeping, babies put to bed, bars mostly closed. You still broke a sweat when you moved but the breeze was there to cool you. You could feel it, as soon as you lifted your arms. Hello, there. Christina was ahead of me, going down the steps, when Dolly called for me to come back up, as if there were something we'd left behind. When I got there, she led me around a corner, leaned against a wall, and held me, putting her hands on my head and pulling me down into a kiss.

"Five years ago, cherry boy," she said, nodding in the direction of the steps Christina had taken. "No competition. You're mine."

"I believe you," I said. "Tell me, Dolly. Do I stand a chance down there?"

She nodded and smiled. "No."

VI

Colonel Peter Parker

I always wanted to get back to Manila. It would be the last trip I'd take, I thought. It would have pleased me to see those Bataan mountains around sunset, out past the ships in Manila Bay. You used to be able to see Corregidor, on clear days, if you knew where to look. Now that I knew that I wasn't going anywhere, it pleased me to picture the boys there. Sure, that was then and this was now. But some things never changed. The weather, say, the heat that turned you sleepy and stupid at noon, the cool that revived you in the early evening, priming you for beer and horny mischief, and the way the rains came later on, hammering on tin roofs, turning streets into rivers. I wanted them to know what that was like. I wanted them to see how money worked, what it means to be rich and not deserve it and poor, piss-poor, and nothing you could do about it. I wanted them to be strangers, surrounded by strangers, by people who looked at them, and thought, okay, how can I use these Americans? I wanted them to be smiled at, seduced, hustled, used, to learn the meaning of the word *maybe*, to see what people will do when they're willing to do anything. I wanted them to get sick and get well down there, to be homesick in the morning and go native at night. And at the end of it all, I wanted to know I could save them.

They could fly it in three hours, Guam to Manila, with no land in between, only deep ocean and an imaginary line that separates a place that happens to be part of the United States—the Marianas Islands—from a place that used to be part of the United States, but not anymore, the Philippines. And down in the water, that line between first world and third, the lucky and the unlucky, the kitchen and the cockroaches. You've got to cross that line at least once in your life, or you're not human. My father had the Depression: he knew what it was like losing it all and starting over. I had the war, not just the fighting and the prison camp but the hold of the *Nagasaki Maru*, praying that the American torpedoes wouldn't miss. Albert and Chester and Ward, too, were part of a generation that never learned how bad life can be. So, for them, the Philippines was perfect.

Have you ever been to Guam? (There's a line to try on folks, if you ever need to clear out a room.) Home was in a ranch house in Agana Heights, a sprawling air-conditioned place that suited me fine, three bedrooms, den and TV room, industrial-size kitchen with twin deep-freezes that could embarrass a mortuary, a kitchen nook where we ate all our meals, a dining room no one dined in, a living room no one ever lived in, and a garage that I converted into my office, plenty room for my secretary, plus any lawyers or accountants I might be needing. I needed them plenty, sometimes, but not as much as they needed me and they didn't mind it a bit, working in a garage.

These days, there was another room in the house that had a hospital bed and a pharmacy of pills and a dialysis machine, all mine, and a Filipina nurse, full-time. She came when Sheila was dying and she agreed to stick around for my exit. Two one-way tickets to punch. Lupus erythematosus. If it sounds familiar it's because Ferdinand Marcos had the same disease. He lived with it awhile and stayed ahead of it awhile. You go down, you bounce back up. Eventually, though, the bouncing stops. The boys knew that I needed treatments but I never named the disease. I just had "off days," now and then, the way an athlete might go on the injured list with a torn muscle or a sprained ankle. That's how Chester and Albert thought of it, which was just as well. I had some pills, too, for when the off days took over.

I couldn't travel much. I hadn't planned to, but there's a difference between choosing not to travel and being told you can't and it's the difference between a quiet life at home and house arrest. You looked at things differently. This house, for instance. My last. No more moving days for me. That sickroom was the room that I entered alive, one of these days, and came out dead. That hospital bed which I peeked at from the hallway, that was my deathbed, waiting for me, all neatly made up. Nobody knew the exact time of his death and no one wanted to. But I knew the place.

Granted, it's not exactly a news flash when you learn, at the age of seventy-two, that you're running out of time. Everybody did. The boys kept it light around here, disorganized and noisy, phones always ringing, cars in the driveway, people knocking on the door or not bothering to, just coming in to sleep on couches and eat. Till they left, my nurse spent most of her time cooking pork barbecue for Chester's freeloading compadres. We had our own way of speaking about my problem. If they asked me how was I feeling and I had a bad day, I'd say, "Don't ask." If it was an okay day, I'd say, "Next question." On a good day, they'd ask me that same question and I'd fire back, "None of your damn business!"

I'd been getting weekly phone calls from Baby Ronquillo, telling me more than I needed to know about how Graceland was doing. She sent me copies of the bookkeeping, she sent me photographs, newspaper clippings, tape recordings. She pleaded for me to come visit. Maybe she sensed I couldn't travel or maybe she wanted me to tell her that I couldn't and explain why. There was also the chance she really wanted to see me. Her driver would pick me up at Ninoy Aquino Memorial Airport, Baby promised. I could stay at her home. "I have an entire mansion to myself, Colonel Parker." She made it sound like she was sitting alone in a heart-shaped bed, doing her nails, waiting for me to call. "You have your own bedroom, your own bathroom, a maid, a *lavandera*, a driver." My old flame. In at the beginning, in at the end.

When Chester came up with this Elvis idea and Dude went along with it and they found Professor Ward Wiggins singing in a pay toilet, I realized I needed a partner in Manila. I was too sick to handle both ends of the deal.

Several dozen Guam-based Filipinos were more than happy to suggest investments, from mining to mariculture, garment factories to five-star hotels. Joint ventures, limited partnership, tax holidays, repatriation of profits: I heard it all. But when I said I was interested in a bar nightclub, the M.B.A.'s went blank. A bar nightclub? Yes. Not a hotel, then? Or a golf course? No, a bar nightclub. Not in Manila, either, not in Cebu, Palawan, or Mindoro or any of the islands marked for tourist development. I wanted to open my bar in—are you sitting down?—Olongapo. That's right, the liberty port, the Navy town, the big bad Babylon of the Philippines. So, in the end, I called Baby Ronquillo.

We'd done business before. Twenty years ago, when Saipan was opening up, I started importing labor from the Philippines for the new hotels they were building along the invasion beach, Chalan Kanoa to Garapan. I brought in construction workers, electricians, plumbers, gardeners, waitresses, entertainers, you name it. Back then, I'd looked into Baby's background and it was quite a story. She'd come out of nowhere. She'd done what was necessary. She was a piece of work. And play.

"One final question." This was in my suite at the Manila Hotel, fifteen years ago. We'd spent the day planning how to bring Filipinos into Guam and Saipan, where they were needed, that's for sure, needed if not welcome. No one seemed to have told Pacific Islanders that those hotels they wanted to build and get rich off of required laborers. Two jobs per room. Modern hospitals required doctors and nurses, those bars and karaoke parlors, those farms and fishing boats, they all generated jobs that locals didn't want or couldn't do. And then there were the maids—even the welfare cases on Saipan hired maids back then, $150 per month. So we were bringing them in by the planeload, Baby and me. She handled her end, I handled mine. Money was in the air.

"One final question," Baby Ronquillo said. We'd signed contracts. We'd eaten a room-service meal, shared a bottle of Piper-Heidsick, we'd opened the curtains for a view of the bay at sunset. By day, the bay stinks, but at night it twinkles.

"What's that?"

"Have you tried a Filipina?" I loved her nonchalance, as if she were asking, had I revisited Corregidor.

"Not lately," I said. "I'm married."

She nodded gravely. "This is good, to be married. Everybody should marry, someday. I hope to myself." She laughed. "Many times. Nevertheless . . . you haven't?"

"Like I said. Not lately." Sheila and I had been together thirty years and I hadn't stepped out on her, not once. But here was Baby Ronquillo, kicking off her shoes and walking across the room toward me and I guessed she'd be right against me in a minute and that would be it, case closed. But she stopped, just out of reach, and let me look at her, at what I could say yes or no to. Take a good look. At a body toned and tuned and taken care of, but a peasant body to start with, generous here, strong there, hair that was bunched in the back of her head, though a wisp of it had come loose around her ear and she was kind of playing with it, wrapping it around her finger, as if waiting for me to say whether she should tuck that bit of hair back in or let it all come tumbling down.

"How far down does it go?" I asked.

Later—a couple years later—I asked Baby Ronquillo whether we'd have gone to bed if we hadn't done business, if we'd met at a party or a dinner. Or if the business we'd done hadn't gone well.

"Of course not," she said. She thought it was a foolish question, the idea of sleeping with someone just because you liked the looks of them. It wasn't just silly, it was frivolous and wasteful. It was kid stuff and Baby Ronquillo, as I came to discover, took life seriously.

"So it's all about business?" I asked. Baby on top. Did I detect a small change of expression as she felt me enter? Her hair brushed over the tops of my legs. Amazing.

"My colonel," she said. "One thing, it leads to another. We negoti-

ate. We agree. We sign contract. Your name, my name. Now we . . . we dot
the *i*. No?"

"That's it?"

"Yes . . ." I could feel her moving. "And we cross the *t*."

Baby and I got together often in the late seventies and early eighties,
when the Japanese were turning Saipan into Florida. During that time, she
was married twice, once to a Marcos cabinet minister, once to a Chinese-
Filipino banker. Never mind. Baby was faithful—to old lovers. We managed to dot the *i* and cross the *t*.

Saipan was full, pretty much, by the late eighties. Enough hotels, resorts,
duty-free shops. Too many, probably. The Filipinos kept coming—by
1990 they outnumbered the locals, the Chamorros—but the big real estate deals and construction projects were over and I'd taken my money
out, just ahead of court rulings that challenged outside ownership of land
through local proxies, my usual method. Locals complained they were losing their culture. Besides, a recession was choking off investment from
Japan. So Baby and I lost touch. The last time I heard from her was a fax
she sent when Sheila died and I thought that was kind of classy, her
condolences, like you never apologize for the things you do or the love
you have.

I didn't hear much from Baby after that. No business, no pleasure. It
was that simple. But I heard about her. The woman who'd started handling
an endless stream of copycat Filipino bands—you name it, we play it—
was an international commodities trader now. A competitor. In Singapore
she competed with Tamils and Sri Lankans, in Malaysia with Indonesians
and Pakistanis, in Saudi Arabia with all of those, Egyptians and Palestini-
ans as well. In Europe she competed—but only in some categories—with
Turks, Algerians, Tunisians. They got the manual labor. But no one
wished to leave their child in the care of an Algerian maid. Those demure,
English-speaking Catholic Filipinas owned the market for maids, also for
entertainers, everywhere in hotels, at resorts, on cruise ships, the Manila
band, the Manila masseuse, hostess, dancer. Some categories stayed con-

stant, others rose and fell. It was a commodities market. People's labor—people themselves—were commodities, like coffee and pork bellies. An oil glut, a revolutionary Islamic government, a tariff or a value-added tax or a change in quotas on television sets, all affected the lines of people outside her Shipshape offices, the newcomers and repeaters, the virgins and whores. Once, people moved freely from place to place, settling new lands. No more. They couldn't enter as citizens. They could not come as slaves. Baby's business was somewhere in between. And Baby's business was good.

As soon as I contacted her about doing something together in Olongapo, Baby had a Guam lawyer sniff around for what he could dig up about me. She may have loved me once, but she wanted all the information she could get, business being business. She wanted updates, suits, filings, recent figures, whatever there was. She didn't get much and, knowing her, she was aching with curiosity, practically humming "We've Only Just Begun" when she sent me the monthly totals from Graceland. When she called, she never failed to ask, "How can I better serve you?" It was a business question but she made it sound like she was proposing sex. And she was. They went together, for Baby Ronquillo. Sex and business got stuck together a long time ago. Both were about screwing someone and getting paid for it. "What do you really want?" she asked, long-distance, from Manila. Bedroom and boardroom, all the same to Baby.

She was good. I put $100,000 into Graceland and I had $30,000 back after six months. I wouldn't have been doing that well if Baby didn't think there were bigger deals yet to come. If she was cooking the books, she was doing it in my favor. Bars and nightclubs didn't make that kind of money. She was out to impress me. And commit me. And—just warming up—she hooked Dude.

Those first months, Dude did nothing but complain about the dirt, the food, the heat. It was one pitiful letter after another, and late-night phone calls, like a prisoner calling a lawyer. Then it stopped. Suddenly. Totally. Disturbingly. No news was not good news, not when you send Albert and

Chester Lane to the Philippines. For several weeks I sat tight, fighting off the urge to call. And then the phone rang at one in the morning and for once it wasn't one of their old friends, looking for one of the Lane brothers. It was one of the Lane brothers, it was Dude, looking for me.

"Uncle Pete?"

"Where are you, son?" I made myself sound calm. At least it was him calling, not the police, the embassy, or some funeral parlor. Damn, when you're young and the phone wakes you in the middle of the night, you worry about your mother and father. When you're old, you worry about your kids. So I told them never to call, put it in writing. When the phone did ring, though, I worried that much more. And I worried when it didn't. That's family for you.

"In Olongapo. We just finished for the night."

"How's it going down there?"

"Going good, Uncle Pete. You were right about this. It's going real good."

"I'm glad to hear that, son."

"I know my letters sounded down. We arrived and the place hit me kind of hard."

"I guessed it would."

"Culture shock, they call it. A whole world of hurt out here. It wasn't my fault. But still . . ."

"I only wanted you and your brother to see it. I never figured you could cure it."

"I'm better now. That's why I'm calling. You know Mrs. Ronquillo? The lady who set things up for us down here?"

"Yes."

"She's gone way out of her way for me. She practically adopted me. She's had me over to her house. . . ."

"Yes . . ."

"Well, she makes movies down here. They're not great movies. But she's starting to use me in them. She sees that I'm an actor more than anything, that Elvis is just a part I'm playing. Not like Ward. We've got to talk about

Ward. Uncle Pete, sometimes it feels like Jonestown down here. It's getting weird."

"Tell me about yourself, son. You're family. He's not."

"Little parts. Walk-ons, really, a couple lines. You want to hear the first?"

There was silence. My son getting into character, I guessed. Then it came.

"*I have ways of making her talk.*" More silence: coming out of character. "How'd you like it, Uncle Pete?"

"I've heard it before," I said. "But I can't say I've heard it better."

"It's a start. Mrs. Ronquillo signed me to a contract. She says she wants to develop me."

"Did you sign it?"

"Sure. But I haven't told you the best. Baby's dream, she says, is to make a film that will break out of the local market. Not just sex and violence but drama, character-based drama. That's what I've been working on."

"You mean you're writing?"

"Every minute I get, Uncle Pete. I don't go around the clubs, I don't chase women anymore. They don't chase me. I barely drink beer."

"I'm happy to hear that, son. You're making me happy."

"Happy's just the start, Uncle Pete. I'm going to make you proud."

I choked up then, I barely finished the call. Then Dude sent me the contract Baby Ronquillo had gotten him to sign and I choked up again. Basically, she owned exclusive and continuing rights to represent him forever, anywhere, no matter what. I was going to have to do something about that; he'd signed his life away to Baby.

Then, Chester. They'd never invented a game that Chester Lane couldn't play. I don't mean basketball, football, track, and swimming. Those were snaps. I mean you could take Chester to a bullfight or a jai alai court and he'd be out there doing fine. He could fish, fix cars and toasters. But he couldn't read or write much. Hell, back when Sheila was alive, just barely, Chester took a piece of mahogany into shop class and turned it into a serving tray that was beautiful, polished, even, and straight. Except he put a message on it that he carved himself: TO ANT SHEILA, LOVE FROM CHESTER. My wife looked at that. It was the last time in her life she laughed. Then she told me Chester would be attending the University of Guam.

Well, a week after Dude told me about his career in movies, a letter came from Chester. The penmanship was beautiful and not a spelling error in the whole thing. After one sentence, I knew Chester had found himself someone or someone had gotten to Chester. It was hello from the pearl of the Pacific, the beautiful islands of the Philippines, and he really loved it down there, more than he could put into words, which was why this was not so much a letter as an invitation. Did I remember what I had told him, about how if you were nice to people, they'd be nice to you? Well, he'd found that to be true. It hurt him to remember the way he'd sat around and laughed at Filipinos, at their accents and their manners and their attitudes, like they were household appliances, not people. He loved the place, the country, the people, and—yes—one person in particular that he wanted me to meet. Love, your son, Chester.

That letter walloped me. I figured he'd sow wild oats down there and the worst that could happen was a dose of clap or some girl said she was having his baby, nothing that couldn't be fixed. But he was nicer than I'd told him to be. He went and fell in love. In Olongapo, of all places!

Now, about Elvis number three. I hadn't heard a word from Ward Wiggins. But he appeared in photographs that Baby sent me, performance shots. I studied those photos closely. Ward Wiggins wasn't family but I still wondered about him. He hadn't just changed careers, he'd changed his life, almost like a suicide, throwing his life away. And there he was, down on his knees, clutching himself like he'd been shot in the gut, ready to fall face-down on the floor. Hard to describe the expression on his face. Sometimes, in the newspapers, you see a photo of somebody, usually in Africa or Asia, and the face is all twisted by emotion, so you know they're feeling something extreme, only you can't tell what, joy or pain. You just can't tell, until you read the caption. They look the same. That was the look I saw on Ward's face, like he'd traveled right to—or past—the edge of something enormous.

Then, on a Sunday morning, I had the paper in front of me, the *Pacific*

Daily News, and I was checking for people I knew, the headlines, the obituaries, the weddings, the police blotter. And—damn—there they were right on page one.

SACRED OR PROFANE?

Elvis "Trinity" Draws Crowds,
Controversy at Subic Bay Base

There was a picture of the three of them, onstage, in costume. The caption identified them as three Guam-based entertainers, Chester Lane and brother Albert, both of Agana Heights, and Ward Wiggins, recent professor of English, University of Guam. Then the article began by describing Olongapo, the base, the anything-goes reputation that made it the liveliest town in the Philippines, a town that had seen everything. Or thought it had. Till three American Elvis Presley types came to town and opened up and nobody gave them a chance of making it, not in this cutthroat city of a thousand nightclubs. Coal to Newcastle: in the Philippines, they export entertainers, they don't import them. But the Elvises had taken over the town, selling out every night. They had a following of faithful who came to see the show again and again, enlisted men and officers and even officers' wives. "Sophisticated Manilenos" made the pilgrimage to Graceland by bus, limousine, helicopter, and—the latest thing—yacht. Foreign tourists had joined the parade, Japanese, Taiwanese, and Korean, in particular. But the local folks liked Elvis too, and not just the fan club of "winsome hostesses" who provided "various services" in and around Graceland but also street people, jeepney drivers, students. Every night, even though the place was sold out, they converged on Graceland hoping to glimpse "an Elvis they are unwilling or unable to distinguish from the late original." That was a little snotty I thought, and so was the description of Graceland: "part coliseum, part funeral parlor, part brothel." That sounded like high-octane mix to me, all right. Still, despite the wise-guy attitude, the writer liked the show. "An undeniable, even eerie power . . . séance, revival meeting, roadhouse jam and grand opera . . . an uncanny and oddly persuasive blend of naive melodrama and drop-dead musical talent."

Not everybody in Olongapo was cheering. Rival club owners complained, some of them anyway. And some Filipino teachers. "America's final imperial gesture," said one. "Cultural rape." "One more American too many." And this from a women's group: "Prostitution with music is still prostitution. Rape, serenaded, remains rape." And then a local priest weighed in. "Appalling. . . . Beyond the point of sacrilege . . . popular songs turned into psalms, song cues into homilies, nightclub into shrine, bar girls into acolytes and Elvis Presley into a rhinestone messiah." He called their club "Disgraceland."

That was plenty news from the Philippines, I thought. They were doing better than expected down there. I put the paper down, sat thinking things over. It wasn't until I got up, I saw another story near the bottom of the page, trailing the one that I'd been reading. A little box of a story, about Ward Wiggins.

BURNING LOVE?

OLANGAPO'S ELVIS

IS ARSON VICTIM

Somebody had tried to kill the man. That night I called Baby Ronquillo.

"Are you alone?" I asked, soon as she picked up the phone.

"Colonel, my colonel! What if I were not alone?"

"I'd get down on my knees and pray you didn't have one of my boys on the mattress."

"No, my colonel. Better. I have one of them under contract."

"I saw that contract, Baby. Didn't you hear, they outlawed slavery?"

"No, they haven't. Only changed the name."

"Tell me, you put any film in the camera when Dude walks in front?"

"He's not so terrible," she said. "Colonel, it's good to hear your voice. I think about you often."

"Listen, Baby. It's hard for me to travel these days."

"Oh?" she said. "Legal problems?"

"Lethal problems. You'll see. I want you to come to Guam. And soon as you can."

"We'll make some business?" She perked right up. I loved the way she spoke. Make business, make love. I said yes, we'd make business. And she said she was on her way.

Part Three

They are in the deserts of Saudi Arabia and the freezing waters of the Arctic. In the entertainment joints of Japan and the AIDS wards of US hospitals. In the hotels of London and the brothels of Amsterdam. In opulent villas in Rome and oil tankers in the Mediterranean. In factories in Taiwan and casas in Spain. In a car assemply plant in Malaysia and a nuclear plant in Syria. In schools in Africa and newsrooms in Singapore. In apartments in Hong Kong and factories in Seoul. In the nightclubs of Saipan and of Abidjian in the Ivory Coast.

"The Overseas Contract Worker,"
Philippines Daily Inquirer,
January 1, 1995

Ward Wiggins

I always believed—and Malou believed it too—that when you're happy you shouldn't examine your happiness too closely. It'll fall apart on you. If you start looking back, into the times before, finding all the mistakes you've made, bad luck and off-timing, you see how fragile your happiness is. How rare. Then, if you look ahead, you see all the things that are just waiting to bring you down. So you focus on one day at a time, try not to think about the past that's waiting to catch up to you. Or the future, waiting to mug your joy.

Those weeks before Colonel Parker struck were the happiest I'd been in years. And the house-burning was part of it. A lot was made of it at the time. Headlines that screamed: OLONGAPO ELVIS/ARSON VICTIM. Headlines that snickered: BURNING LOVE? It was scary, I admit. We might have died and— even though we lived—it gave me pause, knowing there was someone out there with that much hate. Or maybe love. But in the end it didn't matter. Because we were happy. Happier. Happiest.

We'd been at a party down the beach, the baptism of Elvis Presley de Ocampo. I gave them the name, I paid for the roast pig, and we'd sat out late, talking story like they do here. Whatever happened to? Where are they now? I loved the way it felt, that you could sit out in a lean-to on the beach and you could travel the world, because these people had connections and histories in Saudi Arabia and Kuwait, Brunei and Taipei, Guam and Tokyo and San Francisco. Or we talked history, back to Marcos, back to Magsay-say, further back, to the Huk rebellion, the Japanese, back, back, Quezon,

Arthur MacArthur, the Spaniards, story after story. It reminded me of a bit I'd used on Father Domingo on how you could stand twenty hundred-year-old men in a row and the man at the back of the line could have seen Christ. Twenty men between the life of Christ and the life of Elvis. Then I'd lean forward and clink beer bottles with him. "That's progress for you," I'd say.

I tried staying as late as I could but even then we were among the first to leave the party. It's frustrating but it came with being Biggest Elvis. It would be a different party after I'd gone, just like after a priest pushed back from the dinner table and said he had to brush up on the Sunday sermon. That was another line I could use on Father Domingo, another item in the comparisons I kept making between us, our competition for Olongapo's tarnished soul. I couldn't resist throwing lines his way, lines that were only half-ironic, as if we were practicing the same trade, working in the same shop, in business together. He was Hertz, I was Avis, he was Coke, I was Pepsi. I'd think about it sometimes and say, now Ward, you've got to stop saying things like that. Lay off the irony: it doesn't travel well. The trouble with irony is you can never tell how far it goes or where it leads. To more irony, I guess. To the fact that down deep, I believed we were in the same business. And, what's more, that I was winning. And he was losing. He knew it, too.

I should have backed off, but something in him invited challenge. We were locked into it. We liked and needed each other and we couldn't stay away. I can still see the play of expression across his face, the sighs, winces, head shakes, the glances upward, as if he were asking God, what did he do to deserve Biggest Elvis, Dude Elvis, Baby Elvis, right here on his doorstep? Wasn't it punishment enough to be born Filipino, to be a priest in a liberty port, to be assigned to a particular parish celebrated, across the world, for its blow jobs? Did he have to face a fat, bejeweled, hairy-chested American, an Elvis Presley incarnation—*not imitation, Father, I said incarnation*—who aped the church's rites, liturgy, sacred music, and who offered himself—and his two early selves—as a new Trinity? Who died and resurrected himself four nights a week in front of packed houses, beer on premises, women to eat in or take out? The whole grotesque situation had gotten as bad as it could get, he thought, and then—*hot damn, Father*—it got worse. The bright, winning Christina, his cherished sister, fell under the spell of the infant Elvis, who—worse yet—turned out to be a youth whom he could not resist liking, no more than he could quite avoid friendship with the dangerous and subversive Biggest Elvis.

Before, his life had been difficult. Now it was torture. In the morning, within the walls of his church compound, he'd breakfast to the sound of Baby Elvis, conducting pro bono music classes in the elementary grades, whole classrooms harmonizing "Love Me Tender." Driving to Olongapo, he passed the part of Barrio Barretto that was becoming known as Elvisville. He could see Elvis scarecrows in the fields, he'd be caught in traffic behind jeepneys named Jailhouse Rock and Kid Galahad. And, in town, he confronted Graceland itself, all pink and white, tour buses pulling into parking lots, sidewalks clogged with out-of-town, even out-of-country visitors whom I insisted—only half-ironically—on calling pilgrims.

It was too much. Yes, he liked me. He liked the talk. He liked the music, the visits to Graceland, the Sundays at my house. His emotions had been cruelly mixed and it must have been hard, I later decided, for him to order the burning of my house. With me in it, though I no longer slept alone.

Malou and I saw the flames from half a mile away. No other house was near us. We knew that was our place burning and that it was too late to do anything.

"That's us," Malou said. We didn't hurry at all. If anything we walked more slowly. More thoughtfully.

"I know," I said. Strange, but I was enjoying the moment. We were walking hand in hand along the beach and that was the first time Malou had walked that way with me. We'd spent nights together, we'd traveled, back and forth, to Graceland. We went to Manila, Baguio, Agoo, Mindoro, tentative little forays, bit by bit expanding the world we shared. But she withheld a lot of herself: the family I never met, the childhood undiscussed, the old lovers unmentioned. Those were her rules. The curtain came down whenever I asked. So it was me, remembering books I'd read and lectures I'd given, and Malou listening. So there we were, strolling along the shoreline, leaving footprints in wet sand while our house was burning. I knew that something was coming. You couldn't be Biggest Elvis without paying a price. The world gets back at you, I believed. But—that moment—it didn't bother me.

We thought it was a case of theft or vandalism. That was before we found that the back and front doors had been wedged shut, in someone's hope that we'd be sleeping inside. When we saw that, I couldn't help thinking of Father Domingo Alcala. I couldn't avoid it. He topped my list. He was the list. In no time at all, I convicted him. And in the next moment, I forgave him. Biggest Elvis forgave. And felt sorry for the pain I'd caused him. That my friend Alcala was the instrument of my undoing, that bothered me. Someone else should have come along. An anti-American. A thief. A rival bar owner. Or—as the newspapers later suggested—a music lover. Not him. Not a friend.

We spent the rest of that night at Elvira's apartment, the same place everyone else from Graceland went when they had trouble. A half-dozen of the Graceland girls were sitting around the kitchen when we walked in. I went to sleep to the sound of their voices, rising to shrieks, falling into whispers. I was asleep—I was dreaming a dream of graduate school and discovering there was a language requirement I hadn't fulfilled—when Malou came into the bedroom. It wasn't much before dawn. I woke to find her kneeling at the edge of the mattress, which sat on the floor.

"Wake up," she said.

"What is it?"

"I want to tell you how I feel," she said. That got my attention. Malou told you things reluctantly, a little here, a little there, bits and pieces that were out of order, sometimes contradictory, as though she hadn't gotten her story straight yet.

"Go ahead, Malou." God, how I loved saying her name! She'd lit a candle in the corner, turned off the air-conditioning, opened the window, so we could catch a breeze.

"I am scared."

"Of what?"

"Of everything. I don't like depending on you. Or anybody. But I do. I don't like loving you, I don't like the idea of it. It feels like a mistake. But still I go with you. I've lost control of the situation."

"I hadn't noticed that," I said.

"I'm afraid something will happen. And there is nothing I can do."

She fell silent. I reached out to her to touch her and felt tears on her face. That shocked me. And her. As soon as I felt them, tried to wipe them away, she turned her head away. "I hate weakness," she said.

"Whatever is coming, we'll handle it."

"Easy to say."

She got up and walked over to the window and stood there for a while, looking down at the street, and that was when I said to myself that there was nothing I wouldn't do for her. Malou at the window, wind ruffling the curtain, someone blowing a needless horn in the street, a rooster crowing, in the hour when night thinned and the lights at last went out in Olongapo. I knew I was in love and I knew I couldn't tell her. Then I saw her take both edges of her T-shirt, pull it up, to dab at her eyes, and then she pulled it off, over her head, and walked toward me in the half-light.

"Please," she said. A new line, from Malou. I glanced toward the door. I'd heard them talking out there, before I went to sleep. In this house, there was always someone awake. And the walls were thin.

"They might hear us," I said.

"I don't care." She came into my arms and she was trembling, anxious, urgent. Malou was a subtle, able lover, always, but always in control, like an athlete who played just hard enough to win. That night she was out of control, raucous, and, frankly, noisy. She wanted everyone to hear us. And they did.

"You should burn your house down every night," Elvira said to me when I stepped out of the bedroom later in the morning.

A man who works around prostitutes is a pimp. At the start of my time in Graceland, I worried about that. There was no way I could ignore the business of the place. The more I got to know the girls, the worse I felt about it.

There wasn't much consolation, either, in knowing that I wasn't a customer myself. The money they made, the drinks they sold, the bar fines went into our salaries. I tried to make the best of it: the food I ordered, night after night, was part of it, the loans I made, the doctors' bills I paid, the money for phone calls, family presents, tickets home. Atonement, I called it. Malou called it reparations. But it got me only so far. Even in my most jovial mood, it sometimes felt like I was starring in some dark, touring version of *The Best Little Whorehouse in Texas.*

Then some good things started to happen and if they didn't answer all my doubts, they made them less pressing. The word of Elvis spread. We sold out, night after night. We raised our prices and people kept coming. The girls raised their prices too. Now they were Graceland girls, elite, snooty, choosy. And they dressed the part. Jeans and T-shirts, rubber flip-flops were ancient history, as unthinkable as serving warm beer and glasses full of ice cubes.

Most hostess bars paid girls out of drinks and fines. No action, no money. They were there on consignment. Unusually, Graceland paid a minimum wage, just for showing up, provided they passed muster with Malou: they looked good and had their health card. They were ahead before they started. They could do pretty well serving and selling drinks. That was an improvement. Then the big change came. I noticed it one especially busy Saturday night, lots of money in the house, foreign tourists and high-rollers from Manila, we're talking serious money, the kind of night the other bars dreamed of, action, traffic, all the business you wanted, two or three customers a night, two or three girls per customer. And yet, at closing time, most of the regulars were around the jukebox, waiting for my food to arrive.

"What goes on here?" I asked Malou. "Doesn't anybody go out anymore?"

"They prefer not to," she said. That cracked me up: a line right out of *Bartleby the Scrivener.* Just say no. Here in a town that always said yes, if the money was right.

"What's happening?" I asked. The Graceland women were looking better all the time. Afternoons, I'd seen salesmen coming in with clothing, racks and suitcases, and I don't mean Frederick's of Hollywood. Conservative, tailored, dress-for-success stuff.

"Some of the girls went out," Malou said, glancing at the sheet where she recorded bar fines. It had some names on it, but not as many as I'd have expected. Thirty out of sixty had hooked up with someone. Any self-respecting American sorority would have a better batting average, any Saturday night.

"They do as they please," Malou explained. "They don't always go with the customers. They make enough money as it is. What you see is the result."

The result I saw was a dozen beautiful women waiting for the food I ordered. Talk about happiness. Graceland was changing and they were changing too. Graceland was in a state of grace.

"These foreigners come in," Whitney said. "And they think they can have us . . ." She put a lovely tapering hand on my knee to emphasize her point, snapped two fingers of the other hand. "Have us like that."

"You know what I say to them?" Now it was Lucy Number Three. Malou's sheet told me that she'd had a doubleheader that night. If Whitney was fashion-model stunning, Lucy Number Three was our goddess of sex. "Whitney has the face that launched a thousand ships," Dolly had said, "and Lucy Number Three has the body that will sink them." Lucy Number Three had the figure you see in cartoons. She was one of the ones who didn't just tolerate sex, she enjoyed it. Her tricks were contests, conquests. The customers left her, not just poorer, but smaller. She intimidated people. So I was surprised to hear her speak.

"This American . . . officer . . . he is drunk . . . he wants me to go with him . . . to his car outside . . . in middle of show . . . Dude Elvis is singing 'I Want you, I Need You, I Love You.' The American sings along. I tell him he should be quiet. He looks at me, says okay, we go outside now. . . . I tell him, he should go to Subic City."

"There are many other places for him," Whitney declared.

"We are not that kind of girl," Lucy Number Three said. "Necessarily."

All of a sudden, we had a talk show going. First they were confiding, then they were bragging about the guys they'd turned down, the customers they'd told off. They were competing, topping each other. I knew that this late-night jukebox bunch were in the minority. Some of our girls would do any-thing. But these were the elite. Can I say it? The role models? They set the tone and the tone was changing. Suddenly, hearing them talk, I was smiling.

"Other bars . . ." Priscilla was speaking. She'd been "married, or some-thing" to an Australian, Malou had said. She'd gotten overseas and she could have stayed. Her English was good but she rarely wasted it on some-one who wasn't a customer. I'd never had two words from her. Until now. "Other bars the girls *attack* the customers. As soon as the American sits down, one girl is in his lap, another is giving a shoulder massage, number three wants drinks for the table. Other bars, the girls ask, ask, ask. The cus-tomer says yes or no. At Graceland . . . ," she turned and nodded at me, "the customer asks, the girl says yes or no."

"And we know who made this happen," Whitney said. Before I knew it, she leaned into me and planted a chaste kiss on my lips. Startling. "Biggest Elvis."

Happiness.

When I got back to the beach the day after the fire, my neighbors were sorting through what was left of my house, separating smoked metal from charred wood. They stood around, as if in mourning, as if it were their fault. They told me they'd help me rebuild. They wanted me among them, they said, though they were sure there were many other, better places I could go. These weren't Graceland customers either. They were people who fished a little, farmed a little, waited for checks from relatives who were working overseas. They lived in houses they put together after every hard wind. But they liked having Elvis around. Happiness.

I said I'd pay for the lumber, the roofing, the wiring, the plumbing. And their labor. And the property. In Malou's name. I guessed that we'd be back in a matter of weeks, they were that anxious to have me. After the other neighbors left, I talked awhile to Santos. He was the old man who'd met me on the trail with his fighting cock, which was the first time I knew for sure that there was magic around me. Santos didn't sleep much, he now told me, and almost never at night. The older he got, the less he slept. When he died, he said, he expected that he wouldn't sleep at all. He wasn't joking and I didn't laugh. He wanted to spend the nights on the porch of my next house. He would watch while I slept, he said. I had just thanked him when I saw Father Alcala walking toward me.

"I'm sorry for your trouble," he said. He looked as if he'd had his own house burned. He was red-eyed and ashen-faced and unshaven. We'd both been up all night but I'd had Malou. God knows what he'd been wrestling with. Guilt, probably.

"I'm sorry for *your* trouble," I said, staring at him closely. "I wish I could offer you a seat."

"You're all right?" he asked.

"As you see," I said. "We were down the beach, at a baptismal party."

"I was invited there," he said. "I forgot."

"Elvis Presley de Ocampo," I said. "The hits just keep on coming."

This spawn of Elvises bothered him, I knew, but he managed a weak smile. I should have left it at that but out came one of those half-ironic, half-funny—half-assed—lines I couldn't resist around him. "Don't worry, Father. It'll be a long time before we catch up with all the kids in this country named 'Jesus.'"

He nodded, too polite or appalled to respond. Still, I wasn't done.

"We're gaining, though." I was usually the kind of man who thought, too late, of things he should have said. Around Father Domingo, I said things that I later realized I should have withheld.

"I've been missing you," I said. "You don't come to Graceland anymore."

"No," he said. "It doesn't feel right."

"I want you to know that I'm sorry that whatever is happening . . . is happening." Awful sentence but I saw him nod agreement. He needed me a little more than I needed him. "I consider you my friend," I said. "No matter what."

"So am I," he said. "I'm sorry too."

"I know I've given you some hard times," I said. "Those wisecracks of mine. I pushed them too far. Once you start with that kind of—"

"I'm glad you survived," he interrupted. At that moment, I think he was glad. Though he didn't look that way, walking away from me.

* * *

Sometimes I thought that it would go on forever, I was that happy. Other times, I was sure it would end: nobody was supposed to stay happy that way, that long. And my happiness was just mine. It was like the songs we sang, something that was passing, bit by bit, words and music, into the public domain. I think first of Chester Lane, who was in love the way people weren't supposed to fall in love in this wised-up age, in this of all towns, chastely in love in a place where sex cost the price of a six-pack. Everybody who met Chester worried about him, and with reason. He was innocent and the flip side of innocence is ignorance. You can't have one without the other. So everybody worried, that he'd get picked off by some shrewd little hustler who'd trade ring-wise screwing for a green card and a ticket to the States and would end up breaking Chester's heart. Or maybe he'd find some female version of himself, someone equally naive, and then they'd both get taken advantage of. If they lived in the Philippines her family would be all over him, and if they left, then another kind of disaster would result because you couldn't picture Mr. and Mrs. Chester Lane hacking it on the mainland. She'd be homesick and miserable. And he'd be broke. I doubted the Elvis act would travel. What else would Chester come up with? Summer camp counselor? But then God dropped all his other projects and Baby Elvis hooked up with Christina.

"He thinks the world of you," Christina told me, the first time we met. She never set foot in Graceland but orders had come from Baby Ronquillo that we should do a concert at a college in Baguio. Somebody owed somebody else a favor, I guessed. I resisted special appearances. We had something special going at Graceland and I felt uncomfortable before an audience that didn't have Malou in the corner by the jukebox, or Dolly organizing tables full of drunks, or Whitney peeking out from one of the VIP lounges, scanning the room for Mr. Right. But Malou said we couldn't say no to Baby Ronquillo. So we formed a convoy—a van and a jeepney—and headed north.

Malou shrugged me off when I asked her to come along. "Why would I want to do that?" she asked. Baby Elvis brought Christina, though. And we sat together in the van. Dude was there too, stretched out in back, sleeping. Christina was tall for a Filipina, a little like Whitney, but where Whitney was languorous, Christina was lean and athletic, straight up and head-on. I liked the looks of her but I wasn't expecting much in the way of conversation, considering who her boyfriend was. "Hi, darling, what's your favorite food?" Not a peep out of her, for those first miles, up the hill and out of Olongapo, then into the rice country of central Luzon, through fields of volcanic ash, headed for Tarlac. For a while Chester and I discussed the night's program. We were headed for a church-run college and so we replaced some of the sexier songs—"Jailhouse Rock," for instance—with "Crying in the Chapel."

It was hot inside the van and there was something about riding through the Philippines provinces that stupefied you, something about the endless fields and villages. The land itself was tired, so you got tired too. All the green and open places were claimed, stepped on, used, as if not only the farmers in the fields, not only the water buffalo that dragged plows through the mud, but the land itself were a beast of burden, carrying more than it could bear. After a while, there was nothing new. The cities that we drove through were forlorn Mexican-looking places, built mostly around bus terminals. They came and went and before long I was nodding off, my head against the window, a line of drool forming at the side of my mouth. Falling asleep, I heard our driver honking at everybody—warnings, greetings, insults—playing the horn like an instrument. I slept awhile but I stirred when I sensed a change in the ride. We were going uphill, going around curves that pressed me against the window, to my right, and against Christina, to my left. Now we were among mountains, the kind of landscape you see in old westerns, a river full of boulders, a hillside of more boulders, ready to let go, and pine trees here and there, and tufts of grass along the stream. The air was cool now and smelled of trees. Still groggy, I looked to my left and saw that Christina was studying me. No telling how long. I felt spied upon.

"You awake?" Chester asked.

"I guess if I answer I'm awake," I said.

"He says he's awake," I heard him tell Christina. "You can ask him now. Ward, she's got a question for you."

"Yes."

"Was Elvis a drug addict?"

"Where'd you hear that?" I asked. "From your brother?"

"Was he?" she repeated.

"He didn't think so."

"I asked you," she said. "You have studied his life?" No nonsense. She'd bristled when I implied her brother was using her. Now she stayed right on me. You could teach for a long time and not have a student stay on you like that.

"Well," I said. "He took a lot of medicine. He had prescriptions from a number of doctors. Tranquilizers, sedatives, uppers and downers. They might have killed him. It's not entirely clear. Heart arrhythmia, the report said."

"That means . . ." She glanced at Chester to make sure he understood. "His heart stopped. That would be arrhythmia. It means you're dead. That is like saying you are dead because your heart stopped."

I was wide awake now. I saw that Chester had found himself a substantial woman. In the back of the van, Dude kept snoring. He'd been replaced. And he knew it.

"All right," I said, determined to give Christina the respect she deserved. "Elvis' position—if you'd asked him—was that he was not a junkie. All the drugs he took were prescribed for him. They were legal drugs, legally obtained."

That was the way I'd once spoken in classrooms, with a certain finality, a tone that said, all right that's enough class discussion for now, let's move along. I wanted to keep talking, now that I knew she was worth talking to, but about other things, the school she taught at in Subic City. Her brother. That world—I still didn't understand it—of down on your knees Saturday night, down on your knees Sunday morning.

"What you say doesn't make sense," she said. Quiet and polite . . . and direct. "What if the drugs were legal? If a man shoots someone with a legal weapon, it is still murder. And if he drinks himself to death with legal whiskey, he is still an alcoholic. So?"

I turned away, out the window, to hide the smile on my face. Going up, up, up to Baguio, the cool-weather retreat the Americans built in the mountains of the Luzon Cordillera. They brought in Daniel Burnham, who'd designed the Chicago Midway, to lay out the city, the park and gardens. There were corn and roses in the markets and, from after sunset until midmorning, you wore a jacket against the mountain chill. I liked the way Christina had stayed on me.

"Sounds like she got you," Chester Lane, the famous logician, decided.

"Maybe so," I said. If this woman loved Chester Lane, he was the luckiest man on earth. After a while, it was Chester's turn to rest. Christina just told him to get some shut-eye and, like that, he closed his eyes and was gone. As soon as that happened—the kid tucked in and put to sleep—she gave me this look that said, okay, now let's talk.

"So how's your brother?" I asked.

"Lonely. He was lonely before you came. Now he's even more lonely."

"I'm not in control of what's happening here," I said. "This Elvis thing . . . and how he feels about it. We're just . . . you know . . . out there. Bumping into each other."

"If you worked together . . ."

"It's not that way," I said. "I wish it were. With gods . . . it's not the more, the merrier. There's only so much belief around. Faith. Hope. Only so much." I glanced over at Chester, curled up in a position that would torture a contortionist, sleeping like a choir boy. "How are the lessons?"

"They will never end," she said. "Not if it's up to my brother."

"What, then?"

"It's up to me, I think."

The Baguio Concert was just okay. I remember a basketball court, bleachers left and right, chairs on the floor and the stage we played on at one end, underneath a hoop. Chester charmed them. I spooked them. And—to my surprise—Dude did best. He'd been on automatic pilot in Olongapo but he did a "Peace in the Valley" that went from poignant lyric to gospel shout and back again. It gave me goose bumps. Still, the trip confirmed what I'd felt all along. We were an Olongapo act and I couldn't wait to get back there. The backups and setup crew wanted to stay overnight and into the following morning. I couldn't blame them. Baguio was a resort, Olongapo was a dump. But then Christina volunteered to drive the jeepney and take us back down the mountain. We'd leave at midnight and, with luck, we'd meet dawn on Magsaysay Street.

"Jeez, I don't know," Dude said. "She doesn't look old enough to have a license. Besides, did you see some of those ravines on the way up?"

"Stop worrying," Chester said.

"Worrying? I wouldn't trust your girlfriend on a bicycle that didn't have training wheels."

"Well, you can stay," Chester replied. It was the sort of thing he'd never have said a few months ago. Dude knew it. And Dude gave way.

"You want me to stay here by myself? In this fresh air?"

"The place isn't uninhabited," Christina countered. Dude looked at me for help but I wanted to get back early. I wanted to surprise Malou.

"Well," said Dude, "I've heard of plane crashes, motorcycles, cars. Overdoses and shootings. But a jeepney crash." He looked at Christina. Christina looked at her watch. "Rock and roll heaven." Dude jumped into the back of the jeepney . . . and right out. "What is this shit?" he shouted. You couldn't see out the back of the jeepney, or the sides. It was loaded with dark bundles, baskets, corrugated boxes, and more of it was lashed onto the roof. We looked like refugees.

"Christina did a little shopping," Chester apologized. "Down to the market. They grow vegetables up here you can't find down below."

"Corn, cauliflower, beans, eggplant," Christina said, as though checking a manifest.

"How many people is she feeding?"

"Cabbage, cucumbers." She reached for a bag next to the driver's seat, opened it, and held it out to Dude. "Strawberries," she said.

Dude reached in, inspected, swallowed. Then he smiled at her. He had a devastating smile, when he smiled. Now it felt as though he were smiling at his brother's wife. Looking back at it now, I realize that Chester and I were what we were. We stayed the same. But the man in the middle was always changing.

"Got many more of those?" he asked. She handed him the bag. "Okay," Dude said. "Let's roll."

It was better we went down the mountain road at night, the Marcos Highway, when darkness saved us from seeing what we were going to hit, head-on, and how far off the road we were going to fall. I've heard people say you can tell the character of a nation from the way it handles traffic: the tension between public interest and self-interest, discipline versus anarchy. I could tell a few things about Christina, that was for sure. I knew that she could downshift, that she could take curves, calculate passing distance, the speed of oncoming objects, and that—while she did this—she could feed us strawberries and make us sing. We all sang and the idea—her idea—was that we could sing anything that was *not* by Elvis.

I was supposed to go first. There we were, whipping around curves in the dark, because trucks went grinding past in low gear, dogs rushing off the road. We zoomed past sari-sari stores and *carinderias,* caves of light surrounded by potted plants where people sat out all night enjoying the cool, showering and smoking and playing guitars and tinkering with cars. Because all this late-night craziness was taking me back to Malou, because I was racing down a mountain to be with her at dawn, I sang Joe Cocker's "You Are So Beautiful to Me," every whiskey-throated word of it. A pledge of love to her.

"Hey, I got one," Chester shouted, launching right into "Blue Suede Shoes."

"Chester," I interrupted. "That's a Presley song and you know it. It's part of your act."

"Don't matter. Because Carl Perkins, Jr., recorded it first!" Chester Lane, master disputant.

"The idea," Christina explained to her new ward, "is to do a song that Elvis *never* sang."

"Oh. Okay." Chester kept us waiting for a minute. Then he started giggling. "This is ridiculous. I can't think of any song that isn't by Elvis."

"I know what you mean," I sympathized. "It's when they say, now don't think of an elephant, whatever you do, don't think of an elephant. And of course, what do you think of?"

"I don't know," Chester said. "What?"

"Oh, shit," Dude said. "Christina, he's yours. You've got 'im. Forever. Bring over the adoption papers, I'll sign 'em. He's yours. Forever."

"That's it!" Chester exclaimed. "I've got it." And from out of nowhere, out of the night air over Luzon, from the web of sound waves coming from ancient jukeboxes on distant planets came "Pledging My Love," a forty-year-old song by Johnny Ace. The word "forever" reminded him. "Forever my darling . . ." It won't happen often but whenever I hear that song again, I'll be back in that vegetable-loaded jeepney, winding down the mountain, racing out onto moonlit plains—"promise me, darling, your love in return"—the perfect cone of Mount Arayat lifting out of rice fields near Clark Field, the road narrowed by drifts of volcanic ash from Mount Pinatubo— "for this flame in my heart dear"—Chester singing to Christina, feeling his way through the song, as though he were coming up with the words on his own—"will forever burn." He stressed the "forever," for our benefit.

"Wow," Dude said after a while. "Really dodged a bullet on that one, little brother. Sang the hell out of it too."

"Your turn."

Dude didn't hesitate. "This is for no one in particular." He was the only one of us who wasn't in love, I realized. And, in an instant, the just-dead Roy Orbison was with us, somewhere south of Angeles City, closing in on Bataan Peninsula, that gorgeous, sad voice, echoing in me, reaching for those last high notes in "Crying."

We drove in contented silence after that and all I can say is that I loved the feeling in that jeepney, that relaxed intimacy the three Elvises could never find in a bar or around a table. Lately, it seemed we were together only onstage. Professionals. But I believed we were more deeply tied. Three in one and one in three. I dreaded the thought of going onstage alone. I prayed it would never come to that. I couldn't picture Biggest Elvis without them.

"How's it going?" Dude asked Christina. "You're not tired or anything?"

"No sir."

"No need to call me sir," he said. "I'm not in the Navy."

"I'm fine, then . . . Dude," she said. She laughed when she said it.

"Road's straight," Dude said. "Not much traffic. How far are we from home?"

"An hour, only."

"Good. Then it's your turn to sing."

"I cannot sing!"

"Bullshit. I haven't met anybody in this whole country who can't sing."

"There's Dolly," I said.

". . . Or didn't *think* they could sing."

"All right, then," Christina said. "But it's an old song. It goes back to the war, I think, soon after the war. Promise you'll help, if you know the words."

She started in a thin scared voice that got bigger when we came in to help her and so my last memory of that trip is how we headed downhill into Olongapo, around curves, past Dolly's house, black sky thinning into gray, three professional Elvises and a convent-raised schoolteaching jeepney driver, singing "You Are My Sunshine."

Christina's first stop was the Lane brothers' apartment. That was awkward. The two kids ought to have time together alone. I suggested to Dude we stretch our legs a minute and he took my cue. We walked around the corner from where the jeepney was parked.

"I feel like hammered goat shit on a flat rock," Dude said, stretching and groaning. "But I'm sorry to see it end. In a way."

"I know what you mean."

"Not that I'd want to do it again," he quickly added. "I see a way out . . . a way out that's up . . . I'll take it," he said. "Nothing personal. You know that."

"I know," I said. The trip felt over. We walked back to the corner, in time to see Chester standing on the driver's side of the jeepney, leaning inside to kiss Christina. On the lips only, I was sure, and with his eyes closed.

"Damn," Dude whispered. "How often do you see that on the streets of Olongapo? They do short-time around here. They don't do young love much."

"They might be all right," I said. "They might make it."

"In this country, maybe," he said, frowning. "But isn't that like failing in the rest of the world?"

His eyes met mine. He wasn't talking about Chester. He was talking about me, about all the Americans who came here, hanging out and staying on, the beer guts, the wrinkled faces, the shit-eating smirks. The getting laid.

"I'll take you home now," Christina called out, "if you're ready."

We'd thought we'd be back in Olongapo in time to eat breakfast. Whitney was in the kitchen alone when I stepped into Elvira's apartment. She was at the table, the image of a student pulling an all-nighter. She didn't hear me come in, she was that far into what she was reading, and she jumped when she saw me standing in the doorway.

"Biggest Elvis!" she said. "You scare me!"

"All the time?"

"I'm reading this book all night and I cannot sleep." She held up a copy of *The Shining*. "Is this true story?"

"Made-up story. Not true," I assured her. "But there is truth in it. Maybe." I'd just given Whitney the benefit of an entire course I'd taught. And Whitney was appropriately perplexed.

"I'm still scared," she said. She gestured toward a closed door off the living room. "Malou, she is sleeping in there."

"I brought back some strawberries." I put two bags on the table, stained where the berries at the bottom had soaked into the paper.

"I'll wash and put sugar," Whitney said. "You go see Malou. And put sugar."

I knelt down beside her, kissed her on the forehead. Just the way I'd pictured myself doing it. She scowled, as though I'd interrupted something deep, opened her eyes reluctantly.

"Oh," she said. "You came back."

"Close your eyes."

"They were closed," she complained, "until you—"

"And open your mouth."

She obeyed, though with the same enthusiasm you'd give a dentist. I put the strawberry in her mouth. She swallowed and went back to sleep.

Chester was in love, I was in love. Not Dude. Like the Elvis he performed, he was a restless character, not a kid anymore, not a living legend either. He occupied that uneasy middle ground which, come to think of it, most of life is like. He despised the things he did—the way Elvis himself despised those stupid movies—and he wanted things he couldn't put a name to. His ambition was huge and vague. He wanted to be somebody, he just didn't know who.

Dude called himself a Presley imitator, disregarding my request never to use that word. *Imitator, mime, clone, act, shtick, gimmick, trick,* he went out of his way to derogate who we were and what we did. And where we were. We were the biggest fakes on a street of fakes, surrounded by Filipino Tom Joneses and Patsy Clines and Kenny Rogerses. So he screwed his way through half the Graceland staff and when he got done screwing he felt worse than before. Then he started running to Manila on weekends. He came back red-eyed and hungover. It was only a matter of time, I guessed, before he'd leave. But Baby Ronquillo started giving him bit parts in movies—parts that were so bad he entertained us, reprising his roles, late at night around the jukebox. He passed around the scripts, assigned lines for some of the girls to play. I can still see him, playing opposite Dolly, each holding a script.

"Get away from me," Dolly says. "You frighten me."

"This is just the beginning," Dude sneers. "I'll teach you the meaning of fear."

"But . . . but . . . where do you come from?"

"From hell."

"Go back to hell, then!"

"I'll take you with me, woman!"

I see Elvira playing a seduction scene with Dude. This was typecasting. Elvira comes over to where Dude sits at a table. She leans against him from behind.

"What do you want?" Dude asks. Sullen. Arrogant.

"I want some . . . ," Elvira stretches luxuriously upward, then bends down, her cleavage hovering around Dude's ears, "exercises."

"What kind of exercise would that be, lady?"

"Something hard. . . ." Elvira says. And it goes on from there, the Grace-land Studio of Dramatic Art.

"Biggest Elvis," Whitney asked me, after watching a few cameos from Dude's new career. "These movies Dude is acting in . . . ?"

"Yes."

"They are not good, are they?"

"Well, what do you think, Whitney?" Sometimes it seemed Whitney was coming out of a lifelong trance. Sleeping Beauty, wide-eyed with wonder. I knew her story. I knew more about her than I did about Malou. Born in the Divisoria, the clogged, noisy Manila market district. Her father finished a contract in Bahrain, landed in Manila, took her shopping, raped her. The mother sided with him and Whitney was gone. She'd made her way to Olongapo, thinking that waitresses actually served food, that hostesses were polite, well-dressed women who showed customers to tables.

"I'm thinking people do not talk this way," she said. "Also, I do not care about these people."

"I think you're right," I said. And watched her nod and walk away, teacher's pet.

There were scripts all over Baby Ronquillo's house and Dude brought them to Graceland by the armful. They landed next to the jukebox and now I saw the girls at Graceland reading through them. Partly, they were looking for funny bits they could do after closing time. They liked that. More than that, they sensed that this was Dude's way of apologizing for his first weeks, when he'd marched them in and out of his apartment, marking notches on his gun. They put that behind them and turned to looking for—Dolly said— "something which might be good for Dude." They didn't find much. The market for American heroes was way down. The stuff they read was awful. If Dude wanted to make a mark, he'd have to write the role himself. Everybody agreed about that. Baby Ronquillo, the girls of Graceland, Dude himself. And that was when he came to me for help.

"It's not that I don't have ideas," he said. This was offstage, watching Albert do a version of "Old Shep" that had customers sobbing on hostesses' shoulders. "But the good ideas that I have won't work here. And the ideas that I have for here . . . aren't any good. Which is why I was hoping we could talk."

"Sure."

"It's against your interests, Ward. I want to be up front with you. The minute I hit, I'm gone."

"So what have you come up with?" He was holding some papers, I noticed.

"This is rough," he apologized. "Okay. I liked the idea of going with this Elvis thing. Baby liked it too. It's right here for us. She owns the damn club. And it brings in an American audience. *And . . .*"

He stopped, looked down, looked up. "I'm not kidding myself. That's something you can't afford to do around Baby Ronquillo. If it's my idea and I'm in it, she figures she can get to Uncle Pete for financing. She wants that real bad."

"Still—there's no getting around it—you need a story."

"Yeah. Pain in the ass, but there you have it." He shook his head, sorted through his papers. "Okay. Number one is Elvis—that's me—is working in a place like this. He gets captured by drug dealers and held for ransom."

"That's it?"

"Yeah. Basically."

"That's all?"

"For now. So? What do you think?"

"Let me hear number two."

"Well, number two is he gets captured by communist guerrillas and held for ransom."

"Is there a number three?"

"He finds out that the guerrillas are really drug peddlers. It's a kind of combination."

Dude had a short list of villains and heroes: kidnappings, carnappings, hijacking planes, hijacking drugs. He knew the stuff was bad. When he went onstage after our first discussion, he was angry at me and at himself. It took guts for him to throw out his own ideas, night after night. I admired the way he kept working at it, like a prisoner filing appeals, hoping to write his way out of confinement. He read newspapers, hunting for stories. He talked to Graceland women, not only about godawful scripts he brought them. He asked about their lives, where they came from, how the towns they came from were run. He wanted to know about the crimes that they didn't make movies about, illegal logging, land-grabbing, rigged elections.

"I haven't got it yet," he told me one night. "But I'll get it."

"I think maybe you will, Dude."

"Life's so damn sloppy. It doesn't come in stories. Sometimes I think if only a voice came out of the sky and said the beginning, the end, if they just gave me that much, I'd have it knocked."

"That's half the game. Where to start. Where to stop."

"Only place you find those signs is in a cemetery."

"Maybe that's where your story begins," I said.

"I got it!" he announced the following night. "It's that line about the cemetery. We begin at Graceland. The real funeral, the real Graceland, I mean.
That long line of limousines. People crying on the sidewalk and selling shit.
That's all under opening credits, maybe. And then—bingo—we see Elvis
pulling into a town like this . . . bars and whores and guys with guns. Ever
notice how some of these towns look like movie sets? Like that Mexican
town that got shot to pieces in *The Wild Bunch*? Anyway, the audience
doesn't know . . . the people in the town don't know . . . whether he's real or
not. . . . And Elvis sets up shop, real small, a couple girls and a mama-san
who's like Miss Kitty in *Gunsmoke* and it goes okay for a while but this is a
corrupt town . . . racketeers and gunmen—"

"You'd better write it down," I said.

"But I haven't told you the ending yet." I knew the ending but I let him
tell it. "The end is like the beginning. Another funeral, only this isn't in
Memphis, this is in a Philippines cemetery, like the one outside town, with
all those whitewashed above-ground mausoleums. We see another Elvis in
another coffin . . . *and* . . . we still don't know. . . ."

"I like it, Dude."

"You shitting me?"

"No," I said. And I saw him rush back to work, back to the apartment
that Chester told me was wallpapered with plot descriptions, character
sketches, scraps of dialogue, Dude's movie, up against the wall. He paced
the room at all hours of the night, Chester said, put things up and took them
down, crumpled them up, flattened them out again. So, in the end, Dude
was happy too, in his way. It hadn't occurred to him yet that the Elvis he
had written, the Elvis he buried in Memphis and resurrected in the Philippines, was Biggest Elvis. The man in the coffin was me.

"I saw that guy," Chester said one night. "What's his name?" It was Saturday night, between shows, another of our booming, bountiful Olongapo
Saturday nights. We'd slipped across to Soul City. Billy Bowers had a room
upstairs he called his private club. We liked to sit there and look down on

the street. It was enough to make us feel like kings, no lie, because we saw a whole line of buses creeping by, packed with out-of-town customers, and limos and jeepneys and once in a while a horse-drawn *calesa,* all coming up to Graceland. The sidewalk was jammed, tour leaders holding up flags to keep groups of Japanese and Taiwanese together. They were there for us. So were the Navy and Marines. The street kids and vendors. The beautiful people, in from Manila, the spoiled and expensive women who had doors opened by drivers and then you'd see a leg come stretching out from inside, pointing a four-inch heel at the Olongapo sidewalk, like an astronaut on the surface of the moon, then that tapered leg, soon followed—double your pleasure—by another one just like it. Oh, it was fine, sitting and watching the people come to Graceland.

"Who are you talking about?" Dude asked.

"This driver guy. The one in the Hawaiian shirt."

"Jimmy Fiddler. Works for Baby. She didn't tell me she was coming."

"He just went in."

"Did you see her?"

"Only the guy."

A customer who desired the use of a VIP lounge could watch the entire show from behind tinted glass. The idea was to take in the entertainment outside and be entertained yourself, in the lounge, in other ways. Some people really liked it. They liked having sex while we were singing. Their act and ours moved together, their high notes and ours, hurtling toward climax. Maybe it was kinky. I thought so. "Don't knock if you don't try," Elvira reproached me. Her Brunei sheik loved to have her in the VIP lounge. To him it was serenade, ballet, drama, porn-film fantasy, undressing Elvira while Chester sang "Are You Lonesome Tonight," climaxing during "Battle Hymn of the Republic."

It was unusual, though, for a customer to keep the VIP windows closed. More often, the lounges were celebrity seats, first-row balcony, high-rollers, drinking, waving down to their buddies who were sitting on the main floor. Tonight was one of the rare ones: one of the VIP lounges stayed closed, all night long. Person or persons unknown. Our show was solid but we found our eyes wandering to that dark-glassed booth and we all felt something ominous, especially at the end of the show, during "American Trilogy." Usually, if there was something sexual going on up there, it ended when our show ended, sometimes earlier, and, as we stood onstage, taking bows, the glass would slide open and the VIP customers would join in the cheering. And if the girl up there had a sense of humor—Elvira, say, or Lucy Number Three—we'd stand there and applaud them, one performer saluting another. Consummations, high and low. Tonight, the dark glass stayed shut. That hadn't happened before. Suddenly it felt as though the three of us were in a police lineup.

"What's going on up there?" I asked Dude.

"Spooked me," Chester added.

"How should I know?" Dude protested. He was the most disturbed. He'd made a point of knowing Baby Ronquillo.

"Well," said Chester, "she's your . . ." He didn't know how to finish. Friend? Sponsor? Manager? He groped and turned to me for the right word.

"Are you two screwing?" I asked.

"No!" Dude answered. "We're business partners. Look, if you want I'll go see." He started to walk out of the dressing room.

"Don't go, Dude," I said, touching him on the shoulder.

"You don't want me to?"

"No," I said, keeping my hand on him, not to restrain him so much as to brace myself against what I was feeling. "Something's coming."

"What?"

"I don't know. Whatever it is, we don't have to go running after it. It'll come."

Thirty minutes later, it came. It came walking into the now empty Graceland, where the three Elvises and the regulars were gathering, waiting for food. As Graceland's fortunes improved, the so-called midnight snack had turned into a late-night buffet. No more paper plates and cartons, plastic bags of soup. We now had tablecloths, serving trays, plates, and cutlery.

And, though some of the girls couldn't resist joking about something that was neither completely soft nor convincingly hard, everyone knew the meaning of al dente. We were laughing together when the future came at us, walking with a limp. Jimmy Fiddler, a.k.a. Daga, the Rat, working his way among empty tables, singing, dancing a little as he got closer, if a lame man can dance. He stopped right in front of Malou. She looked down at her figures, ignoring him. He reached into his pants to adjust his genitals, humming "These Are a Few of My Favorite Things."

"There's ladies here," Chester said.

"Oh really," Jimmy answered. He glanced at one Graceland woman after another. He saved Malou for last. "Where?"

"Was there something you wanted?" I asked.

"A couple new knees, if you could arrange that, Biggest Elvis," he said. "A white Christmas. The love of a good woman. That's for starters. Meanwhile, Baby Ronquillo wants to see you three."

"When?"

"Now. Upstairs."

When I saw Baby Ronquillo sitting in the VIP lounge, I thought of advertisements you see for airlines, an important-looking woman waiting in a frequent fliers club for the first-class passengers to be called. She had that sober-suited, adult-mature-sophisticated-professional-woman look. The leather valise, a Federal Express envelope and a pile of faxes in front of her, a designer date book, a Cross pen, and yet . . . it didn't quite work and maybe it wasn't intended to. Something about Baby Ronquillo contradicted her appearance. The way, for instance, that she looked at me, appraising, measuring, weighing, the way the girls of Graceland did. Rejecting: she did that too, in my case. But I sensed that, in the right mood, with the right man, Baby Ronquillo could shed it all. She was still from Olongapo. She wore the garments of affluence the way maids and mailmen wear uniforms at the start of X-rated movies, costumes they would lose on command, except that Baby Ronquillo had gone from actor to director. She was the one who called "Action" and "Cut."

"I know it's late," she said as soon as we came in. She glanced at her watch the way politicians do when they signal that there won't be much time for questions after they've finished speaking. "I'll be brief. I just returned from Guam, where I visited Colonel Parker, at his request."

Albert and Chester exchanged looks, saying nothing. Dude had noticed there was no special greeting for him when we walked in. She'd nodded us all onto the couch, a low couch, great for fellatio, I imagined, but bad for meetings. Our knees were in our faces. Jimmy Fiddler looked down, way down on us, from the doorway.

"He sends you his love, of course," Baby continued. "He has followed your progress. I've reported to him all along. He's very happy for you. And I don't mind adding that, in light of the checks I've been remitting, he's happy for himself. He congratulates the three of you."

"How is he?" Chester asked.

"He told me I'd be asked that," Baby said. "He told me you'd probably be the one who asked."

Dude flinched at that a little, hearing Uncle Pete had forecast that Chester would be the one to inquire about his health. "Yeah," Dude added. "We've been wondering."

"What he told me to say is this: none of your damned business."

The brothers smiled and nudged each other. Chester flashed me a thumbs-up.

"He wishes he could travel here to see you but that cannot be. 'My boys are the ones who do my traveling for me,' he said." Now she paused and awarded each of us a smile. "Colonel Parker's wish is that you travel even more, that you take your show to other places, and that you extend the success you've enjoyed here in Olongapo."

"Hold it," Chester said. "He wants us to leave Graceland?"

"Yes," she said. "For a while."

"How long?"

"Four months only. I have your bookings for the first three months. The fourth month is still being negotiated. You'll travel with your Olongapo band and crew. My office will be in constant touch. Everywhere you go, someone will meet you."

She handed us our tickets and a typed itinerary. I scanned the names. Hotels and resorts in Brunei, Penang, Kuala Lumpur, Singapore, Colombo, Bangkok, Hong Kong, Taipei, Okinawa. Arrivals and departures, local contacts, the next four months of our lives. And nothing I could do about it, no appeal possible. It's not that the act couldn't travel. We could go wherever they sent us and put on a show. It was that the act *shouldn't* travel. That's what I wanted to say. But Colonel Parker had kept his distance and Baby Ronquillo wouldn't understand. You had to be a certain kind of smart, to understand Elvis, or a certain kind of stupid.

"It's a great chance for you to establish yourselves," Baby said. "We're happy for you."

When she looked at the three Elvises, though, she didn't see much cheer. We sat quietly, trading glances, trying to figure out what it meant. Chester was thinking about Christina, I was wondering about Malou, Dude didn't know where his movie career had gone. That was when I started speaking. I'd meant to stay calm and logical but in a minute it was as though someone else were speaking in my voice, the way you hear yourself in dreams sometimes, saying unbelievable things, awful things, so that it's a relief to wake up and know that no one heard but you.

"You don't get it," I said.

"I beg your pardon, Mr. Wiggins?"

"Don't Mr. Wiggins me."

"But isn't that—"

"You know who I am. Biggest Elvis! That's Baby Elvis and that's Dude Elvis. And we're not an act that you can just put on the road when you feel like it. We're not an *act* at all. We're for real. We're the real thing."

"The real thing? You don't mean to—"

"That's exactly what I mean. There's something in us that's special. You don't know. You don't know how it all got started. Dance, music, religion, drama, poetry, it all came out of the same place once, around the same campfire, out of the same cave, and it was all one thing and it was magic. And that's what we've got. That's what came together here. Here, in the last place you'd expect, which is also the perfect place, the only place. And you . . . you traipse in here and you say you want us to play in a hotel someplace!"

Chester was looking at me, startled, Dude had his head in his hands. Jimmy Fiddler was enjoying watching me come apart and Baby Ronquillo smiled, the way a nurse smiles when she pulls out a syringe.

"I know what you think," I said. "This is show business and that's entertainment and here's another gig. But we're more than that. You sat through our show. Couldn't you feel it? How could you not feel it? We took a leaky, moldy, money-losing, piss-poor whore bar and we turned it into Graceland!"

"Which I own," Baby Ronquillo said.

"No, you don't. You own an old movie theater. A dump. A blow-job emporium. A nothing. We made Graceland."

"Could we put this to music?" Jimmy Fiddler asked.

"It's hard for you to grasp, I guess. In a country where everybody's portable and everything's for sale and the national hobby is immigration law, well, maybe you think it's odd or funny or crazy that someone would come here and do what we did and that we'd want nothing more than to stay and keep on keeping on. You don't get it, do you? Either of you."

"Calm down, man," Jimmy Fiddler said. "You'll be back."

"You said four months," Dude said to Baby. "What about our . . . you know . . . project?"

"You come back with a script and we'll proceed. The Colonel is interested."

"I see," Dude said. He was the most easily mollified, even though the travel didn't appeal. "Four months is a damn long time."

"Then we will be coming back to Graceland," Chester said. "That is so, ma'am, isn't it?"

"Of course," she said, meeting his stare and smiling right at him. That's when I felt the dread surge into me. The way she spoke to Chester was the way you speak to a kid when you're moving to a new town and you promise him that his friends from the old neighborhood will be friends for life, no matter what. She wasn't lying, exactly. She was just waiting for Chester to outgrow the question.

"What about the girls?" Chester asked. "What'll they do for four months?"

"I'll take care of them, I promise. I was one of them myself once. Don't worry about the girls of Graceland. They will be here to welcome you when you return." Now Baby started assembling herself, getting ready to go. "Do not worry about our Filipinas."

The last line about not worrying about the girls of Graceland was aimed right at me. I got the message, too. She was telling me that I was another American who pretended to care, an outsider who thought of himself as an insider, someone who could afford the luxury of worry before he departed. Well, I could worry or not, I could worry all I wanted, and it wouldn't change a thing. The girls would have to take care of themselves. I could pretend otherwise. But after I was gone, they were on their own.

"Ward! Look at the schedule!" Chester cried out. "We're leaving the day after tomorrow." I couldn't believe it but Chester was right. We weren't just going. We were gone.

"You work fast," I said to Baby Ronquillo. She gave me a curt nod. I didn't interest Baby. She changed men the way she changed clothes and when she looked at me she saw yard sale. She saw out-of-shape, out-of-fashion. "I'll see you two tomorrow," I told the Lane brothers. "I'd like a word with Mrs. Ronquillo. Alone."

Chester and Dude nodded and walked out. Dude cast a glance at Baby on the way out. He got nothing back, that I could see. He was an employee, leaving the boss's office. Meanwhile, Jimmy Fiddler lingered in the doorway.

"I said alone." I gestured at Jimmy. He stared back at me, unimpressed.

"Jimmy has my confidence," Baby said.

"But not mine."

"All right, then," she said. "Jimmy." Jimmy turned to leave. That turn was what I wanted to see.

"He can stay," I said. "It won't take long. The first thing I want to say is I don't believe what you said. This grand-tour business. We're being boosted out of here. I think there's more than you're telling me."

"It doesn't matter so much what you think."

"What if I refused to go? What if I stayed?"

"Stay here? In Olongapo? In the Philippines? What about your visa, Professor Wiggins? Your papers? No, I don't think you'd prosper here. What do you think, Jimmy?"

"It would be a struggle, Professor Wiggins," Jimmy said, mock sympathetically. "I wouldn't recommend it. Truly."

"And the boys need you so," Baby added. "Why do you see this in a negative way? This is an opportunity! A gift!"

"All right," I said. "But there's one thing I have to have. Listen carefully. There's someone on your staff, a woman."

"Yes." Now she was interested. The whiff of sex enlivened her.

"Malou Ordonez."

"My bookkeeper. She's very good."

"We've grown close."

"Really? That surprises me. She seems . . . a tomboy?" She gave me an appraising look. Picturing me and Malou together. "She's very good with numbers, Malou."

"That guy"—I pointed at Jimmy—"has been harassing Malou. It started before I came. It's continued while I've been here. I don't want it to happen after I leave."

"Jimmy!" She feigned shock. "Are you in love again?"

"My foolish heart . . ." Jimmy responded, shaking his head, holding up his hands.

"Jimmy's forever falling in love with the wrong women," Baby said, in a boys-will-be-boys tone of voice.

"He's threatened her, Baby. And it was on your orders. You wanted to know about Colonel Parker. So he leaned on her to find out what she could from me. Which was clumsy and unnecessary and dumb."

"Well," she said. She stopped, looked at me. She marked me for an enemy, right then. She'd offered to slap Jimmy's wrist for me, if I'd been willing to pretend he'd gone after Malou on his own. An Olongapo crush had gotten out of hand: nothing broken that couldn't be fixed. Plenty more where she came from. But I had specified Baby's involvement and she didn't like that. "Well," she resumed, "that's all over now. Colonel Parker and I have gotten to know each other again . . . without assistance."

"So you have," I said. "But I want your gofer away from Malou."

"No problem," Jimmy said. "No hard feelings. I got this habit of falling for the wrong women, like she says."

"The wrong women?" I asked.

"The ones I can't have."

"She'll have my number wherever I'm staying, Jimmy. Phone and fax. It's a small world. You look at Malou, I'll know."

"I said no problem. All right? There's a difference between what's on-stage and what's not. Don't get carried away here, Wiggins."

"Stay away from her," I said.

"Sure, Mr. Biggest Elvis. Word of honor."

Graceland was empty when I came downstairs. The girls were gone, the food cleared away, the lights out on the jukebox. Graceland was closed for the night and it would be months before I saw it filled again. That's what Baby Ronquillo said. It felt longer to me. It felt like forever. I stood there for a while, picturing what it had been like on all our good nights that had been getting better and better all the time. I felt the magic of a full house, when the whole world came to Graceland. I pictured the three of us onstage, the three Elvises. I thought of the Original. Who wouldn't want to be brought back to life that way? Maybe they weren't lying. Maybe we'd be back in no time, reopening triumphantly. But it didn't feel that way. I'd gone into Elvis, maybe too far, but before this came along my life felt small and second-rate. I wanted a bigger life and this was where I found it. And what happened to me was something I'd passed along to others. I saw the girls of Graceland, Dolly clowning and mimicking our act, Elvira vamping, Whitney reading Stephen King, Lucy Number Three taking a bow in the VIP lounge, Priscilla, the former schoolteacher, advising an officer not to use "hope-fully" at the start of sentences. And more. I saw Malou sitting in the corner by the jukebox, the way she looked before we met, distant and puzzling, waiting for something which I hoped was me. Maybe I was right. Maybe.

"Oh, what a beautiful morning," Jimmy Fiddler sang when he dropped by to take us to Manila.

"I've got a favor to ask," Dude said. "Do you think you could get us all the way to Ninoy Aquino Memorial Airport and not say anything all the way?"

Jimmy nodded and passed us the key to the trunk, where we deposited our bags, our wardrobe: guitars and capes, belts and leather, pink and black suits, the tools of our trade. The backup band followed in a van.

We left Olongapo quietly, on a drizzly gray morning that matched our mood, rain like sweat dripping out of heaven's armpit. Smoke from garbage fires curled up into the rain. I asked Jimmy to drive down Magsaysay Street. Outside Graceland they were taking the three cutout Elvis figures inside. Baby Ronquillo worked fast. And Jimmy was driving us out. He was right after all. He was a stayer. We were transients. We could pretend, if we wanted, that we were going out as winners, moving on to bigger and better things. You can always do that, make death itself feel like a promotion, as if you were moving on up. But Olongapo was where I had wanted to stop moving.

"She says she'll take care of all of you," I had told the girls the night before. I'd found them sitting in Elvira's kitchen. One look told me that the word was out about our leaving.

"Baby Ronquillo takes care of Baby Ronquillo," Elvira said.

"She said not to worry."

"It doesn't matter what she say," Dolly replied. "You should know this by now, Biggest Elvis. She say yes, she mean maybe. She say later, she mean never." Was it just me or was there a new directness in the women's responses, a certain edge that signaled awareness of my departure?

"All I can say is I'll come back, I promise." I meant it for all of them. Especially Malou. I didn't know much about her past but I learned—from Dolly and Whitney—that there'd been an American officer she'd lived with

who'd gone away. I wanted her to know I wasn't like that. But she sat quietly, adding some invisible columns. And my words sounded false as soon
as I said them. My promise to return. Another American, sailing away, another woman on shore, yet another replay of *Madame Butterfly*. All the bad
plots in the world were waiting to ambush us.

"You could come with me," I said to Malou, later, in the bedroom, but it
sounded lame, like a hypothesis, a theoretical possibility. "I mean, I want
you to come," I amended.

"I don't think so," she said. She had practical arguments, the house we
were building on the beach. Someone had to look after that. You couldn't
just walk away, not in the Philippines. As soon as you were gone, things
changed. You were here or you were not. It was that simple. We were supposed to be talking about the house but I read a deeper meaning into every
line. Including the last, as I went out the doorway at dawn. "Good-bye,
Biggest Elvis."

So, nine months after our advent, the three Elvises departed Olongapo.
We splashed through puddles. We got caught in traffic near the Victory
Liner Bus Station. Three more Americans leaving the city of easy come and
easy go. The tide rolled in, the tide rolled out. Inhale and exhale, that's the
way it was here. Nobody held their breath, not in this air. Maybe, if Father
Domingo had it right, all the Americans were leaving. That would be something to see. Then again, if I saw it, all the Americans wouldn't be gone. I
wondered if they'd be working on the beach house today. Malou had said
you had to watch them every minute. I pictured her, sitting in Elvira's
kitchen, talking things over with the others. Word was that they'd be bringing new groups into Graceland, versions of the Beatles and Rolling Stones.
They'd stage a "battle of the bands." Or maybe Hank Williams, father and
son, sharing a night. Could Judy Garland and Liza Minnelli be far behind?
Nat and Natalie Cole? John and Julian Lennon?

We headed uphill, past Dolly's house. Kids in school uniforms walked
along the road, her kids among them, I supposed. You always leave a piece of
yourself behind, they said. But it wasn't true. I left nothing behind on Guam.
Except a marriage. Olongapo was different. Why couldn't I believe what

Baby had told us, take her plans at face value, that this was a reputation-building tour, a local group goes regional, a market breakout, and happy endings all around?

My problem was that we hadn't asked for this. Someone had decided we should go. Baby or the Colonel or someone else. Father Domingo? Someday, I'd learn. It was something about money or power. What else? But by the time I found out what had gone on, it would be too late. We were fine in Olongapo. So fine. Two of us in love and the third with a movie deal. Magic every night. Malou.

Our last night in bed wasn't so good. I wanted something memorable, but it ended up like that last meal I'd talked about, just barely touched. We were both off. My problem was that I knew I was leaving. As for Malou—I was gone already. She was shutting down on me. I was in her arms, I was inside her, but I was gone. Our old argument came back to me. Do we live—and love—as if every night might be our last? Or as if we'd live forever and the nights would never end? The truth—as some of my so-so students used to say—was somewhere in the middle. Live as though you've got . . . a while. Nobody dies tonight. Nobody lives forever. But never say that you're making love for the last time. And if that last time comes, don't even try. It's already over. Rouge on a corpse. Heading for the airport, I wondered if I was showing Malou how right she'd been about Americans. I was going to be different, I thought. Partings weren't forever, sadness wasn't required. I'd be back. I'd show her. Promise.

The Elvis Trio

Chester Lane

Some places I'd heard of and some I hadn't. The night before I left,
Christina got out the atlas so we could figure out where I'd be traveling and
she told me what she knew about all those places, starting with Brunei. I
forget what she said. We ended up just spinning the globe, closing our eyes,
and seeing where our fingers landed, taking turns. Wondering what it would
be like to live there. She always knew more about where the finger landed
than I did. Except, of course, when my finger landed in the ocean. Then
there wasn't anything she could say. So the idea was, when this happened,
we kissed. And there's a lot of water in the world.

Albert "Dude" Lane

They told me that the people in Brunei were loaded. They had oil. They
were like Arabs. They worshiped Allah and they hired Filipinos to work for
them. All kinds of work, they told me. A Filipina won a beauty contest and
she got invited to Brunei, a short-term contract on the Sultan's public relations staff. Uh-huh. "Brunei beauties," they were called. Elvira did a turn
or two down in Brunei and had the sheik to show for it. It was her kind of
place. Money talked but not too loud and not too late at night and definitely

not at the hotel where the Elvis Trio began its grand tour. Brunei was the place where we ran into something we never had seen before. Empty seats.

The stage was at one end of a big dining room and the only door to it was what the waiters used, coming in and out of the kitchen. Biggest Elvis shook his head as soon as he saw the place. He decided we might as well come in from the front, the same route diners took on their way to tables. The plan was, Chester would barrel-ass in, like always, and I would do some kind of cocky strut and Biggest Elvis would make his usual grand entrance, "Thus Spake Zarathustra" ricocheting off the rafters, a spotlight finding him in back and following him, all sweat and sequins, as he marched into the arena. That was the plan, anyway.

"Look at this, Dude," Ward said when we peeked through the doors five minutes before showtime, our musicians already onstage, warming up with period rock and roll.

"Oh shit," I said. My heart sank. The room was half-full. What was worse, they were seated around the sides and toward the back, like students who didn't want to get too close to the professor.

"They're eating," Ward said. And, God, he was right, it was a damn supper show. I don't mean that they'd finished their meals and were lingering over coffee, waiting for the show to start. I mean, they were chowing down. Some of them had only just sat down and were looking at padded leather menus the size of Rand McNally's road maps and others were just coming back from the damn salad bar. The waiters were flaming steaks at one table, mixing Irish coffee at another, it looked like high school chemistry class in there, blue arcs of flame leaping from glass to glass.

"Maybe that's what Uncle Pete wants us to learn," Chester said. Count on him to be constructive. I say, I'm covered with shit, don't tell me it's roses.

"Learn what?" Ward asked. He was irritated.

"About being professional," Chester said. "Dealing with all kinds of audiences and situations."

Ward looked at Chester like he couldn't believe what he was hearing. Or maybe what he couldn't accept was that what we were doing was a profession. To Ward, what we did was a lot more than a profession. Or it had been. And tonight it was going to be a lot less.

"You know what I mean," Chester persisted. "What they say. 'The show must go on.' "

"The show must go off," Ward said. "I think that's the plan."

Chester didn't get it. Neither did I. But the more we looked inside that room, the worse it felt. Our backup band—Efren, Rudy, Roman, and Roger—seemed out of place, like they should be playing dinner music instead of oldies-but-goodies. Then we heard an announcer offstage announce the arrival of an act that was the talk of the Philippines. That got no response. Nobody in Brunei cared about what they talked about in the Philippines. The Philippines were servants' quarters, that's all.

"Give it your best shot," Ward said, clapping Chester on the shoulder.

"Always have," Chester said. Black slacks, pink stripes, pink jacket, black stripes. "Always will." And off he ran, God bless him, down past some customers bribing the maître d' to seat them a safe distance from the stage, down past a bunch of empty tables, and then it happened and it's fair to say that this was a no-fault accident, that collision of Chester sprinting toward the stage and a Filipino waiter wheeling a cart full of desserts, cakes and toppings and cut-up fruit, to a table of already-stuffed customers, Chester looking like he'd dived head-on into a banana split.

"They're laughing," I said.

"Why not?" Ward asked. "We're funny."

Chester Lane

After Brunei we came to Singapore. I'd never seen a city before and Singapore was an eyeful, those buildings downtown, like Oz, high towers that shone like mirrors during the day and were lit up all night long, poking up to heaven and saying, up close and personal, in your face, God. I felt real country, walking around that town. Everything that was outdoors was a garden and everything inside was air-conditioned. Even what was old looked new, the opposite of the PI, where what was new looked old, overnight. It made Manila look like a big, dirty joke.

We played in the lounge of a hotel on Orchard Road, a smallish room that attracted what Dude said was Chinese yuppies. The guys looked like the kids who ran student government, only they'd traded their slide rules for cellular telephones. All through the show we heard those phones ringing, right in the middle of Ward's soliloquy, in the middle of "All My Sorrows." Another time, the phone went off right after Dude asked, "Are You Lonesome Tonight?" "Obviously not," he said. He made a joke out of it, see.

The biggest surprise came next. The hotel, it turned out, was only half of our Singapore booking. The rest was on a ship. It seemed the Singapore government was worried that not enough of the right kind of people, the young professionals, were getting married and having babies, so they set up these free three-day cruises, romantic cruises to nowhere. You got up to three cruises. Three strikes and you were out.

We were the talent for the love boat. We sang lots of slow Hawaiian things. We posed for pictures. And, the second night, just an hour before show time, down in his cabin, Ward suggested we should help things along by trying to say something about love in between our songs, something out of our personal experience, how we felt about love and maybe what our particular Elvis would have said about it. An improvisation, he called it.

"Holy shit," Dude protested. "Is this a cruise ship or a Quaker meeting? We have to get up and testify?"

"You don't have any thoughts on this particular subject?" Ward asked.

"I've got *plenty* thoughts! Stay away from the girls when the fleet's in. There's a thought. Never pay the girl more than twice the price of a bar fine and the next customer will thank you. That's another thought. Get the girl out of the house before you go to sleep. Or nail her in the morning, before she pees. How am I doing, coach?"

"Just think of what your Elvis would have said about love," Ward advised Dude.

"Are you kidding? Sign a no-fault divorce contract, that's what he'd say. He'd say he liked them once and he liked them young and what he couldn't do, he liked to watch."

"I hear he loved his mother," I said. "That's something."

"Thanks, Chester. I rest my case."

"That's enough," Ward said. "All in favor raise your hand." It was two-to-one. One brother—me—voting against the other. And with Ward. What surprised me was how nicely Dude took it. A few months ago, he would have been pissed off big-time. Now he just grinned. I now think he was grinning because he knew we didn't have much longer. So he could be charitable.

"You guys . . ." Dude said. "Only once, right? We'll never do this again, this public service spot. We'll never even talk about it."

"Never again," said Ward.

"Shit!" Dude started pacing back and forth, running his hand through his hair and coming up with fingers full of shiny mousse he wiped on the bedspread. But he wasn't mad, not really. "Shit!" He frowned, then he laughed. "Would you believe it? I've got an audience of wallflowers whose idea of a hot Saturday night is a visit to Computer World . . . and I'm nervous."

"Heartbreak Hotel," "Teddy Bear," "Blue Suede Shoes," I did the fast stuff first and I wowed them, I guess, but when people who can't dance watch someone who can, there's always bad vibes. They think if I can dance, then I must be stupid. Then I stopped, grabbed a towel, mopped off, and just held the same microphone I've been known to throw, juggle, wrestle to the floor, but now I leaned against it for support.

"I'm in love right now," I said, "and it's the first time. And the last time." And suddenly I was into it, I wasn't just Chester Lane talking about a woman named Christina, I was Elvis talking about Priscilla and I was everybody who ever felt what I'd been feeling. "I'm not so much," I said. "There's some things I can do—like you've seen—and lots of things I can't. Which you won't see."

I glanced off the side, where I saw Dude beaming at me, laughing some, thinking of all the things I couldn't do.

"Most anything with writing in it," I said, "or numbers. I've heard some people say there's only one right person for you, one in the whole world, and others—including a close relative of mine who will be appearing in a minute—say no, gosh no, there's not just one, because if there's only one, think what the odds are against finding that one."

Now I started strumming a few slow chords. "One or more than one, I don't know. But I found mine and I'm singing this for you, Christina." And I sang "Loving You," like I was singing it into a phone with her at the other end. That's how it was for me, on the love songs. There was the audience in front of me. And the audience I saw when I closed my eyes.

After that, it was Dude's turn and he was rougher than usual, meaner and sulkier. Not the marrying kind, for sure. Then, after "It's Now or Never," his turn came.

"They tell me three voyages is all you get," he began. "Now, how many— tell the truth—are on this voyage for the first time? Tell the truth, now."

We saw a scattering of hands. Not many. And not many more when Dude asked about a second voyage. No need for another question, the third-times were more than half the room. Some of them were good-humored about it. Why settle for one voyage when the government was good for three? But some were embarrassed. They felt like losers.

"This isn't the love boat," Dude said. "It's the voyage of the damned. Well, three days isn't long enough, that's what I think. We should stay at sea until everybody's paired off, everyone. I wonder how long that would take?"

I heard some nervous laughing in the audience. Some. Even when he was being nice, Dude had an air about him, laughing with you one minute, at you the next. He could turn on you in a wink. The people sitting in front of him knew it too. He could be dangerous.

Dude sang a song that night he'd never done before. It usually belonged to Ward. It was maybe the best love song Elvis ever made, called "Don't," a simple melody that Elvis just slides and glides all over, light and easy one moment, dark and husky the next. Ward said it was "a song of innocence and experience, perfectly balanced," and I believe he got that right.

The song was out of character for Dude and it was out of character for our audience of Singapore young professionals. Still, the dance floor filled. And then everybody was dancing close, nobody was too busy or too cool or too ugly, needed a smoke or a trip to the john. They were all out there and that was Dude's doing. Our whole act was like that, when it was good, the way it brought feelings into people's lives.

"I can't follow that," Ward said. I agreed but I was too involved in watching Dude to say much. I was about ready to cry, seeing how he got into that song. And then, the way that last "Baby, don't say no . . ." hung in the air. And everybody just stood around when he finished. They didn't applaud or shout encore. They just waited for him to sing it again. When he finished the second time he wiped his face and eyes with a towel, leaned forward in a bow, and walked out toward us.

"Don't make me do that again," he said to Ward. "Ever."

"Don't worry," Ward said. He was smiling. "Unless, that is, you want to finish the show."

"Come on, little brother," Dude said to me. "Let's see what Biggest Elvis does on the subject of love. I've been wondering. . . ."

"That was my song you sang out there," said Ward. "That's what I was going to do."

"Now, Professor. Didn't you tell us to poach? To extract music from time and place? To interrogate the texts? Well, I just gave a song called 'Don't' a pretty good interrogation out there tonight. The third degree. But you can interrogate it again, if you want."

Ward shook his head, the way teachers do when their students act up on them. Then he stopped, looked into a showroom that still hadn't gotten over Dude's performance. "Serves me right," he said. He looked puzzled. He scratched his head. He moved his lips, but nothing came out. Onstage, he did the things he usually did, "Suspicious Minds" and "Return to Sender" and "Can't Help Falling in Love." He put a lot into them too but I couldn't help wondering what he'd come up with at the end of the show, when we were supposed to talk about love. I saw him walk back and talk to the musicians awhile. They nodded, after a bit.

"Love songs," Biggest Elvis said. "When I was in my twenties, I went to all my friends' weddings. I was best man twice and usher half a dozen times. And, after church, there was always a reception at a restaurant or hall or under a striped tent in someone's backyard. It was June. Always June. But the custom was the first song the band played was for the bride and groom. Their song and they danced it alone, with everybody looking on. Taking pictures. Smiling. Songs like 'Love Is a Many Splendored Thing' or 'True Love' or 'Tonight, Tonight.' "

When Biggest Elvis mentioned those songs he sang a little bit of them, just tossed off a line or so. He had the audience now, not like Dude had them, by the short and curlies, but he had them wondering what was coming next. So did I.

"A marriage medley," Ward said. "I've lost touch with all those people. Not even a Christmas card, anymore. But whenever I hear those songs, I wonder how they're doing and whether or not they made it."

A pause. A question he asked himself. A decision to take a chance.

"I attended my own wedding and it was my turn—our turn—to dance. I left the choice of song to the woman I loved. And she chose a song by the Carpenters, 'We've Only Just Begun.' "

There was a sprinkling of applause from the audience. Some Carpenters fans out there. You never know.

"I knew right there, right then, that something was wrong, something that couldn't be fixed. And I was right. And it was wrong. And ever since I've thought that if we'd only gotten the song right, we'd be okay. Years pass and now I'm Biggest Elvis. And this time I've got the right song. And the right woman for the song. And so this is to her. And to you."

Biggest Elvis took a deep breath and sang and the band just stood there because the decision was that he'd sing it alone, a capella, and it was "Unchained Melody," and this one was too good to dance to, they just stood and listened to him, saw him standing tall, then folding down onto his knees, like he was praying, and when he got done it was like a hymn, nobody applauded, and that was the way Biggest Elvis liked it, even at Graceland. Silence, he said, was the ultimate applause.

"Okay," Dude said when Ward came back to us. "Better than okay."

"We'll never have another night like this," he said.

Albert "Dude" Lane

After we finished up in Singapore we flew to Malaysia, where we had two weeks at a hotel in Kuala Lumpur, their capital city, and another two in a beach resort at Batu Ferringhi, which is on the west coast, near Penang. And that was when things began to fall apart, big-time.

Maybe Uncle Pete was hoping that we would see the world while we were touring. For a while, we tried. But it didn't come natural. In Olongapo, we'd gone our own ways. We each took our own tour of the Philippines. What we had in common was those two shows a night, four nights a week, and that was plenty. Now, on the road, Ward went into his professor act and organized these field trips. We walked through fish markets and flower markets, markets that opened at the crack of dawn or stayed open all night. We saw monkeys and birds for sale. We visited bat caves and snake pits and enough Buddhist temples to last a lifetime. And we drove poor Ward out of his mind. We were like two kids again, in the back of the family car. "He touched me!" "He started it." "Is there a bathroom here?" "Are we there yet?" "Is this it?"

We missed Olongapo. Would you believe it? There wasn't a city we visited that didn't make Olongapo look like a dump and not a country that didn't have thousands of Filipinos in it, legally and illegally, and grateful to be there. But we missed Olongapo. Chester missed Christina and Ward missed Malou. That was easy to see. What I missed was the Olongapo buzz, the action and angles and connections and deals. I'd taken my work along with me and yet, with all the time we had on our hands, I couldn't write a word.

Something was missing. So I put my paper away and watched cooking shows on cable TV.

Ward could be full of more shit than any human being I've ever met and I told him so, more than once. But sometimes he was right. He'd said the act wouldn't travel and, when we traveled, I believed him. We were just another band from the Philippines. That we were an American band from the Philippines didn't make it any better either. Maybe worse. Not even the local Filipinos, the contract workers, came out to see us. Oh, sure, sometimes we filled the house, but with tourists, sunburned and goofy. Other nights, the rooms were half empty. Through it all, the management kept smiling at us, treating us well, pleased as punch to have us there, apologizing to us for the poor audiences, instead of us apologizing to them. It was off season or a national holiday or there hadn't been time to give us the promotion we deserved. I knew what they were paying us. They had to be taking a hosing. Why were they so nice to us? I wondered. And I'm the one that solved that particular puzzle. We were in Sri Lanka by then.

Chester Lane

Colombo sits right on this beach that runs forever. The city just stops and the ocean begins, waves rolling in from like halfway around the world. Mornings in Colombo, six A.M., I'd walk along the beach with Ward, joining all the other folks who got up for the first light and the breeze, walking, stretching, flying kites, and there were crows all over the place, swooping and cawing, like breakfast was late. In Manila, the morning feels like, oh, hell, here we go again, like the eighth inning of a ball game the local side can't win. The mornings in Colombo felt like the beginning of the world.

"Any luck last night?" Ward asked one morning. We'd both been trying to call Olongapo. He'd tried Elvira's apartment and the phone just rang. Same thing at Graceland. He'd been trying so often he could tell, he said, just from the way the phone rang that no one would be answering. You call a place where someone is home, he said, and the phone sounds perky and hopeful, like it knows it won't take more than two or three rings before someone comes along and says hello. Other places, it sounds like a lost cause from the first ring. That's the way his phone calls to Olongapo were sounding.

"I got through," I said. "Father Domingo answered the phone and I asked for Christina. And he hangs up. That's expensive."

"I'll try. Maybe he'll speak to me. We were friends."

"There's another thing," I said. "Dude brought a woman into the room last night. I was asleep, the light snaps on and he's there with her, asking if I'd mind sitting out at the swimming pool for a while. Then this woman whispers something to him. And Dude—my own brother—gives me the strangest look. 'She says she'll take care of both of us. One at a time . . . or . . . same time. It's your move, little brother.' "

"What did you do?"

"I ran out of there and sat outside like he suggested."

"Good."

"It didn't feel so good to me. I felt stupid. And another thing . . ." I caught myself wincing, choking up, forcing it out. "I wanted that woman myself. Ward, she had this thing on, like she was rolled in a fancy curtain, needed unwrapping, and skin which was like polished wood and these big eyes and I sat down at the pool, saying why the hell not why shouldn't I, it's there for you, right for the taking. . . ."

Dude was waiting for us downstairs in the lobby of the Lanka Oberoi Hotel and he acted like he'd been waiting for us awhile. "Come with me," he said, "right now."

He led us out of the lobby, toward a wing of the hotel that was still under construction. They used it for workers and staff quarters. That's where they put the low-ranking foreign help, Chinese cooks and Filipino entertainment, our guys and a bunch of others. The Filipinos were all in one room, with luggage and mussed-up beds and the clothes they performed in hanging from a line in the bathroom. When we came in, they were all there, just hanging out, the way overseas Filipinos do, as if they were two ships at sea, the crew of one coming onto the deck of the other to talk awhile.

"Hi guys," Dude said. "You know the other Elvises, Ward and Chester." He nodded at us. "These guys belong to Jun Velasco and the Music Messengers. That's Jun over there."

Jun was a good-looking, Spanish-type Filipino, hunkered down next to a hot plate, poking into a pot that had fish in it. Three other guys and a girl made up the rest of his group. We all said hello.

"I talked to Jun last night," Dude said. "It seems his group was playing here before we came. And, after we leave, they'll be back playing here. Meanwhile—"

"Hey, I'm sorry you got laid off," Ward jumped in. "If there's anything—"

"Just listen," Dude said. "Don't talk. Listen." He nodded at Jun. "Just tell Biggest Elvis what happened around here. The same as you told me."

"Mr. Pandit is the entertainment manager," Jun said. "He is telling me that a special contract is bringing you from the Philippines for two weeks. I'm asking about our contract." Jun was young enough not to be automatically polite to Americans. He hadn't stood up when we came in, he'd stayed busy stirring that pot of dead fish they were looking forward to. He hadn't said "sir" yet either.

"I'm thinking where do we go? Also . . . why do we go? Because we are doing well here. We are doing better than you do now." Jun hadn't liked giving up the stage. He thought he was good. And he didn't say how much he loved our show. "Mr. Pandit says no problem. We stay here. We get paid. I say okay. But how can they pay for two band when they can only use one?"

He was satisfied with what was going on in the pot. Now he rocked back and forth on his haunches and sat down. Filipinos, whenever they're together, it's not like they're sitting around. It's more like they're camping out.

"Mr. Pandit tells me this time the hotel will be making money. He is laughing. If no one comes—if every table is empty—no problem. The band's agent guarantees money for every show. I'm wondering, what kind of band is this? Then, you come."

*   *   *

After we left the Filipinos, we walked down to the swimming pool, the same place I'd sat out last night. It was still early. They were hosing down the concrete and cleaning ashtrays on tables. And there were crows all over the tables, making double sure cigarette butts weren't bread crusts. Mainly what I remember about Sri Lanka is the crows. It felt like they'd be the last birds left on earth, when the robins and the hummingbirds were gone. The meek wouldn't inherit dippity. At the end, it would be crows and cockroaches, with nobody watching.

"So I got a little drunk last night and there's this woman down at the end of the bar," Dude said, "and I said to myself, I deserve a break tonight." He reached out and mussed up my hair. "Sorry to disturb your sleep, little brother."

My sleep wasn't what he'd disturbed, though. It was what I thought, after he woke me up. And what I wanted, while I sat out back by the swimming pool.

"It seemed like a good idea at the time," Dude said. Now he faced Ward. "I guess you could say I was feeling like a whore. But at least there's this. We're not just another Filipino band, out scuffling for a living. We're special. We're sponsored. We're a no-lose situation. We're a no-fault accident. I was wondering why they were so glad to see us. Why they couldn't be nicer." He stopped awhile. Thinking, I guessed. Then he smiled at me. Not a nice smile. The same smile I'd seen last night, when he offered to share. "Anyway, she got her money's worth. That woman."

"She what?"

"Got her money's worth, I said. She told me so." I didn't like the look on Dude's face, that punk sneer. I'd seen it before, but only onstage. That was acting. This was something else.

"She paid you?"

"That's . . . entertainment!"

I looked at Ward to help me decide whether Dude was putting us on. I wasn't sure. Neither was Ward.

"Little brother, when the market for Elvis concerts dries up, you can re-cycle your talent. There's a lot of women out there who loved Elvis. There's action for all of us, all three. They start out with the young Elvis. That's you. They get me next. Yum. And then they wind up with Biggest. It's like a Red Cross lifesaving class. You go from beginner to intermediate to advanced. And if the money's right you can do it in one night."

"What's become of you, Dude?" Ward asked.

"What's become of me? You're the one who's always saying how we have an advantage over the Original. We can get closer to people, we don't seal ourselves off behind gates and bodyguards. We meet the people on the peo-ple's terms. Am I right? They can get closer to us than to him. They can touch us. Sit on Saint Elvis' lap . . . attend ceremonies with Saint Elvis . . . walk with him and talk with him. Well, I just took it a step further, Profes-sor. I put on my leather for her and I let her take it off and I say this is my body, darling, broken for you, come have a little piece of it. Or a big well-marbled hunk. And you're asking me what happened?"

Dude's voice trailed off and his anger drained out of him. We all just sat there. After a while, he shook his head. "Okay, I'm sorry. Ward? Chestnut? It didn't happen that way. Okay. It really didn't. I was bullshitting. Okay?"

"Then how . . . did it happen?" I asked. He smiled at me but he didn't answer. So I guess I'll never know.

Albert "Dude" Lane

So we were tourists. We were on a free vacation. We kept on playing in Hong Kong and Macau and Taipei. We should relax and enjoy it, Ward said, look at that Hong Kong harbor, the way the water caught the neon signs off the skyscrapers, and the hills were piled high with lights, and the ferries scut-tled back and forth in a place that never rested. Or check out those lost, pretty Portuguese buildings in Macau, a little bit of the Mediterranean sur-rounded by high-rise condos and casinos, an ancient harbor stuffed with landfill, pipes and dikes and cranes. We took it in, we nodded respectfully, we even spent a day at a Taipei museum the size of Fort Knox, all of China on display. But we were wondering what was going to become of this.

What was Uncle Pete thinking? Did he figure we'd never find out he was footing the bill? Did he reckon that, once people caught our act, they'd be anxious to have us come again and to pay for what we'd given away? A free Elvis sample, was that the idea? That's what Chester decided, after he'd given it some thought. I said, yeah, sure, Chestnut, I guess you scoped it out. He was happy again, he cheered right up.

There was another way of looking at it, though. Uncle Pete had backed us up every step, starting with when we dragged him down to the Tiger's Cage. He'd done it all, from Guam to Saipan to Olongapo. So far, so good. It was wild oats, youthful adventure, seeing how the other half lives. But then—just maybe—it got out of hand, out of his hands, anyway. Other things took over: Ward Wiggins, Olongapo, Graceland, Elvis. It had given me the willies, sometimes, when I saw what had happened in Olongapo and it might have done the same to Uncle Pete, long-distance, one son fixing to make a movie, another planning marriage, and eldest Elvis going ten rounds with the Catholic church. I doubted Uncle Pete would put up with that for long. Or that Olongapo would be there for us when the tour was over. I felt it down deep, down in my legs and stomach, in all the places that you feel *before* you think.

We tried to call Olongapo. We should have known better. You'll never get a Filipino to figure out how a telephone works. At home, you sit by your phone, you get more wrong numbers than right and usually it's the same person making the same mistake again and again. They dial numbers like they pray the rosary, the same fingers over the same beads, hoping that sooner or later they'll get through to heaven, no matter how many times they hear it's a wrong number. And when you try calling the Philippines, it's even worse. Now you're the one on the rosary. Dial a prayer. Pray for a dial tone. Static, silence, disconnects, maids and children. It broke my poor brother's heart, trying to get through to Christina. He kept the number by the hotel phone, tried every night. Until the night in Taipei I got Ward to try for him. "Don't ask for the girl," I said. "That's the mistake. Ask for the priest. Your buddy. He won't talk to Chester. But he might talk to you."

"Where's Chester?"

"Down moping in the lobby."

"Shouldn't he be here? If I get through?"

I gave Ward the look I gave him when I wanted to link right up to him: one smart man to another. "He might not like what he hears."

"Okay, Dude," he said. He knew what I meant. We were at that stage where things were happening that we couldn't control. So no news was good news and what you didn't know wouldn't hurt you . . . for a while. This time the phone call went right through. Ward identified himself. "Your old friend." He said we were in Taipei. He said he missed Olongapo. He missed Father Domingo, he said. Sure, they'd had problems but they were friends. That's how he would feel, if it ended tomorrow. He said that poor Chester had been trying to get through, again and again, it was breaking his heart and whatever stand Father took on the marriage, couldn't he at least let them talk awhile, while they were so far away? Then Ward heard something that must have startled him. His face turned serious. He listened, just listened, not saying anything more than yes and I see and I believe you and good-bye. And when he hung up, he looked around the room, to confirm that Chester still wasn't around.

"He says that when Chester called he told him that Christina wasn't there. He says that's the truth. And he didn't mean she's not by the phone or not in the house. He means she's left. . . . She took off."

"Christina took off? His own sister? The schoolteacher?" It came as a surprise, till I thought of the way she'd driven us down from Baguio that night.

"She packed her bags, he says. He didn't go into it but I think he leaned into her one time too many about Chester."

"No clue where she went?"

"That part was odd. He was thinking, all this time, that she was with us. So when Chester called again and again, Father thought he was rubbing it in, that Christina was with him, with us, in a hotel room someplace."

"No way," I said. "Not her."

"Anyway . . ." Ward walked over to the hotel window and swept open the curtains. Taipei was spread out below, a hive of lights, like all the other hives we'd been to by now, Singapore, Kuala Lumpur, and Hong Kong. "Anyway, she's out there someplace."

"Maybe just Manila," I guessed. But I doubted it. Christina wasn't going to take small steps. "Best not to tell Chester."

"I agree." We decided we'd say we got through and the good Father opened up a little and told us Christina decided to go back to the provinces for a while, visit relatives, breathe clean air, think things over. The Chestnut would buy that, we decided. He was easy to lie to.

"She'll be all right, I bet," Ward said, still looking out at the city. "If they get together again, it'll be because she finds him." He closed the curtain. "That's one couple I have hope for."

Ward left it at that but I knew what he wasn't saying. He hadn't gotten through to Malou and he hadn't had any mail either. There were all sorts of reasons why that could happen but I believed in trying simple explanations first and the simplest was he hadn't gotten mail from Malou because Malou hadn't written. That woman was a bad case of frostbite. I thought so from the start, seeing her next to the jukebox, using it like a reading lamp, not listening to the music, just keeping track of bar drinks and bar fines and VIP lounge rentals, wearing an I-don't-care expression. It didn't surprise me, no mail from Malou. Or that the only one Ward heard from was clueless little Whitney, who asked if he could send her some paperback books.

Chester Lane

We never watched more television than when we went out to see the world. It's not supposed to be that way and when you think about it, it doesn't make a lot of sense. It's like sitting around Disney World reading a Mickey Mouse comic book when the real thing is right in front of you. Or something like that.

Still, we worked late and we slept late and the day was already half-dead when we got up. Who felt like rushing off to visit a Korean temple? I liked the foreign-language MTV shows. Ward was a female volleyball connoisseur. "I love the way those Cubans spike it." Dude favored the exercise shows. The one from Hawaii had some women working out on a grassy lawn in front of a beach. Those were tanned, muscular women. But his favorite was from India, where this perky dark-skinned girl jumped around in pistachio and black exercise tights, like a flavor of the month, announcing—in a British accent—how splendid everything felt. Dude loved her a lot. He wondered what the bar fine might run, on someone like that. So, this particular afternoon, we were cruising around the channels, Dude looking for his aerobic Indian girlfriend.

"Stop!" Ward shouted out. "Go back. I think I saw Olongapo."

We dropped back three channels, cooking, kung fu, business news, and there was an airplane view of the base, with the ship-repair facility right in the center, and I heard the announcer saying that Subic Bay was America's largest military base and that, when combined with Clark Field, it represented the biggest payroll in the Philippines, pumping $370 million into the local economy, directly and indirectly employing half a million Filipinos.

"It's a documentary is all," Dude said.

"No, it's not," Ward snapped back. "It's an obituary."

More footage from the base. The bay, beaches, golf courses, housing areas, and hospitals. And the announcer: "This transplanted America had its other side, a neon wilderness of bars and massage parlors that gave Olongapo a reputation as a sin city . . . and the most famous liberty port in Asia."

"That's us!" I shouted.

Now we were looking at Magsaysay Street at night, home sweet home, bumper-to-bumper traffic, crowded sidewalk, miniskirted girls in doorways, security guards.

"Where's Graceland?" Dude asked.

"It's probably file footage," Ward said.

"I thought I saw Lucy Number Three," I said.

"This isn't a home movie," Dude told me. They brought on some Filipino guy who said the bases were imperialist, militarist strongholds that had no place in a sovereign nation.

"Here it comes," Ward said.

First they showed a shot of Clark Field, before and after Mount Pinatubo blew up. "The abandonment of Clark Field focused attention on the Subic Bay base. U.S. and Philippines negotiators had agreed on a ten-year renewal of the Subic lease for more than $250 million per year. Philippines President Corazon Aquino, herself an earlier bases opponent, submitted the bill to the Philippines Senate but gave the treaty only lukewarm support. Today, by a margin of one vote, the treaty was defeated." Shots of demonstrators. BASES MUST GO. Nuns and students mostly.

"Holy shit," Dude said.

"How did Washington react to the treaty defeat?" the anchorman asked the on-the-spot reporter. "With surprising mildness," the lady said. "Certainly, the Pentagon would have preferred to retain the base. But with the Soviet threat receding—and with the level of rhetoric on the rise in Manila—along with the price tag—planners here decided that it might be time to go. They could live without the base." Now the anchor was back. "The shut-down of America's biggest naval base is already under way. It should take about a year. That's our report."

We sat in front of the TV while they showed the Subic footage again under closing credits and played this sad old song from World War II, "Now Is the Hour." We saw the harbor full of ships, the sailors crossing over the bridge into town, a whole jeepney full of guys waving and hoisting beers as they headed out to the cheap dives along the coast. Then the show was over and some ads came on and we still sat there.

"What are we waiting for?" Dude asked. "Instant replay?"

"I still think I saw Lucy Number Three," I said.

"This doesn't change anything," Ward said. "Not for us."

"You mean," says Dude, "accustomed as we are to playing half-empty houses, we should feel real at home in an abandoned military base. That what you're getting at, coach?"

"It can work. . . ."

"Of course it can. Why just confine ourselves to Olongapo, though? There must be bigger, better ghost towns for us to haunt. What's the scene in Cam Ranh Bay? Maybe they could use us in Chernobyl." Dude shook his head, smiled, stopped himself. Time was, Dude would go right after Ward, get in his face when he talked about the three Elvises and how time flowed in circles, not straight lines, about creation and re-creation, about what those words meant and how they were linked. Dude would shake his head or make a sawing motion, like he was holding a violin. Now he smiled in a sad kind of way, like Ward needed to be let down gently.

"It can work," Ward said. "That's all I'm saying. I hate to see the Navy go. I liked it fine, when the fleet was in. But I think we can hold on." He thought about it some more, picturing something we both couldn't see. "They come to us from all over. They come to Graceland. It happened once. We weren't a sideshow. We were a destination attraction. Am I right?"

"Maybe so," Dude said.

"We've got to get back to Graceland. That's all."

"We've got to look after Biggest Elvis," Dude said to me that night. We were backstage in Seoul, right before showtime, and, as Dude spoke, he gestured over to where Ward was sitting in a corner, sitting on a stool, in kind of a daze. He was in costume, Biggest Elvis threads, but he looked more like a wrestler waiting to go into the ring, ready to get pinned. Jukebox music drifted in from outside, cigarette smoke, and the noise of the hard crowd that was waiting for us.

"What's wrong with him?"

"You haven't noticed? He's doing more and more sad songs. No more 'American Trilogy.' At the rate he's going, he'll be a blues singer."

Dude was right. No one who was seeing our show for the first time would notice. If they'd never seen him raise the roof in Olongapo, "rolling the stone from the mouth of the cave," they wouldn't miss what we were missing, that big triumphant I'm-here-forever, I'm-not-leaving, I'll-never-die.

What's more, they were prepared to accept that, at the end of his life, Elvis might be kind of down. But it bothered us, even if it meant the true facts of Elvis' life were taking over. But here he was, singing "That's How Your Heartaches Begin." Every night. Loser music.

"Listen," Dude said. "If this Elvis thing is over, like I think it is . . ."

He stopped and shook his head, nodded at Biggest Elvis, who sat on a dressing room stool holding a bunch of cheap scarves that were part of the act. Ward used to wipe sweat off his face and throw those scarves at the girls in the audience at Graceland. Lucy Number Three had the biggest collection. It was like throwing the bride's garter at a wedding. The Graceland girl who caught the scarf was said to be a cinch for double bar fines that night. Now it was more like crying towels.

"When this ends, we've got other things to do. I've got deals waiting. You're halfway married. We'll be all right. We're young. We've got Uncle Pete. It's all in front of us. But him . . . what's he going to do? Where will he go? It's like we do what we do . . . and he is what he is. We can change what we do. But he can't change what he is."

"Biggest Elvis . . ." Now that I thought about it, it seemed a strange thing for a person to be. It wasn't a trade. You couldn't say Ward was a professional entertainer, someone who could do different songs and styles. He only did one thing. He did what he was.

"We just have to look out for him," Dude said. That night, second show, I saw just what he meant. It was one slow, sad song after another. The crowd was getting restless and, I've got to say, this was a rough crowd to start with. The servicemen were tougher than the guys at Subic, it seemed to me, and the girls—half Filipinas, half Korean—were always on the hustle, not like Graceland, where they teased and kidded around. You say a bar is a bar and a bar girl is a bar girl, you can say that, but I say there are differences. There are always differences, I think. Anyway, these guys had come out to drink and maybe get laid, not cry in their beer about old girlfriends. Well, Ward was closing his act with "Are You Lonesome Tonight." If it came after something fun and fast—"Burning Love," say—it would have knocked

them out. But they were knocked out already. So Ward was going into the
first part of the song,

> Are you lonesome tonight,
> Do you miss me tonight,
> Are you sorry we drifted apart?

and we knew he was thinking about Malou, who he hadn't heard a word
from. I'll say this for Ward. Whatever he sang he got into it and took it as far
as it could go.

> Do the chairs in your parlor
> Seem empty and bare?
> Do you gaze at your doorstep
> And picture me there?

In the middle of "Are You Lonesome Tonight" there's a spoken part, which
is usually real moving and sexy,

> You know someone said that
> All the world's a stage
> And each must play a part . . .

and it goes on from there, so that it comes as a surprise when he says
"honey, you lied when you said you loved me." It doesn't sound angry but it
is. Or isn't. Because then he says he'd rather put up with those lies than live
without this woman he loves. Then he goes back into the song and it's high-
powered. But not tonight, this last night in Korea. The military had had
enough of Elvis and too much of Biggest Elvis.

"It was Shakespeare," somebody shouted.

"What's that?" Biggest Elvis asked.

"It wasn't *someone* who said all the world's a stage," the guy fired back.

His friends didn't try to stop him. They were cracking up, laughing and high-fiving. "It was Shakespeare, you asshole!"

"So it was," Biggest Elvis said. "You know the play?" That stopped the heckler. His buddies looked to see if he knew the answer. He didn't and he was done for the night.

"*As You Like It,*" Biggest Elvis said. "Set in the Forest of Arden. The seven ages of man." Then he walked offstage and went straight over to the table. The guys were hunkered down in a circle, as if saying, hey, we didn't mean nothing, we're just out drinking beer.

Now Biggest Elvis signaled to the band, so they played some slow music, harmonizing behind him. "It goes like this," Biggest Elvis said. And then he recited this whole long thing I'd never heard before, but I've looked it up. I've even tried to memorize it, but no luck, so far. Anyway, it's about the different parts of life—a lot like our act, really—and how you wind up, like you started, an old person just like a baby, shitting on itself and crying in the dark. Dude thought Ward had gone over the edge but I thought it was one of Biggest Elvis' biggest moments, standing in a hostess joint that was a lot less classy than the one we called home, standing there in a sequined jumpsuit, pulling that Shakespeare stuff out of the air and reciting it, beat by beat, while the guys played "Are You Lonesome Tonight."

"There you have it," he said when he was done. "Was there anything else you wanted?"

"Hell no, buddy," one of the guys said. "It's all right."

"Yeah, man," the heckler said. "You just go do your act. We're sorry."

Biggest Elvis got back onstage and finished the song. Everybody applauded. It's not often you see someone get so close to the edge.

"Ward, that was great," I said when he came off.

"I think it was pathetic," he said. And he walked on by, out back.

"I think you're both right," Dude said after Ward was gone. "Great. And pathetic. The thing of it is, next time it'll be a little less great and a little more pathetic."

"Next time?"

Albert "Dude" Lane

I'm not the kind of guy who kids himself. Or, if I do, it's not for long. So I'd be the first to grant that what happened to us might have happened anyway, as sure as what goes up must go down. But, about halfway through that so-called tour, I sensed we weren't just fighting the law of gravity. Someone was helping the law of gravity along.

Baby Ronquillo had told us that the tour was put together fast, so there might be some loose ends along the way. But in Korea, that hotel we stayed in was second-rate and the bar we played in was a dump. I wondered if that wasn't the plan. Then we flew from Seoul to Narita. There were a couple of flights a day, Narita to Guam, and it would have been easy to give us a break to visit home and look in on Uncle Pete, but our flight was for Saipan and from Saipan we were supposed to rush off straight down to Palau because a new hotel was opening there, a very big deal, and we were supposed to open the new hotel. So all we had was an hour in the transit lounge at Guam and when we tried calling home, nobody picked up. There we sat at three in the morning, elbow to elbow with hundreds of Japanese tourists. I looked hard at Chester and he looked at me. We were a taxi ride from home. We could have walked away from the whole thing, straight out the door. "Thanks a lot, Uncle Pete, we been there, seen it, done it, and now we're prepared to get serious about our lives." But there sat Biggest Elvis, all heavy and sad and heartbroken and I guessed we'd be staying with him awhile longer. I also guessed it wouldn't be long. Something was happening to Biggest Elvis. It was about his weight or maybe about the way he carried his weight. He was never svelte. He packed the weight that the role required. He used to joke about it. Sitting down to eat, he'd say he was "going into wardrobe." An extra portion of ribs, another pile of rice, a double scoop of ice cream was "putting on some makeup." He carried it pretty well at the start. It was happy fat. But now he was sagging, just sagging all over, up and down, inside and out, looking more and more like those last sad pictures of the Original, all bloat and jowl, like this was someone he had an appointment to catch up with. In for a penny, in for a pound.

South from Guam, we stopped at Yap, where there were shot-up Japan-ese fighters on the airstrip and they sold betelnut at the airport store and some of the guys on the ground crew had red mouths that matched their loincloths, teeth and wardrobe all coordinated. We always talked about how our act moved through time, but that was the time of Elvis' life. Now it felt like we were reeling backward, way back, out of control, and that if we turned on a radio we'd hear Glenn Miller playing and getting interrupted by an announcement that Pearl Harbor had just been bombed. Sometimes, in spite of what Ward said about the importance of the past, how it enriched and renewed—a rap I'd heard about a hundred times—it still seemed like an awful lot of luggage we were carrying around. People think it's easy be-ing an oldies-but-goodies act, dressing up in someone's clothes, stepping into their shoes and songs. But sometimes I didn't want to be part of what was over with, even though Ward said that nothing was ever over. I wanted to be new and young and clueless. I wanted to pretend the whole world be-gan on my birthday.

Palau was something else from the air, this whole mess of green islands in a huge lagoon, so many leftovers from the Garden of Eden, with cause-ways that connected the islands, and fishing boats outside the reef and metal roofs winking up into the sun, to tell you that there were people around. Not many people either, and none of them were to meet us at the airport. That hadn't happened before. We waited around while the crowd thinned out and the plane we came in took off and then we got a taxi to take us to a brand-new hotel that was supposed to be waiting for us to christen it with song. Only they weren't expecting us at the hotel. When we told the desk clerk that we were the Elvis Presley trio, she went blank.

"Elvis Presley is dead," she informed us, as if that settled things. Then she asked, did we have reservations? Ward said no. We always let him han-dle the messy details. Before this, he'd have had a response when the woman said that Elvis was dead. He'd look astonished. "I hadn't heard. Are you sure?" Or he'd look sad. "Why didn't they tell me?" Or indignant. "I'd be the first to know!" Or he'd lean forward and whisper to her. "But I came back." This time, though, he stayed quiet. Did we desire an ocean view room—she pointed through the lobby toward where some Filipinos were stuffing palm trees into the ground near the swimming pool—or would we prefer the garden view? That was out near the road and the parking lot. And all Ward did was shrug and walk away, dumping his butt into a chair, leaning backward, looking up at the overhead fan.

"You don't understand," I finally said. "We're the Elvis Presley show. You hired us. We don't pay to stay here. As a matter of fact, you pay us."

"Just a moment," the clerk said, and out came a busy-looking Japanese man, barely polite, who admitted, yes, this was where we were booked. But he'd canceled, he said. The hotel, as we could see, was half-finished and ten percent full. He hadn't heard from our manager, Ms. Baby Ronquillo. He still awaited her response. He agreed, as a professional courtesy, to give us lodging while he sought to reach her again. The cost of the lodging would figure in any later settlement, of course.

"So . . . no show?" I asked.

"Who for?" the manager replied. "There are thirty guest now in hotel. They go scuba diving all day. They come back tired, eat, go sleep."

"Suppose you invited local people," I suggested. "Introduce them to the new hotel?"

"Not a good idea," the manager said. His meaning was clear. This place wasn't for local people, not today, maybe never. I figured we should leave now. But the next plane to Manila wasn't for three days. We'd have to buy tickets and—when I asked the manager for the registered packet that had waited for us at every other stop—we got a shrug. Our salary had been deposited in the Philippines all along but expenses and onward tickets were sent everywhere we went. Except Palau.

After a long back-and-forth, they agreed to throw in three days of meals—alcohol at our own expense—and gave us keys to some rooms that weren't quite finished. There were empty soda cans in the bathroom, a tube of putty on the bottom of the bathtub, a pile of wood shavings in the corner, waiting to be removed or maybe to stay forever underneath a carpet that was rolled up, out in the hall. And there was a hole in the wall, like a giant empty mailbox, where the air conditioner was going to sit.

All the rest of that first day, I tried to reach Baby Ronquillo. She was out of the country. Why wasn't I surprised? This wasn't a string of accidents. We were being fucked over, not up. The following morning I went to the local government, to the office of the president of the Republic of Palau, and explained the jam we were in. Maybe the president was an Elvis fan, I don't know. They turn up in the oddest places. So the next night we gave a free public concert at the local high school, in a crowded auditorium that doubled as a basketball court, and that night was a sauna.

Knowing then what I know now, I should have paid attention to every minute, filing it away for forever. We'd sagged some lately, I admit, but that night in Palau we were pumped up, knowing that we were singing in exchange for tickets that would get us out of there, singing for our freedom almost. There were a couple of other things, besides. There was a challenge in the air. We sensed something about Palau, something sullen, something that said, hey, you came here, you came to my island, you came to me. So how big a deal are you, if you're here? How big—really—could you possibly be? To come to a place that isn't yours, a small place where you don't belong? And with what? With funny costumes and old songs, that you want us to pay for?

Even Ward perked up, one last time. They were the youngest audience we'd ever faced, grade school, high school, community college. They hadn't paid to see us. The choice was between us and homework. But as soon as we saw them, laughing, restless, noisy, chewing betelnut and popping gum and snapping open soda cans, fanning themselves with papers while overhead fans slapped at locker-room air the way a lazy cow swooshes its tail at a swarm of flies, as soon as we saw all that, I think the three of us decided to see if we couldn't just kick ass.

We did the hard songs we hadn't done for a while. Chester did "Good Rockin' Tonight." I unloaded on "Jailhouse Rock." Ward couldn't quite tear himself away from "Are You Lonesome Tonight," his recent theme song, but then, when his act could have ended, he brought us all onstage for "American Trilogy," half-horseshit, half-holy, I used to say, but this one night we traded off on it, back and forth, the three of us, like it would never

end. And yet we knew it was ending, I swear we did, that this was our last
stop and that's why we kept singing, because we didn't want to let go of it,
because when we stopped that would be it for us. So, in the end, Ward won
another argument with me. I was the guy who said that those old songs
would go flat, the more we sang them. But here we were, end of the road,
end of the world, and we were never better. We had them, just like in Olongapo. On the way back to the hotel, driving across a causeway with the windows open and the tide high and the warm wind coming in off the lagoon,
we kept singing. We sang all the way back to the hotel, where Baby Ronquillo was waiting.

"Your uncle . . . your father . . . Colonel Parker died," she said.

Chestnut and I were flying back to Guam where Uncle Pete's ashes were
waiting for us to take them out to sea. Ward walked us out to the parking lot.
He wanted to go to Olongapo. We knew why. When it came time for us to
split—which meant split up—he just stood there, looking at us. I remember
that hot heavy air, that greenhouse tropical morning, that sense of sharing
our lives for the last time.

"Thanks for everything," Ward said. "For putting up with me and all."

"I'm thanking you," I said. "We had a real good ride."

"I know."

"It's more than that," I said. "We were good. We were better than I ever
thought we'd be."

"Well . . ." Biggest Elvis fumbled. He took compliments badly.

"Let me just get this over with, damn it," I said. "I gave you some shit,
especially at the start. But in the end you were right, Ward. We had magic.
And you were the magician."

"Not me. The time and the place."

"That's what a magician does. Finds the time and the place. You did
that. And I'm thanking you. Uncle Pete used to say that if you were good at
something, no matter what, you wouldn't settle for anything else that was
second-rate. So that's what I'm taking away from this. Thanks."

"You guys are talking like it's over," Chester protested. He was a wreck. I was hurting, but not like Chester.

"Not as long as you remember," Ward told him. "Then it's not over."

Ward Wiggins

"The night they announced that the Senate rejected the bases treaty, late that night," said Billy Bowers, "is when it happened."

I saw black smoke stains around Graceland's doors and windows. I saw carpet puddles and broken glass around the bars. The sinks and coolers were gone, the chairs and light fixtures also. The balcony level, where the VIP lounges had been, had collapsed down into the main showroom and part of the roof had followed. Malou's jukebox was still there, the front bashed in, where someone had reached in to steal the records. The back bar and dressing room had been picked clean too. The place dripped and stank and I knew no phoenix would be hatching out of this pile of ashes. So, a small moment of silence among the rot and drips. Elvis had left the building.

"I'll tell you what was in the newspapers," Billy said. "Some radicals burned you out. Torched the last stronghold of American imperialism. A symbol of exploitation. Like that priest says: 'Disgraceland.' The will of the people. All that bullshit."

"You don't believe it?"

"Hey, friend, what do I know?"

"That's what I'm asking."

"The fire department? They showed up before the fire started. They were out back, drinking beer. There's important people own the neighboring buildings."

"Say it, Billy."

"I'm saying nothing. But I've been around."

•   •   •

At the Palau airport earlier that day, I had seen Baby Ronquillo sitting in the department lounge. She was by herself. The dozens of Filipino contract workers waiting for the same flight kept their distance. They worked for her, after all. But I didn't, not anymore. I sat down right next to her. Then I just stared out, as if we were next to each other on a subway or a bus.

"I'll miss him," she said, after a while. "You don't know."

"Colonel Parker."

"He was one of the old-time Americans. The ones who never apologized. That was their way."

I wondered why she was telling this to someone she'd never see again. Then I saw that the question answered itself.

"You don't know this," she continued. "How . . . fragile . . . you Americans are. The most fragile. The Japanese never change. Nor the Chinese. A Frenchman or a German, they stay as they are. But the Americans . . . I always knew they wouldn't be around forever."

That's when she stopped and she didn't say another word, from then until the time they called us out to the plane to Manila.

When I had pictured the girls of Graceland, I saw them in Elvira's apartment. I saw Dolly cooking and Whitney reading a paperback, Elvira and Priscilla and Lucy Number Three looking through magazines, ransacking closets, trying on clothing, and Malou just sitting there, being Malou, watching it all, waiting for the right minute, waiting for me. They'd had plenty to talk about, I bet. After the treaty rejection, there'd have been endless roundtables about where to go and what to do. That was the talk I wanted to hear. What next for the girls of Graceland, what next for Biggest Elvis? I still thought we were in it together, that I'd come walking in, throw my bags on the floor, hear them arguing out in the kitchen. I'd surprise them. Whitney would jump up and hug me. "Did you bring me any books, Biggest Elvis?" Dolly and Elvira and the rest, even Lucy Number Three, they'd all embrace me. Malou would let all the others get to me first, watch-

ing with deadpan eyes. "So," she would say, "you've come back." I'd sit at
the table, take my place among them, order out for food and say, "All right,
let's start putting it all back together."

Elvira's apartment was the best in Olongapo. It had a fountain in front,
even though it was dry and filled with mango peels. It had a circular driveway. It had a doorman who told me that the place was empty. The gentleman
from Brunei had stopped paying rent and Ms. Elvira was gone. I could look
for myself if I wanted. Graceland was next: a burned-out ruin that wasn't
worth tearing down because there wouldn't be much action on Magsaysay
Street for a while. Soul City was open but empty. Billy was small-time, no
live music, only a few girls who came and went as they pleased. He could
hunker down, live off his retirement, run his bar out of a refrigerator. Up and
down the street, the biggest places were sunk or sinking, the Corral, Foxy
Lady, Disco Inferno, Plato's Cave, Heavenly Harbor, Miss Liberty, a long
row of boarded windows and tattered awnings and signs that offered bar/
restaurant fixtures for sale.

It wasn't just the bars and nightclubs either. The restaurants and barbershops were folding up, the T-shirt and sandal makers. No more gaudy silky
jackets, no more carved water buffalo. I'd guessed—and hoped—that it
would get wilder and wilder here, as it came nearer to closing time for Uncle
Sam. I was looking for a crescendo, a countdown, the last week, the next to
last night, the last, the twelfth of never. But the base was just dribbling away.

I left my luggage with Billy and took a jeepney out to Barrio Barretto, to
the neighborhood that had been known as Elvisville. It started raining as I
headed down the path toward my house, a hard rain that sent people scurry-
ing for shelter, except for some women who were doing laundry in the
stream. It didn't matter to them, those sheets of rain.

Wet past caring, still I hoped that I'd see a house or half of a house coming at me out of the rain. Just something that would tell me Malou had been
taking care of business while I was gone. I would stand in a doorway,
maybe, shelter under half a roof, considering the decisions that Malou had
made. It was all going to be her design—she'd enjoyed making sketches—
and I wondered what she'd pictured for us.

If I lingered upon my anticipation, it wasn't because I really believed that something would be waiting for me on the beach. I could feel in my bones that nothing was there. But I wanted to remember what I'd been hoping all those months, I wanted to review those pictures that I'd carried in my mind, the way I might remember the words of a song I wouldn't be singing anymore, "Auld Lang Syne," on the eve of a new year I wouldn't be around to see the end of.

So: nothing. The old burned-out house had been cleared away. The makings of a new home, the cement blocks, the piles of lumber, the metal roofing that I'd seen piled there, the day before we left to Brunei, those had also vanished. There was nothing to show that I had ever lived there. Or ever would. I stood there for a while—not long—and headed back up the path. And then, at the very place where he'd stopped me once before, on a moonlit night, at the very beginning of the magic, the old man was waiting for me. Santos: I was glad I remembered his name. He'd kept his promise to watch over my house, he said. Day and night, he'd stayed there, sleeping on—or under—the same plastic sheet that covered the lumber. But the workers stopped coming. No one told him why. Then the landowner said that the woman Malou had never come to pay the agreed price. And, one day, some people came, more than he could talk to, and the pieces of my house disappeared, up and down the beach. Here, he said, handing me a piece of paper that was wet and much folded, like an old treasure map, the names of the people who took and a list of things that they had taken. So I could get back what was mine. I nodded and thanked him and said that what was lost was lost and I didn't think I'd be living there anymore, but wherever I went I would never find a neighbor as good as he had been. I made a mistake then. I reached for my wallet. He shook his head and slipped off the trail, back into the muddy field, and walked away.

"Santos!" I called out after him, hating myself for offering money. At the end of it all, I made a beginner's—a dumb tourist's—mistake. He stopped and turned toward me. "Thank you. Thank you." He waved and disappeared into the rain, which was harder now. I couldn't see if the Elvis scarecrows were still standing in the gardens.

•   •   •

I dried off and changed clothes at Billy's place, in an upstairs room that
some girls once used as a crib: a bed, a crucifix, a bucket of water, austere
as a monastery cell. I spent three days there, trying to get a line on Malou
and the others. I asked jeepney drivers, guards, street kids, regular customers, departing military I saw on the street. At nights, I cruised the bars
that were holding on, all the way from Olongapo to Subic City. I found a few
of the girls working in other clubs and they told me about others, who'd
gone back to the provinces. But no one knew about the gang at the jukebox.
They'd left early, before Graceland burned, they'd left together and that was
all anybody knew.

I tried Baby Ronquillo. If they'd gone overseas, as I suspected, chances
were that Shipshape had placed them. She'd promised to take care of Graceland girls and maybe she'd kept her word. I called Manila and got nowhere.
"Who may I say is calling?" "What is this in reference to?" And—rudest of
all—"I'll see if she's in," followed by the response that she was in a meeting, or out of town, or overseas. Could someone else help me? No one could.
Job placements were privileged information. And so forth. I called Baby
Ronquillo's home and got past the maid. A man came on the line. He didn't
identify himself but I recognized his voice.

"Where'd they go, Jimmy?" I asked. "Malou and the others?"

"Somewhere across the sea," he sang. "I guess. Who the hell knows?"

"Do you?"

"Give it up, Biggest Elvis."

"Just point me in the right direction. I'll take it from there. And I'll never
bother you again."

"The right direction? Where would that be? Hong Kong and Tokyo and
Taipei are north. Singapore is south. Kuala Lumpur is west, Kuwait and
Saudi Arabia and Europe, east and west, depends which way you travel.
The world being round and all."

"Where'd they go? Please?"

"Anywhere there's a squealing baby or a drooling grandparent, a pile of dirty dishes or laundry, a runny nose or a stiff cock."

Before long, my search felt foolish. It felt foolish when people recognized me, Biggest Elvis out of costume, out of work, another big American lumbering around the sidewalks of Olongapo. I didn't like the looks I got, even from the Graceland girls I found working in dirt-floored dives, serving warm beer with ice cubes. So, their looks seemed to say, you're still here. You want anything? Want me? One morning—my last in Olongapo—I took an inch of sideburn off my face. After that, people weren't so sure about me. Even Father Domingo Alcala had trouble recognizing me.

"I thought of you the day the Senate voted down the treaty," he said. I'd come late in the afternoon, waiting on his porch when he came back from his walk. He recognized me by my voice. Then he grabbed my hands, held them, said he'd missed me. He gave me dinner, brought out cognac. "I talked to you, Biggest Elvis. What I'd worked for had come to pass. All those years of speaking and marching and letter writing. But I pictured you. We talked. I said to you, *See, my people tell you that money isn't everything.* And you laughed back at me and said, *That's only because we didn't offer enough of it.* You were there. And you were there the night that Graceland burned. I was there, watching your . . . your temple . . . turn to smoke. And I thought, well, that's two victories in one day. Next to me on the sidewalk are some Graceland girls and they were crossing themselves and weeping. And you were there."

"Well," I said. "It's over now. . . . Just for the record, Father . . . who burned Graceland?"

"The same man who burned your house," he said nonchalantly. As though he'd been reading sports pages and I'd asked him the score. I couldn't tell whether he was admitting to two crimes or to none.

"Who is that man?"

"The American who works with Baby Ronquillo. The Rat. You know him, I think."

"You're sure?"

"This is what I hear," he answered. "This American is taken with Malou. Crazy about her, as you say. Crazy, also, without her."

"Where are they?" I asked. "Any ideas? All my friends?"

"Christina, too. God knows."

We talked for hours. There were big plans for Subic, Father Domingo said. Tax-free manufacturing zones, duty-free shops, tourist hotels, international airport, the Philippines competing with Singapore and Hong Kong. He had his doubts. When it came time for me to go, he walked me out to the main road. Already barrooms had turned into pool halls and grocery stores. Some were people's homes. Like that, Subic City had gone from being the nastiest place on earth to just another Philippines town. Remarkable, how quickly the place had changed, as if the difference between good and evil were no more than the clothes that you put on, and took off, depending on the situation. The Americans were gone now. But if they came back—I had to wonder—how long would it take Subic to become what it had been? And, if it happened, if those great gray ships returned to port, would the people here chase chickens out of the cribs, rewire the jukeboxes, restock the coolers?

"It's quiet here now," Father Domingo said. "A man can sleep."

I climbed into a jeepney named ROMPIN RAMBO. This was the start of the route, so I sat up front next to the driver and waited while other people crammed in back.

"I'm sorry to see you go," he said.

"Well ... anyway ... whatever you call what happened to us ... you won."

He seemed surprised at that. Then he shrugged, like a student who'd been called upon in a class he was having trouble with. It was as though he were asking what I meant, conceding victory to him.

"The winner is the one who remains in possession of the battlefield when the contest is done," I said. "That's the definition, no?"

He heard me out. Then he checked out the field he'd been left in possession of, which he'd be seeing for the rest of his life and which I was seeing for the last time. A wide spot on the highway, a jeepney pickup zone, people hacking and coughing as they sardined themselves on board. Night falling on a village that was all his, boarded windows and small shops where jukeboxes once had blossomed, when the fleet was in.

"Another definition," he said. "The winner is the one who moves on. The loser stays. Where are you going?" Father Domingo asked. It felt as though he wanted to go with me, wherever I went.

"I don't know," I said. "I'm like a Filipino after all. Spin the globe, I might be anywhere."

Part Four

But that was in another country and besides, the wench is dead.

Marlowe,
The Jew of Malta

Ward Wiggins

Sunday is the slaves' day off. It starts happening in the late morning on both sides of the harbor, Hong Kong and Kowloon, two or three Filipinas parking on the sidewalk, two or three more on pedestrian overpasses near the Star Ferry terminals. Through the afternoon, they keep coming, more every minute, so that if you watch it for a while, it's like a time-lapse sequence in a film about our crowded planet. A dozen Filipinas become a hundred, a thousand, dozens of thousands, a Woodstock, a refugee camp, a revival meeting. They meet and multiply as the sun mellows over the harbor, as office buildings catch the last of daylight, Victoria Peak mansions gilded with gold, and down below, almost as if they've come out of some underground world, the overseas workers converge and claim the empty heart of the city.

They crowd together—safety in numbers—sitting on sidewalks and on roped-off streets. The parks are closed to them; so are the fountain patios in front of skyscrapers. Roped in, roped off, the Filipinas keep on coming. You hear their voices from blocks away. It happens every Sunday, both sides of the harbor, in Hong Kong and a dozen other cities, from Jeddah to Singapore. They are tolerated, not welcomed. They come to work in places that need them, where they do not belong.

How could I not be among them, every Sunday, when I would leave piles of uncorrected papers, walking from my studio apartment near the Victoria Peak tram station, taking my walk before supper, when the city cooled off, down to Hong Kong Central, to see the Filipinas sitting on a street lined with closed boutiques—Armani, Salvatore Ferragamo, Wedgwood—lining up to place overseas phone calls, sending money home from mobile bank offices? How could I not be among them, eating, gossiping, just sitting around and staying off the grass? One afternoon wasn't too much to gamble with, one hour wasn't too much to walk and hope and wonder about Malou, all the days and miles that had come between us.

I'd gone back to the States from Olongapo, back to New Jersey, where I'd stayed with my sister, married and the mother of two, who lived in the same town I'd grown up in. New Jersey's curiosity was limited. There was no question they asked I could not have answered after one week in the Philippines, questions about food and weather. That covered it. There was no way Biggest Elvis could get a college teaching job. My transcript was old, my recent employment unimpressive. I had to come down the ladder a step or two, to high schools and prep schools. I called placement services, I read ads, and a month after arriving in New Jersey I left it, for a foreign school in Oman.

In a game of spin-the-globe, it was an odd place for a finger to land. I had a comfortable, sterile apartment to which I added not one trace of myself. In the community of overseas educators—adventurers, misfits, missionary types, ex–Peace Corps volunteers, bedraggled trailing spouses—I was another character. For my birthday, my colleagues gave me picture frames, encouraging me to decorate. When I left Oman four months later, the frames stayed behind, with the same pictures they'd been bought with: bright, smiling women, winning children, dogs, sailboats, flowers.

I was funny in other ways, as well. Oman is where Biggest Elvis melted away. I started my walking at the edges of the day, before sunrise, after sunset. Then I ran. Sometimes—madly—I ran in the middle of the day. That gross, gorgeous oversupply of flesh, that I-don't-give-a-damn excess that dripped from my cheeks and pressed against my belt, disappeared. Why, I sometimes wondered, do we picture romantic, self-destructive types as lean and haunted? Show me the fat man, and I'll show you someone tempting fate.

Spin the globe. I had an affair with a fellow teacher whose contract had outlived her marriage. Fortunately, her contract ended before mine. There was truer love in Subic City in back of the Blow Hole Bar than there'd been between us. I didn't sing anymore, not even at parties. Spin the globe. Endings are for movies and mortuaries. Stories don't end. Love and friendship don't end, or curiosity and wonder. I was almost as far from Olongapo as it was possible to go. Look here, look there—at the quality of light, the color of the land, the feel of the air, you wouldn't think you were on the same planet. The nights in Olongapo were heavy, liquid, sexy things, all sweat and perfume. The sun set but the heat lingered past midnight and the air never changed. In the desert, the temperature dropped fifty degrees, the air was clean and clear and, if you drove out of town, the stars were there for you. Your thoughts traveled high and far. All the way, in my case, to Olongapo.

Spin the globe. Whatever I found, I didn't find an ending. Half a world away, there were plenty reminders. There were Filipinos everywhere. You couldn't fly around the Middle East and not see them at airports. I'd noticed them flying home at the end of contracts, carrying cardboard boxes with stereos, electric guitars, cans of sausage, chocolate-covered macadamia nuts, four-foot teddy bears. And somewhere—taped to their stomachs, sewn into their clothing—there'd be wads of $100 bills which their relatives peeled off, one at a time, in a matter of weeks. I'd spot them on the return, too, back to their "three-d" jobs—dirty, difficult, degrading—smiling all the way, surging toward customs and immigration. Where the lines were slow. The whole world knew they couldn't be trusted. Was there a race held in less regard? They faked passports, forged contracts, changed names, traveled in disguise, under pseudonyms. The newspapers were full of it. At an athletic meet, a Philippines team marched in, marched off, melted away. In Hong Kong and Singapore they manufactured slugs to cheat the telephone companies. In Malaysia they jumped from contract to contract. On departing for Saipan, they swallowed bags of marijuana and crack, landing with drugs in their bowels. They were all over the world, my old friends. They could be anywhere.

Day in, day out, you were as likely to be talking to a Filipino as to an Omani. The Philippines were home to an army of mercenaries who fought not to win but to survive, and every airport, every immigration booth was their beachhead. They did what was necessary to go wherever they could. Their uniform was a Snoopy T-shirt, blue jeans, and running shoes, their packs were cardboard and Naugahyde, their specialty was whatever they could get someone to pay them for.

And I was one of them. Granted, I carried that coveted passport. The country they dreamed of, I called home. I worked for better money, got assigned an apartment in a compound, not a cot in a barracks. My place had walls around it, theirs had barbed wire. Still, we were working in the same market, we had the same bosses, we were out there taking chances in the world. And on Sundays, at dusk, in parts of Muscat, I went out and walked among them. Slaves' day off.

I cut an odd figure. They'd be sitting around by the dozens, bantering in a language I had never learned, so that they sounded like birds, crowded into the branches of a single tree. They'd be eating, reading letters, passing around months-old newspapers and magazines, singing. They'd look up at me as I passed, look cautiously, because foreign predators passed among them, foreign males looking for women to buy. I smiled and nodded and kept moving.

No endings in life, no real closure. Things die down, not out. Pictures came to mind, sounds that were echoes. Biggest Elvis, exiled and much reduced in size, remembering Graceland. On Magsaysay Street, I'd found a place that I'd needed and—I would always believe—had needed me, where ships sailed in and women came down to meet them. Now that they'd vanished into the Philippines diaspora, I saw that there was something special about the women of Graceland. They'd lived in a rough town, practiced a degrading trade. They put themselves on the line and when it was over, they didn't go home. They wouldn't. They moved on and out, joining millions of other Filipinos overseas. I wondered what the odds were against my ever finding them again, Malou or one of the others who'd gathered around the jukebox. Or maybe just someone who had seen me onstage. The odds were bad, I thought, on any given Sunday. But it seemed unreasonable, statistically unreasonable, that my long shot would not come home. Also, though fairness didn't come into it, it seemed unfair—outrageous—that I should never see, or at least hear about, Malou again. I couldn't accept that. I found myself saying her name sometimes, just saying it to myself. Malou. An oath, a curse, a song, Malou. Wondering how you are, Malou, and wishing you were here.

There were nibbles. Once, when I was visiting Riyadh, out on a Sunday, a Filipino walked over and asked me if I'd ever been to Olongapo. When I said yes, he nodded and walked away, before I could follow up. Maybe he'd settled a bet. And once in Dubai, passing a construction site near the airport, the frame of a building swarming with Filipinos, I heard someone singing "Are You Lonesome Tonight" just as I walked by. I stopped dead. The singer stopped too. The digging, banging, hammering, riveting kept up but the singing stopped. Someone had recognized me. I scanned the place, looking at one worker after another, but no one waved and nodded. I resumed walking and the singer started up again, only now there were a couple of them, joining in on "Suspicious Minds." I stopped, they stopped. I moved on, they sang again. They were singing till I passed out of earshot.

After the school term ended in Oman, I accepted a similar job in Hong Kong. I missed the Pacific. If an ocean can be your home, the Pacific was mine. Oman had been comfortable and they'd have been happy if I stayed. There were schools in Rome and Munich, also. But I missed the noise and the neon and the smell of cooked pork mingling with diesel, the crowded sidewalks, and the . . . action. So I went to Hong Kong and the Filipinos were there ahead of me, more than one hundred thousand of them. So my Sunday walks continued.

Do not think of me as altogether melancholy, stepping among people who came from a place where I'd been a kind of king, living off memories, looking for lost love. It wasn't quite like that. Say what you will about Filipinos or repeat what everybody else says: that they are hapless but tenacious, undisciplined but persistent, "too stupid to be useful, too smart to be helpful." But, more than any other people I knew, they were of good cheer. They sang in their chains. (No wonder the people who hired them thought so little of them.) The thousands of maids who sat on streets and sidewalks around Statue Square ate and laughed, held hands, smiled, sang. I felt good, wandering among them, even if the lightning I was hoping for didn't strike. And then, one afternoon, after I'd been in Hong Kong for three months, it did.

I'd looped around the square, crossed the pedestrian overpass, gone across the harbor to Star Ferry, walked the promenade in front of the Cultural Center, had tea in the lobby of the Peninsula Hotel. Then I crossed the harbor again and was on my way home—feeling better, always feeling better, than when I started out. But I paused near where a group of Filipinas stood in a circle, singing hymns. There was nothing pious about it. It was more like a pep rally for Jesus, one maid with a megaphone shouting verses, dozens of others following, some of them getting into these dancing, sexy little moves that would have worked fine in Olongapo, but now they were going out to the Almighty.

I can feel him in my head!
I can feel him in my heart!
I can feel him all over me!

I watched them for a while, noticing how they put themselves into it, pointing to head, pointing to heart, then hugging themselves, to show Jesus' all-over love. Out of nowhere, I wondered about Father Domingo. I remembered how irritated he'd been when I asked him what was the difference between saying God was love and love was God. Now I realized we weren't enemies. We were allies. We were the ones who tried to make sense of life, who traded in meanings and endings, who raised our voices in prayer and song. From thinking about him I got to thinking about the others, all the ones I'd been missing and looking for, in my way. Maybe it was lost love. Maybe it was unfinished business. But it stayed with me.

Filipinos look alike. They resemble each other more than most people do. The hair, for instance, is always black and almost always straight and fine. Their skin is usually light, though not white, their bodies short and slight, their eyes always brown so that what marked one from another are the nuancey things, a matter of nose and cheekbone, a small turn of figure.

So a Sunday never passed that I did not see someone, sometimes several someones, who might be Malou. Or Whitney. Or—more rarely—Elvira. Or any of the others.

I can feel him in my head!
I can feel him in my heart!
I can feel him all over me!

They cheered and applauded when they were done and—with Jesus still offstage but one song closer to returning—they started another. I sensed that someone was standing behind me, what's more, had been standing there for a while, and then I heard a voice I recognized. And a name.

"Biggest Elvis?"

"Dolly?"

It was awkward. She couldn't resist approaching me but, when it turned out her guess was right, she regretted it. She was with a guy, an Australian named Geoffrey Gilchrist. She said he was her husband. It sounded made-up. He gave her something between a smirk and a smile before he nodded to me and glanced at his watch.

"We worked together in the Philippines," Dolly explained. "In Manila."

"That so?" He wasn't interested.

"He was my boss in Manila." She gave me a hard look, to make sure I caught the message. Olongapo was our secret.

"It's more like she was my boss," I replied.

"She's a natural boss, all right," Gilchrist said, dropping an arm around her shoulder. "Honey, we're late."

When I heard that, I decided to take my shot. I didn't have long and if I postponed—if I asked for a phone number, made an appointment—I knew she wouldn't be there. This was it, and this was all.

"Dolly . . . after I left . . . where did you go?"

"Biggest Elvis . . . " she floundered.

"Biggest Elvis?" the Australian asked. "What are you, buddy? A porn film star?"

"Just an English teacher," I said. Dolly nodded her head gratefully. "And I used to sing a little on the side."

"Oh." Now he'd lost interest completely. "Doll? We've got to go."

"Where did you go?"

"America," she said. "That's what they told us."

"Where?"

She shook her head again and again, not wanting to tell me because she knew if she told me, I'd go. Or maybe she just didn't want to remember.

"I left and ran way. The others are still there."

"And Malou?"

"Don't go, Biggest Elvis. You wouldn't like what you see."

"Where, Dolly?"

"All right." She leaned forward, though I saw no need to whisper, but she was still afraid. And then she gave me the name of a place I recognized, the piece of America that the girls of Graceland had gone to. The following day, I bought my ticket to America. Back to Guam.

Guam. "Where America's Day Begins." The slogan of the island. The beginning of my story. And the ending. The green rugged hills below the plane, rutted red clay roads leaning to tin-roofed boondock farms. Coastal highways looping around coves with nests of hotels. Land, lagoon, reef, and the deep sea where Colonel Peter Parker had gone. As soon as I arrived, I rented a car, found a hotel, and went looking for the other two thirds of the Elvis show. Peter Parker's name was still in the phone book. The new owner—Chinese, from the sound of his voice—gave me the name of the realtor who'd handled the sale and he told me where to go, to a boatyard in Apra Harbor.

I couldn't help smiling, walking out toward the moorings, looking for a boat named *Graceland II*. That would be Chester's doing, all right. I liked the idea of seeing him again, of surprising him. Though I was his senior— and his boss—I'd fallen for him like everyone else. Chester was living on the *Graceland II*, the realtor had said, taking fishermen out after marlin or escorting tourists up to some uninhabited islands north of Saipan. He was doing well, the realtor told me: he'd hooked up with some of the hotels. Now, standing there, I heard hammering inside what looked like a yacht to me, and guessed that somewhere inside, Chester was at home.

"Yo, Baby Elvis," I shouted. "Come on out here, cherry boy!" I liked reunions. When the past comes back at you, when you hear your name in a crowd of strangers, we say what a coincidence or small world but what we feel and don't say is that maybe our lives make sense, there's a script around somewhere, with a pattern. And an ending.

"Biggest Elvis!" He came flying over the side the way he used to hurtle onstage at Graceland. Paint on his T-shirt, oil on his jeans, sawdust in his hair, he threw himself into my arms and just held on, bouncing up and down, like we were heroes of a game we'd played.

"Where have you been?" he finally asked.

"I've been away. Oman."

"Oh, man is right. Where?"

"Chester!" a voice sounded from behind. "You should invite Biggest Elvis on board." And then it was my turn to see that if you go around surprising people, you get surprised yourself. Christina was standing there.

"Welcome aboard, Biggest Elvis."

"Not so big anymore," Chester said. "God, we've talked about you."

"We've got some catching up to do," I said. Then I looked at Christina, a shade darker than I remembered. She was smart, not just in the head, but smart all over, the way a ship is smart. Or a captain. "I'm glad you made it here."

"Made it?" Chester asked. "She was here waiting for me. She came to Uncle Pete's funeral. We buried him off the boat. The way he wanted. Out there. What he called the deep end of the pool."

"He called me," she said. "Only two weeks before he died. Sent a ticket. Wanted to see me."

"She came, she saw, she conquered, just like in Shakespeare," Chester announced. "Papers, contract. Local sponsor. Which she don't need anymore, of course, now that she's got me."

I looked from him to her. I was slow, I guess. I wasn't expecting so much happiness, so fast.

"Funerals aren't the only ceremonies we've had aboard the *Grace-land II*," Christina said.

"We missed you that day," Chester said.

At dusk, they took me out of Apra Harbor, around the north side of the island, Chester at the controls, Christina cooking down below. Chester was surprised I hadn't heard about Dude. Dude had made it, by God, in Hollywood. He was in a series called *Intruders*, not a starring role but enough of a continuing part to get him on the cover of *TV Guide* with some other people, even if his head was where the mailing label usually landed. He played a rock star's bodyguard and—this was wild, Chester said—he did Presley bits on the side, all the time. Later, Chester showed me a tape which had Dude come crashing through a window into a room of crack manufacturers, drawing a gun, and asking them, "Are You Lonesome Tonight?"

"He calls all the time," Chester said. He glanced in at the shore. "He's due in this week. Local boy makes good. He'll want to see you. He's always asking about you. What I think, he's sorry about the grief he used to give you."

"You tell him we're fine . . . even. And give him my best."

"He says he owes you." Then he peered in at the coastline, looked left and right. "This is where we dropped Uncle Pete off at," he said. "We got married in the same location. I figure he wanted what was best for us. I'm not sure how it worked out for you. Dude's been wondering too. He asks about you all the time. We stepped into an inheritance. And you hit the road."

"It had to end sometime, Chestnut," I said. "Nothing lasts."

"Our thing didn't end, though," Chester said. "It just kind of got stopped. You know?"

"Yeah," I said. "Sometimes I feel a little cheated. But not by you." And now I gazed north, into gathering darkness, at what might have been a light on an island, or a ship at sea. It hadn't been easy looking for people who might be anywhere. But I was closing in.

"I miss it," Chester said. "Those nights. I hear it was a bad place and it had to go. I hear it from Christina. She must be right. And what did I ever know?" He hesitated, thinking over what he said and, maybe, what he was going to say. Chester looked comfortable at sea. I'd cross the Pacific with him, no problem. Till we hit signs and traffic at the mouth of the harbor. "Here's what I know," he said. "We didn't open up that base and we didn't shut it down. We went there and we lit it up. The three Elvises. And I'll be damned if I'll ever forget."

Christina brought chicken adobo, rice, from down below. Beer for me, coffee for Chester. "She's making it happen," Chester said. "She does the bookkeeping. She links up with hotels. And now we're talking to these other groups. Eco-tourism. There's islands up north of Saipan. Some empty, others got a family or two. Some of them are volcanic. I don't mean that's how they were formed. I mean, that's what's happening right now. They're cooking, Ward, they're boiling over and it's something to see. Uncle Pete got a couple fifty-year leases up there, all of one island and a chunk of a couple others. That'll give us something to do, for a long time. You ever need a place, you come too."

"You could live on the beach," Christina said from below. "A black sand beach at the end of the world."

"I tried that once," I said.

"Try again," Christina said.

I was halfway down the dock, headed to my car, when Christina came running after me.

"I almost forgot this," she said, handing me an envelope addressed to Chester Lane, attention: Biggest Elvis. The handwriting had the ornate, naive style I'd seen on letters that Olongapo women sent to the States, to AWOL lovers and absent fathers, trying their luck in a lottery with no mercy. "It came months ago," she said. "We advertise sometimes in the newspaper. Our address is there."

"Thanks. . . ." American stamps. No return address. Cancellation indistinct.

The bulge of the envelope told me the letter was long, probably written over a period of days and weeks. I'd seen that before too. Writing kept the girls busy, in the heat of the day or the early part of the evening, waiting for the customers to come. These women had a lot of time on their hands.

"I saw her," Christina said.

"Saw?"

"Your Malou." Those two words paralyzed me. I could walk through crowds of maids forever. I could look everywhere, what the lawyers call "diligent search." I could ask old friends, go back to familiar places. On my own terms. It's one thing to send signals into space, time after time. It's another to hear back.

"At the airport," Christina continued. "I picked up a party of visitors we are taking to the northern islands. I was waiting outside but I can see into the transit lounge. She was there. . . ."

"And . . ."

"It was Malou, sitting there. Quiet. Maybe she was sleeping. She wears what she always wears. The jeans, the T-shirt. The hair is under a baseball hat. She sits alone. No one is with her. That I can see."

"Going where?"

"In transit," she answered, a little abashed by my intensity. "I'm sorry, Biggest Elvis. I thought maybe I should not tell you. You would have so many questions."

"You didn't see where . . ."

"My party came," she said. "And the flights from Guam go in every direction. I'm sorry."

"I didn't mean to . . . snap." I patted the envelope. "This might help."

"Dude comes from Los Angeles the day after tomorrow. We will go out on the boat. You can talk. You can sing. An Elvis reunion."

"Could be," I said. "Could be I'll have something to sing about."

Whitney Matoc

DEAR BIGGEST ELVIS.

I do not know if you will ever be receiving this but maybe sometime you are wondering what did ever become of your old friend from P.I. This is Whitney. The thin girl. "The worst lay in Olongapo." SMILE. Now you remember me? Always bothering you for book to read. I'm having so much to tell you and about where we are going and what has happen to us. Even if this letter never get to you, I have to say. Best part of my day is when I write to you. Or night. I'm feeling better even if you never are reading this.

Graceland goes bad after you are gone. We are having local band dressed up as outsider, as Beatle and Rolling Stone. Battle of Band, they call it. But, Biggest Elvis, is same band. Those guy are only changing their cloths in back. A junk act, Dolly says. So businesses goes away. Many girls leave and nobody is caring. We are not Graceland anymore. We have twenty girl and some of these girl do anything. Biggest Elvis, they don't even go to V.I.P. lounge anymore, they go right under table for b.j. and nobody say, not here, upstair, please.

We sit around jukebox at night, and we hope things get better if our three Elvis come home. We are wondering if you bring, balikbayan boxes for us. You know what is balikbayan box? Big box of gift overseas worker bring home from Saudi, toys and stereo and duty free thing. I'm only hope you are coming soon. With many paperback books, I hope.

Biggest Elvis, I'm standing on the sidewalk the night that Graceland burn. I'm cry. Father Domingo from Subic City, he is there. What for, you cry, he say. I do not answer but I cry for us because I know you are not coming back, you three guys, and I'm not seeing you nevermore. When you are here, I grow, I learn something, I read and talk more and I am not just the worst lay but I am also Graceland girl. Customer pay other girl to do monkey business. With me, sometime they pay to have picture taken, only sitting at table. They use some other girl for mickey mouse.

Baby Ronquillo come to us next day after fire. She does not have to do anything, she say, no obligate, but as special favor to our group she will arrange overseas contract, good job in U.S. Commonwealth. "UNDER AMERICAN FLAG," she says. What kind of job? Waitress, hostess, cultural dancer kind of thing, she say, in brand new restaurant that is very classy place, very classy customer. Not like Olongapo. Plus we have American citizen for boss. "We go with customers?" Dolly is asking. No, no, waitress and hostess and cultural dancer, you seat people, you serve food, you sell drink, you dance, you talk sweet talk. After that, Baby say, is up to you. For Ms. Malou she offer another kind of contract: bookkeeper at construction company, building golf course and vacation home.

We talk all night, after that. Elvira does not want to go. But she has big problem. The Sheik—you are remember that guy?—is going to be Brunei ambassador someplace. So no more part-time local wife in Olongapo. No more shopping trips. Priscilla wants to go. Nothing for us here, she say. Dolly is needing money for her children. She will leave the children with her mother in provinces. Life is cheap in provinces but is not free. Dolly will go. Everybody is almost agree. Then we hear someone laughing at us. It is Lucy Number Three. You remember Lucy Number Three? So many night, she take my customer, thank you, she say. And I say thank you, Lucy Number Three. Lucy Number Three is very quiet. You remember her t-shirt? LESS TALK—MORE ACTION. Very tight t-shirt. I'm thinking you remember.

"Cultural dancer? This is what they tell us for our contracts. This is what they tell us, so we can tell ourselves. Cultural dancer. Pretend name. It's okay for me. I am ready. But I'm not fooling myself about cultural dancer. My eyes, they are open."

Now everybody is afraid and feeling bad. We worry, what Lucy Number Three say is true. Newspaper is always telling bad things happening to Filipinas overseas. Sex slave, women in cage. Deported, pregnant, with Arab baby. Now maybe this is happen to us. Maybe better we stay in P.I. This is what we are thinking, until Ms. Malou speak.

"My eyes are open," Ms. Malou says. "I will go. And I go alone, if it comes to that. But I will tell you what I think and then you decide. If you do not come, I will go alone." Oh, Biggest Elvis, she speak soft but she is strong and everybody listen. "We spend all our lives waiting for someone to rescue us. Every time the fleet sails in, everytime the door to Graceland opens, everytime someone gives a smile or a tip or talks to us in a nice way, we are full of hope, we are asking is this my chance? Is this special? Is this someone for me? We spend our lives like this. Always waiting. Waiting in doorway, at table, at bar. Waiting while we are on our backs. Or knees. Will he come back? Will he ask for me? Will he even know me? Or remember my name? Now I tell you I'm finished with waiting. I don't want a man to rescue me. I'm going to America. Not the real America, but the beginning of it. The beginning of America. It is an island. We know islands. It is Catholic also. Our color skin, our kind of hair. Our weather. But they are American citizens. I'm going."

Biggest Elvis, now Malou walks over to Lucy Number Three. "You are right, maybe, about cultural dancers. What they write for isn't what they want. But what they want isn't what they get. That's the game. That's the way." Then Malou looks at all of us. "We are women. Some of us, first we use the body, then we use the brain. Others, first the brain, then the body. That's the way . . ."

Malou is our leader. She is so calm and strong. In the next day, she help with arrangement. We take loans from Baby Ronquillo to pay for tickets and processing and placement fee. Very expensive. It scares me, I am owing 50,000 pesos before I start. Maybe I will be rich girl later! But now, so poor! And I worry. I still see Lucy Number Three laughing about cultural dancer.

Also—excuse me—I wonder about Malou. Why is she the one who convince us to go? All the rest of us, we have got nothing. We are nothing. Bad girl, nasty girl from Olongapo. But Malou is bookkeeper and manager, not hostess. And also, she has you.

We are silly when we leave. We make joke. Filipinas going to America, laugh all the way. And it does not take so long. Three hours only and we are in Guam airport. Still plenty joke. We try perfume in Duty Free shop, all kind from France, and scarves and handbag, watches and jewelry. Elvira spend Sheik money to celebrate. Is only traveler checks, she says. I do not buy. Biggest Elvis, my contract with Darling Enterprise pay $300 per month and I am going to spend nothing until I pay my loan to Baby Ronquillo. Almost five month, that will take.

Next flight is very short. I sit at window I can see the island soon. Biggest Elvis, it is so small, ocean all around. I am thinking I will see resort hotel on beach, tall building with plenty tourist, like in VCR tape of Elvis concert from Hawaii. I am remembering swimming pool and garden and waterfall and fountain and flower everywhere. But we land at airport in boonies, Biggest Elvis, and a woman named Darling is coming there to meet us.

Mrs. Darling is fat now and she don't care. She wear tight white slack and t-shirt. She don't care but I think she was sexy girl once. Now, maybe sexy still, but not so pretty. Not needing to be pretty, because now she is boss. She has husband named Gregorio who come over a minute while we are waiting for our baggages and he is like the wife. Handsome once but now also he don't care.

"He looks pregnant," Dolly says in our language. He wear his belt very low, leave room for his belly which go out in front of him, like it is looking for food and beer and the rest of him comes along too. Gregorio use his belly like Elvira is using her titties, at Graceland. The sun is hot and the road is dusty on this island and the people watch us pass. They do not smile or wave. They only look. Another shipment from the P.I. Another delivery. And now we are scared. So small a place.

Our boss, Mrs. Darling, is nice at the start. She smile plenty. She likes the looks of us, I think, especially Elvira and Lucy Number Three, and me.

Priscilla and Dolly she is not so sure. Is asking how old they are. Malou is riding up in front of truck. We are in back. "Mind first, then body," Lucy Number Three says, when she sees Malou in front. Lucy Number Three is strong. Elvira is crying in back of truck. Elvira likes taxis and limos.

"This is not good," she says. "This is mistake. I don't like how they look at us."

"Let them look all they want," says Lucy Number Three. "You are cultural dancer."

Mrs. Darling stops truck outside construction site, with buildings and equipments inside fence, for building new golf course for Japanese. Wire fence runs all around and inside are buildings with plenty Filipinos, cooking and washing, sleep and play chess because it is Sunday afternoon. A guard sit by the gate, also sleeping.

"They keep us like prisoner," Elvira say.

"It is a work place," Priscilla says. "They have tools and supplies inside. Need to keep people out. Same as in P.I."

"Keeping us in."

"Same as in the Philippines," says Lucy Number Three. She is waving to the men inside. Malou will live across the street from labor camp in house with Filipina nurse and schoolteacher. House is new but wood was never painted. I'm feeling a little bit sorry for Malou but only for a while. I tell you exactly how long, Biggest Elvis. Ten minute. The time it take to drive to Darling Resort and Disco Club. It is just like inside construction site. The ground is dirt and puddle, the main building is in front and in back is long narrow building, sit on cement blocks, wooden sidewalk along the front and five rooms, with a door and a window. The building is pink. And a fence is all around. The place is like barracks. No woman ever sleeps in this place before me, I can tell. Only some Filipino guys. A picture of Jesus is on the wall of my room and the picture is moving, a piece of electric wire goes back and forth and when I walk over the whole picture move because the wire is tail of a rat who jump on floor and run out door. Jesus picture covers a hole in wall. I walk outside, shaking. I look at dirty yard and fence where guard is sitting. I walk in back where ocean is. Beach is rough, all sharp stone. The waves come in, big and noisy and the island give them punch in stomach, says stay away from here. So we have fence on three side and ocean on four. The ocean is fence too.

Mrs. Darling is still nice. Tell us to make ourself comfortable and rest from long trip. Later that night, after we eat, we should come over to club for meeting. Sign outside club says watch for grand opening, SEXY DYNA-MITE DANCERS FROM MANILA. Lucy smiles. No talk about cultural dancer. Inside the club is puddle on floor and small stage with poles up and down and smell from toilet and paint can on the bar. Inside is Darling and Gregorio sitting at table.

This is new business, she say, and we are partners and team. If they are making money, we are making money and everybody is happy. If we are lazy girl, then no money. Up to us. Some good Filipinos on this island, some not so good. Our big opening is one week and we have so much to do before then. Clean and paint and polish and make everything extra nice. I look at Elvira when I see that we are supposed to do janitor work. Elvira look at floor. Dolly speaks.

You say what you want from us and you say we work together, Dolly says. Mrs. Darling nods. Husband don't say anything. He just look at us, one after another. Biggest Elvis, you know how customer look on slow night when he choose a girl and we pretend we don't notice? Gregorio look at me in that Olongapo way.

I'm needing some things from you, Mrs. Darling, Dolly says. I need screen in my window, for keeping mosquito out. And new mattress also. Cock-roaches in my mattress now and it sits on floor, no springs, no bed. And no water in toilet or sink, only oil barrel with plastic bucket in corner. I'm need-ing sheet and towels and I'm wondering where is dressing room in night club. Also, I'm wanting my passport back, Mrs. Darling. You take at airport to help with immigration, thank you very much, but we like to have our pass-port back.

Biggest Elvis, from this minute, Dolly is finish. She is finish before she start. It is taking one month before she go but after she speak, so brave, they know Dolly is troublemaker. She is bad girl. Now, Darling and Gregorio

speak in their own language, back and forth. When Darling speak she is not
so nice no more. We invite you to our island, she say. We pay your recruit
fee. We pay your ticket. We meet at airport, give you food. We do this with
our own money. This is how you are thanking us, my husband and me, before we begin? We are good friendly people. Ask anybody. Friendly island.
But we bring you here for work, not play. We don't want to hear all the time
complaint. You work, we work. We don't want no bad, lazy girl here. We
work together, make your room nice. The more money, the nicer we make it.
We fix bar together. For start bedroom is dressing room. Or make change in
toilet.

The passport, Dolly ask. You get when you need, Darling say. I keep in
safe place, no worry. How come, first day you arrive, not lifting one finger
yet, you ask for passport?

Later we go have talk in Elvira's room. No better than my room but, like
in old days, we go to Elvira's place. Elvira saying we should complain about
our room and this nightclub. Lucy Number Three say complain to who?
About what? Cockroaches? No running water? Dolly says no. We complain
about our passport. Too early to complain, I say. Wait until club has grand
opening, maybe better then. If not, we call Baby Ronquillo and she will
help us.

I say this and everybody is quiet. What did I say? Dolly and Priscilla
look at each other, Elvira and Lucy Number Three.

"Whitney," Priscilla say. "You borrow money like the rest of us from
Baby Ronquillo, no? What for, please?"

"For placement fee. And airplane ticket. Like all of us."

"Yes. Like all of us. And like all of us you hear Mrs. Darling tonight. She
talks. You listen? And hear . . . what?"

"We work hard. We not complain. We make money when business
is good."

"Yes?"

"We open one week, grand open and—"

"We hear that, Whitney. Anything else?"

"And she pay plenty money for . . . oh . . ." Now I see that Baby Ronquillo is not our friend and not Mrs. Darling's friend and Mrs. Darling is not our friend. Baby Ronquillo collects twice for tickets and fee. And Mrs. Darling will make us pay double.

"I'm sorry. Sometime, I'm feeling stupid."

"On your good days?" Priscilla asks. Then I'm crying, Biggest Elvis, and she is hugging me. And I'm thinking it does not matter so much about our passport because we have no place to go. I almost say it and decide no. Maybe they will laugh at me again.

We decide, no complain yet. We will wait until we have something to complain about. And, during the next week, we are work hard every day. We never leave that place. We are not permit to leave except on Sunday and Sunday we arrived so we spend whole entire week like busy beaver. We scrub bar, bathroom and sink, we shampoo and vacuum carpet, we polish stage, we wax bars and windex windows and wipe glasses. And we are wondering where do customers come from? This is hard question. Sometimes whole hour go by, all we see is few pick up truck go down road, Filipino worker in back.

Then, opening night. We truly work hard to make a success. But still we wonder, where our customer come from. Filipino boy works with us—bartenders they are—tell us we need to work hard because plenty competition. Maybe four more places down the road. Some of those places have pool table, some have karaoke. We do not. We have girls. "SEXY DYNAMITE DANCERS FROM MANILA" So do other place. What do we have that is different, Priscilla ask.

"Room in back," he says. He is talking about MY room. We take customer to our room. Short walk, short time, plenty money. Other place, girl go into car. Or to beach. Or hotel room. For us, only short walk from club to rooms. Now, Biggest Elvis, I feel sick. But when the night come we are all dress up at six o'clock but very few customer, one table only, local guys, drinking beer, not noticing us, except Gregorio, the husband. He is not dressed for opening.

We Graceland girls are at table, sitting together, very quiet. Now, I don't care about work hard, make lots of money. I'm wishing no one come, all night long. At seven o'clock a band comes, local, and begin to play cha cha music. Mrs. Darling arrive, eight o'clock and by then we have two full tables, then four, more cars and trucks coming outside, headlights across the wall, every time that happen, my heart sinks. Full house. Local people. Golf people. Some Japanese and real Americans also.

"Why you sit here?" Mrs. Darling say. "Is time for work!" Three of us should sit with customer, she say. She point to Dolly and Priscilla and me. We should sell drink to customer. They buy drink for you. You go with them. Why do I need to explain to you, you girls, you are from Subic, you are not from convent. Time to be making money. And you two—Elvira and Lucy Number Three, you dance. Who you want, I dance with, Elvira asks. On stage, Mrs. Darling says.

So this is what happen to us, Biggest Elvis. I sit at table. I ask permission first. I sit there and they do not talk to me. They tell me to get beer. They talk in their own language and put arm around my shoulder and touch me. Come sit on lap, come give me a taste. And while this is happen I see Elvira and Lucy on stage, in purple light. Lucy Number Three, no problem. She has dance before. Lucy Number Three has so much experiences! But not Elvira. She never perform in public. She is champagne lady, not beer. And this is beer place. Beer on floor, beer on table, beer smell in air, beer trail from table to toilet.

People love Lucy Number Three. She move up and down around the pole. She slide, she curl, she wrap herself, she pretend all kind of thing, make people laugh, make people horny. And Elvira, she does not do anything, she only stand there, moving back and forth to the music, sway a little bit this way and that, trying to copy Lucy Number Three but not good. And then Lucy Number Three laugh at Elvira and start taking off her clothes. Elvira, she runs off stage, out back door. Mrs. Darling go out after her. I leave table and go back door. I can hear Mrs. Darling shouting at Elvira. You undress, she say, you go all the way. I'm not bring you to stand and pose. She shout for two or three minute. Elvira says nothing. She goes back on stage and people cheer very loud. They are thinking that this is part of act, Elvira is pretending to be shy kind of cherry girl, that she only pretend not wanting to do this. This is turn on for them, Elvira has great body, you remember, but she take clothes off, she fold and put in pile one by one, it is like she is in doctor office, waiting for exam and it hurt me to see this, how she just standing there while these people in dirty t-shirt and jeans and rubber sandal cheer.

Later I dance, with Dolly and Priscilla and I must go naked too. I'm so happy you are not there to see this. And then we go with men. Now I'm worst lay here. We are take out girl. We are fucking machines. Even me. The customer pay $100 and take us to our own room. We close curtain and do monkey business and open curtain and someone is already there, waiting for next. I hate. They treat us like animal here, animal in cage, cage inside fence, island another cage because no passport. No place is my own. No place to hide. Also, no money. Darling keep all money. She keep track of money. She cut our monthly wage. She gives us $150, not $300, and piece of paper to sign. She says paper is receipt. Dolly reads. This is no receipt, she says. This says we accept lower wage, is okay with us. So we take money but do not sign. Mrs. Darling says Dolly is troublemaker.

For next Sunday, we make plan. I will walk to Malou's house to talk to her about what can we do. Malou is smart. They don't keep Malou in cage. She will help. Dolly goes to police, to local government. We walk everywhere, we look a little crazy, Dolly and me, all along road. Cars and trucks pass by, blow horns, throw garbages, shout at us. They like to see us in nightclub or in bedroom. They do not like us in the open, in public place. Sometimes they offer ride but that only mean they are drunk and wanting to take us into boondocks for monkey business. We can hear beer can rolling in back. We see these drunk red eyes, that way they talk about us, the way they move, after drinking, reaching for zipper, cannot decide whether to piss or screw, they are getting some message but they cannot read it and, piss or screw, it is all the same to them, go to bathroom or come to us.

When I go to Malou, no one is home. "It doesn't matter," Priscilla says when I come back. "She won't do anything." She is our friend, I tell them.

She was with us at Graceland. "She kept count of what we made," Priscilla says. "That is all." Then Dolly comes back. She tells us the police laugh at her. She goes to mayor house. The wife will not let her inside. She goes to house of labor official. Come back Monday.

Next Saturday night, place is busy. Many people from Guam and Saipan. This island is place to go for fun. Save money on ticket to Manila. And Darling Bar is most popular place, just like at market, when fresh shipment of fish comes in, everybody is running over to see what is there. Mrs. Darling complain during the week but on weekend she make money. She is always wanting more money. Never enough. She decided to have what she is calling raffle. Everybody pay $20 only and winner gets a girl. Lucy Number Three is prize number one, Elvira number two, Dolly number three.

Biggest Elvis, this night is bad. Some people say what we do is bad, no matter what or where or how or why. But at Graceland we come in the afternoon and we leave at close, unless we stay behind and talk with you. If customer is taking us out, he talk to us. After he pays bar fine, he pays us. And when monkey business is over, we are in our own place, not in some cage like animal. Sometimes customer is nice. He makes friend with us. He take us to restaurant or maybe we have breakfast. And you maybe remember, in back of bar, wall is covered with postcard from all over, Navy guys saying hello baby, how are you, wish you were here, really. All bullshit, we say. And we laugh. Those crazy guys! But we smile too. Here, no smiles. Never ever.

Dolly comes over to me while we are dancing together on stage. "Tomorrow night I will not be here," she says. I ask what she does mean. She don't say. Then we are all on stage and Mrs. Darling make Lucy, Elvira, and Dolly stand up front. Biggest Elvis, she makes them be naked. She tried to sound like beauty contest, announces third prize, second prize, first. "Number One, Lucy In the Sky With Diamonds." And winner is old drunk man. Loud cheer from his table, people asking is old man able to handle Lucy and old man—he should be home with his grandchildrens—he say no, no, he like to try. "Number Two Elegant Elvira, What You See Is What You Get." A big short guy—he look like sumo wrestler—blows Elvira kiss. "Number Three prize, a Night In The Dolly House." And somebody laughs and I do not see what Dolly is doing. She bend down, look away from audience and, before I know what she is doing, before anybody know, she shit on stage.

Darling scream and run toward her, also Gregorio, but not fast enough because Dolly turn around and pick those dirts up and it hit Gregorio and it go out into audience and Dolly don't say anything, she just laugh and show her hand to the audience and run finger over her hair and over body. This is Dolly, always so smiling and funny. "The leader of the pack." Now she is like this, Biggest Elvis, and it hurts me to see. Mrs. Darling and Gregorio drag her out back, tell band start playing, free drink, but we can still hear Dolly laughing like crazy girl. People don't like. They leave. Even winners, not staying for prize.

We are still in club, closing, when a car comes in the gate and these guys take Dolly away. Biggest Elvis, I don't know what happen next. That was the last I see of Dolly, maybe ever. Cloud of dust and headlight going away down road. I don't know. One of our Filipino boy talk about "the midnight special." I ask what is this, maybe they kill her in the boondocks. Who would know? You hear talk, all the time, bad things happen. He says midnight special is flight from Guam to Manila. People who make trouble, they put on flight: deported. Sometime, they stop on the way to the airport. Have party. Maybe this happens to Dolly. Maybe that is why she rub her dirts in her hair: to keep the men away.

After Dolly goes our life is the same. Week nights, nothing happen. A few young boys and old men. Local. Sometime, Mrs. Darling and her husband send for me to their house. They want massage, both of them. Why me, I ask. I am not so strong. Because you are lazy girl, nobody miss you if you leave bar, they say. Last week I go to house and Gregorio is alone and he is wanting . . . you know what he is wanting. Not only because I am woman or Filipina or bar girl but because I am Whitney and he has his eye on me from first day at airport.

So, Biggest Elvis, this is story of the girls at Graceland. Maybe I'm not doing favor, writing you this letter, making you feel bad. This is not what you want for us, I am sure. Not what we want, when we go to "AMERICA."

But I'm thinking you are only person in the world, caring what is happen to us. One time, you know, I finally find Ms. Malou. She is so smart, I ask what should we do. She tell me we come so far already, we need to work hard and keep hope and save money. And maybe the right man come walking through door. But I do not believe this. She does not believe what she tells me, I think. I do not believe. The door has open many many many so many time and men come through but, Biggest Elvis, it is never the right one. Goodbye. Always remembering you and Graceland.

Whitney

Ward Wiggins

Spin the globe again, not even a spin, just a nudge. I kept staring at the island out the plane window, not letting it slip away when I wasn't looking. The colors got brighter, the lines grew sharper, details of coast and cliff.

What you had to remember about islands in this part of the Pacific was the depth of the sea they came out of, four or five miles down. So they were all mountains, survivors, tough guys. They came off the floor of the ocean like uppercuts, thrown in anger from way down below, from dark buried places under endless pressure, the whole weight of the ocean bearing down. Up they came, propelled by God knows what, up toward the lightening of the water, the breaking surface, daylight, the Northern Marianas. That wasn't the end of it, though. No sandy lagoons and lazy atolls here, these islands broke water and kept going, punching up into the clouds, forcing rain, as if they were making heaven cry, evening some ancient score.

Closer now. A coastal road came into view, curving along a shoreline that was lava and coral, dark and sharp-edged. Waves crashed against rock, water pounded into underground caves, geysering upward out of blowholes. There were cars on the road. Inland, uphill, I saw steep hillsides, rough-looking cliffs, and, at the center of the island, green uplands, almost like meadows, with plowed fields and smoke coming off of brush fires.

In the late seventies, the Northern Marianas—that was all of the islands north of Guam—had voted to become a United States Commonwealth. Before then, they'd been part of a United Nations Trusteeship. Then the trusteeship split up. You had the Republic of the Marshall Islands, the Federated States of Micronesia, the Republic of Palau, all still tied to the United States, depending on Washington for aid, but at least with the appearance of sovereignty. The United States offered—and the Northern Marianas accepted—a different kind of deal. Outright U.S. citizenship. Permanent. Washington wanted military options, access to bases on Tinian and Saipan. It was cold-war thinking; a fall-back perimeter, if we got moved out of Japan and the Philippines. The Marianas wanted in. So a little America was born, halfway around the world. Born and boomed. Location was everything. Japanese hotels sprang up on Saipan. Garment factories sewed made-in-USA labels on shirts and sweaters assembled by Chinese and Filipina women on Saipan. Real estate went crazy. Everybody was in the business, joint-venturing, leasing, agenting, commissioning. The money poured in and, as usual, the Filipinos followed the money, first to Saipan, then to the other islands.

Coming off the plane, I inserted myself in a party of sport fishermen, Guamanians and Statesiders. I chatted them up while we passed through customs and immigration. We talked about marlin while we waited for our baggage. They were a jovial, weekending crew, out for a good time. They talked golfing and fishing and hinted about nightclubs "where they go the whole nine yards." Fish by day, philander by night. It was all the same, except at night they didn't throw the small ones back.

The airport people gave us priority. Filipinos to the back of the line. Filipinos took checking—papers, passport, contracts. That was a lesson I'd learned in other places. Never get in line behind a bunch of Filipinos, or you'd be waiting for hours. They were still there when I followed the fishermen into a hotel van parked outside of the airport terminal. My pals were raring to get started. I sat among them. The air here was hot and green. They said the island was like Guam and Saipan used to be, and Hawaii, once upon a time, see it now, my friend, get it while it's good, before the Japanese take it over and price it out of reach, golf condos and sashimi, they've got plans for this place, megabucks, and the locals will be nigger-rich before you know it. I listened and laughed. The bullshit was comforting. Then I glanced out the window, toward the terminal, and what I saw scared me.

Jimmy Fiddler. Jimmy the Rat, the man of Malou's nightmares, and mine, was leaning against the door of a red pickup truck while a group of Filipino Oversees Contract Workers climbed in back. Wrinkled khaki pants, rubber sandals, aloha shirt. Cigarette in one hand, Styrofoam coffee in the other, saying something like snap it up, come on, let's move it. When they were all aboard he moved to the front of the pickup and talked through a rolled-down window to someone who was sitting inside. I might be wrong, I thought. Whitney's letter made me jumpy. But it seemed to me he looked my way, nodding toward the van where I was sitting, shaking his head as if to say, guess what came walking off the plane?

Something was wrong at the hotel. I noticed it as soon as we arrived, something they were trying to cover, the way stewardesses patter to passengers when a plane that's in trouble turns back to the airport. It took twenty minutes for me to check in and—though I didn't have any luggage—some of my buddies waited another twenty minutes before their gear got to their rooms. Leaves floated in the swimming pool. On patio tables, cats foraged off plates of sashimi that had been left out the night before.

I asked the waitress what was happing, when she brought a lunch menu. A Filipina. She seemed nervous. "Problems," she said, taking off. Most of the staff were from the Philippines and what was happening looked like what you might expect would happen if most of the slaves got sick. No disaster, no dead stoppage, just a slow fraying around the edges, cosmetic details going first, more serious things later. Decay, from the outside in. Not many people were around. And the ones who were all seemed to be doing someone else's job. That was odd, because if you ran a place with Filipinos, you ran it with lots of Filipinos, two of them for every job. "Cheap and worth it." Even back in the PI, overstaffing was chronic, provision of employment being the whole point: standing around and looking busy. Here, no one was standing around. And the people who were working were under strain. "Some kind of strike," one of my buddies said. "Skeleton crew. Buffet dinner tonight. Apologies all around."

Sure, no problem, a rental car was available, but I'd have to pick it up myself. So, that afternoon, after the worst heat had passed, I walked into the village to a gas station where I rented a Nissan that had chicken bones in the backseat. The manager, a local, looked like he was filling out his first rental agreement.

"Bad people is the problem," he told me. "They come here and complain and they lie. They should thank us. They are lucky to be here."

"Is it about money?" I asked.

"It is about Filipinos," he said. "You know those people?" I shook my head. "Let me tell you about Filipinos. A Filipino is a problem. The more you hire, the more you need. You solve one problem, you make two. They get sick at home and homesick when they are here. They don't belong. Was better here before they come."

"Okay. If they go, who washes your rental car?"

He tossed the keys on the counter. "Tank is full going out, full coming back."

I drove slowly through the village, weaving in and out of side roads, around the church and hospital. On islands, you drive cars the way you wear clothes. They identify you. Park your car outside a bar, the island knows that you're drinking. Leave it on a beach, they know you're fishing. Drive a rental car, you announce that you're a tourist. They watch you pass, they know you'll pass again, what goes around comes around on an island. They'll see the car again. They won't see you.

I was watching for the red pickup truck I'd seen in the airport. I didn't know what I'd do when I found it. Park outside? Wait for Jimmy? Look for Malou? Park down the road, sit inside until dark, and then what? Creep up to windows? Whitney's letter was four months old. I wondered what would be left of Malou and the others. It might be too late for Biggest Elvis to the rescue. Too little and too late. The ending I'd missed might not be ahead of me. It might be in the back someplace, on an unmarked night or day that I'd passed through, not knowing.

Jimmy the Rat and Malou. Could it be? I'd been wrong about him, I guessed. I'd written him off as a hot-weather mutant, a local character, a misfit who couldn't make it in his own country and set himself up someplace else, never at the heart of things, always working the edges, like a scavenger bird along the waterline, feeding on what the tide washed in. A truly marginal guy, a con man who mostly conned himself, believing that wherever he went was the inside track. He wouldn't get past the airport in Singapore, Hong Kong, or Japan, but the Philippines was perfect, for a career minor leaguer.

That was right, as far as it went. But I'd missed a lot. The way he focused on Malou. I guessed we had that in common and it made me uncomfortable. He'd fallen for her too. He'd cared enough to burn the house we slept in. And—if I had it right—he had followed her here, faster than I had followed her. Maybe he'd induced Baby Ronquillo to send him, so he could look after business, and have Malou as well. Maybe he hated her that much. Or wanted her that badly.

I drove for hours, I looped and circled through the afternoon, through a gaudy Marianas sunset, a full hour from orange and gold to deep, final purple. But I didn't see the truck. And I didn't want to ask. If he knew that I was looking for him, he'd come looking for me. Then, when darkness fell and stars came out and color TV screens bloomed in houses along the road, I saw the Darling Bar, right along the beach. I saw the fence, the main building, the long low structure in back, everything that Whitney had described. A car and truck were parked in front, the place was open. I saw the banner, tattered now, SEXY DYNAMITE DANCERS FROM MANILA. So this was what it all had come to.

One table of drinkers sat inside and they looked like they'd been there for a while. They stopped talking when I walked in, gave me a good looking-over, resumed talking when I sat at a bar and ordered a beer from a Filipino who'd been working one of those newspaper puzzles, how many words can you make out of these letters. You're supposed to finish in twenty minutes. He was making a night of it.

The stage where Elvira and Lucy Number Three and Dolly had stood naked was empty now, cardboard boxes piled high. They were three beautiful women, I remembered, and they must have been something to see. I hated to think of them standing there like that. I hated knowing that this was what it had come to. At Graceland, the sex had happened offstage, after hours. It happened before I got there, it would have happened anyway, whether or not I was there. That's what I had told myself. I was taking things as they were. And I made them better, I honestly did, for a while. Now it had all turned bad. Or—I had to ask myself—had it been that way, that bad, all along?

There's nothing deader than a dead bar. I ordered another beer and sensed a ripple of curiosity behind me. Two beers in a place like this didn't make sense. It was like sitting in someone's empty cellar and calling it a night on the town. I walked over to the men's room door. It was locked. Quarantined, maybe. I could smell fermenting piss through the door. The last man to leave hadn't flushed.

"Sir," the Filipino said. "Outside." I stepped out back. Just one light was on in the building. I thought of walking over for a look but the drinkers were watching me. I went around the corner, pissed, and returned. One of the local guys was waiting at the bar.

"Over from Guam?" he asked.

"R and R," I said. I gave him my name, first name, and he gave me his: Gregorio. He wasn't unfriendly, he wasn't evil. He was beery, fat, and wasted. "I heard this was the place to go. If I wanted a takeout girl."

"All finished." Like a bakery that had run out of bread. "New bunch coming soon. Next week, maybe."

"That's good for you," I said. "What about tonight? Are there any other places around?"

"This is bad time," he confided. "The Filipinos make trouble. What you call strike."

"Takeout girls on strike? Are you kidding me?"

"Stupid," he said. "Not only girls. Construction, farmer, waiter, fishing. Complain about everything. Contract. Mistreat. Bullshit. They are so lucky to be here."

"Where are they all?"

"In construction compound. Nineteenth Hole Corporation. Out by airport."

It was the one part of the island I hadn't driven to that afternoon. And the first time, when I'd arrived, I hadn't noticed much, other than the Rat. A sense of fences, sheds, heavy equipment. Talk in the van about golf and megabucks. Heat and dust and spilled oil and laundry flapping in the wind.

"They went yesterday. Take over inside. Lock gate," Gregorio said. "I think, we lock gate for good. And throw key. Police are there."

"Well, shit," I said. I didn't want to take him any further. "High and dry on Saturday night."

He nodded. My tough luck. I could see him preparing to change it, though, when he looked toward the building in back, the motel, the barracks, the coop.

"We got one girl, still," he said.

"Bottom of the barrel?"

"No, no, she is very beautiful. Only little bit . . ." He searched for the right word. "Used." At least, that's what I thought he said. He invited me to take a look and decide for myself. The takeout charge was $100 only, payable to him. In advance. Then I walked across the yard, climbed unpainted wooden steps, knocked on the door.

"Coming soon, sir." I heard her straightening up inside, the way kids clean up when parents knock. Then the door opened. She was wearing white shorts and blouse. Eyes downcast. I was a figure in the doorway and it didn't matter about the expression on my face. She had great legs, I noticed, to my shame. I guess I'd never seen her in shorts, back in Olongapo. Then I saw her face. She'd been used, all right. Maybe the word that Gregorio had mumbled wasn't *used*. Maybe it was *abused*. Or *bruised*. Whitney had a sunset of a shiner, all around her left eye.

                             ⁕   ⁕   ⁕

"Come in, sir, if you wish." I stepped inside and she closed the door behind me. Then she moved over to the window and closed the curtain: lavatory occupied, room in use, fall in line, first come, first served; first served, first come. I approached her from behind while she was still at the window. I put my hands on her shoulders. I could feel her flinch, a reflex she couldn't disguise, involuntary protest at whatever was coming. Then I turned her toward me, put a hand under her chin, slowly raised her face. Her eyes were closed, the swollen one and the other, the good one, that reminded me of how she'd looked, back at Graceland. "Open your eyes," I said. "Whitney, it's . . ." I couldn't make myself say the name. It stuck in my throat. Biggest Elvis: a couple words to choke on. She looked up, half-expecting another in a line of frauds, like this mini-America she'd landed on. She wouldn't finish the sentence for me until she was sure.

"Biggest Elvis?"

"Yes . . . used to be. Got your letter."

After that, she was in my arms, close. I guessed she didn't want me to see her face. She held tight and there was no way of knowing how long she'd have kept on holding me like that. She had a lot of crying in her. It took a shout from outside to interrupt us.

"Hey buddy," Gregorio shouted. "Sale or no sale?"

I stepped outside, down the steps to where he was waiting for me. Even then, I guessed that if we drank together or went fishing, I could like Gregorio. Gregorio wasn't evil. He was a fat, beery, bullying small-time guy who'd become American without knowing what it meant and gotten rich before he knew how to handle it. His fat, happy time would be short. Once that golf course got going he'd be on the sidelines, complaining how big outside money had ruined his island.

"Somebody treated her rough," I said. "That eye of hers . . ."

"So?" he asked. His buddies were outside, standing around a pickup truck. "You going to fuck her or paint her picture?"

That was the moment in the movie where Elvis slugs the guy. I'd always wondered what it was like to hit a deserving, unsuspecting fat man as hard as I could. But I reached for my wallet and handed over a $100 bill.

"I'm taking her out of here."

"Sure, no problem," he said. "Drop her off when you finish." A horn sounded outside. "You're missing the real action. That girl, she's nothing."

"What's that?"

"Out at the labor camp. We're going to take our island back."

"You said police were there."

"Local police, I said." He winked at me. "No problem. They work for us."

As soon as I got back to the room, I saw that Whitney's bruised eye was just the beginning of her hurt. Some other things might never heal. The other Graceland girls were tougher or shrewder. Whitney had been miscast in Olongapo but the others had protected her. Here, it was like throwing a ramp model into a mud wrestling pit. While I'd been talking to Gregorio, Whitney had pulled a cardboard box from under her bed. She'd spread out a pile of paperbacks on top, like the squares of a quilt she'd been working on. The books were used, some with missing covers, the kind of random assortment that people leave behind in hotels: *The Eiger Sanction*, *The Way West*, *A Bridge Too Far*, *Dead Cert*, *The Final Days*, a dozen others.

"Biggest Elvis, I read them all," Whitney reported to me. "Some of them I read more than one time."

"That's good," I said. Right then, when she'd pulled herself together, I fell apart. Deep inside, I started weeping for us. For all the books I hadn't brought. For all the letters that the girls wrote, to guys who went away and never answered. For all the time she'd been in pain, while I'd been gone.

"You test me," she said. "You ask me anything, Biggest Elvis. I know all the story."

I turned away and covered my face. Behind me, she continued.

"This one," she said. "*Bridge of San Luis Rey*. It is happening long time ago in Peru. There is old bridge across very deep canyon in the mountain. One day, they have accident. Bridge breaks and some people die. Accident, no? But we learn the life of those people and we see, maybe this bad accident make sense."

"We're leaving here now, Whitney," I said. "I'm taking you out."

"Okay."

"Is there anything you want to take? You won't be coming back."

"My clothings," she said. "And can I take my books?"

Before we went to the hotel, I wanted to drive out to the airport, to the construction site the Filipinos had taken over. It looked nasty out there. There were pickup trucks along the road, some police cars and a fire engine, red and blue lights flashing, and dozens of people looking into the fenced compound where maids and waitresses and hostesses, domestics and farmworkers had gone, turning the place into a fort and interrupting construction of a Japanese-financed golf course–vacation home community that was supposed to be the equal of anything in Hawaii. We kept our distance but the locals were drinking. Some of them had guns. So far, the cops had kept them out of the compound. But they were local cops.

"The other girls go," Whitney said quietly. "I'm afraid. I do not want to be hurt some more. And someone will be hurt here, I am thinking."

I agreed. The Filipinos had locked the gate and blocked the entrance with graders and forklifts. Smudge pots and scrapwood fires burned around the inside of the fence and there were lights inside. They had a generator.

"How many are in there?" I asked. Surely not all, I thought. There'd always be some who backed off. It would be wrong to assume they were all in on it. Every Filipino on the island wasn't mistreated. Some were all right, others were almost like family. Others took mistreatment for granted, part of what you put up with for the money you sent home. No matter how bad it got, they would keep coming. Keep trying. Keep making the same mistake. They knew it. Everybody knew it.

"Maybe half," Whitney said. As we drove away, I saw more cars and trucks coming up the road. And somewhere between the airport and the hotel, I decided what I was going to do. Or try to do. A plan formed while we drove through the night, Whitney sitting next to me as if we'd been on the road forever, quiet and relaxed, on an interstate that went on forever, miles and exits precisely marked. Maybe I'd been right when I guessed she'd been damaged for life. But now I wondered if I might not be in for a surprise.

"How old are you, Whitney?"

"Nineteen," she said. "Teenager still. Just a kid, no?"

"Yes."

"And you, Biggest Elvis? How old, you are?"

"More than forty." I heard her laugh. "What's so funny?"

"Double, my age."

We came into the village, which seemed emptier than before, though it was only eight o'clock. The action was going to be at the airport in the wee hours, after they were drunk and before they fell asleep. There was no need even asking Whitney. Malou was inside the fence, I knew. She'd organized it. The generator, the fires, the forklifts behind the gate: that was Malou's kind of thinking. Calculated. Organized. "The result is what you see."

I marched Whitney up to the front desk, said this was my guest, she'd be staying here with me, they should give her a key to the room and anything else she wanted. The clerk was surprised at the fuss I was making, bringing a takeout girl up to my room, but he obliged.

As soon as we got to my room, Whitney disappeared in the bathroom. From the sound of it, she filled the tub all the way to the top. It would take more than a bath to wash off what had happened to her here. But it was a start. After a while, I heard her singing. "We Are the World." Taking all the parts, hitting some, missing others.

I was on the phone and for the first time in a while, I had some luck. I got through to Chester, who was out on the *Graceland II*, north of Guam, and Dude was with him, a TV celebrity, just in from LA. I told them to come, and soon. Something had to be done but it wasn't a solo act. I needed them here. When Whitney came out of the bathroom, a towel wrapped around her, I said I was going out to the construction site.

"Some friends of ours are in trouble," I said, "and if I'm there it might not happen." I did not mention Malou's name. Whitney already knew what Malou meant to me and it seemed cruel to remind her, after what she'd gone through. She was so relaxed and easy around me. I couldn't bring myself to ask about Malou. She seemed so happy but the chances were she'd be on her own again, alone. "If there's someone around who cares . . . an outsider . . . the worst things might not happen," I said.

"Okay," she said. But when I said she should stay here, rest, order from room service, maybe buy a pair of sunglasses at the gift shop, she shook her head. She didn't want me walking off, leaving her by herself. "I'm going with you," she said. She looked around and shuddered. "Not stay here."

"Are you sure?"

"I go with you," she said.

I parked at the airport, well away from the other cars and trucks. We walked toward the construction site, lit up like a carnival or county fair, where there might be fireworks later on. I could hear music, from a gaggle of ghetto blasters and car radios. Closer to the compound I saw that things had gotten worse. The police were still there and I saw a priest circulating through what looked like a collection of tailgate parties, but that didn't stop the crowd from cheering when someone dashed out, ran toward the fence, and lobbed a rock into the compound. The Filipinos didn't return fire. They stayed back from the fence, in buildings and in the shadows, though a couple of them were hunkered down right by the gate, inside a shed. When we got closer, Whitney put her hand in mine.

"You want to go back?" I asked. "Sit in the car at least?"

"No . . ." I realized there wasn't a place on this island where she'd feel safe alone, not the inside of a u-drive or the lobby of the police station or my hotel room. Every beach, every dirt road into the boondocks had bad memories.

"I come with you," she said. She hesitated, her voice got even quieter. "Maybe you need me."

I wondered what she meant by that, but by then we were among the cars and trucks, the beer cans and barbecue. At first no one paid much attention to us. They were concentrating on the compound. Waiting for the right moment. Working up to it. How often did this happen, I wondered, uneven contests in out-of-the-way places? Mismatches, unreported, no referees, no rules, no reporters, all the advantage on the side of the home team. I didn't kid myself that the people on the outside were villains and there was only virtue inside the fence. Or that, if the sides were reversed, if the Marianas Islanders were poor and away from home, if the Filipinos got suddenly rich, things would be any different. Still, I knew what side I was on tonight.

We stopped where the last row of cars pointed in toward the compound, headlights on. Now it felt like we were in a drive-in, waiting for the movie to start. Standing here, we were among spectators; in a few steps we'd be actors. Here, I was still the man who walked around Hong Kong Sunday afternoons. Whitney was the girl in the VIP lounge, looking at the action down below, the show just starting. But now I knew where I was headed. Biggest Elvis' last show. The Original had been booked into Portland, Maine, the first concert after he died. If it came to that, to dying, this was going to be better than Portland. Better than Graceland.

"Well," I said to Whitney.

"We go inside," she said.

Two hundred feet separated us from the gate, a red-clay field, rutted by heavy equipment, half-baked by heat. We were halfway there before the people behind us reacted.

"Sir," a cop called out, "you don't go in there." He didn't move to stop me, though. "Fuck you, man!" the owner of the Darling Bar called out. "Fuck her too!" Then someone said something in Chamorro—surely to the effect that Whitney had been amply fucked already—and they settled for laughing at us, heaving a few Budweisers our way. Garbage after garbage. What difference, one used hostess, more or less. If some dumb American allowed himself to be conned into escorting a takeout girl into the cage, so what? He'd paid in advance. Still, I hoped that my being there would worry them. The outside witness, the inconvenient American. Clueless. Hapless. Annoying.

The gate was chained and shut. Whitney said something in Tagalog and one of the guys behind the fence hustled off to the main building. When he came back, someone else was with him. She nodded at Whitney.

"Hello, Biggest Elvis," Elvira said, as if we were back at her apartment.

"Hi, Elvira. Are you in charge here?"

"I'm help. You want to see the big boss?"

"I think you know the answer."

"Okay," she said. She nodded and they unlocked the gate, opening just wide enough for Whitney to slip through. The people behind us expected that. What surprised them was that I followed. That brought another volley of rocks and bottles. They didn't want an American around. Pain in the ass. Nothing they threw hit us, but some rocks clanged off the roof of the construction shack where we were headed.

"We call her the commander," Elvira said. "Just like in the movies." We followed across a sidewalk of wooden planks, left over from when it rained. I saw Filipinos huddled next to tool sheds and trailers. "Biggest Elvis!" someone called, and I waved to Priscilla. Then she started explaining who I was to the others. Biggest Elvis again. It was as if I'd gained thirty pounds, as if my sideburns were growing, like the hair on a werewolf's hands, as if I were covered with sweat and sequins, with Dude and Chester offstage. Could I be blamed, then, when Elvira led me to the trailer and held open the door for me and when Whitney slipped her arm out of mine, as if to say that this was where she'd leave me—could I be blamed for thinking I'd step inside and see Malou running things?

"Biggest Elvis." She looked up from her desk. "They cut our telephone. I'm wonder what took them so long."

"Lucy Number Three," I said. And that was all I could say. She was the last one I expected to see in control. *Less talk—more action.* I was surprised she'd gone inside the fence at all. She was the gamest—and gamiest—of the Graceland girls. The others were forced into the business, or drifted in. But Lucy had been born for it. Or so I used to think.

"You are surprised, Biggest Elvis," she said.

"He's surprised," Elvira answered for me.

"He expects someone else," Whitney said with a look that was like nothing I'd seen from her before, a look that was pitying and knowing and—would you believe it, on Whitney's bruised child-beautiful face?—wise. "He expects Malou."

"Someone should tell him," Lucy Number Three said.

"Maybe," Elvira suggested, "he knows already."

They were watching me, the three of them, waiting to see if I could catch on, catch up. Or would one of them have to come back and get me? I'd gotten to know them well, all those nights at Graceland. I liked them and—what wasn't quite the same thing—I liked knowing them, their style, their quirks and humors. And maybe I'd congratulated myself on discovering they were likable and human, as if that discovery were to my credit as much as to theirs. But if I was watching them, they were watching me, night after night, watching me fall for Malou. They'd kept quiet about what they were thinking, from then till now.

"Okay," I said. "She worked for Baby Ronquillo back then. And now. She still works for her. Is that it?"

Lucy Number Three nodded. Whitney looked like she might break into tears, as if she were deep into a story with a sad ending, the tale of Biggest Elvis and Malou.

"So," I said, "she's on the other side of the fence more or less."

"She makes us borrow money for tickets," Elvira said. "Illegal. She collects recruitment fee. Illegal. Employer here is supposed to pay. Did pay. Reduction in salary, change in job, all illegal. Taking passport. We complain. Nothing happen. She work for them. She does not work for us. She works for Baby Ronquillo."

"She works," said Lucy Number Three, "for Malou."

I stepped over to the window, resting my head against the screen. When my marriage fell apart, I'd had months to sort it out. Long walks, hours in bed, books to read or music, and sometimes I stepped into a car and drove around Guam all night. I wasn't going to have that long, for Malou.

Malou. When I'd thought about her, it had been things I wanted to re-member. Now the other things came rolling in. From the first night—at the Scrabble board—when she'd said "I'm surprised you know that word"—to all those nights of talk and slow dancing and flaring argument—"Why me, when there are so many women from which to choose?"—to the day I'd stood on the empty beach where our house was supposed to be, what had happened had happened because of me, out of my longing, my need. Not hers. Not especially. She was the most skeptical—factual—numerical per-son I'd ever met. She'd never believed in the Elvis magic. Not really. The others crossed themselves when I sang "American Trilogy," when death and resurrection blew through Graceland, two shows a night. She kept counting. And when the show kept happening and Graceland prospered, it wasn't magic, only clever business. Down deep, Biggest Elvis was kind of a joke, just as Elvis—the Original—had been another joke. An interesting act, but was it the only one I had? Was that it? Was that all? And when the magic compounded, all around me—and who could miss it?—and when neighbors named children after me and farms filled with scarecrows in my image and bar girls crossed themselves and priests denounced me, when miracle followed miracle, she stayed cool. She nodded, she smiled, but she didn't believe. And I wanted her all the more, just because she didn't be-lieve. My skeptical, doubting Malou. I had some moments with her, some wins. There were times when I surprised her, or she surprised herself. That girlish yelp when the ice-cold water came out of my shower or, oh God, that night she stood at the window at Elvira's place, looking out at the street, slipping off that T-shirt and walking toward me with love on her mind. She lost it, once or twice with me. But now I could see how things must have looked, after I'd consented to that absurd tour, after Graceland burned and the base-closing was announced and our dream house was just a pile of boards on the beach. Was this where she wanted to be? She'd hooked up with the wrong Elvis. She should have gone for Dude, the way Dude used to be. Wipe ass and walk away. That was my guess anyway. So Malou had gone to America, this island version of it. She'd done what was necessary and she'd done it on her own, not waiting for a man to rescue her. "And the result is what you see."

Lucy Number Three was in it for the money. She didn't want to move to San Diego. She didn't want to make a better world. She never thought about falling in love. But she did want to get paid for the work that she did. She was the wrong woman to cross. When Darling started withholding pay, shorting her, taking the money up front, Lucy Number Three didn't think, didn't feel, didn't consult. She acted.

"Less talk—more action." They would take over the construction compound, the Nineteenth Hole Corporation, and stop work on the island's biggest project. The New Pebble Beach Golf Course had corporate investors—airlines and hotels, in Japan and the United States. It had deadlines to meet, budgets committed, opening tournaments scheduled. Once work stopped, important people would notice. When they came to investigate, they'd have Lucy Number Three and all the rest to reckon with. They didn't want the world, either. They wanted back pay and illegal payments refunded and passports back and tickets out.

It had to happen fast, if it happened at all. A week's advance notice, or a day's, was asking to be sold out. She talked to the men at the site, she stored water and rice, while a half dozen construction trucks drove around the island, collecting maids and farmers, bar girls, cooks, janitors. They'd all gone inside the gates, locking up behind them, before the locals knew what had happened. Then, from inside, they started with phone calls. That was Priscilla's job, and Elvira's, because their English was better.

They hadn't liked what they heard. The Japanese project manager on Saipan threatened them with criminal trespass, court proceedings, deportation. A Filipino consul reminded them they were guests on the island. A priest pleaded that they avoid violence. They felt lonelier than ever, after that. No one wanted to hear it, no one particularly cared. Overseas workers were plentiful, expendable, replaceable. They complained all the time—

that was common knowledge—and even if what they said was often true, it got old. Loser talk. What they'd accomplished so far was amazing. But now they didn't have anything else planned. Already a sense of defeat, of gallant effort about to be punished, hung in the air. Fatalism and martyrdom were just around the corner.

At ten o'clock we heard there were some people outside the gate who wanted to talk. Lucy Number Three asked if I wanted to accompany her. I nodded. Two other members of the party were Nonoy, who worked for Nineteenth Hole, and Felix, who'd been working on a farm. Nonoy had spent a year in Saudi. Felix was younger but he'd seen me in Olongapo, he said, "with her." And he nodded toward the ones who were waiting outside, standing by a police car screening us from the crowd, roof lights stroking us with beams of red and blue. Three people waited for us. A man I didn't know. And Jimmy Fiddler. And Malou.

Our eyes met. I nodded. She looked at me a moment, taking me in, and nodded back at me. That was all. Our reunion. And then, before I could say a word—and I'm not sure what it would have been—the third visitor took over, an island politician I half listened to while already replaying the fraction of time that had just passed: the red and blue light, like at an accident, Malou and I on different sides of a fence. She was heading where she wanted to go and I had landed where I was meant to be. Olongapo had been a crossing of paths, an intersection, fun and fine while it lasted. But the act wouldn't travel. Another thing: I hadn't stopped loving her. And it didn't make any difference, now.

"We have hundreds of good Filipinos on this island," the politician was saying. "They say they are ashamed of what you do. This is a friendly island. You make trouble here. My people are good people and you provoke them. You come out now, I guarantee your safety. I personally guarantee. But if you stay . . ." Now he leaned forward, as if to confide. "I cannot control them."

"I can control my people," Lucy Number Three said. "You cannot control yours?"

"My people have guns. Also bombs they use for dynamiting fish. I'm just telling you."

"You have police, no?"

"A few. Very tired. . . ." The way he looked at her, I sensed a note of personal appeal. "You used to be such a fun girl, Lucy."

"I have complaints."

"No one made you come here."

"We want settlement."

"If you have a problem, you should talk to Shipshape representative." He nodded at Malou. "She comes here with you. She is a liaison officer."

"No," Lucy said. She stared straight at Malou. "With this woman, I do not talk."

"You have proof of your complaints?" Malou asked. Calm, nonplussed, the way I remembered. "Or only talk?"

"Maybe, we have proof."

"What sort of proof?"

"I'm waiting for the boss, Malou. Not you."

"I'm getting so tired of this," the politician said. "Watch me now." He stretched theatrically. He yawned and yawned again, turning around as he did so, so the world could testify how he'd tried, in vain, to settle things. He raised his hands, he shrugged. "Pretty soon I go home, Lucy."

"Straight home?" she asked back. "Or stopping off?"

The man muttered something under his breath and walked away. Malou followed. No lingering behind for a chat. We'd had our moment. Lucy and the two Filipino guys left for the inside of the compound. Oddly, Jimmy Fiddler stayed behind.

"Saw you at the airport," he said. "I said to myself, there's a guy who doesn't know where show business ends and real life begins."

"I'm figuring it out. In real life, the bad guy gets the girl."

"You still don't have it right, Biggest Elvis," he said. "I could make a career out of watching you get things wrong."

"But only if the arson business slows down."

"Oh yeah," he said. "Sorry about that. The nightclub was business. Your house was different. What I did for love. I didn't like the idea of you two together. I'm a sore loser. So? Sue me. Where are your buddies, the Lane brothers?"

"Headed this way, Jimmy. Coming to entertain the troops."

"Here?" he asked. "I love it." He stood there for a moment, as if there were something else he wanted to say. In a few seconds more, he'd have come out with it. But a horn sounded inside the red pickup truck. Places to go, people to see. Jimmy rolled his eyes and limped away. Now I saw that he wasn't her boss—or lover. He was her gofer. And I felt a little sorry for him.

Whitney came over to me as soon as I entered the construction trailer.

"Too bad," she said, "about Malou."

During the next few hours, they watched us and we watched them. We watched the politician call it a night. He drove off and a dozen cars followed him. The genteel folk, I guessed, and just enough to fill out a hometown jury that could say it hadn't seen what was going to happen next. Rocks and beer cans started in again, music and horns blowing. Then, around midnight, island law enforcement called it an evening. They drove off to cheers, their sirens blaring, lights flashing, as if a crime wave had just broken out on the other side of the island. I hoped I was wrong but I guessed some of them would be back in half an hour, out of uniform.

We were losing people now. Lucy Number Three said there were four hundred of us to start with, inside a compound that was about the size of a football field. With all the sheds and trailers, the heavy equipment, piles of lumber, and culverts, there was cover for everyone. But then one of the men reported that a woman was climbing up the inside of the fence. We went to the window to look. The people outside applauded, honking their horns. She got up to the top, lifted herself over the fence, hung on for a moment, then dropped to the ground on the other side. The same thing was happening in back, but more quietly. Here, people rushed off into darkness.

"No surprise," Lucy Number Three said. Some of the guys asked if she wanted them to try to stop the fence-jumpers. She'd said no: let them go.

But space them out, every twenty minutes or so. The crowd liked watching them, liked laughing at them. As long as they kept coming, one deserter after another, there'd be no attack.

"What are you going to do?" I asked. "This can't go on."

"Stay here," Lucy Number Three replied.

"If they come through the fence, I mean. They have guns, some of them."

"So. We go out, we raise hand, we go back where we were. Only first, I think, they punish us. The women . . . you know what they do. The men, beat up and back to work. But the women . . ."

Now I saw that there was no plan. No secret tunnel, no cache of arms, no one coming to the rescue. They had put it together—the trucks fanning out around the island like so many schoolbuses, the locked gates, the calls for help. But that was it. And now it was going to end badly, sometime between now and dawn.

"Or maybe we fight little bit," Lucy Number Three said. "Some of us. We have knife. If we get close."

"People will die then," I said.

"Maybe," she said. She might have been talking about the chance of rain. We heard another cheer from outside as a couple more Filipinos went over the fence. Bit by bit, we were weakening. It didn't bother her. She saw that I was studying her, trying to figure her out. There was a lot I'd missed. She came over, led me to a corner of the trailer, near a table covered with blueprints, where no one else could hear us. "All the men I have," Lucy Number Three said, "I know that there is a time when I can hurt them. I'm strong girl. I only got to . . ."

She raised her fingers toward my eye, signaling a twist of hand that would leave me blind. Then she nodded at my crotch.

"Or anytime I want, with these naked guy, I just close my hand so tight and squeeze and nothing they can do . . . but scream . . . you know?"

She was so nonchalant about it. As if she were telling me how to pluck a chicken or bone a fish. Even when she flicked her tongue around her mouth and pursed her lips, a Graceland signal that left nothing to the imagination.

"So many times," she said, "I think, what if I close my mouth right now, till tooth touch tooth."

Now I knew that no matter who climbed over the fence, some of them would stay behind with Lucy Number Three.

"You want to go, you can," she said. "Over the fence. You take Whitney, it's okay."

"I want to take you all," I said. "I'll march out of here with you."

"I don't think so."

The bomb was a crude device, of the sort that became common in the islands after World War II, when unexploded shells littered the islands and people stripped off brass and copper fittings, extracted explosive, packed the powder into coffee cans, inserted fuses, and turned reef fishing into a can't-miss proposition. It went off noisily, right at midnight, right against the fence. It didn't do much damage, more noise and smoke than anything, but a couple dozen more of our people left, mostly domestics, rehearsing apologies and downcast smiles. "Sorry, mum," I could hear them saying to their employers. I could hear it already. "They tell us come to meeting for all our Filipino people. I don't know what is about. And when I am at that place they close gate and we cannot leave." That would be the tune. "Those nightclub girls are making trouble."

The crowd inside had thinned out but the construction guys weren't going anywhere and the takeout girls remained too, and a scattering of others, farmers mostly. There were fewer people outside too but that didn't make me feel any better. It meant that the squeamish on both sides had left, the way cornermen and seconds climb out of the ring before a boxing match starts. It wouldn't be long now. And, once it started, it wouldn't take long. A few shots, some scuffles, and, when the fighting ended, the fun would begin: a gamut for the men to run. As for the women: a night to remember, a gang bang, pull-the-train, and then it would all be over, a story that became a rumor. Words like *spontaneous* and *abortive* and *short-lived* would appear in the newspapers, if they covered it at all. Hotheads, outsiders, and troublemakers. A local problem, locally settled. No big thing. Island back to normal. Golf course on schedule.

Now there were more shots and they weren't shooting into the air anymore. A window shattered, a barrel of fuel oil started leaking out near the generator. The workers ran around the camp, killing lights. The whole compound was dark except for the headlights in the cars and trucks that were parked outside. They started moving. They drove off the road, into the burned-off field in back of us, so they formed a circle all around the camp. Then, at someone's command, they moved closer, as if pushing toward a starting line. They blew horns, all at once, like a herd of animals anxious to charge. And we prepared for them. Lucy and Felix, the worker who'd seen me in Olongapo, climbed onto a bulldozer, Elvira and Priscilla joined Nonoy on a grader, others jammed onto the tops of tractors and forklifts, into the backs of dump trucks.

Now it was all set up, a battle of cars and pickup trucks against bulldozers and graders, our heavy lumbering beasts against their Nissans and four-by-fours, not one battle but a dozen skirmishes which could end all over the island, on the road into town, or outside the church, or up and down the airport runway. Or at the end of the island, where there were cliffs. Oh, it was going to be something here tonight, before it was over. And the mood had changed. And everybody wanted it. That's what I could feel. They wanted it now.

"Biggest Elvis," Whitney said. She reached a hand out to me, as if I were helping her onto a dance floor, but she was gesturing to the top of a bulldozer and the other hand was holding a rake. "Please give me boost."

I reached out, not to help her up but to hold her back. "Listen, Whitney. Stay here. Stick close to me and you'll be all right. We'll get to the car."

"Not all right." Even Whitney wanted war.

"You're with me. They won't . . ." It sounded wrong, even before I said it. "They won't come after an American."

"Give me boost," she repeated.

I grasped her by the waist. I pulled her toward me. She came willingly. I held her there. "Don't do this. You can't win."

"You come too," she said. Whitney was feeling brave. I lifted her up on the bulldozer.

"What you are doing?" she asked, looking down on me.

"Watch me now," I said.

We were at the end of waiting. The moment had come. Peace was a drag and negotiations were a waste of time and peacemakers, far from being blessed, were a serious pain in everybody's ass. They were all ready for action. You could feel the hunger on both sides of the fence, the Filipinos mounted on heavy equipment, followed by foot soldiers with knives and hammers and two-by-fours with nails hammered in. I could see it in Lucy Number Three and Elvira, in Priscilla and even Whitney: Let's do it. Let's get it on. I could see it in the people outside, mounted in cars and pickups, drunk and reckless. No stopping it now. Fighting and fucking were two things that no one—not even Elvis—should get in the way of.

And yet. I found that little pocket of time before the engines roared, the whistle blew, that silence before the clash when the only question was who moved first, do they rush in, do we rush out, curtsey or bow? I walked to the front gate and signaled for the Filipino guards to open it, which they did. Then I gestured for them to close and lock it again, which they did not do. They ran off and climbed into some trucks.

So it had come to this. I stood there onstage alone—"emptiness all around"—and an audience watching. Both sides thought that, after opening the gate, I'd make another move. I might go back inside, hop onto a bulldozer and advance, like Hannibal, onto the Marianas plains. Or I might accept the hospitality of my fellow American citizens on the other side. That would disappoint some of the Filipinos but it wouldn't surprise them. It was what a lot of them would do, even now, if they thought it would work. Or I might just walk away. Or go back to the hotel. I was an outsider. I could be at the airport in the morning.

I stood there. There was nothing to do or say that would have any effect on what would happen. I stood there in the no-man's-land between two sides.

"Get out of there, man!" someone shouted from in front. There were other shouts, less polite. I was blocking traffic. "Get that piece of shit off the road." I was like a fan who steps out onto a football field, stopping play, before the stadium guards escort him out.

"You'll get hurt, my friend." This time the warning came from behind, softly. "You'd better go now."

I just stood there, not proudly. Not like I was stepping up toward the gallows—"It is a far, far better thing"—or in front of a firing squad. More like some hapless schmuck, forced into a police lineup, staring at a window he couldn't see through. It was half-assed. It was stupid. It was perfect for a fool such as I.

"Off the road, asshole," someone shouted, and that, I guess, was when my act began. I bowed, a grand sweeping bow that reminded me of how I'd strode on the stage at Graceland during "Also Sprach Zarathustra." It was coming to me now, what I was going to do.

"Get out, Biggest Elvis." Another warning from behind, pleadingly, from one of the Graceland girls. Never mind. Now I had it. Biggest Elvis. The ending I'd been looking for—the grand finale—one show, one night, farewell performance, till the next Elvis came along—there'd be more, I bet—and it started again, the magic.

Are you lonesome tonight
Do you miss me tonight
Are you sorry we drifted apart . . .

No slow build for this performance. I sang at full strength from the beginning, as if my life depended on it. It was hard to know where to turn, with an audience in front, an audience in back. The toughest possible house, between two armies, right in a demilitarized zone. I used to think it was hard, playing to sailors and hostesses, what with beer on the table and sex in the air and money all around. But this was harder: I'd stepped into a fight that both sides were incredibly ready for. I was all that kept them apart. Their irritation with me was all that united them.

Does your memory stray
To a bright summer day . . .

Carry the gospel to the hardest places, right, Father Domingo? At least
they turned off their damned radios. Their ghetto blasters had been si-
lenced. Music hath charms. I thought that I'd be rusty but I still had the
voice, the big voice, and the attention of the crowd, both sides of the fence.
It sounded different out-of-doors. Graceland—poor Graceland—had raised
me up onto a stage, with spotlights and microphones and backup musicians
and—oh, where were they now?—the Lane brothers, Chester and Albert.
This was pure solo. What I'd always dreaded. A solo act. On the road. A
man alone, etc. Car headlights, clouds of dust, a fence behind me. Above
me, night and stars. Around me, the sea. Something lonely and primal in
the sound of my voice. His voice. Biggest Elvis. That guy.

Do the chairs in the corner
Seem empty and bare . . .

Resurrecting Elvis never felt more right. Where else but here? Who else
but me? Second chance for Elvis, second chance for me. Second chance for
the audience. Another shot at intimacy and communion. A couple of bottles
came out from the cars, one flying way over my shoulder, the other rolling
harmlessly at my feet, no harm done, and I dodged them gracefully—the old
moves returning, the lean forward, the backward tilt, the side profile, the
frontal pose, Elvis as willing, easy, target. This is my body, assholes, broken
for you.

Is your heart filled with pain,
Shall I come back again?
Tell me dear, are you lonesome tonight?

When I went into "Heartbreak Hotel"—something a little upbeat, please,
on this night of nights—they knew I wasn't going to be leaving. The bottle

throwers got serious then, and when things hit, they hurt. They hit more often. They weren't into chasing me off; this was about bringing me down. I
had wondered about those scenes, in biblical movies, when people got
stoned. They never danced, never fired back. They just accepted it. They
stood and took it and folded down onto their knees and the rocks kept coming, instant funeral cairn. So Biggest Elvis would be covered by a pile of
Budweisers and Mountain Dews, all set for recycling. But I kept singing. After "Heartbreak Hotel," I felt there'd be time for one more song. I was on my
knees already and wouldn't be getting up. "American Trilogy," then. Because I wanted to complete the circle, to get back to where the magic began,
far enough into "All My Sorrows" and the acknowledgment that death comes
to all of us, Elvis and Biggest Elvis, and I by God made it, though I took
some shots in the head and the taste of blood was in my mouth and no way
would I get to "Battle Hymn of the Republic" . . . that was the good news. . . .
I turned to face the people behind the fence, my people, to see if the girls of
Graceland were crossing themselves again, but I couldn't tell, I couldn't see,
because some headlights were coming at me from the side of the fence, and
then I got hit by a Budweiser that was full. This one's for you! I fell forward,
onto the ground, in front of the pickup, and the funny thing was, I couldn't
tell where that Budweiser came from, from which side of the fence. And, at
the last, I wondered about the guy who picked up that can of Budweiser that
had just hit me. Blood coming down into my eyes, I guessed he'd have foam
and spray all over him, if he opened that particular can. Odd, what things
come to you. How, come to think of it, I'd lasted about as long as the Original. Forty-two and curtains, for both of us. I wondered if Malou was out
there, watching me.

Epilogue

Jimmy Fiddler

He looked like roadkill when we got to him, head first, down on the ground, bleeding from his mouth and out of his hair. Some curtain call. Young Chester Lane jumped out and went right over to him, shielding him with his body, and the bottles stopped coming. It was so nasty, the heart went out of the crowd. What they'd been planning for the Filipinos, they'd given to Biggest Elvis.

And then too, the older brother—Dude Lane, that would be—went right out into the crowd and they recognized him from his piece-of-shit TV show, Guam-boy who made it in Hollywood, right on the cover of *TV Guide*. He shook hands, signed autographs, and did little Elvis bits. The king is dead, long live the king. Another damn Elvis.

Lucky for the Filipinos, I'd say. They get off their heavy equipment and come out the fence to have a look at Biggest Elvis, who's alive, all right, but not pretty. They didn't go to war, which was just as well, because they'd have lost, big-time, and they knew it. They just didn't care anymore, and I couldn't blame them, really.

Earlier that night, I'd dropped Malou at her office, meaner than catshit. This wildcat strike was a mess and she had to get hold of Baby Ronquillo. So after I left her, I was driving past the harbor and that was when the Lane brothers flagged me down, not knowing who I was. Funny, isn't it: I drove them to Olongapo for their first concert and I drove them out to the airport, for their last.

We got there and I've got to admit, it was deep-dish strange, watching Biggest Elvis singing and dancing and dodging beer cans, like a vaudeville act that's bombing. He got clipped in the head, across the mouth, and the dumb shit kept serenading them, down on his knees, the same cornball crap he used to serve up at Graceland. They kept throwing stuff and he was singing and it was as if he wanted it to happen this way, it was all in a script he'd written, a fat peckerhead crooner going out like an Old Testament prophet.

"Let's go," Dude Lane said.

"Where?"

"We have to stop it. They'll kill him."

"But the show ain't over yet," I said. "We still got the 'Battle Hymn of the Republic.' " And the both of them gave me this look, so off we went, and the party was over. Chester lifted Biggest Elvis into the back of the truck, which I'm going to have to hose down later, and while Dude worked the crowd, this little Whitney girl jumps in back and I end up driving the meat wagon to the hospital.

Albert "Dude" Lane

I stayed at the camp all night, even though nothing was happening. I watched the place empty, bit by bit, and I stepped inside. Saw some of the same faces I remembered from Graceland. Same bodies, too. I couldn't get out of my mind what Ward did. It was so corny and theatrical and half-assed. I knew it. He knew it. But that didn't stop him. I saved the day, maybe, working the crowd with handshakes and high fives, hugs and autographs. But Biggest Elvis had fought the main event.

Chester Lane

When the plane came in that next morning, a whole bunch of passengers headed straight over to the Nineteenth Hole Corporation. Lots of locals showed up too, but the rumble had gone out of the them. This wasn't an island thing, anymore. There were outsiders involved: Japanese investors, the Filipino consul, a priest, a couple reporters, and someone from the commonwealth governor's office. You know, I felt sort of sorry for the locals, the way they looked, a little sulky, a little apologetic. The game had gotten beyond them and it was sad, the way they'd lost control of their island. They'd missed their chance, the night before, and that was the end of something they might never get back.

They set up a table inside the compound and a meeting started. It looked bad at first. On one side, you had a suit from Japan and some dress shirts from Saipan and Malou, who was supposed to keep the Filipinos in line, I guessed. Across from them was mainly Lucy Number Three and a couple guys I didn't know but they looked like every other contract worker I'd ever seen, standing around and waiting for instructions.

The Japanese guy, Mr. Kaneshiro of the Nineteenth Hole Corporation, wanted his project back on track, "and not held hostage by unhappy bar girls." The consul apologized for hotheads, the commonwealth guy granted that it was wonderful, how Filipinos were able to better their own lives while contributing to the progress of America's newest commonwealth. And Malou pooh-poohed these "unsubstantiated complaints." Sure, she allowed there might be problems here and there but they were hard to avoid when you brought so many people—all levels of skill, education, sophistication—to a strange place. I loved the way she said "sophistication." Like she owned the word. I couldn't blame Biggest Elvis for falling for her. "Anomalies are inevitable," she said. Then she glanced at Lucy Number Three as if to say, your move, lady, knowing it wouldn't amount to much. Whores complaining about customers. . . .

Then it was Lucy Number Three's turn and, right away, I could see I'd had her wrong. Maybe not in Olongapo: she was what she was. But she was different here. She had her stuff together, in order, names and dates to go with complaints, one after the other, and people standing by who were willing to back her up, story after story. I was watching the Japanese, Kaneshiro. He'd started out ticked off at Lucy Number Three. But then he started giving Malou these long hard looks.

"All talk," Malou said. "They say this and that. No evidence."

Lucy got up. Still a barmaid in a T-shirt that any red-blooded American boy would pay a hefty sum to peek underneath. But more. Plenty more than that.

She brought out a big brown envelope and dumped out a pile of papers, mostly file cards, right in front of the Japanese. "From Shipshape. Evidence. Recruiting record. Loan agreement. Altered contracts. Double billing. . . ." Malou froze. She'd been a careful recordkeeper for Baby Ronquillo, going back to Graceland. But she should have kept these payments off the books. Kaneshiro reached over and picked a card at random. Whitney's card. It showed rake-offs, salary reductions and all. It showed Whitney coming to complain. And nothing happening.

"Evidence," Lucy Number Three said. "Some people do bad things." Now she looked at Malou, one tough woman to another, the sort of look that no man should get between. Stare-down time, I figured. Then Lucy Number Three gives Malou this smile. "And what you see," she said, "is the result."

Well, that was about enough. I decided to get involved. I ambled over to the table. The Graceland girls nodded at me. Malou too, for that matter, I always liked Malou and I never gave her cause not to return the feeling.

"Baby Elvis, what are you doing here?" she asked, but nicely. "This is a business meeting."

"Hi, Mr. Kaneshiro," I said. "It took a minute but now I recognize your name."

"You are . . ." The Japanese was having a bad enough day already. Dealing with someone nicknamed Baby Elvis didn't make it any better.

"Chester Lane. Me and my brother Albert . . ." Say no more. He caught on instantly, jumped to his feet. But the others were in the dark.

"I said to myself, I said, geez, Nineteenth Hole Corporation, damn if that doesn't sound familiar. I was saying that to my wife. She's the one who keeps track of the estate. So I say, don't we own a piece of that? Me and Albert? Thanks to Uncle Pete? and Christina says, well yes. Actually, more than half. Nice to meet you sir, anyway."

Kaneshiro was up and shaking hands and expressing regrets and inviting me to lunch at the hotel.

"I think we should settle this," I say. "Settle our problems and see that the other problems get settled too." He nodded at me. Yes sir. Amen. Right on. "For old times' sake," I said, "and just to show we aren't just in this for ourselves . . . ," I looked at Lucy Number Three, "start with the barmaids."

Whitney Matoc

I'm reading *Misery* by Mr. Stephen King when Biggest Elvis wakes up. He makes groaning noise and feels for his bandages. Then he moves his tongue to where two-three teeth are not present anymore. They are absent.

"Good afternoon, Biggest Elvis," I say.

"What happened?"

"Is something. Everybody is going to make fight and then you are starting to sing and then everybody is throwing cans and bottles at you and you keep singing."

"I know that part, Whitney. After that, I mean."

"Baby Elvis and Dude Elvis come in truck. People go away. Plenty blood for one night, courtesy of you. Now they make meeting today. Settle up. Tonight, Baby Elvis say, tonight you leave."

"*I* leave?"

"On boat. Dude and Baby Elvis go too. And they are saying, anybody else who is wanting to go."

"Do you want to go?"

I cannot answer.

"Do you want to go with me?" he says.

"Yes," I say. "Okay."

"As . . . what? I'm older than you."

"Yes," I say. And I want to tell him all the times I go with guys I never move. Never. Worst lay in Olongapo, worst here. Always. But I don't say this. "You are beat up, not just only old. And I am beat up too."

"So what'll it be, Whitney?"

"We'll see," I say. "Work it out. Like you say at Graceland. Every night you say it, at closing time. 'Evening still is young.' "

Albert "Dude" Lane

We'd put out the word that anybody who wanted to leave the island could go with us to Guam. We were leaving at dusk, because the weather was fine and the moon was full and, well, that's just the way we wanted to go. Sail away, sail away. Like that. Chester and I brought Biggest Elvis down from the hospital. He looked like one of those animals that gets hit by a train in a cartoon, winding up all bruises, bandages, stitches, and crutches. We put him in the captain's chair that Chester never sits in, he's moving around too much to relax. Biggest Elvis wouldn't be moving too much for a while. Christina piled pillows all around him. If Biggest Elvis were a fruit, you'd say, way past ripe. Whitney came along too and, after a while, the original material girl, Elvira, came walking down the dock, like she was walking down a ramp at a fashion show. Biggest Elvis catches me looking at Elvira.

"It was real dumb, what you did last night," I say. "Tacky. Sort of thing you want to say, can we put this to music? Only you were already singing. Till they took your teeth out."

"You take your chances."

"Lot of heart," I said. Not so loud and not so clear, because I was looking down when I said it. Not enunciating, not projecting. Like they say.

"What?"

"You heard me. What you did last night. A lot of heart. Low on brains. . . ."

The way he looked at me, the way he studied me, you'd think he couldn't believe what he was hearing.

"I have a question for you, though," I said. "I saw you last night, getting hit by beer cans and rocks and singing, and I said to myself, that's the ending I've been needing for my Elvis screenplay. That thing I half-wrote. That's it. But what I need to know is, how to play it. If that's the ending, is it happy or is it sad? I mean—not to dance around the point, old-timer—how did it feel, getting buried under a pile of rocks and beer cans?"

"The empties are nothing. Bat them away like butterflies. It's the full ones. Those hurt. And the rocks, of course."

"You know what I'm asking, coach."

"Yeah." He pointed at his head, where they'd shaved away a bunch of hair to sew up his scalp. "That one Budweiser came from inside the fence, I'm pretty sure. The Filipino side."

"Music lovers," I said. He laughed again, though it pained him. I'll give him that. He could laugh at it all, Elvis, Biggest Elvis, the whole bit. But he still believed too, or part of him did, so that—knowing better—he'd put his ass on the line in the middle of nowhere in a fight that couldn't be won. That's the trick. To do better than you know. Or to do good, when you know better. Something like that. In the screenplay, I'll get it right. But he still was ducking me. "How did it feel? How do I write it and play it? If I take it a couple beats further and no one comes to the rescue . . ."

"Well," he said. "It hurt. That's for sure. Not being able to see what was coming. Where it would hit. I won't kid you. It hurt me. And I was scared."

"But that's not all, is it?"

"No," he said. "No, it isn't. Though you could leave it like that."

"I want the rest. . . ."

"Listen, Dude." He stopped, swallowed hard. He'd told me to listen but now that I was waiting, he turned mute.

"So?" I pressed.

"All right."

"It felt all right?"

"All right, I'll tell you," Biggest Elvis said. He tried to smile. "It was godlike."

•   •   •

I figured we'd have a whole boatload of refugees, a regular exodus, a boat-load of slaves, sailing into the sunset. Well, I've got news. It doesn't work that way. Our Filipinas, mostly they were staying. Some, maybe, hopped a plane as soon as they got their back pay and refunds and tickets out. But a lot, including a lot who were inside the compound, decided to stay. Some of them came down to the boat to explain. Including some we knew.

"I come so far already," Lucy Number Three said. "I will be getting re-spect around here."

"We are going to make business here," Priscilla said. I didn't press for details. Sometimes, it's better not to know. Maybe they were opening a bookstore.

"Thanking you for the nice boat ride," Lucy Number Three said. "But no going back for me."

"You know what they say about us," Priscilla said. Actually, I knew a lot of things they said. Including some about Priscilla. But it was her choice. "We never stop trying."

Now, get this. We're ready to leave and lots of people come down to see us off, damn near every overseas contract worker on the island and some lo-cal folk besides. I had a little to do with that. I posed for pictures. I signed autographs. I mugged some Elvis poses, promised to be back to visit the is-land in better times, at fiesta, when I'd see what the place was really like, or when they opened the golf course. They weren't bad people, they insisted, and I believed them. Hell yes. We'd do a celebrity golf tournament when the time comes. They wanted Sonny Bono and Frank Gifford and Heather Locklear. I just told them to make a list and send it along.

The Filipinos were there for Biggest Elvis. The story of his last concert was already turning into legend, embellished by people who weren't even there. Christina led him to the railing, so that they could wave to him and he could return the wave, though weakly, like an aging pope. There were ru-mors all over the island, he'd died during the night. Next thing, they'd be saying he died and got buried at sea, between here and Guam. Or that he died and returned to Olongapo. Things like that. Biggest Elvis didn't say anything to them. We didn't know it yet, but it turned out his jaw had to be wired on Guam. It was all he could do to stand there and give them his blessing, the way he always used to close the show. Then he got a little shaky and Christina led him down below, so he could sleep. Too bad he couldn't stay up a little longer. Right after he went down the steps, the red pickup truck pulled up and Malou got out.

Now, I'd think—most people would—that the Filipino workers would move away from her, like she was poison. That was how I'd direct the scene. Hard, righteous stares. Ostracism kind of thing. The woman without a country. And the boat would sail off, loaded with people we rescued, and we'd see her standing on the shore alone. Bullshit. The Filipinos talked to her, smiled, bantered, like sure she was the villain last night, but that particular play was over and this was the cast party.

"Good afternoon," she said to me.

"Hi, Malou."

"Elvira and Whitney. . . . Anybody else from the Philippines on board?"

"That's it."

"You're sure?" She looked up and down the deck. I sensed she was waiting to be asked aboard. No way. Then she handed me some envelope she said had passports and back money for Elvira and Whitney. They had come up behind me, so I handed the envelopes right over. They didn't say thank you.

"Biggest Elvis goes with you?" Malou asked. I nodded. "He's already on board." Another nod. "Do you think I could—"

"Not a good idea," Whitney said. "He was hurt bad. Now, Biggest Elvis sleeps."

"Oh . . ." She kind of bit her tongue and skipped a beat, it seemed to me. She wanted a meeting, I guess, and now it registered that it wasn't in the cards and their last meeting was something that had happened a while ago, only they didn't know it at the time. That can give you pause, losing out like that.

"Whitney," she said. "Tell Biggest Elvis Malou said good-bye . . . and thank you . . . and . . . sorry." Now she honest-to-God looked like crying and that right away pissed her off. "I feel like a baby, here. . . ."

"Anything else?" Whitney asked.

"Tell him . . . no hard feelings."

Jimmy Fiddler

"Can I come out now?" I asked Elvira.

"Not yet," she said. "Truck is still on the dock." I was down below, listening to Biggest Elvis breathe and groan and fart.

"You noticed how she wanted to come aboard," Elvira said.

"I'll bet she did."

"She nearly cries, when Whitney says Biggest Elvis sleeps. See, Daga, she missed you already. She is crying for you."

"She misses and cries about those file cards and contracts I stole for you."

"You wait until we're out of the harbor," Elvira said, closing the door, so that I'm back in darkness, Biggest Elvis lying in state. After a while, the engines started. We were moving.

"I heard what you said," Biggest Elvis said. I about jumped out of my skin. His speech was kind of garbled, I had to lean forward to catch it. "You don't have to tell me . . . but why did you do it?"

"Damn straight, I don't have to tell you shit," I said. Now that I'd cleared that right up, I talked some more. "I didn't like what was happening on that place. Olongapo was rough, but there were rules. This island was different. Sure, it was whores. But I can still tell the difference between fair and unfair. I was in Darling's the night that Dolly freaked and I always kind of liked Dolly. The way she kidded me. And I saw those Graceland girls getting stripped and fucked over. I mean, well . . . shit . . ."

"You and Malou?"

"I really wanted her. Could I use the word . . . crush? . . . would you laugh at me? First time I saw her, which was like the first time you saw her, same place, all composed and . . . together . . . sitting next to the jukebox . . . I wanted to know her. It's funny. All those acres of snatch around and you want the one you can't have. And then, you had her. But not for long, buddy. Not for long. . . ."

"What were you here? To her?"

"Employee. Just like with Baby Ronquillo. There was a time I had a shot at Baby years ago. And missed. I helped her out a time or two in the early going. You see where that got me. So far . . . only so far."

"And Malou was the same."

"Ditto. It didn't happen. You think you're in charge, with these girls. Then you learn otherwise."

I heard Biggest Elvis give out a deep sigh. I waited awhile, maybe he was back sleeping. That was okay. I didn't have to say it aloud. He didn't know Malou like I did. He hadn't seen the way that woman worked. She wasn't Baby Ronquillo all over again. Baby always came home to the PI. Part of her belonged to Olongapo, no matter what. Not Malou. That woman was outward bound. Before the Graceland girls organized their strike. I would have guessed she'd be taking the whole operation over in a year, edging Baby out. Already, she'd learned Japanese. She'd have run rings around Baby, in time. She'd kept her records a little too careful and she'd put them where I could borrow them, but that was a temporary setback.

There was something else I could have said, if I wanted to give a compliment to the local hero. Being with Biggest Elvis was as close as Malou got to being human. Near miss. He was just unlucky. She'd had one American before. And she'd have more. He was just out of order. He was her second American. If he'd been the first or third: different story. That's all. Even now, if he'd said, okay darling, meet you a year from now on the Golden Gate Bridge, that might have worked. She'd have made it. She'd make it yet. Biggest Elvis was the one I wasn't so sure about.

The door opened, the air rushed in, Elvira motioned me up, like letting a puppy out of a cellar. She liked bossing me around. I keep getting into situations, with women like that. I'm Alan Alda in a Freddy Krueger body.

Ward Wiggins

An hour or so out of Apra Harbor, Whitney and Christina came down to wake me.

"Come on, Biggest Elvis," Whitney whispered. I liked the sound of Whitney whispering.

"I don't know if I can make it up the—"

"We'll help you," Christina said. So they walked me over to the steps. Then Christina took my hand and pulled me upward, while Whitney stayed behind, giggling, pushing me up, hands on my ass. "I give boost," she said.

A moonlit night. A sea like a lake, though we were miles above the bottom of it. In the distance, an island. A landing tower at the airport, red-tipped in the night, and the glint of traffic on Marine Drive. Chester and Jimmy were at the helm. Then Chester left him there and walked over to me.

"They didn't want you to miss this night," he said. "They thought it was important."

"Why?"

"Over here, Biggest Elvis," Whitney said. She led me to the railing, put me against it, fixing my arm on either side. "Is all right?"

"Yes."

Then Christina brought Chester over and stood him next to me. She stood back and looked the two of us over. "That's good."

Elvira was next, taking Dude's hand and bringing him over, into the picture. The three Elvises.

"A reunion," Chester said.

"We are wanting to see you together again," Whitney said.

"Next time is . . . who knows? People like us . . ." Elvira didn't finish her sentence.

"Now or never," Whitney said. Actually she tried to sing it. Then she stopped and we were there, just there, we three under the stars and above the deepest possible sea, in the middle of another perfect moment that wouldn't last but we would take it, anyway. Sea and islands all around us. That where-in-the-world feeling. That sense of life maybe working out.

"Does anybody have a camera?" Chester asked. "With a flash?"

"Man, I hate those red-eye pictures."

"Dude, there's this new kind," Chester explained.

Christina came back from down below, shrugged. "No camera."

"Well . . ."

"Just stand there a little bit," Whitney pleaded. "Just a little bit more."

"Yes," Christina urged. "Please."

"It's important," Elvira said.

"Why?" I asked. "If there's no camera?"

"I know, no camera," Whitney said. "But I'm wanting to remember."

Also Available from The Overlook Press

Gone Tomorrow
978-1-59020-259-3

In Kluge's (*Eddie and the Cruisers*) thoughtful new novel, Mark May, a young professor at an Ohio college, is surprised to be named the literary executor of a recently deceased colleague he barely knew. George Canaris was a literary sensation in the 1960s, but hadn't published anything in 30 years. At the time of his death, he was rumored to be working on his magnum opus, but there is doubt the manuscript exists. While inspecting the dead man's house, Mark finds the manuscript of Canaris's memoir, which provides insight into the man and his work, and even if Mark has doubts about its veracity, it pushes him to arrive at some important decisions about his own life. The novel is suffused with Kluge's obvious affection for books, and has some cleverly aphoristic things to say about the joys of teaching, the pitfalls of academic infighting and the tragedy of artistic expectations left unfulfilled. Although not as witty or biting as Kingsley Amis's academy fiction, this novel combines elements of Citizen Kane and Goodbye, Mr. Chips for a satisfying resolution.

—*Publishers Weekly*

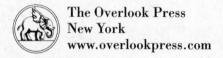

The Overlook Press
New York
www.overlookpress.com

Also Available from The Overlook Press

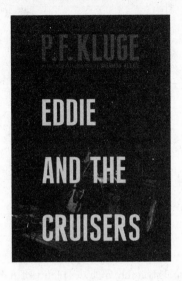

Eddie and the Cruisers
978-1-59020-094-0

"An excellently crafted book. The dialogue is sharp, the book is packed
with exquisite description and a surprise ending."
—*Sunday Journal and Star*

"*Eddie and the Cruisers* seems at first glance to be only a smartly written
novel about nostalgia for the music of the late 1950s. It quickly proves,
however, to be A remarkably good suspense story, full of vivid
characters and some hilarious dialogue."
—*St. Louis Post-Dispatch*

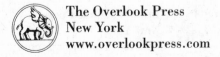

**The Overlook Press
New York
www.overlookpress.com**

Also Available from The Overlook Press

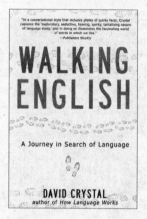

Walking English
978-1-59020-263-0

"In a conversational style that includes plenty of quirky facts, Crystal captures the 'exploratory, seductive, teasing, quirky, tantalizing nature of language study,' and in doing so illuminates the fascinating world of words in which we live."
—*Publishers Weekly*

"Peels back the layers of history compressed into the [names] he encounters or just thinks of along the way—names of places, mainly, but also of abbots, churches, pubs and locomotives… Like passing the afternoon with a knowledgeable uncle."
—*Wall Street Journal*

"Every page of Crystal's book contains some linguistic curiosity or flight of fancy."
—*Financial Times*

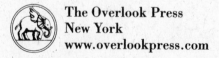

The Overlook Press
New York
www.overlookpress.com